DC SUPER HERO GIRLS

DATE WITH DISASTER

an original graphic novel

WRITTEN BY
Shea Fontana

ART BY
Yancey Labat

COLORS BY
Monica Kubina

LETTERING BY
Janice Chiang

ERGIRL BASED ON CHARACTERS CREATED
JERRY SIEGEL AND JOE SHUSTER.
SPECIAL ARRANGEMENT WITH THE JERRY SIEGEL FAMILY.

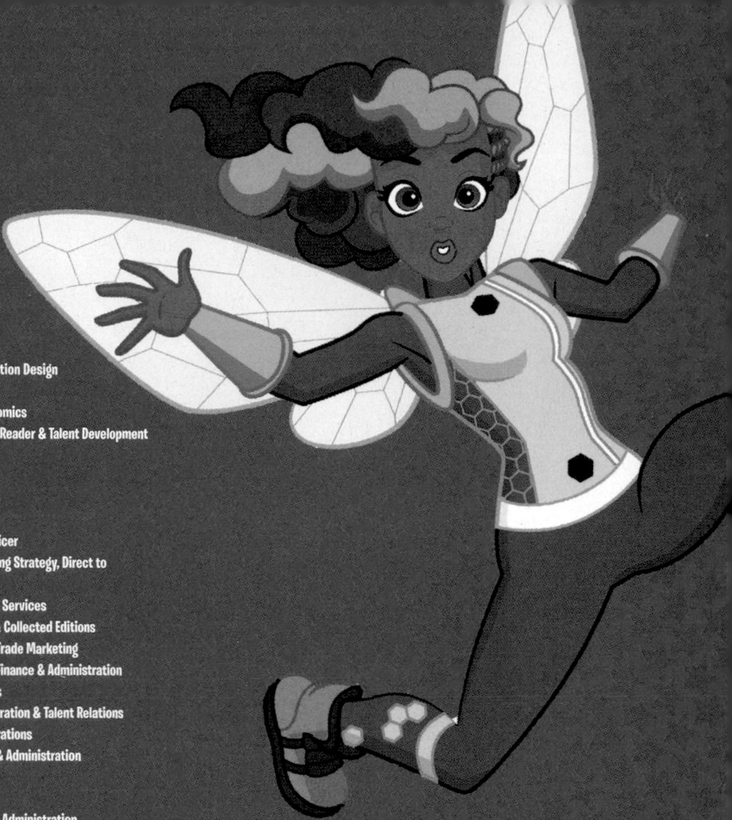

MARIE JAVINS Group Editor
DIEGO LOPEZ Assistant Editor
STEVE COOK Design Director - Books
AMIE BROCKWAY-METCALF Publication Design

BOB HARRAS Senior VP - Editor-in-Chief, DC Comics
BOBBIE CHASE VP & Executive Editor, Young Reader & Talent Development

DIANE NELSON President
DAN DiDIO Publisher
JIM LEE Publisher
GEOFF JOHNS President & Chief Creative Officer
AMIT DESAI Executive VP - Business & Marketing Strategy, Direct to Consumer & Global Franchise Management
SAM ADES Senior VP & General Manager, Digital Services
MARK CHIARELLO Senior VP - Art, Design & Collected Editions
JOHN CUNNINGHAM Senior VP - Sales & Trade Marketing
ANNE DePIES Senior VP - Business Strategy, Finance & Administration
DON FALLETTI VP - Manufacturing Operations
LAWRENCE GANEM VP - Editorial Administration & Talent Relations
ALISON GILL Senior VP - Manufacturing & Operations
HANK KANALZ Senior VP - Editorial Strategy & Administration
JAY KOGAN VP - Legal Affairs
JACK MAHAN VP - Business Affairs
NICK J. NAPOLITANO VP - Manufacturing Administration
EDDIE SCANNELL VP - Consumer Marketing
COURTNEY SIMMONS Senior VP - Publicity & Communications
JIM (SKI) SOKOLOWSKI VP - Comic Book Specialty Sales & Trade Marketing
NANCY SPEARS VP - Mass, Book, Digital Sales & Trade Marketing
MICHELE R. WELLS VP - Content Strategy

DC SUPER HERO GIRLS: DATE WITH DISASTER. February, 2018. Published by DC Comics, 2900 W. Alameda Avenue, Burbank, CA 91505. GST # is R125921072.

Printed by Cenveo, Richmond, Virginia, USA. 1/5/18. ISBN: 978-1-4012-7878-6

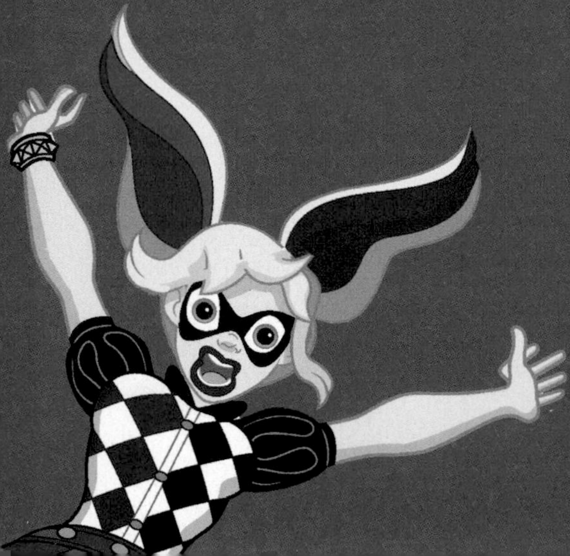

SUSTAINABLE FORESTRY INITIATIVE
Certified Chain of Custody
Promoting Sustainable Forestry
www.sfiprogram.org
SFI-00484

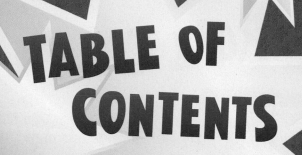

TABLE OF CONTENTS

ROLL CALL

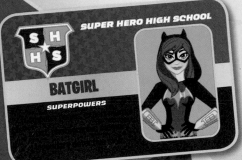

SUPER HERO HIGH SCHOOL

SHHS

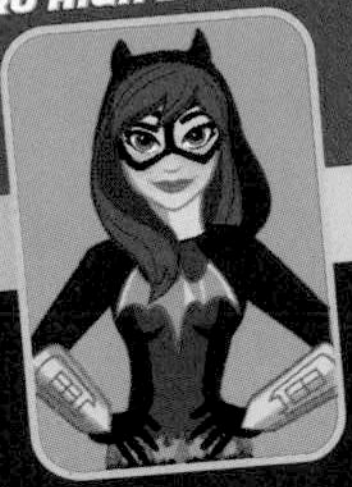

BATGIRL

SUPERPOWERS

SUPER HERO HIGH SCHOOL

SHHS

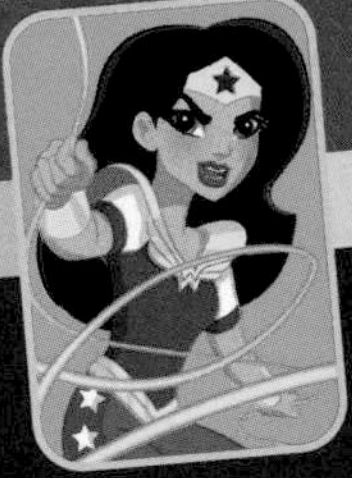

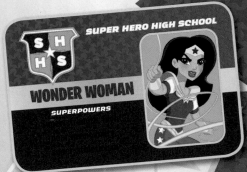

WONDER WOMAN

SUPERPOWERS

SUPER HERO HIGH SCHOOL

SHHS

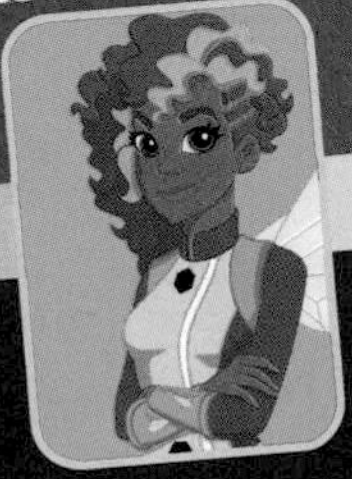

BUMBLEBEE

SUPERPOWERS

SUPER HERO HIGH SCHOOL

SHHS

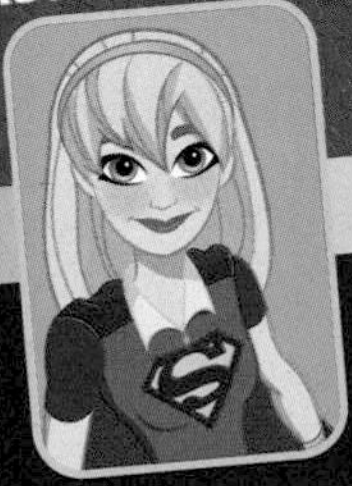

SUPERGIRL

SUPERPOWERS

SUPER HERO HIGH SCHOOL

SHHS

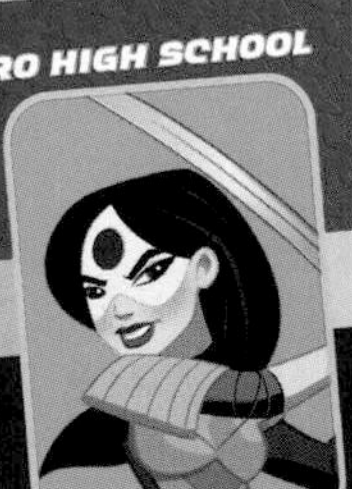

KATANA

SUPERPOWERS

SUPER HERO HIGH SCHOOL

SHHS

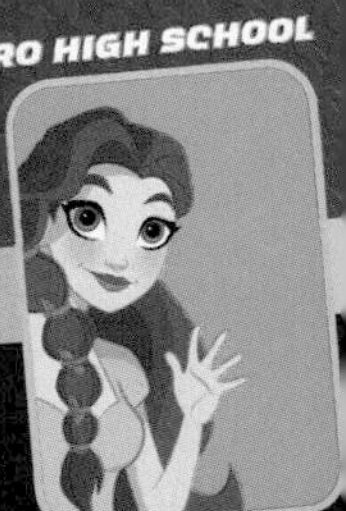

POISON IVY

SUPERPOWERS

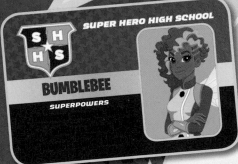

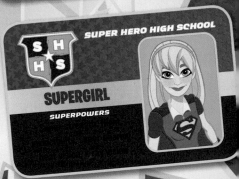

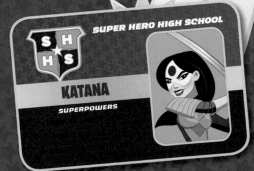

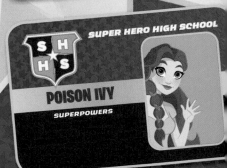

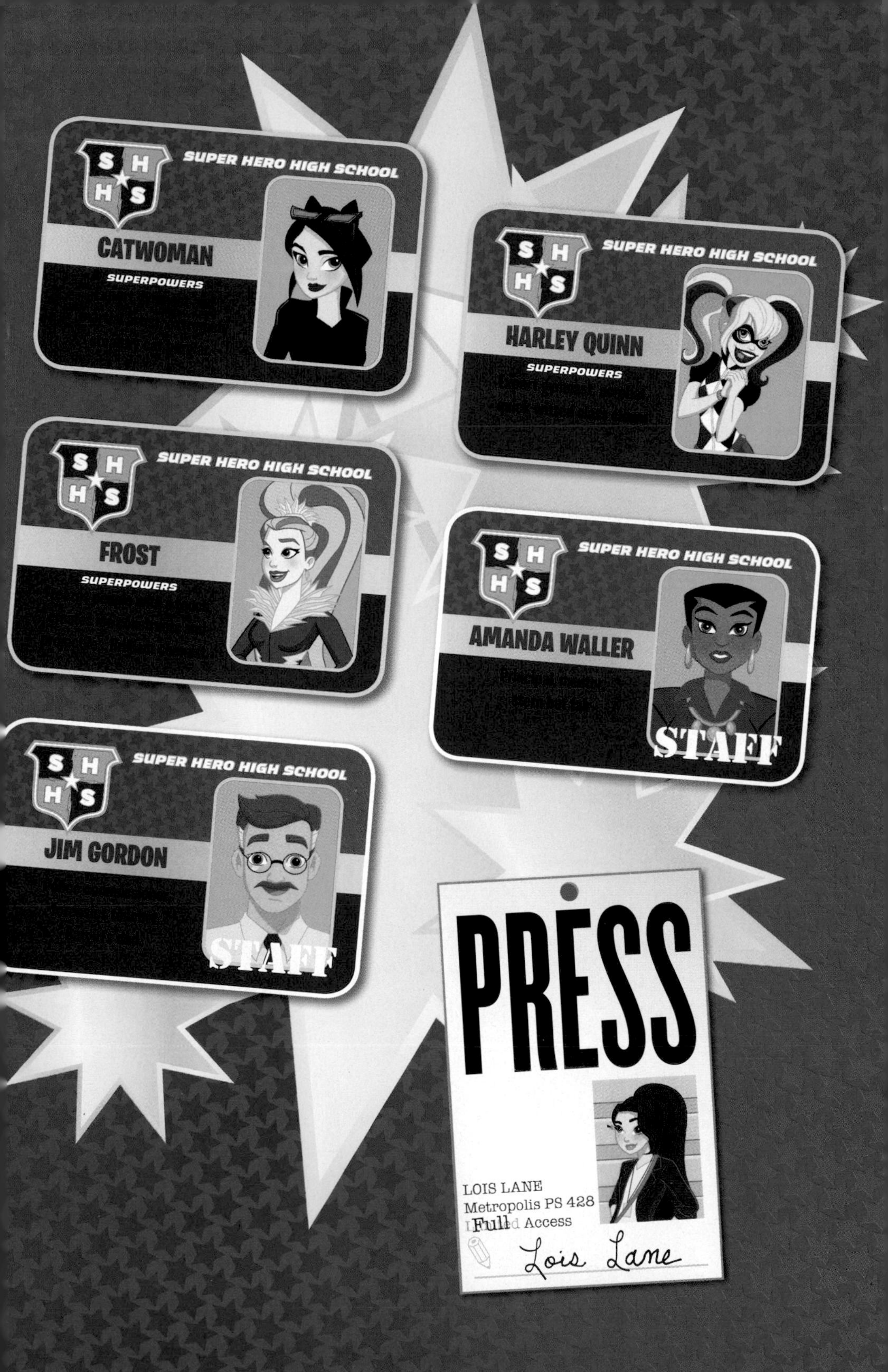
SUPER HERO HIGH SCHOOL
CATWOMAN
SUPERPOWERS
SUPER HERO HIGH SCHOOL
HARLEY QUINN
SUPERPOWERS
SUPER HERO HIGH SCHOOL
FROST
SUPERPOWERS
SUPER HERO HIGH SCHOOL
AMANDA WALLER
STAFF
SUPER HERO HIGH SCHOOL
JIM GORDON
STAFF
PRESS
LOIS LANE
Metropolis PS 428
Full Access
Lois Lane

CHAPTER 1
S.T.A.R. OF METROPOLIS

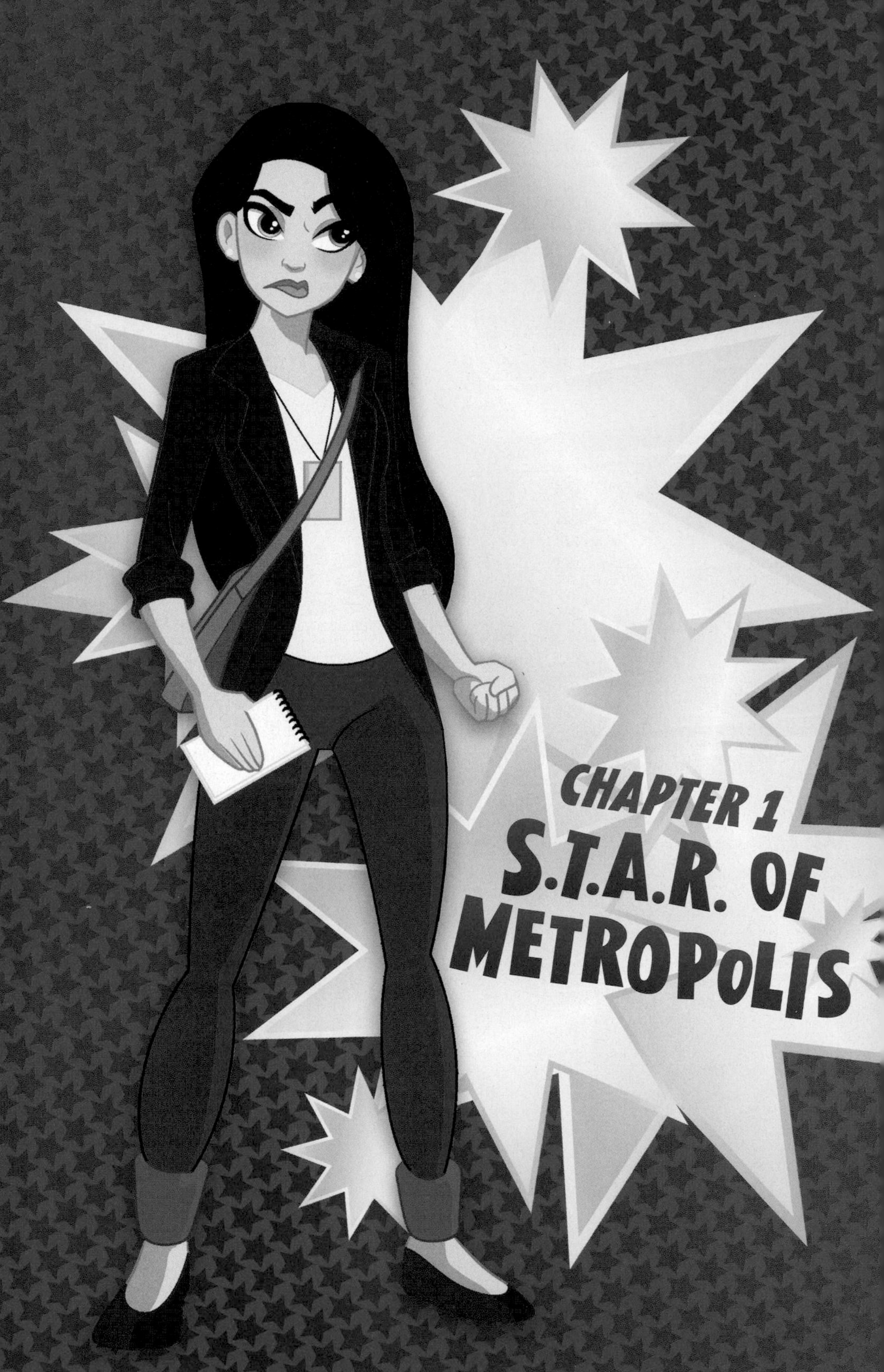

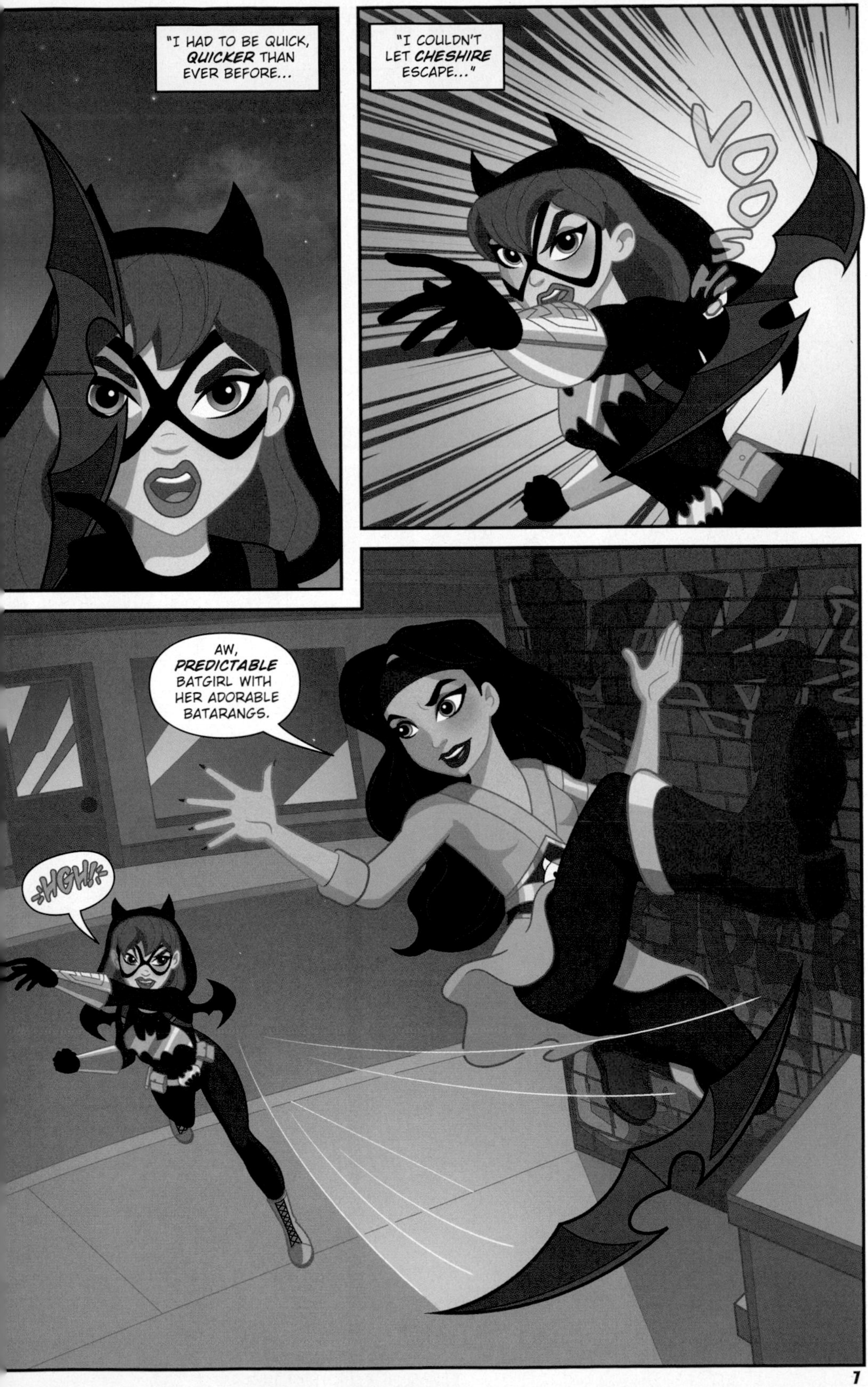
"I HAD TO BE QUICK, *QUICKER* THAN EVER BEFORE...
"I COULDN'T LET *CHESHIRE* ESCAPE..."
VOOSH
AW, *PREDICTABLE* BATGIRL WITH HER ADORABLE BATARANGS.
HGH!

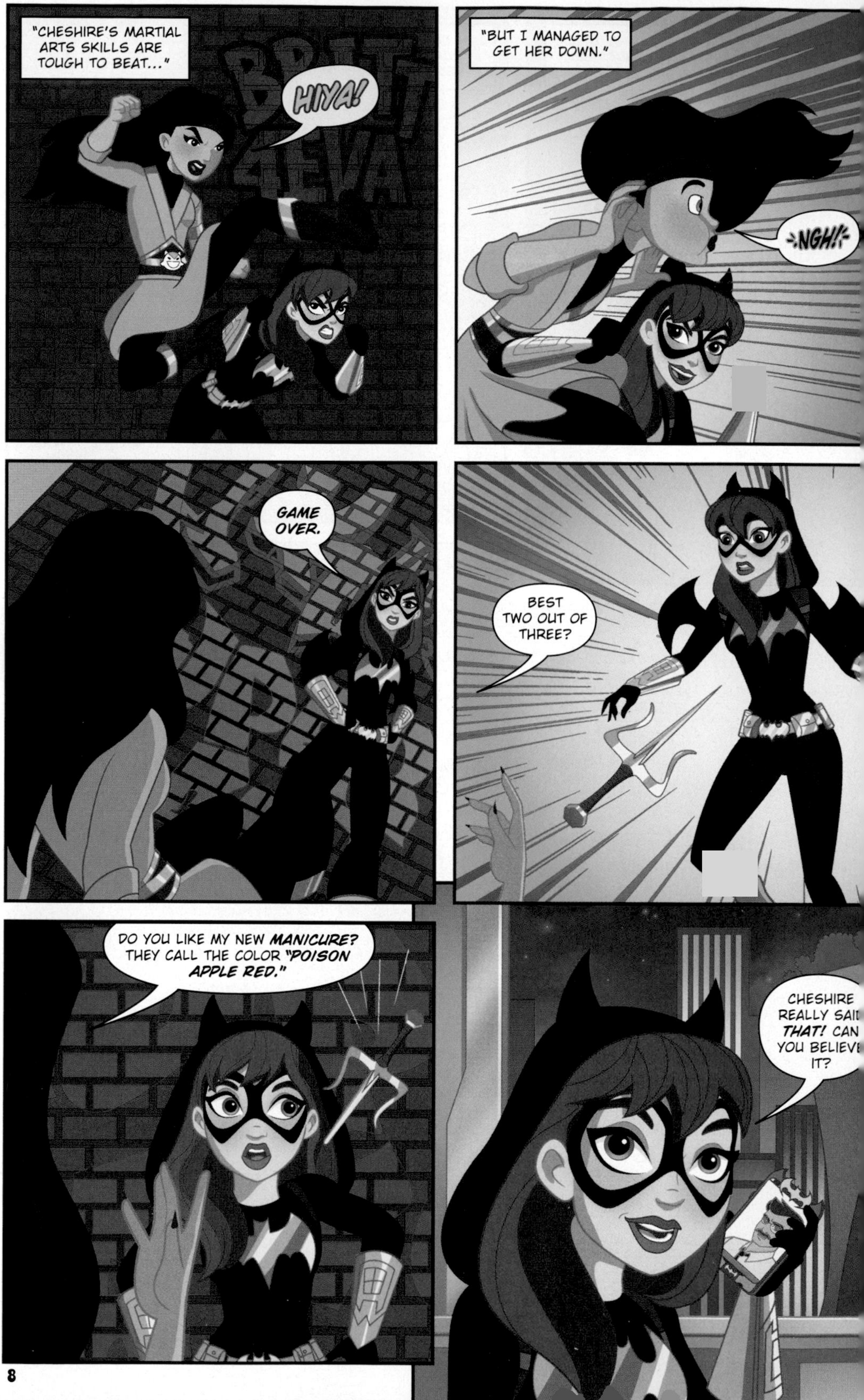
"CHESHIRE'S MARTIAL ARTS SKILLS ARE TOUGH TO BEAT..."
HIYA!
"BUT I MANAGED TO GET HER DOWN."
-NGH!-
GAME OVER.
BEST TWO OUT OF THREE?
DO YOU LIKE MY NEW MANICURE? THEY CALL THE COLOR "POISON APPLE RED."
CHESHIRE REALLY SAID THAT! CAN YOU BELIEVE IT?

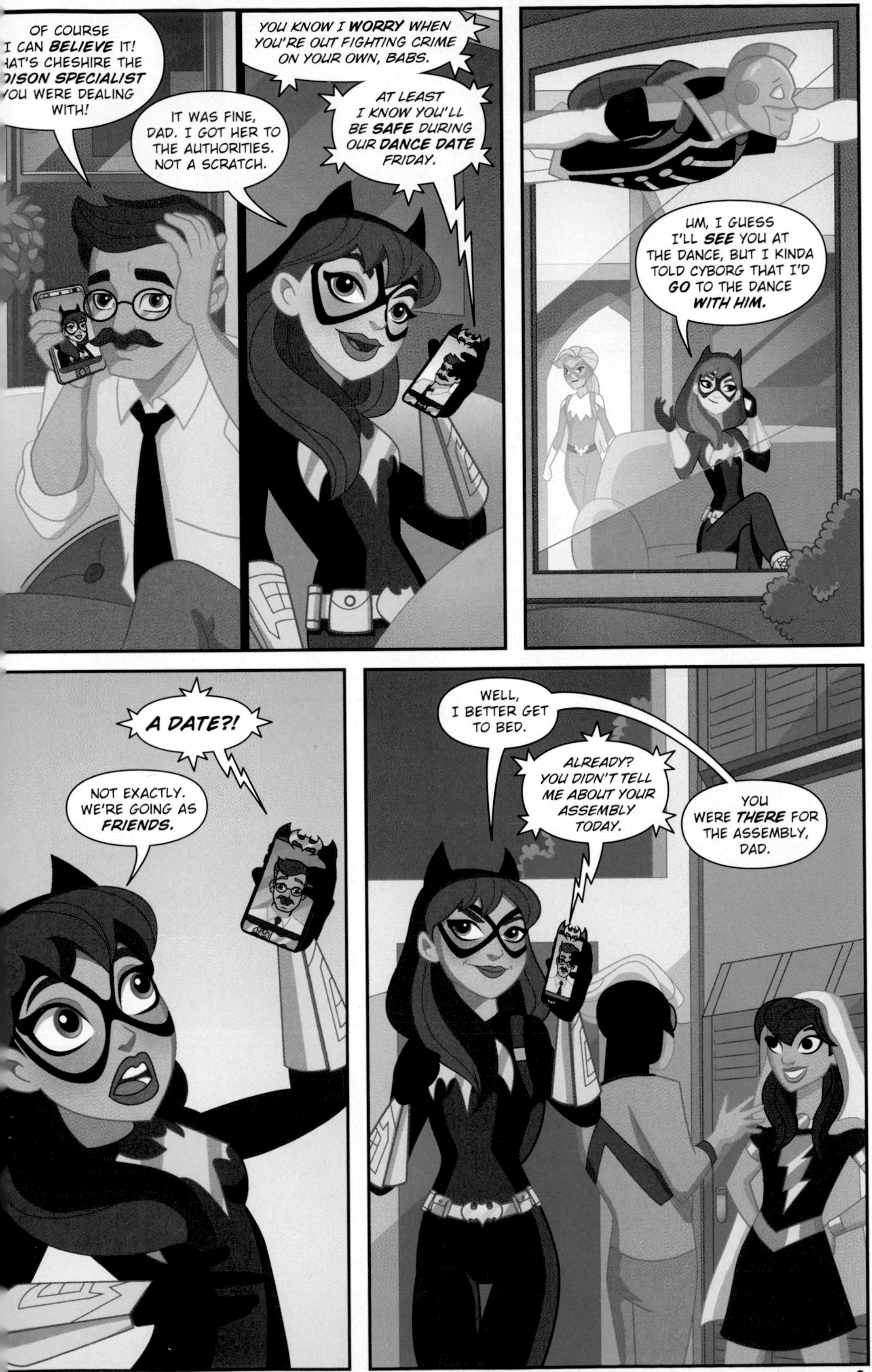

OF COURSE I CAN BELIEVE IT! HAT'S CHESHIRE THE DISON SPECIALIST YOU WERE DEALING WITH!
IT WAS FINE, DAD. I GOT HER TO THE AUTHORITIES. NOT A SCRATCH.
YOU KNOW I WORRY WHEN YOU'RE OUT FIGHTING CRIME ON YOUR OWN, BABS.
AT LEAST I KNOW YOU'LL BE SAFE DURING OUR DANCE DATE FRIDAY.
UM, I GUESS I'LL SEE YOU AT THE DANCE, BUT I KINDA TOLD CYBORG THAT I'D GO TO THE DANCE WITH HIM.
A DATE?!
NOT EXACTLY. WE'RE GOING AS FRIENDS.
WELL, I BETTER GET TO BED.
ALREADY? YOU DIDN'T TELL ME ABOUT YOUR ASSEMBLY TODAY.
YOU WERE THERE FOR THE ASSEMBLY, DAD.

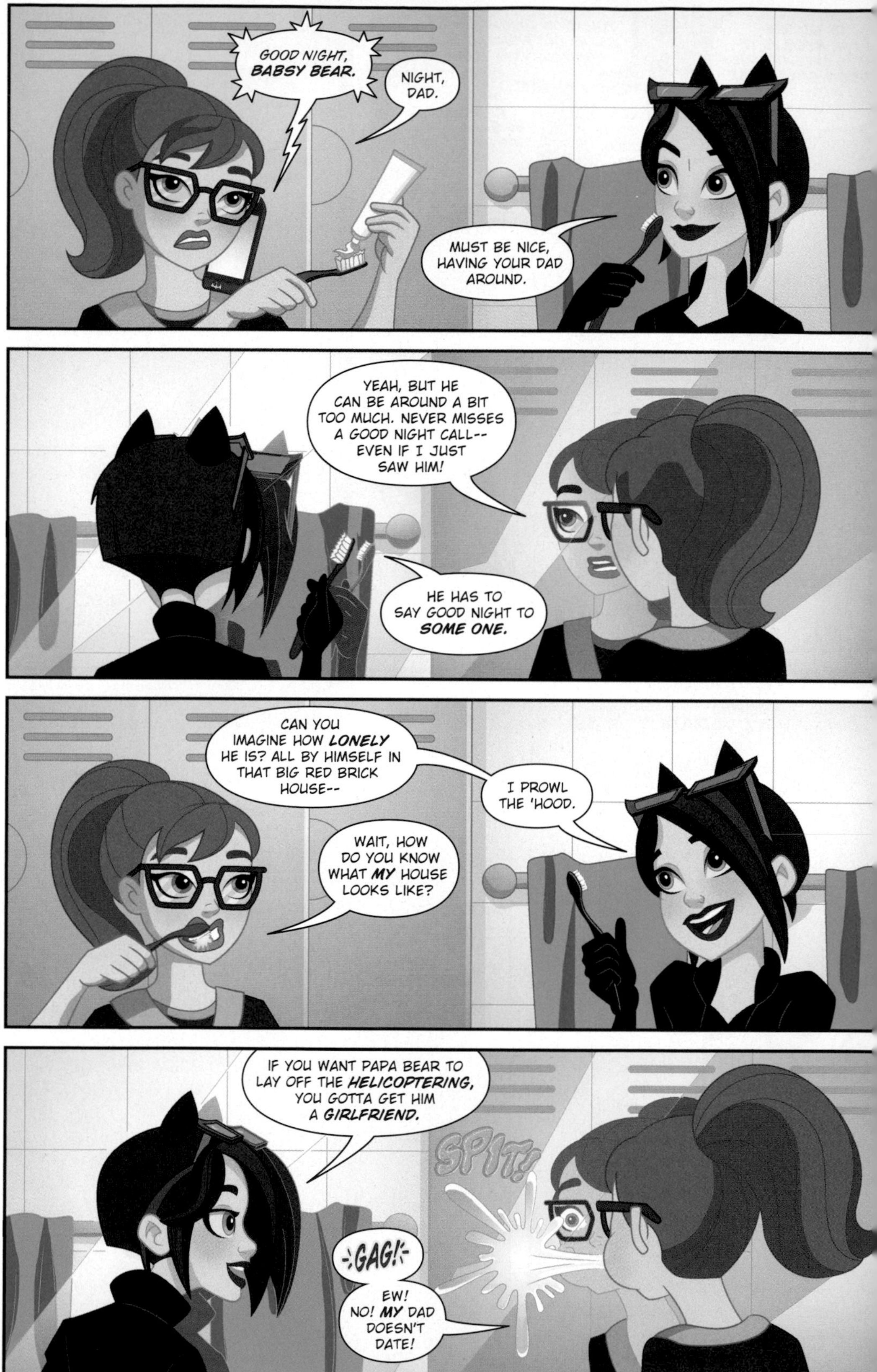
GOOD NIGHT, BABSY BEAR.
NIGHT, DAD.
MUST BE NICE, HAVING YOUR DAD AROUND.
YEAH, BUT HE CAN BE AROUND A BIT TOO MUCH. NEVER MISSES A GOOD NIGHT CALL-- EVEN IF I JUST SAW HIM!
HE HAS TO SAY GOOD NIGHT TO SOME ONE.
CAN YOU IMAGINE HOW LONELY HE IS? ALL BY HIMSELF IN THAT BIG RED BRICK HOUSE--
I PROWL THE 'HOOD.
WAIT, HOW DO YOU KNOW WHAT MY HOUSE LOOKS LIKE?
IF YOU WANT PAPA BEAR TO LAY OFF THE HELICOPTERING, YOU GOTTA GET HIM A GIRLFRIEND.
SPIT!
GAG!
EW! NO! MY DAD DOESN'T DATE!

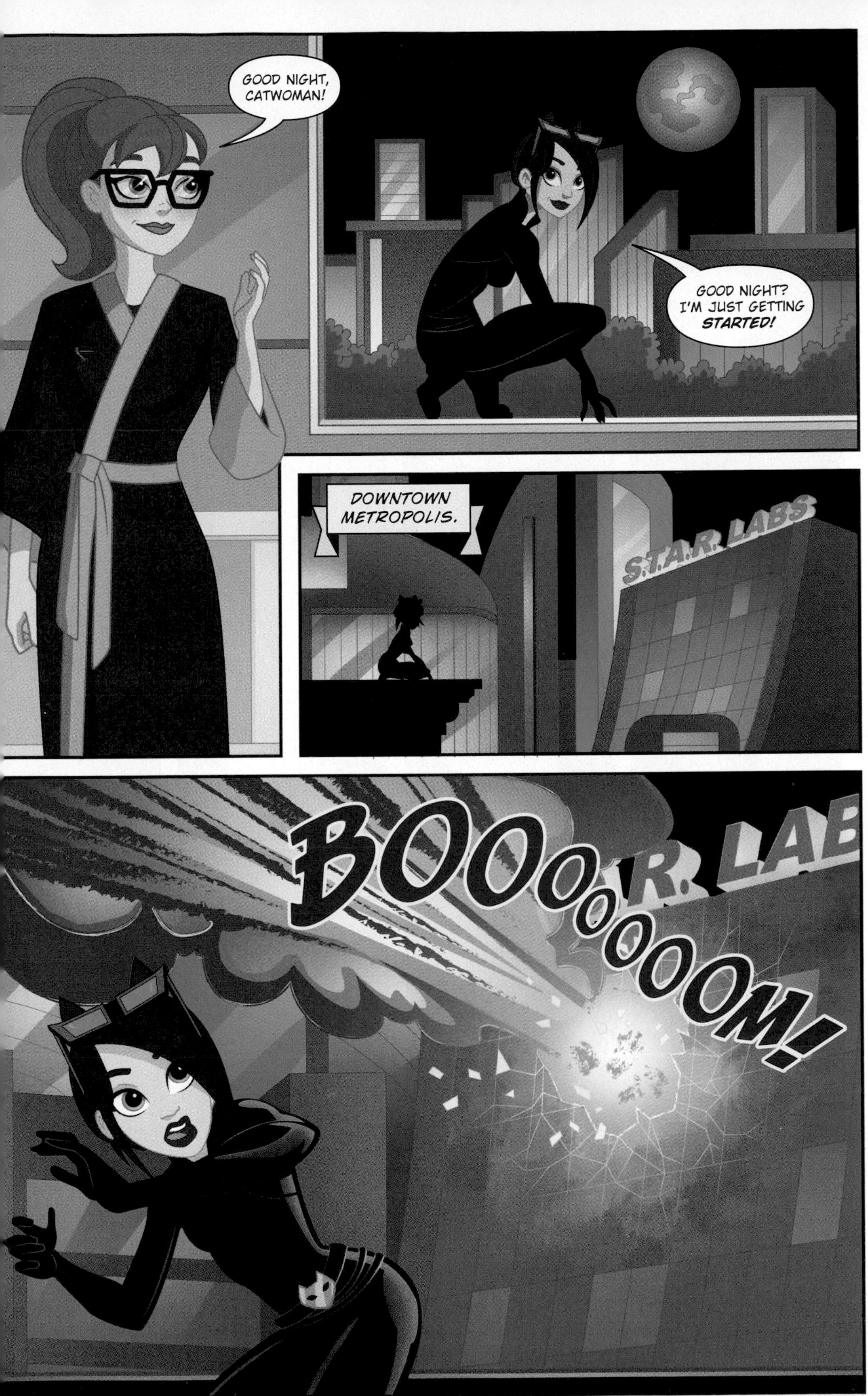
GOOD NIGHT, CATWOMAN!
GOOD NIGHT? I'M JUST GETTING STARTED!
DOWNTOWN METROPOLIS.
S.T.A.R. LABS
BOOOOOOOOM!
R. LAB

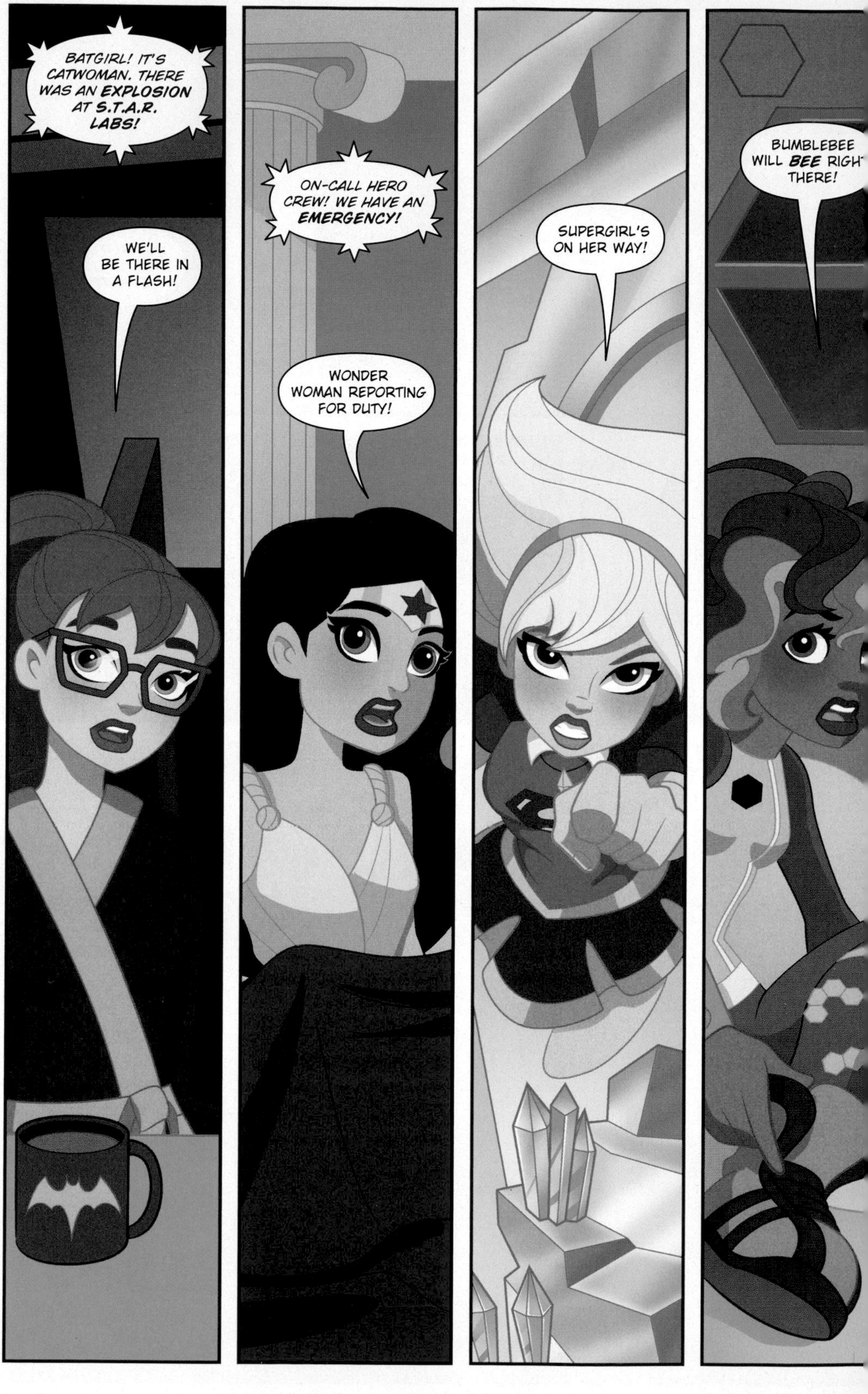
BATGIRL! IT'S CATWOMAN. THERE WAS AN EXPLOSION AT S.T.A.R. LABS!
WE'LL BE THERE IN A FLASH!
ON-CALL HERO CREW! WE HAVE AN EMERGENCY!
WONDER WOMAN REPORTING FOR DUTY!
SUPERGIRL'S ON HER WAY!
BUMBLEBEE WILL BEE RIGH
THERE!

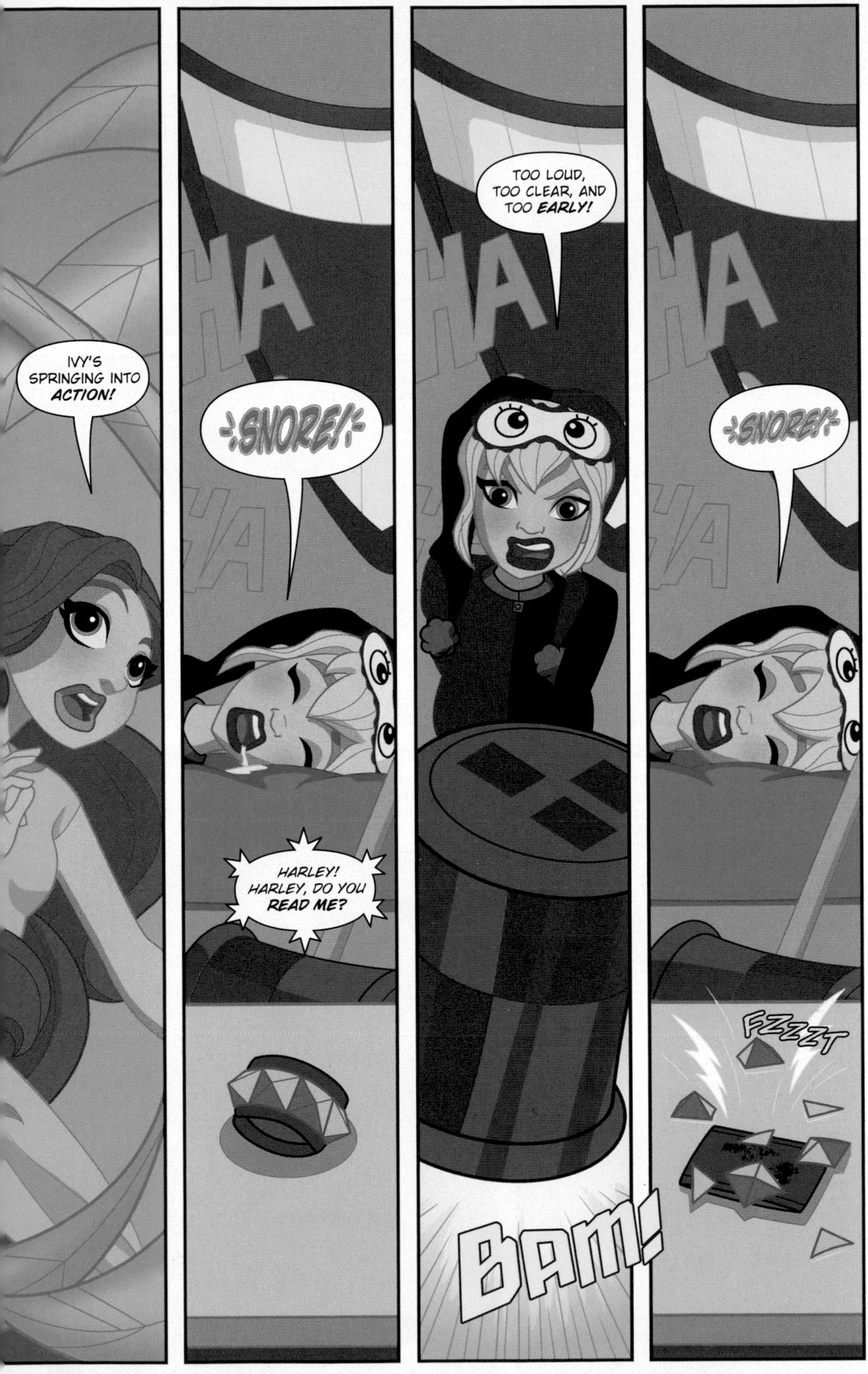
IVY'S SPRINGING INTO ACTION!
-SNORE!-
HARLEY! HARLEY, DO YOU READ ME?
TOO LOUD, TOO CLEAR, AND TOO EARLY!
BAM!
-SNORE!-
FZZZT

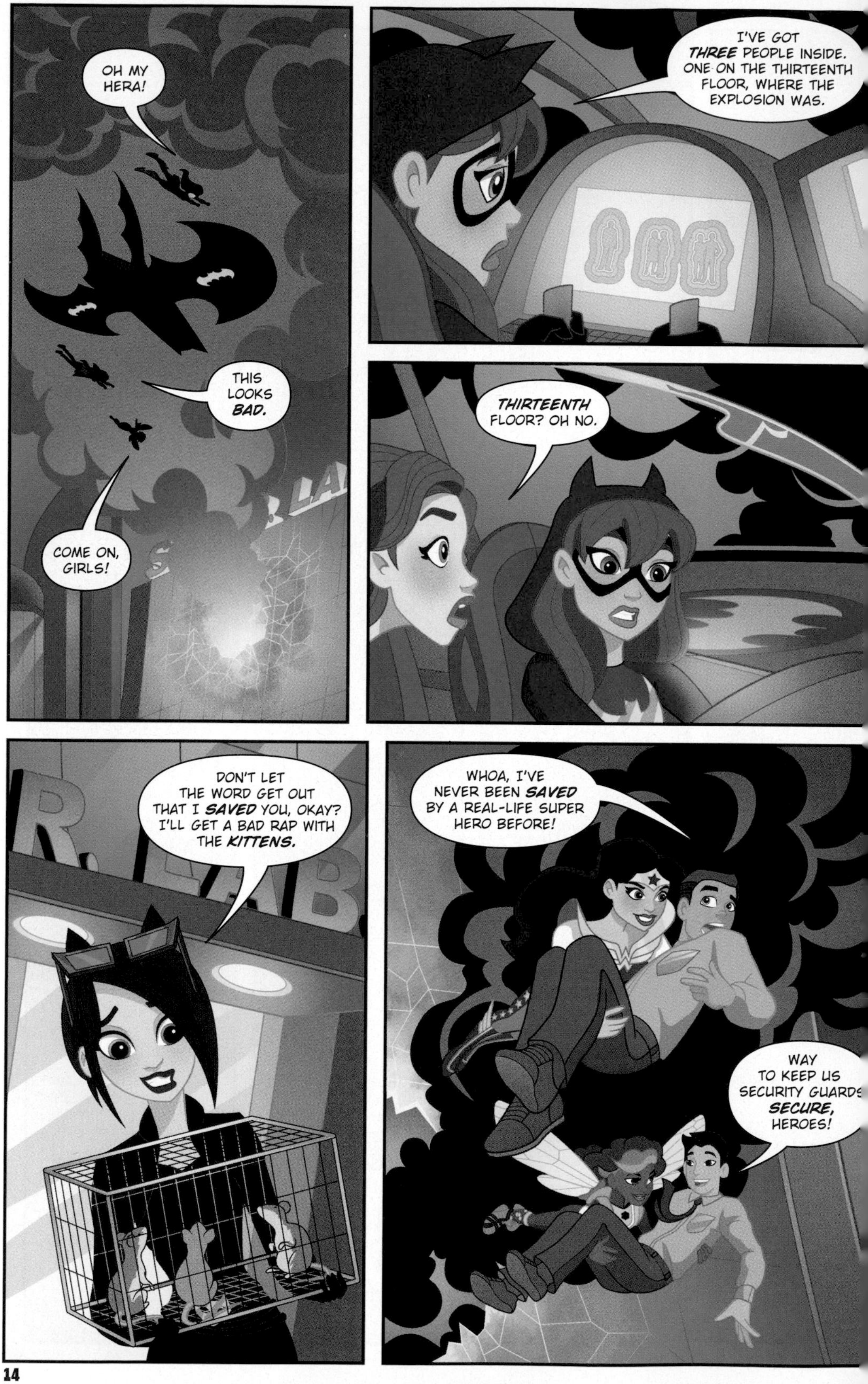
OH MY HERA!
THIS LOOKS BAD.
COME ON, GIRLS!
I'VE GOT THREE PEOPLE INSIDE. ONE ON THE THIRTEENTH FLOOR, WHERE THE EXPLOSION WAS.
THIRTEENTH FLOOR? OH NO.
DON'T LET THE WORD GET OUT THAT I SAVED YOU, OKAY? I'LL GET A BAD RAP WITH THE KITTENS.
WHOA, I'VE NEVER BEEN SAVED BY A REAL-LIFE SUPER HERO BEFORE!
WAY TO KEEP US SECURITY GUARDS SECURE, HEROES!

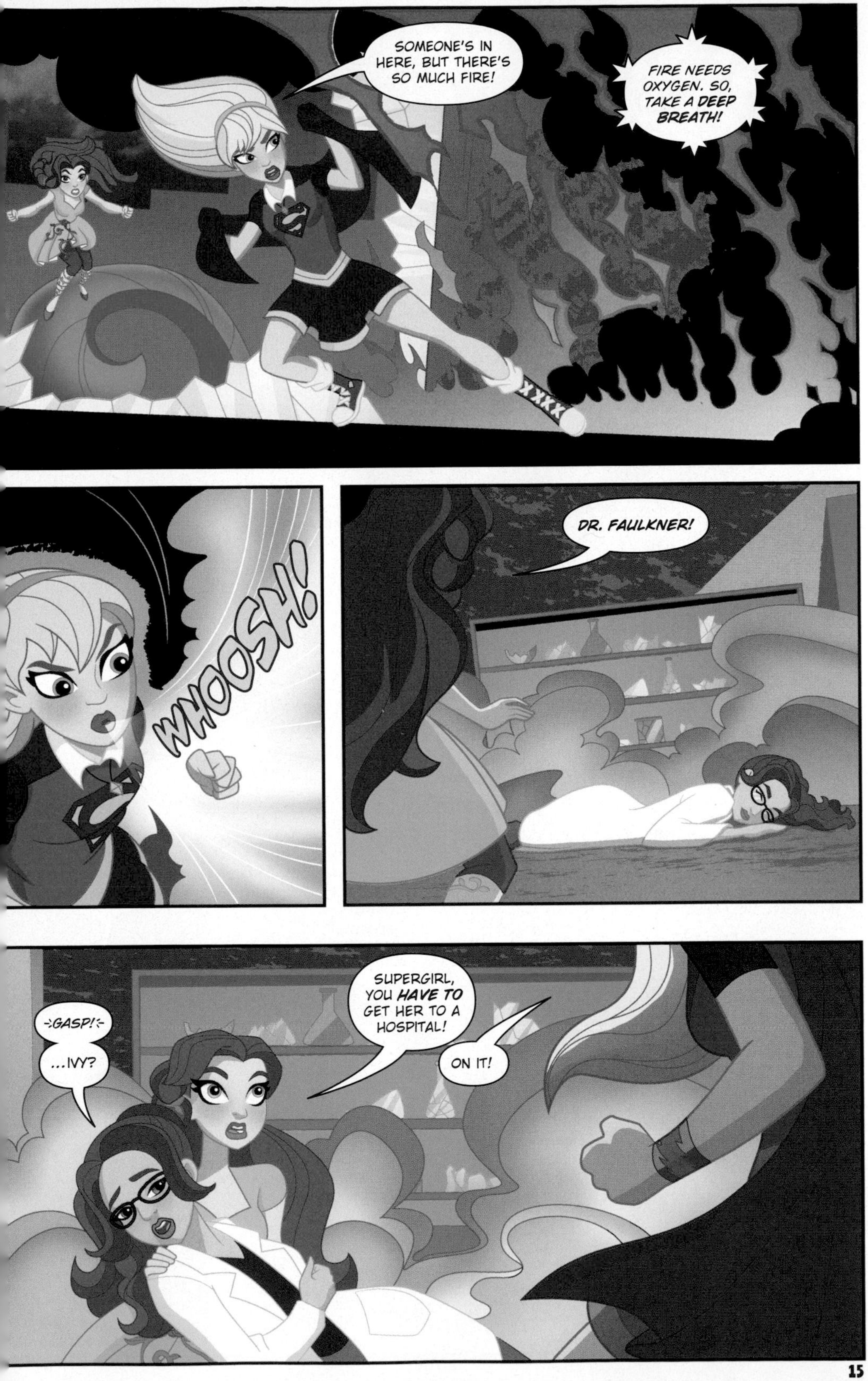
SOMEONE'S IN HERE, BUT THERE'S SO MUCH FIRE!
FIRE NEEDS OXYGEN. SO, TAKE A DEEP BREATH!
WHOOSH!
DR. FAULKNER!
-GASP!-
...IVY?
SUPERGIRL, YOU HAVE TO GET HER TO A HOSPITAL!
ON IT!

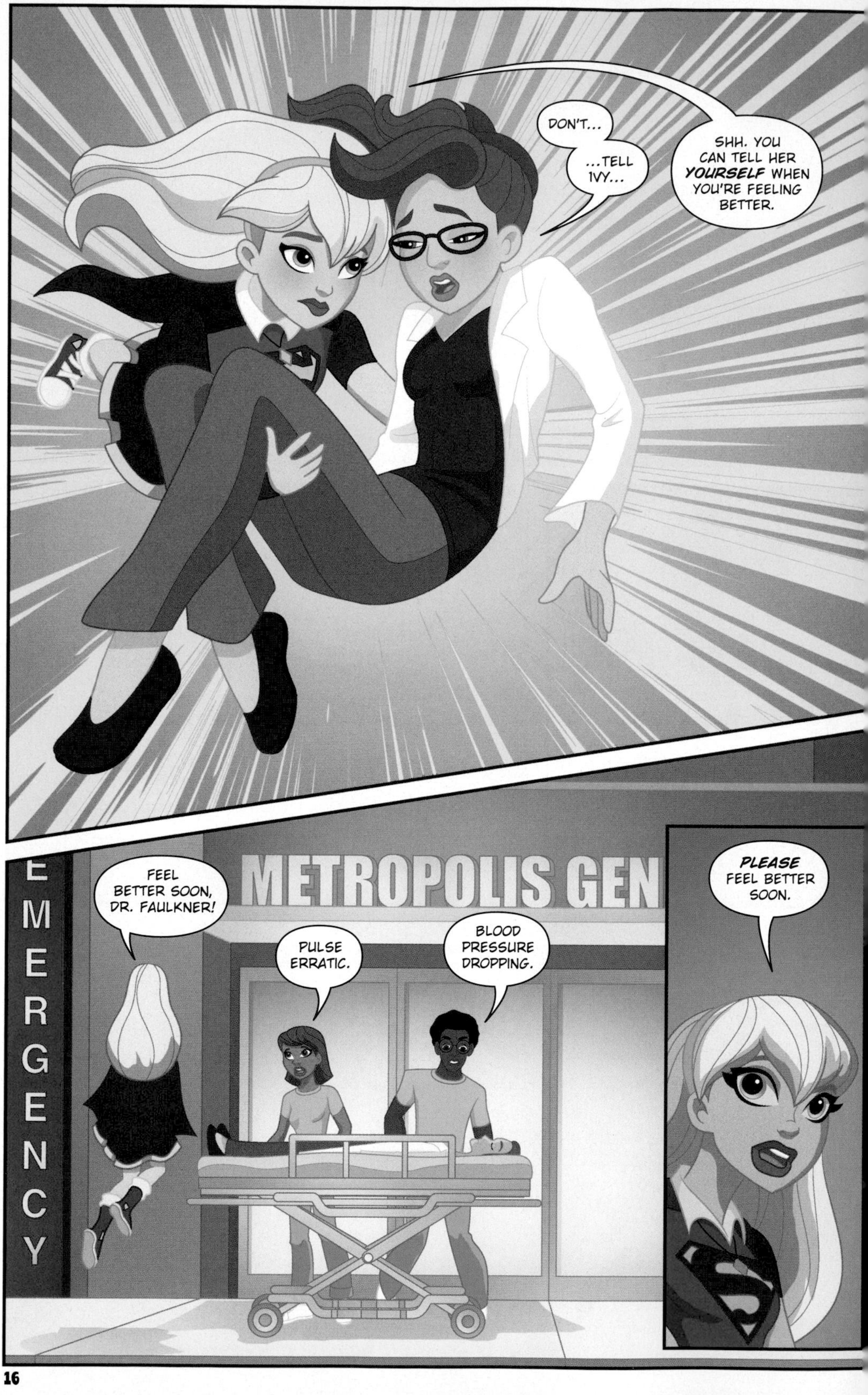
DON'T...
...TELL IVY...
SHH. YOU CAN TELL HER ***YOURSELF*** WHEN YOU'RE FEELING BETTER.
EMERGENCY
METROPOLIS GEN
FEEL BETTER SOON, DR. FAULKNER!
PULSE ERRATIC.
BLOOD PRESSURE DROPPING.
PLEASE FEEL BETTER SOON.

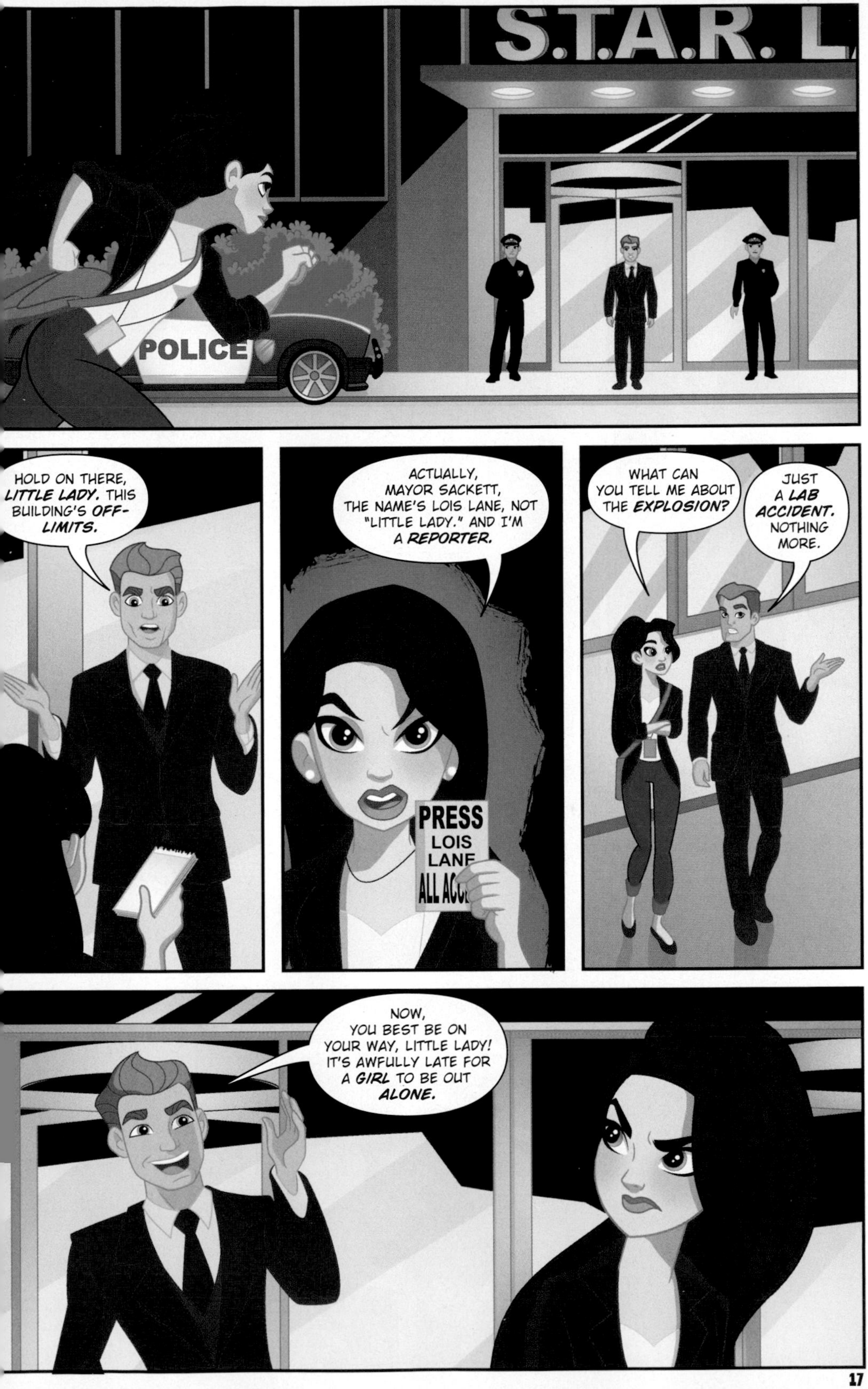
S.T.A.R. L
POLICE
HOLD ON THERE, LITTLE LADY. THIS BUILDING'S OFF-LIMITS.
ACTUALLY, MAYOR SACKETT, THE NAME'S LOIS LANE, NOT "LITTLE LADY." AND I'M A REPORTER.
PRESS
LOIS
LANE
WHAT CAN YOU TELL ME ABOUT THE EXPLOSION?
JUST A LAB ACCIDENT. NOTHING MORE.
NOW, YOU BEST BE ON YOUR WAY, LITTLE LADY! IT'S AWFULLY LATE FOR A GIRL TO BE OUT ALONE.

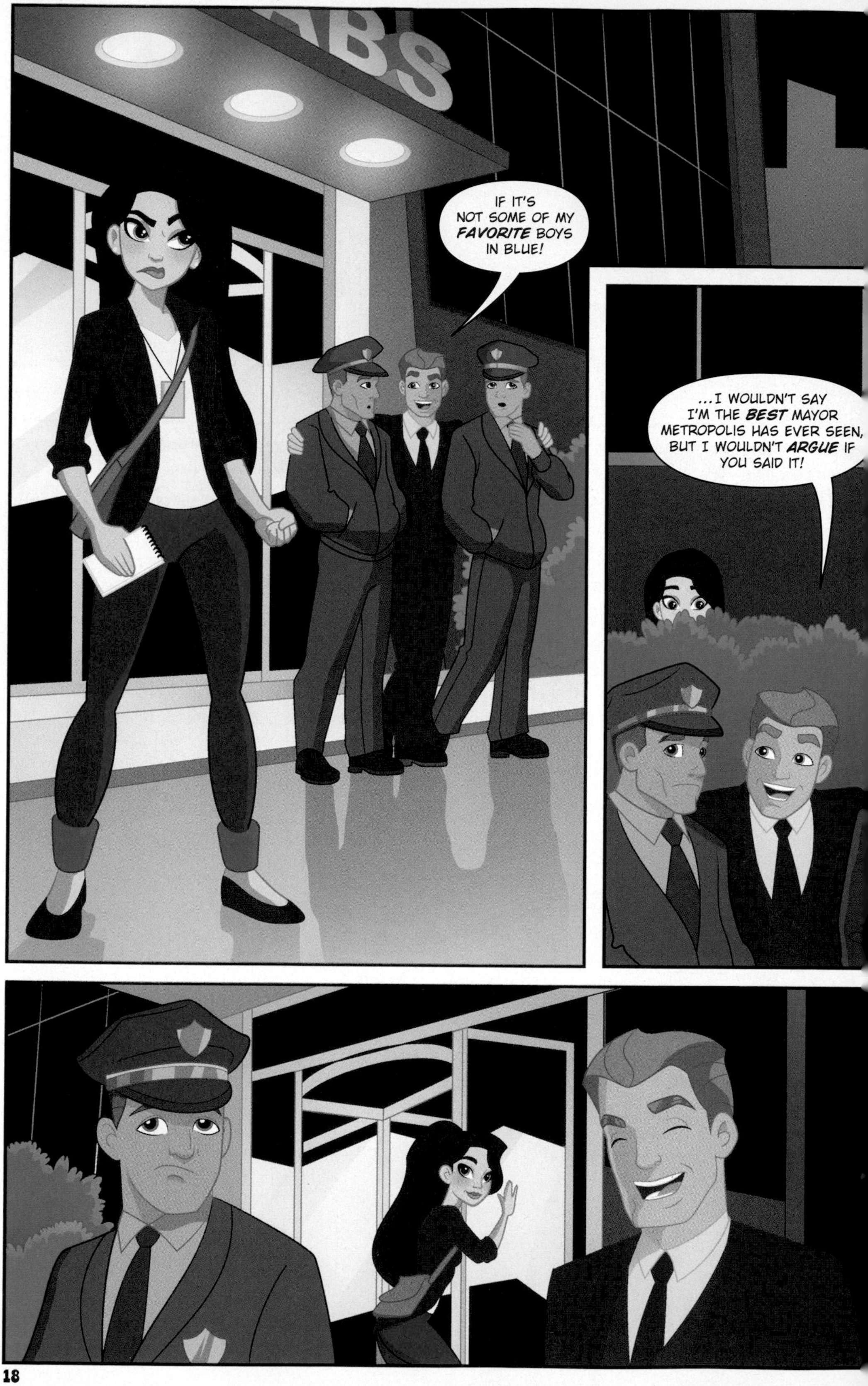
IF IT'S NOT SOME OF MY *FAVORITE* BOYS IN BLUE!
...I WOULDN'T SAY I'M THE **BEST** MAYOR METROPOLIS HAS EVER SEEN, BUT I WOULDN'T **ARGUE** IF YOU SAID IT!

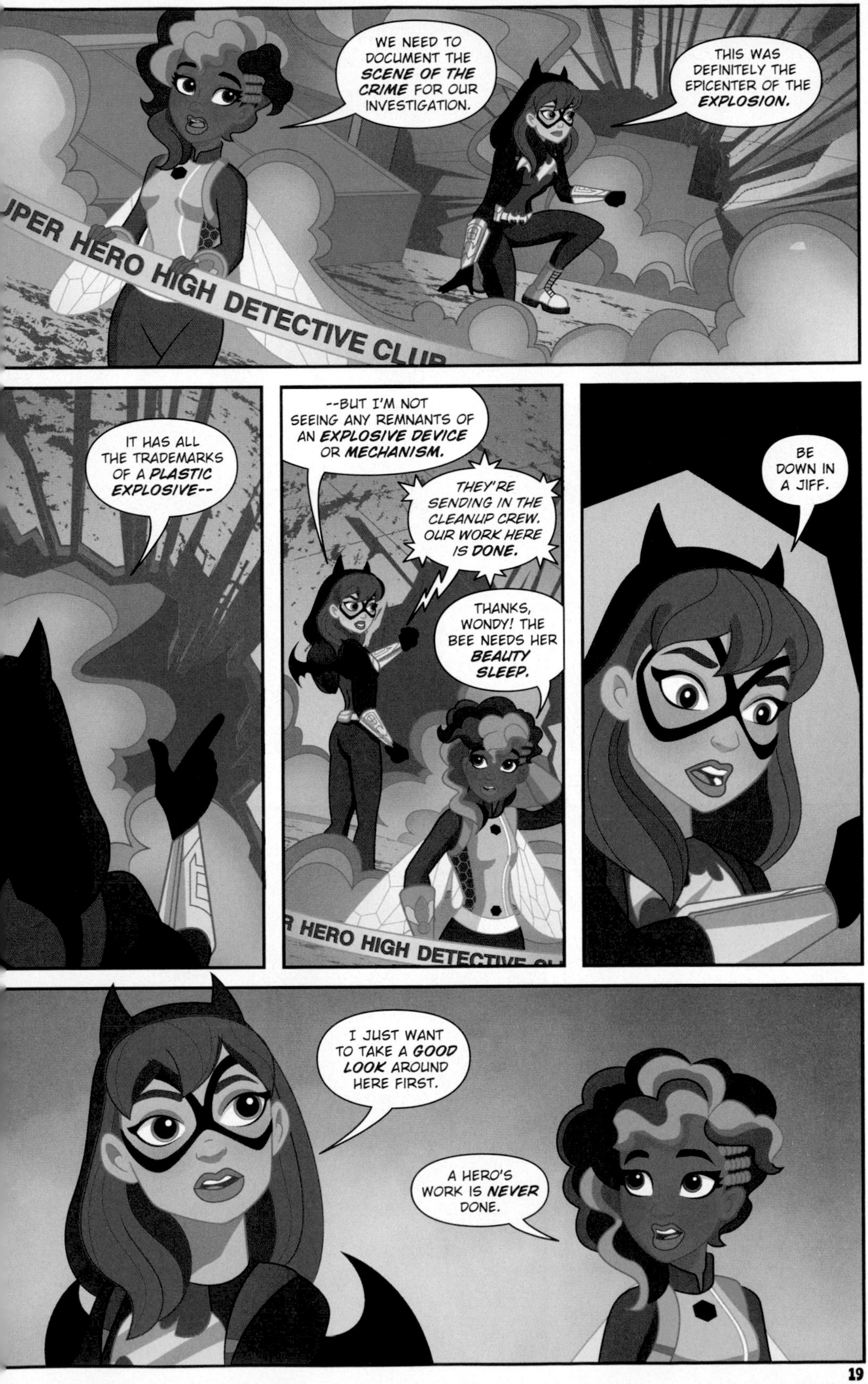
WE NEED TO DOCUMENT THE SCENE OF THE CRIME FOR OUR INVESTIGATION.
THIS WAS DEFINITELY THE EPICENTER OF THE EXPLOSION.
UPER HERO HIGH DETECTIVE CLUB
IT HAS ALL THE TRADEMARKS OF A PLASTIC EXPLOSIVE--
--BUT I'M NOT SEEING ANY REMNANTS OF AN EXPLOSIVE DEVICE OR MECHANISM.
THEY'RE SENDING IN THE CLEANUP CREW. OUR WORK HERE IS DONE.
THANKS, WONDY! THE BEE NEEDS HER BEAUTY SLEEP.
R HERO HIGH DETECTIVE
BE DOWN IN A JIFF.
I JUST WANT TO TAKE A GOOD LOOK AROUND HERE FIRST.
A HERO'S WORK IS NEVER DONE.

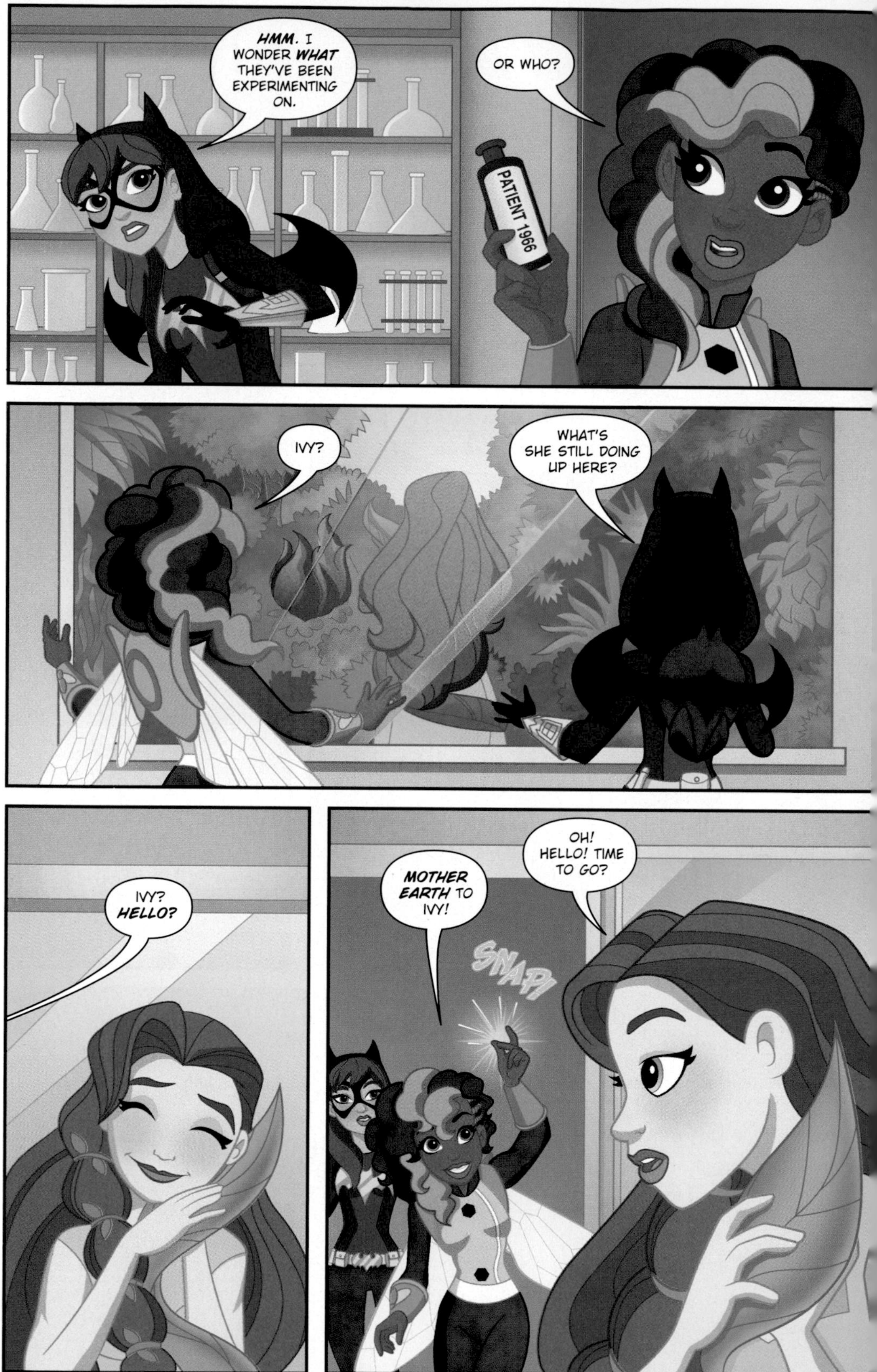

HMM. I WONDER WHAT THEY'VE BEEN EXPERIMENTING ON.
OR WHO?
PATIENT 1966
IVY?
WHAT'S SHE STILL DOING UP HERE?
IVY? HELLO?
MOTHER EARTH TO IVY!
SNAP!
OH! HELLO! TIME TO GO?

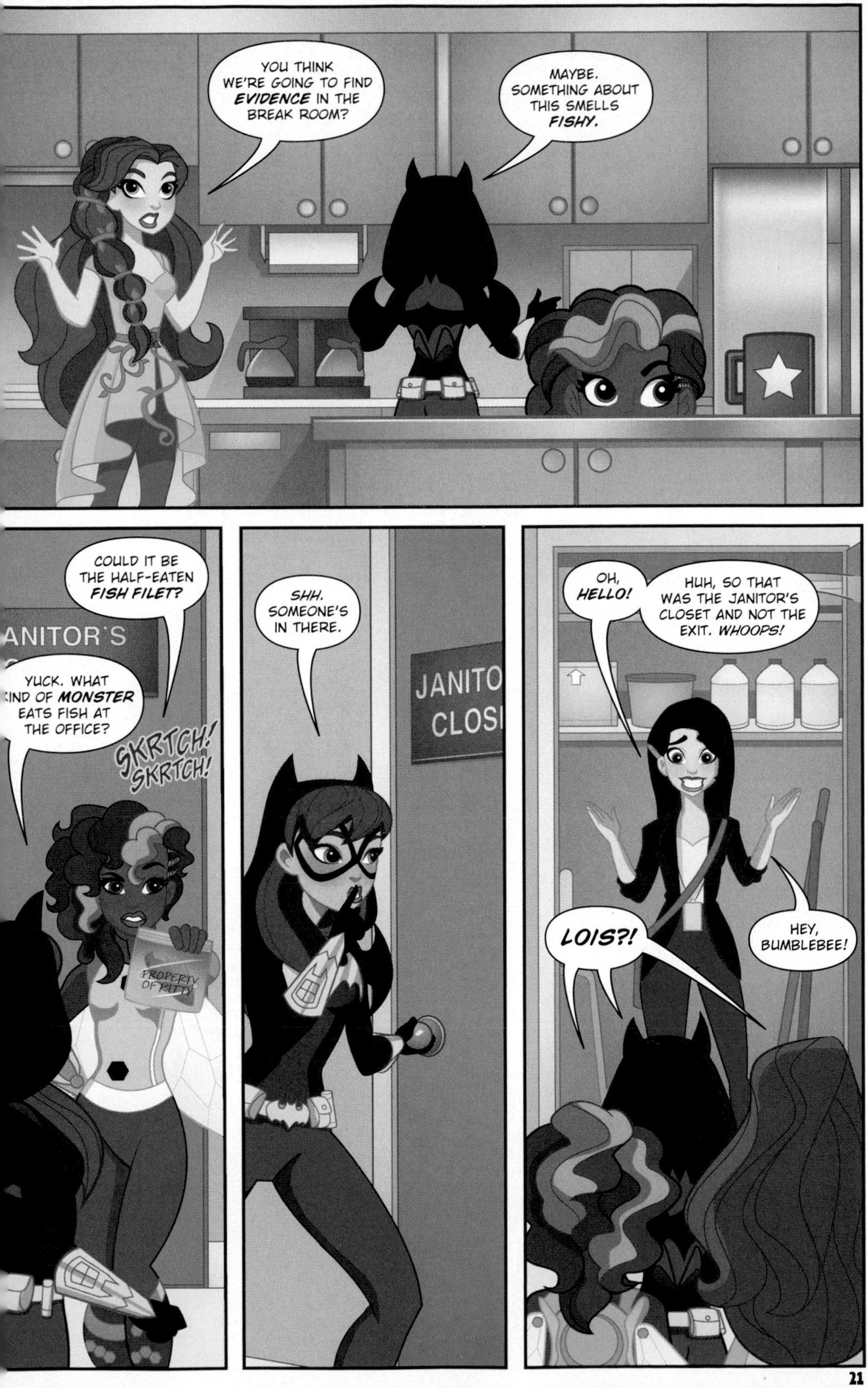
YOU THINK WE'RE GOING TO FIND EVIDENCE IN THE BREAK ROOM?
MAYBE. SOMETHING ABOUT THIS SMELLS FISHY.
COULD IT BE THE HALF-EATEN FISH FILET?
ANITOR'S
YUCK. WHAT KIND OF MONSTER EATS FISH AT THE OFFICE?
SKRTCH! SKRTCH!
PROPERTY OF KITTY
SHH. SOMEONE'S IN THERE.
JANITO CLOS
OH, HELLO!
HUH, SO THAT WAS THE JANITOR'S CLOSET AND NOT THE EXIT. WHOOPS!
LOIS?!
HEY, BUMBLEBEE!

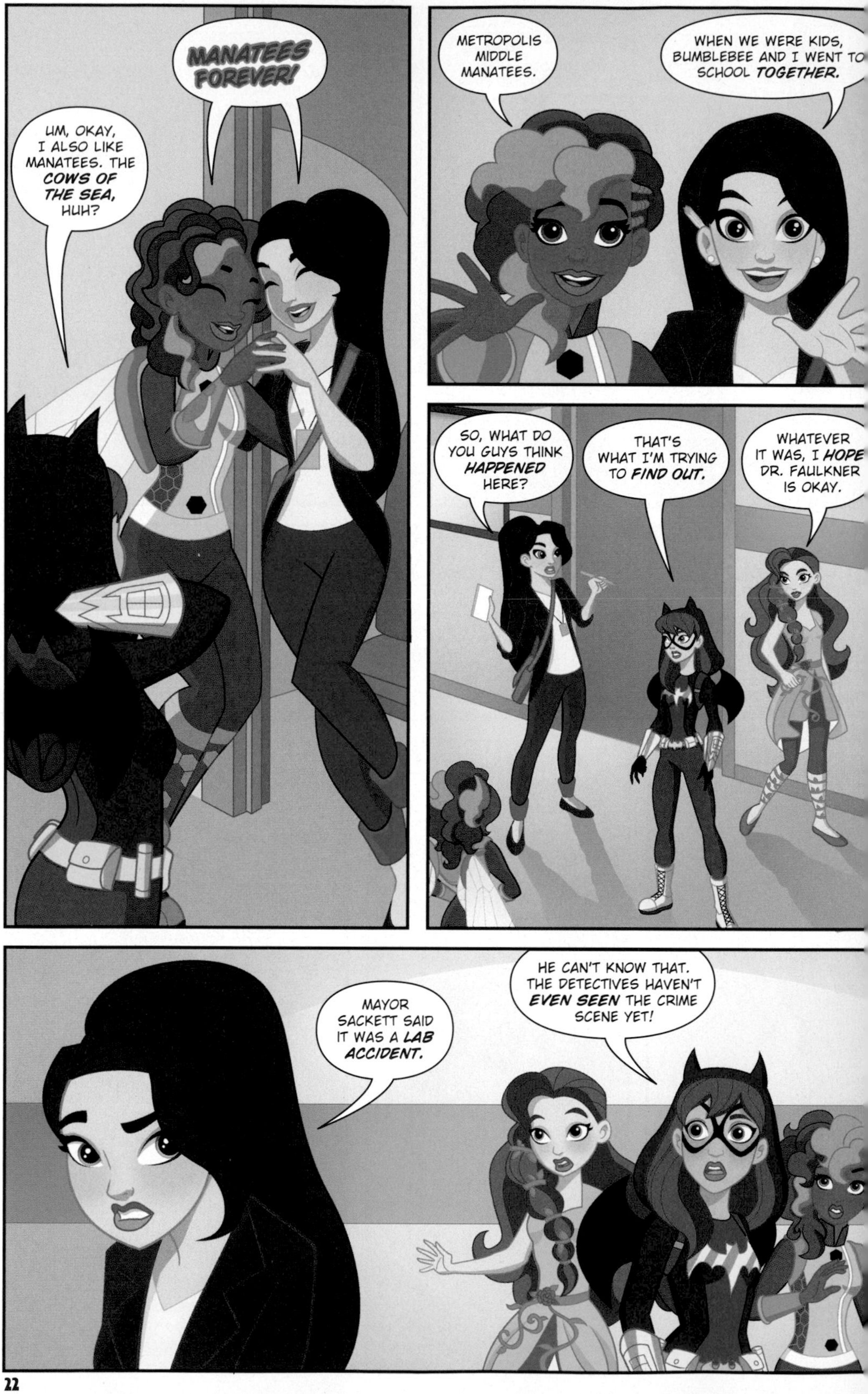
MANATEES FOREVER!
UM, OKAY, I ALSO LIKE MANATEES. THE COWS OF THE SEA, HUH?
METROPOLIS MIDDLE MANATEES.
WHEN WE WERE KIDS, BUMBLEBEE AND I WENT TO SCHOOL TOGETHER.
SO, WHAT DO YOU GUYS THINK HAPPENED HERE?
THAT'S WHAT I'M TRYING TO FIND OUT.
WHATEVER IT WAS, I HOPE DR. FAULKNER IS OKAY.
MAYOR SACKETT SAID IT WAS A LAB ACCIDENT.
HE CAN'T KNOW THAT. THE DETECTIVES HAVEN'T EVEN SEEN THE CRIME SCENE YET!

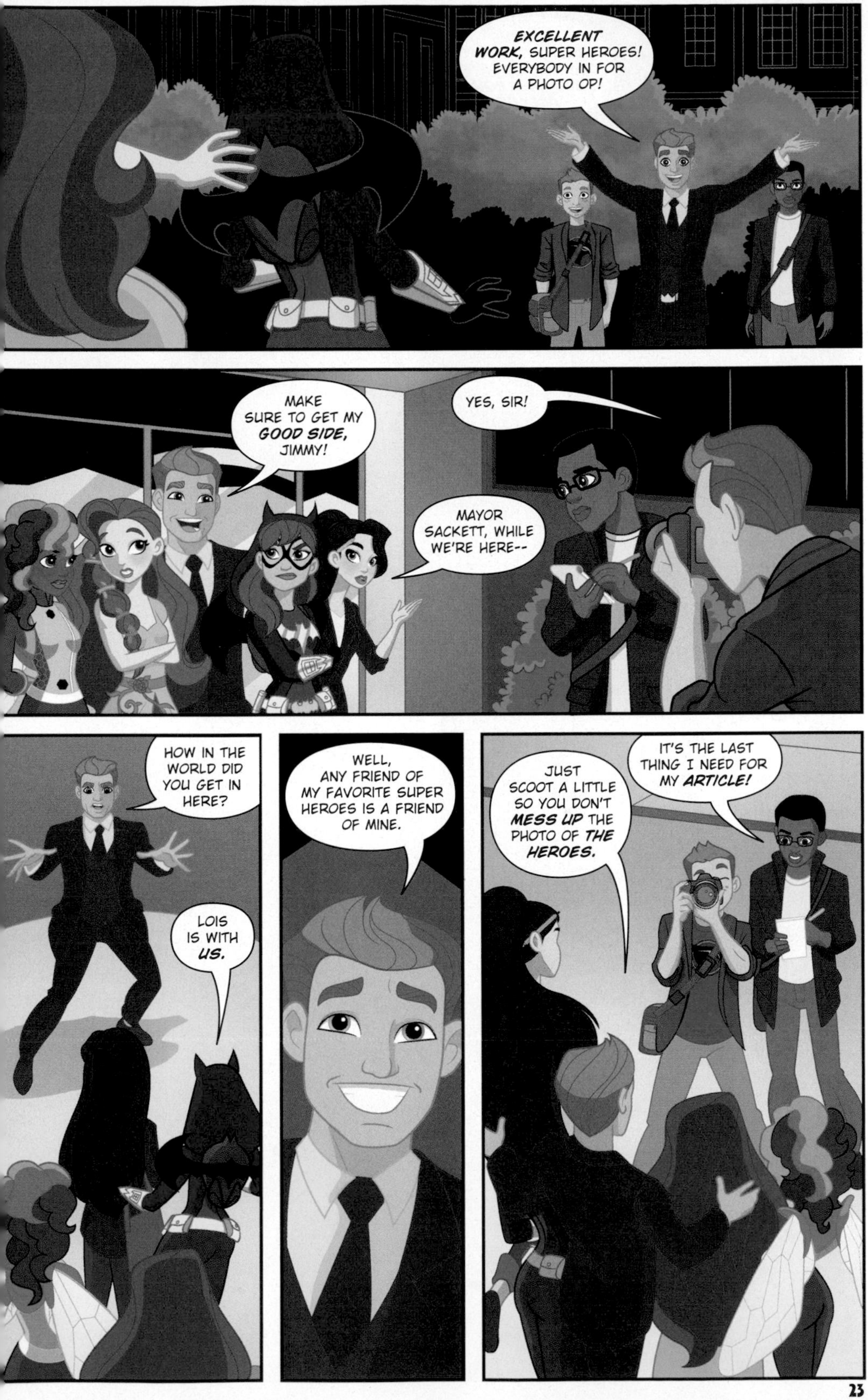
EXCELLENT WORK, SUPER HEROES! EVERYBODY IN FOR A PHOTO OP!
MAKE SURE TO GET MY GOOD SIDE, JIMMY!
YES, SIR!
MAYOR SACKETT, WHILE WE'RE HERE--
HOW IN THE WORLD DID YOU GET IN HERE?
LOIS IS WITH US.
WELL, ANY FRIEND OF MY FAVORITE SUPER HEROES IS A FRIEND OF MINE.
JUST SCOOT A LITTLE SO YOU DON'T MESS UP THE PHOTO OF THE HEROES.
IT'S THE LAST THING I NEED FOR MY ARTICLE!

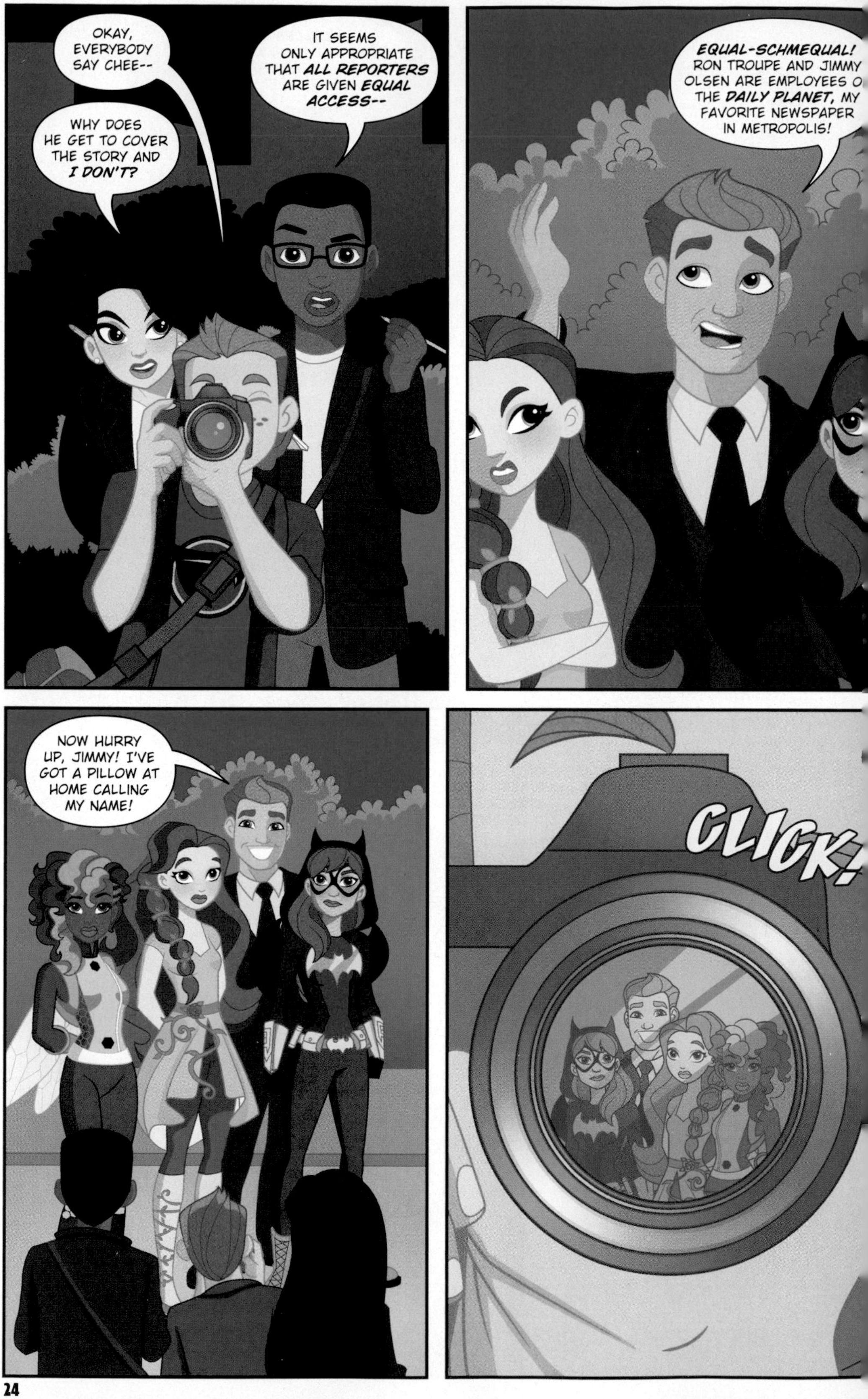
OKAY, EVERYBODY SAY CHEE--
WHY DOES HE GET TO COVER THE STORY AND I DON'T?
IT SEEMS ONLY APPROPRIATE THAT ALL REPORTERS ARE GIVEN EQUAL ACCESS--
EQUAL-SCHMEQUAL! RON TROUPE AND JIMMY OLSEN ARE EMPLOYEES O THE DAILY PLANET, MY FAVORITE NEWSPAPER IN METROPOLIS!
NOW HURRY UP, JIMMY! I'VE GOT A PILLOW AT HOME CALLING MY NAME!
CLICK!

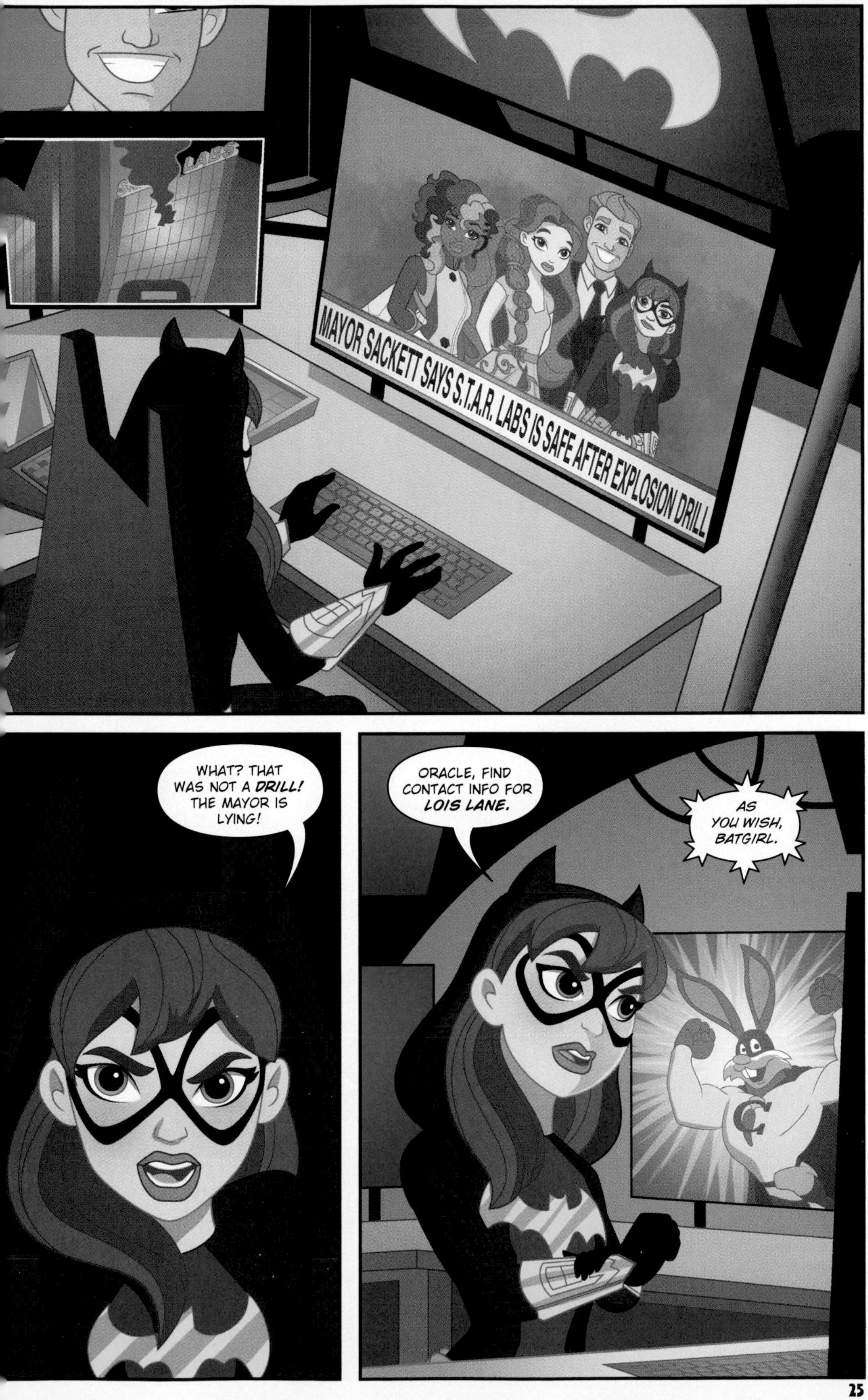
LABS
MAYOR SACKETT SAYS S.T.A.R. LABS IS SAFE AFTER EXPLOSION DRILL
WHAT? THAT WAS NOT A *DRILL!* THE MAYOR IS LYING!
ORACLE, FIND CONTACT INFO FOR **LOIS LANE.**
AS YOU WISH, BATGIRL.

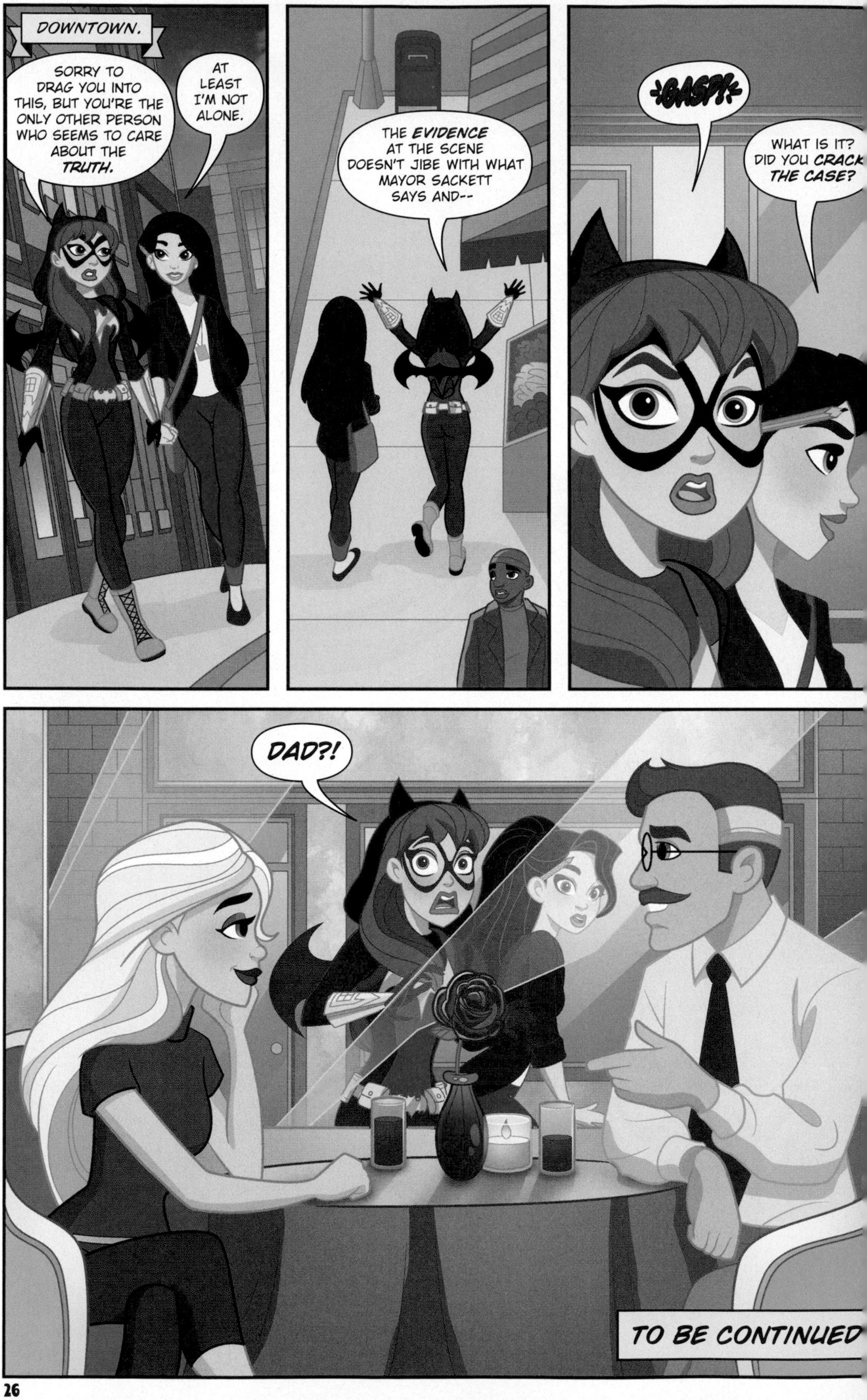

DOWNTOWN.
SORRY TO DRAG YOU INTO THIS, BUT YOU'RE THE ONLY OTHER PERSON WHO SEEMS TO CARE ABOUT THE TRUTH.
AT LEAST I'M NOT ALONE.
THE EVIDENCE AT THE SCENE DOESN'T JIBE WITH WHAT MAYOR SACKETT SAYS AND--
GASP!
WHAT IS IT? DID YOU CRACK THE CASE?
DAD?!
TO BE CONTINUED

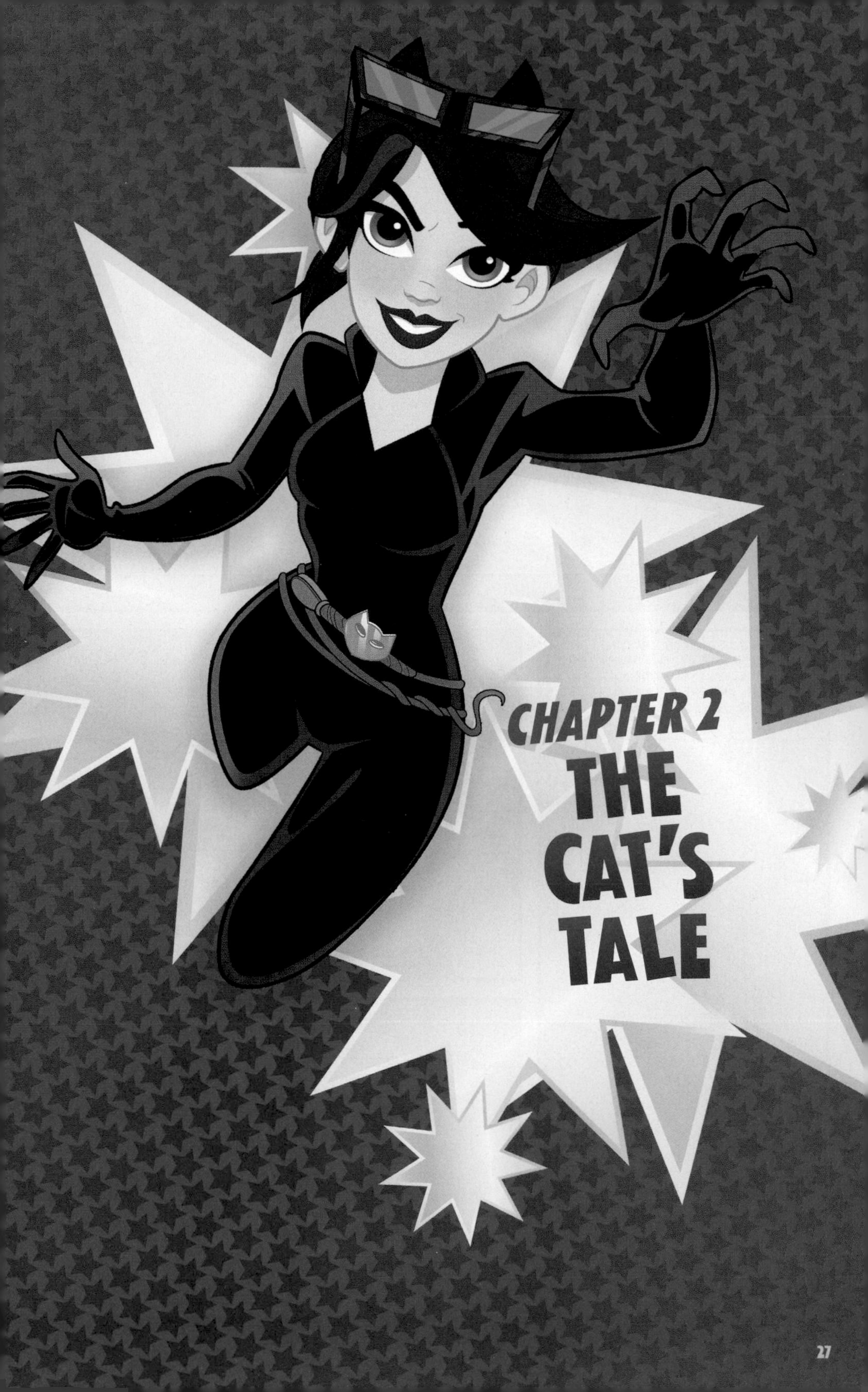

CHAPTER 2
THE CAT'S TALE

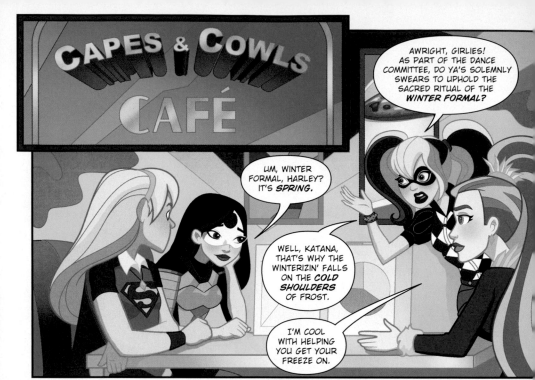

CAPES & COWLS CAFÉ

AWRIGHT, GIRLIES! AS PART OF THE DANCE COMMITTEE, DO YA'S SOLEMNLY SWEARS TO UPHOLD THE SACRED RITUAL OF THE *WINTER FORMAL?*

UM, WINTER FORMAL, HARLEY? IT'S *SPRING.*

WELL, KATANA, THAT'S WHY THE WINTERIZIN' FALLS ON THE *COLD SHOULDERS* OF FROST.

I'M COOL WITH HELPING YOU GET YOUR FREEZE ON.

WE'VE GOT THE KABOOM CANDY COOLER FOR HARLEY. THE GREEN TEA LATTE FOR KATANA. SPINACH JUICE FOR SUPERGIRL. AND THE HONEY SMOOTHIE FOR YOU, BUMBLEBEE!

RIGHT ON, STEVE! THE DANCE COMMITTEE THANKS YOU.

BY THE WAY, YOU GOING TO THE DANCE?

NAH. IT'S THE SUPER HERO HIGH DANCE FOR *SUPER* KIDS, NOT NON-SUPER GUYS *LIKE ME.*

BUT *ENJOY* THOSE DRINKS!

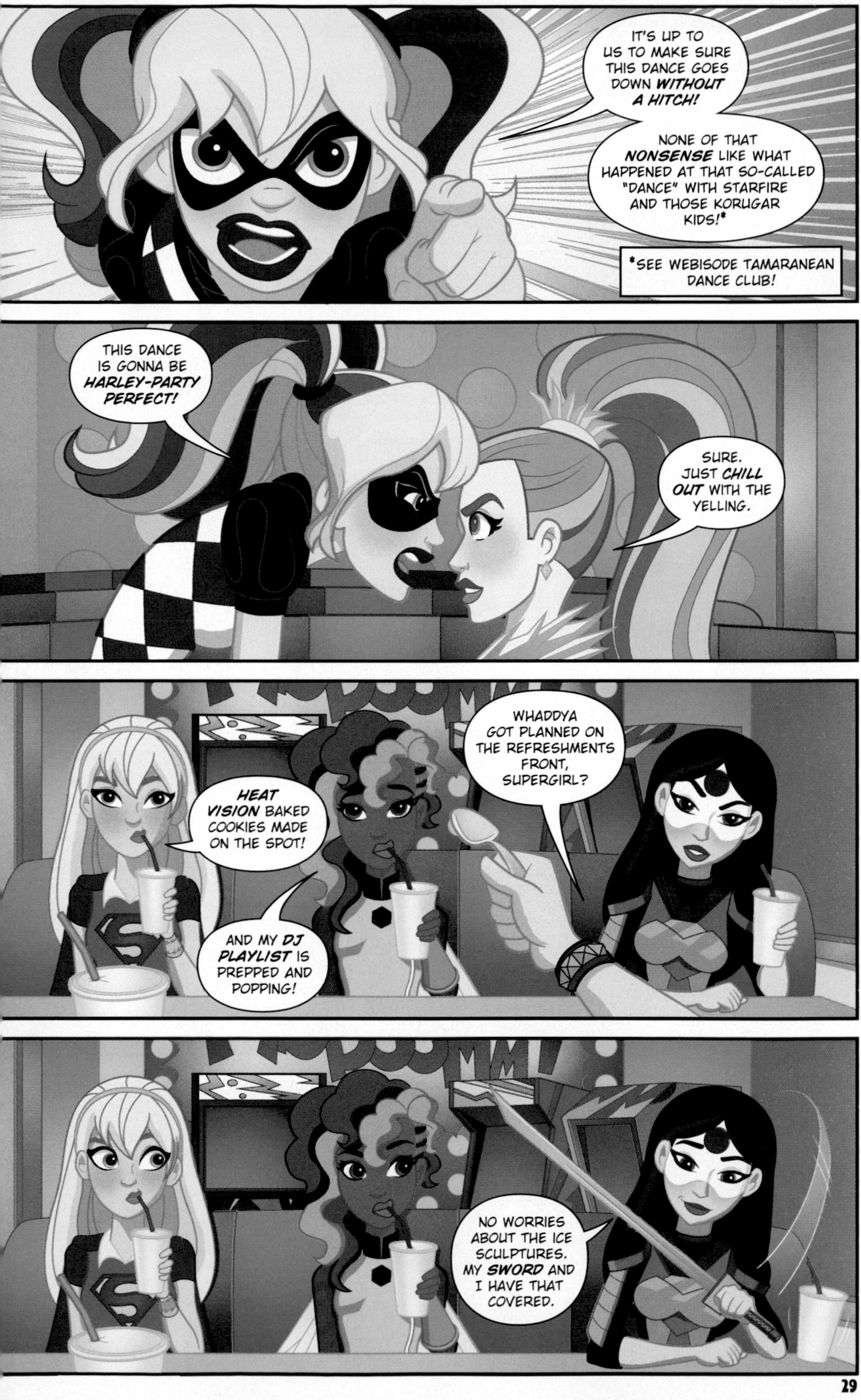
IT'S UP TO US TO MAKE SURE THIS DANCE GOES DOWN WITHOUT A HITCH!
NONE OF THAT NONSENSE LIKE WHAT HAPPENED AT THAT SO-CALLED "DANCE" WITH STARFIRE AND THOSE KORUGAR KIDS!*
*SEE WEBISODE TAMARANEAN DANCE CLUB!
THIS DANCE IS GONNA BE HARLEY-PARTY PERFECT!
SURE. JUST CHILL OUT WITH THE YELLING.
HEAT VISION BAKED COOKIES MADE ON THE SPOT!
AND MY DJ PLAYLIST IS PREPPED AND POPPING!
WHADDYA GOT PLANNED ON THE REFRESHMENTS FRONT, SUPERGIRL?
NO WORRIES ABOUT THE ICE SCULPTURES. MY SWORD AND I HAVE THAT COVERED.

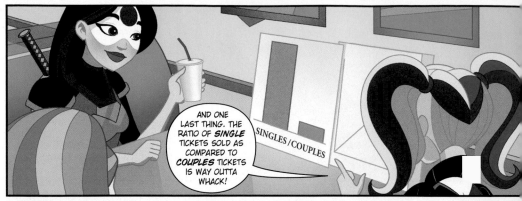

AND ONE LAST THING. THE RATIO OF **SINGLE** TICKETS SOLD AS COMPARED TO **COUPLES** TICKETS IS WAY OUTTA WHACK!

SINGLES / COUPLES

SO, IT FALLS TO US TO DO SOME **MATCH-MAKIN'**!

HARLEY, YOU CAN BARELY **MATCH** YOUR SOCKS.

NO GOOD EVER COMES OUT OF **INTERFERING** IN OTHER PEOPLES' LOVE LIVES.

FINE! YA TWO SOURPUSSES ARE GONNA MISS OUT ON THE FUN.

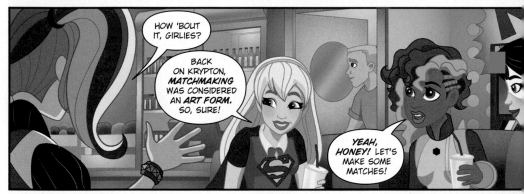

HOW 'BOUT IT, GIRLIES?

BACK ON KRYPTON, **MATCHMAKING** WAS CONSIDERED AN **ART FORM.** SO, SURE!

YEAH, HONEY! LET'S MAKE SOME MATCHES!

♪♫♫

AND I KNOW JUST WHERE TO **START!**

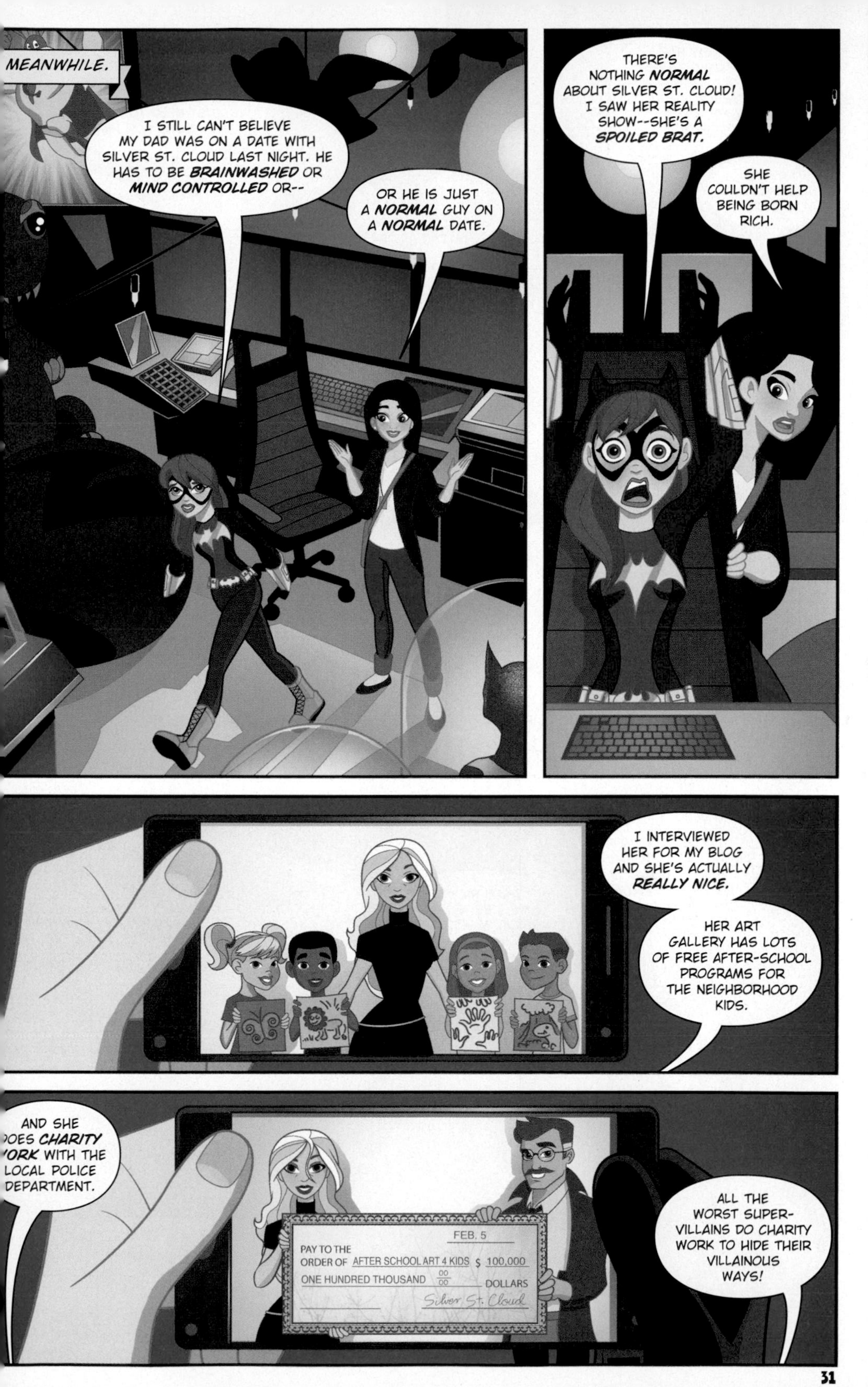
MEANWHILE.
I STILL CAN'T BELIEVE MY DAD WAS ON A DATE WITH SILVER ST. CLOUD LAST NIGHT. HE HAS TO BE BRAINWASHED OR MIND CONTROLLED OR--
OR HE IS JUST A NORMAL GUY ON A NORMAL DATE.
THERE'S NOTHING NORMAL ABOUT SILVER ST. CLOUD! I SAW HER REALITY SHOW--SHE'S A SPOILED BRAT.
SHE COULDN'T HELP BEING BORN RICH.
I INTERVIEWED HER FOR MY BLOG AND SHE'S ACTUALLY REALLY NICE.
HER ART GALLERY HAS LOTS OF FREE AFTER-SCHOOL PROGRAMS FOR THE NEIGHBORHOOD KIDS.
AND SHE OES CHARITY ORK WITH THE LOCAL POLICE DEPARTMENT.
FEB. 5
PAY TO THE ORDER OF AFTER SCHOOL ART 4 KIDS $ 100,000
ONE HUNDRED THOUSAND 00/00 DOLLARS
Silver St. Cloud
ALL THE WORST SUPER-VILLAINS DO CHARITY WORK TO HIDE THEIR VILLAINOUS WAYS!

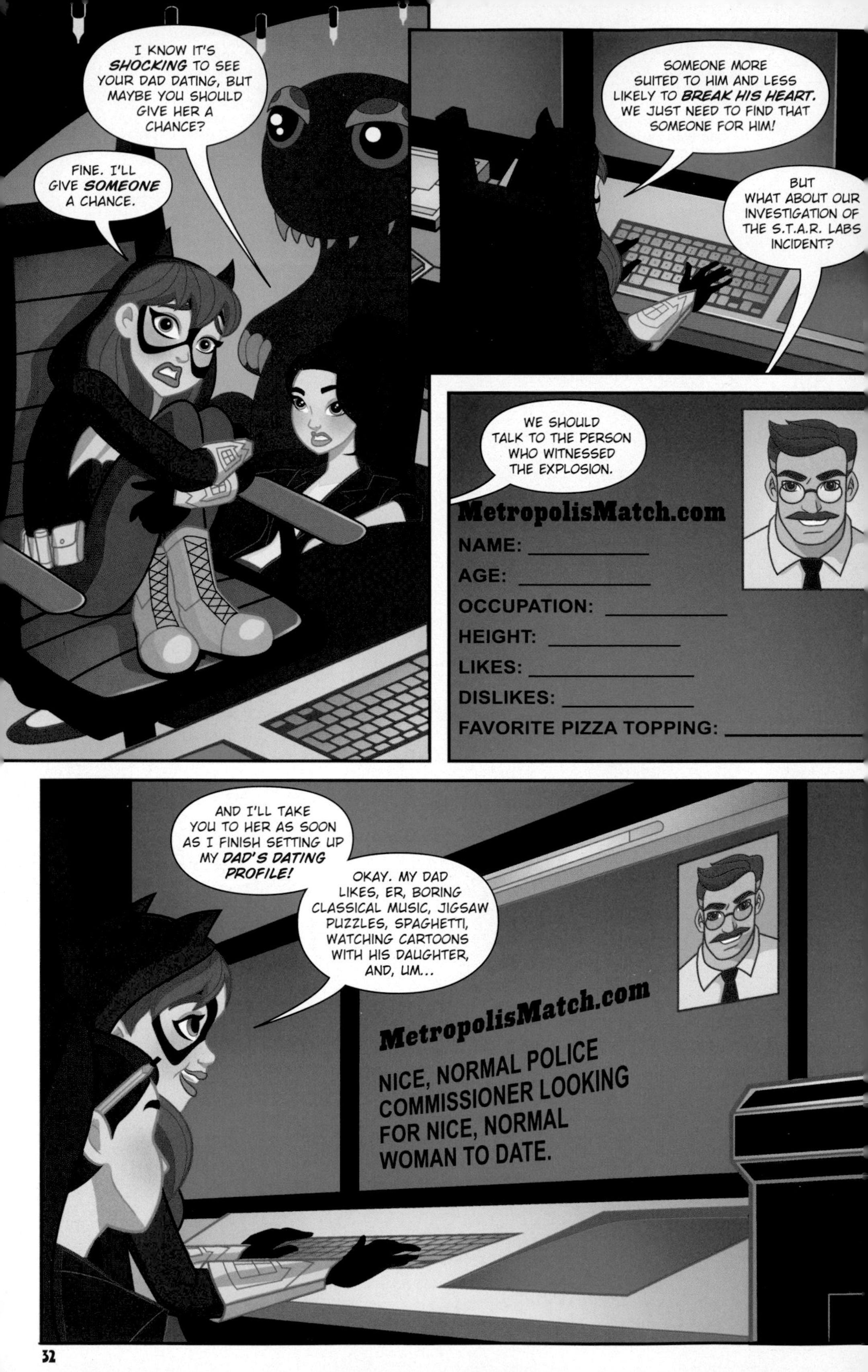
I KNOW IT'S SHOCKING TO SEE YOUR DAD DATING, BUT MAYBE YOU SHOULD GIVE HER A CHANCE?
FINE. I'LL GIVE SOMEONE A CHANCE.
SOMEONE MORE SUITED TO HIM AND LESS LIKELY TO BREAK HIS HEART. WE JUST NEED TO FIND THAT SOMEONE FOR HIM!
BUT WHAT ABOUT OUR INVESTIGATION OF THE S.T.A.R. LABS INCIDENT?
WE SHOULD TALK TO THE PERSON WHO WITNESSED THE EXPLOSION.
MetropolisMatch.com
NAME:
AGE:
OCCUPATION:
HEIGHT:
LIKES:
DISLIKES:
FAVORITE PIZZA TOPPING:
AND I'LL TAKE YOU TO HER AS SOON AS I FINISH SETTING UP MY DAD'S DATING PROFILE!
OKAY. MY DAD LIKES, ER, BORING CLASSICAL MUSIC, JIGSAW PUZZLES, SPAGHETTI, WATCHING CARTOONS WITH HIS DAUGHTER, AND, UM...
MetropolisMatch.com
NICE, NORMAL POLICE COMMISSIONER LOOKING FOR NICE, NORMAL WOMAN TO DATE.

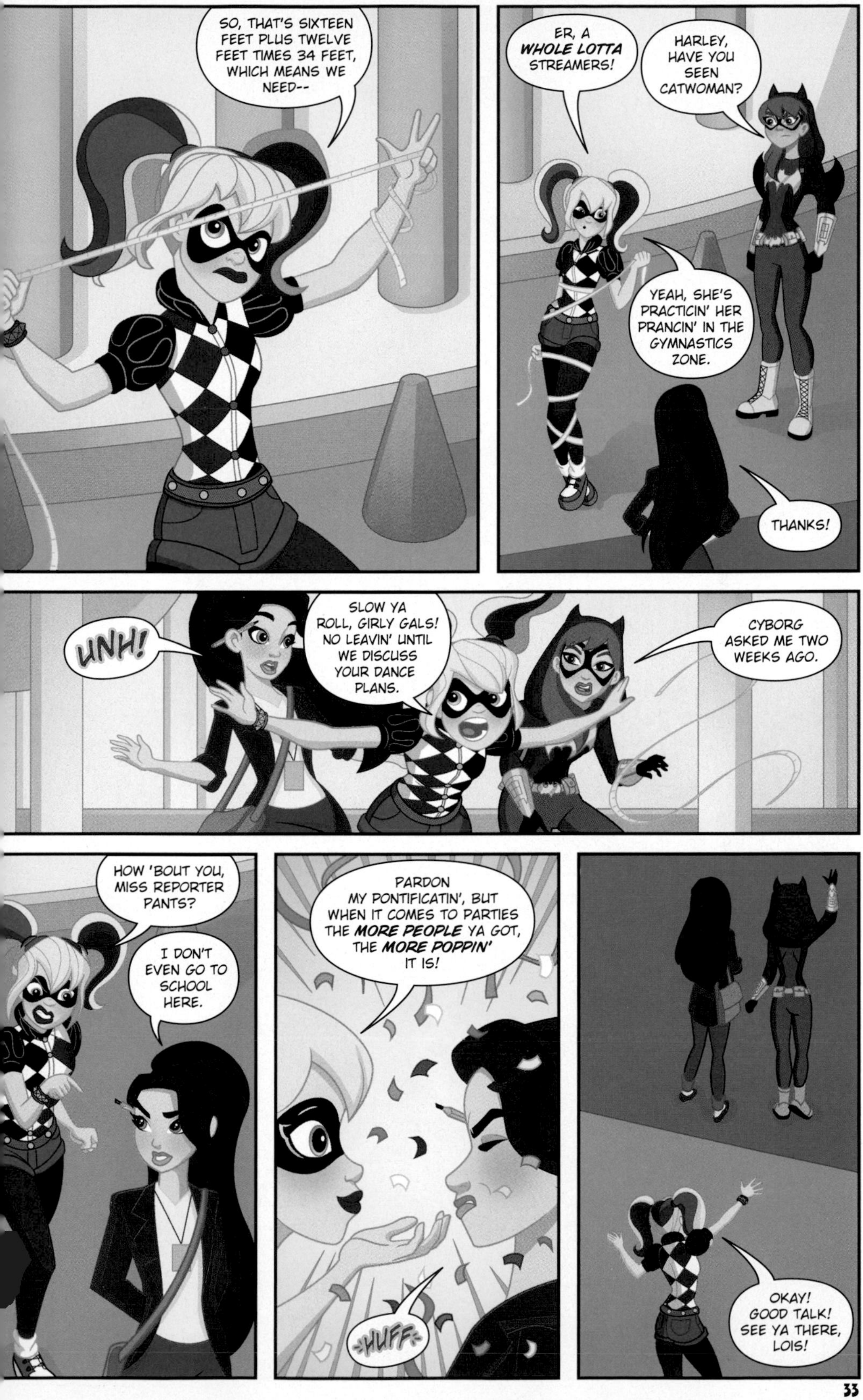
SO, THAT'S SIXTEEN FEET PLUS TWELVE FEET TIMES 34 FEET, WHICH MEANS WE NEED--
ER, A **WHOLE LOTTA** STREAMERS!
HARLEY, HAVE YOU SEEN CATWOMAN?
YEAH, SHE'S PRACTICIN' HER PRANCIN' IN THE GYMNASTICS ZONE.
THANKS!
UNH!
SLOW YA ROLL, GIRLY GALS! NO LEAVIN' UNTIL WE DISCUSS YOUR DANCE PLANS.
CYBORG ASKED ME TWO WEEKS AGO.
HOW 'BOUT YOU, MISS REPORTER PANTS?
I DON'T EVEN GO TO SCHOOL HERE.
PARDON MY PONTIFICATIN', BUT WHEN IT COMES TO PARTIES THE **MORE PEOPLE** YA GOT, THE **MORE POPPIN'** IT IS!
HUFF
OKAY! GOOD TALK! SEE YA THERE, LOIS!

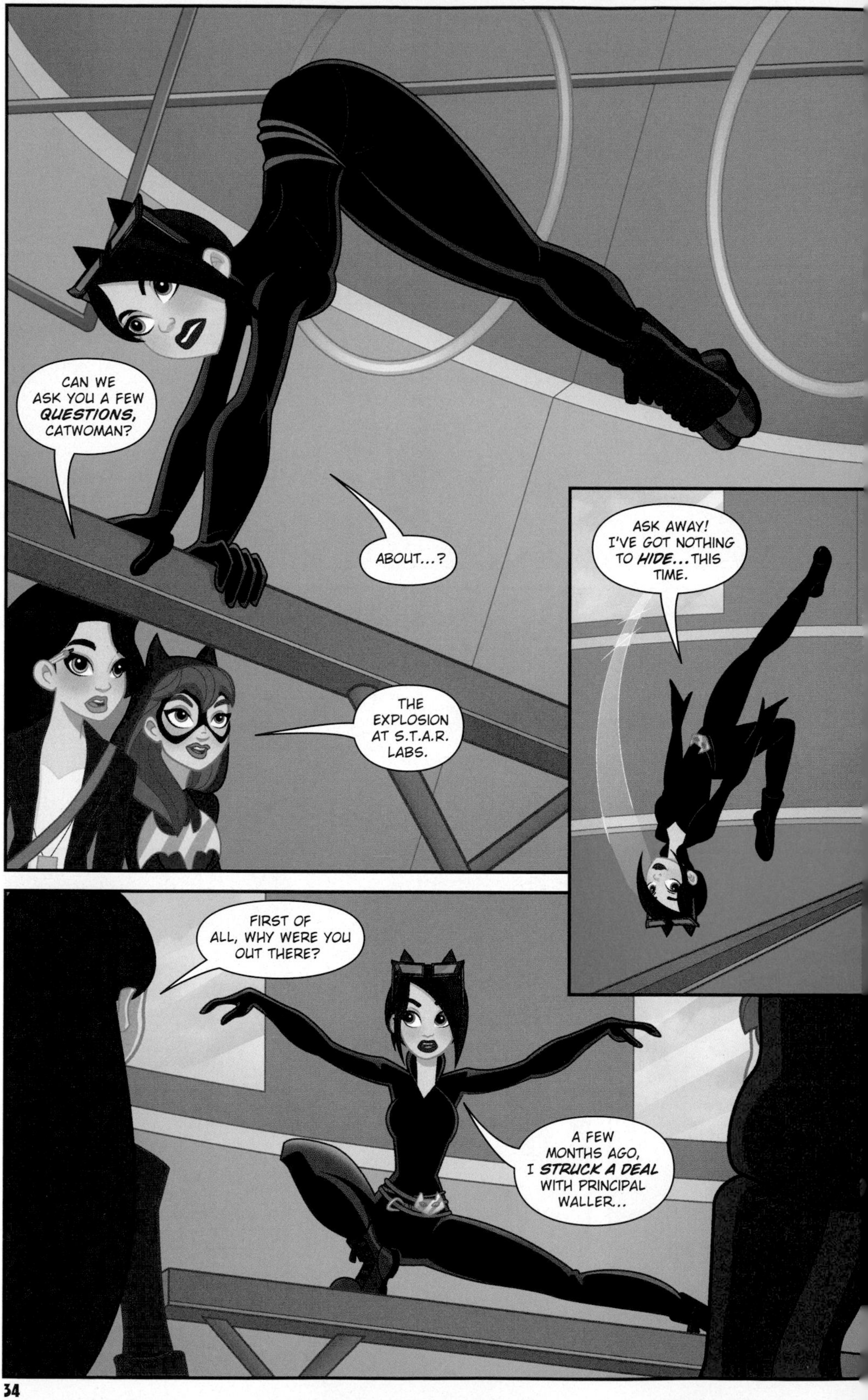
CAN WE ASK YOU A FEW QUESTIONS, CATWOMAN?
ABOUT...?
THE EXPLOSION AT S.T.A.R. LABS.
ASK AWAY! I'VE GOT NOTHING TO HIDE... THIS TIME.
FIRST OF ALL, WHY WERE YOU OUT THERE?
A FEW MONTHS AGO, I STRUCK A DEAL WITH PRINCIPAL WALLER...

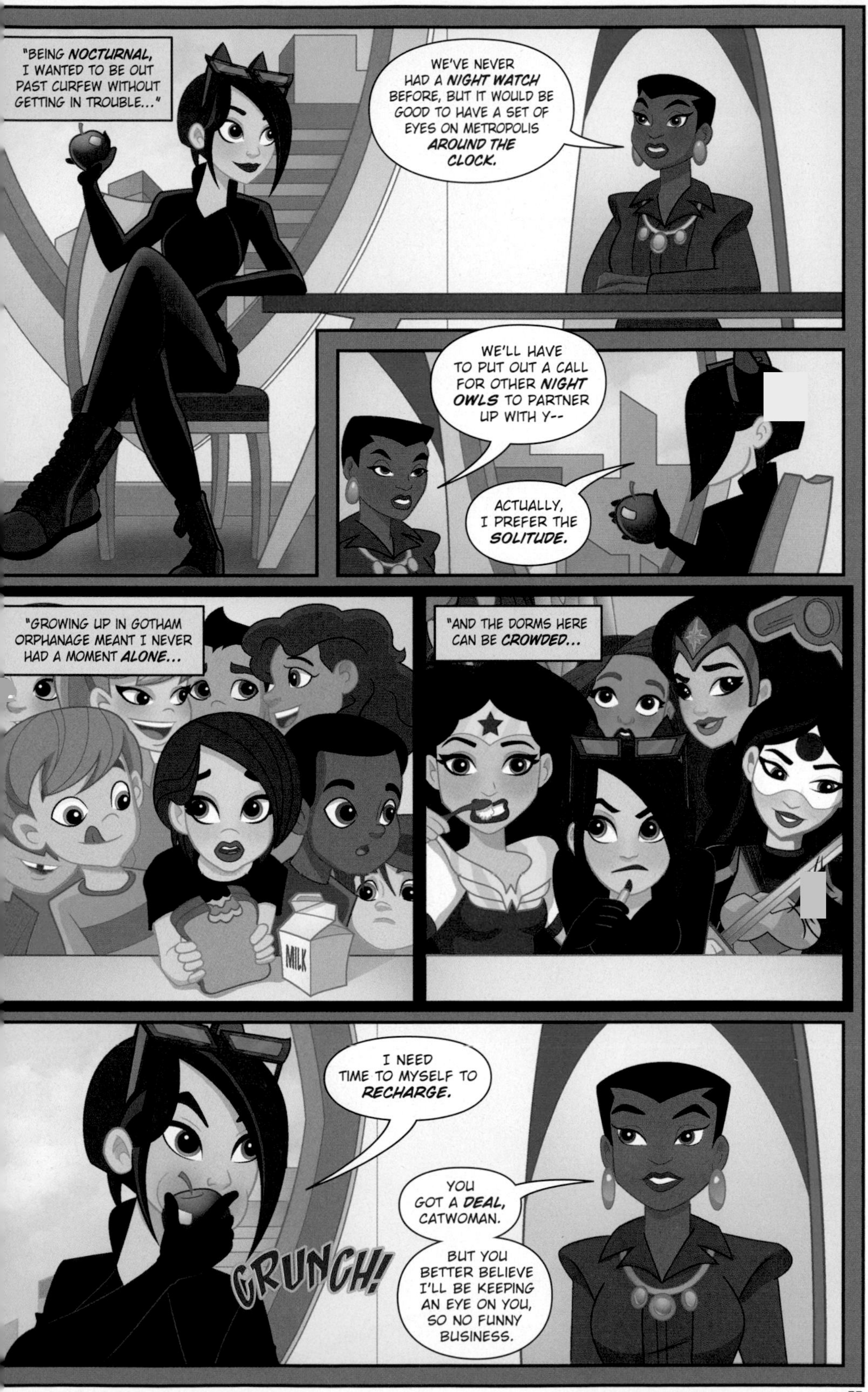

"BEING NOCTURNAL, I WANTED TO BE OUT PAST CURFEW WITHOUT GETTING IN TROUBLE..."
WE'VE NEVER HAD A NIGHT WATCH BEFORE, BUT IT WOULD BE GOOD TO HAVE A SET OF EYES ON METROPOLIS AROUND THE CLOCK.
WE'LL HAVE TO PUT OUT A CALL FOR OTHER NIGHT OWLS TO PARTNER UP WITH Y--
ACTUALLY, I PREFER THE SOLITUDE.
"GROWING UP IN GOTHAM ORPHANAGE MEANT I NEVER HAD A MOMENT ALONE...
MILK
"AND THE DORMS HERE CAN BE CROWDED...
I NEED TIME TO MYSELF TO RECHARGE.
YOU GOT A DEAL, CATWOMAN.
BUT YOU BETTER BELIEVE I'LL BE KEEPING AN EYE ON YOU, SO NO FUNNY BUSINESS.
CRUNCH!

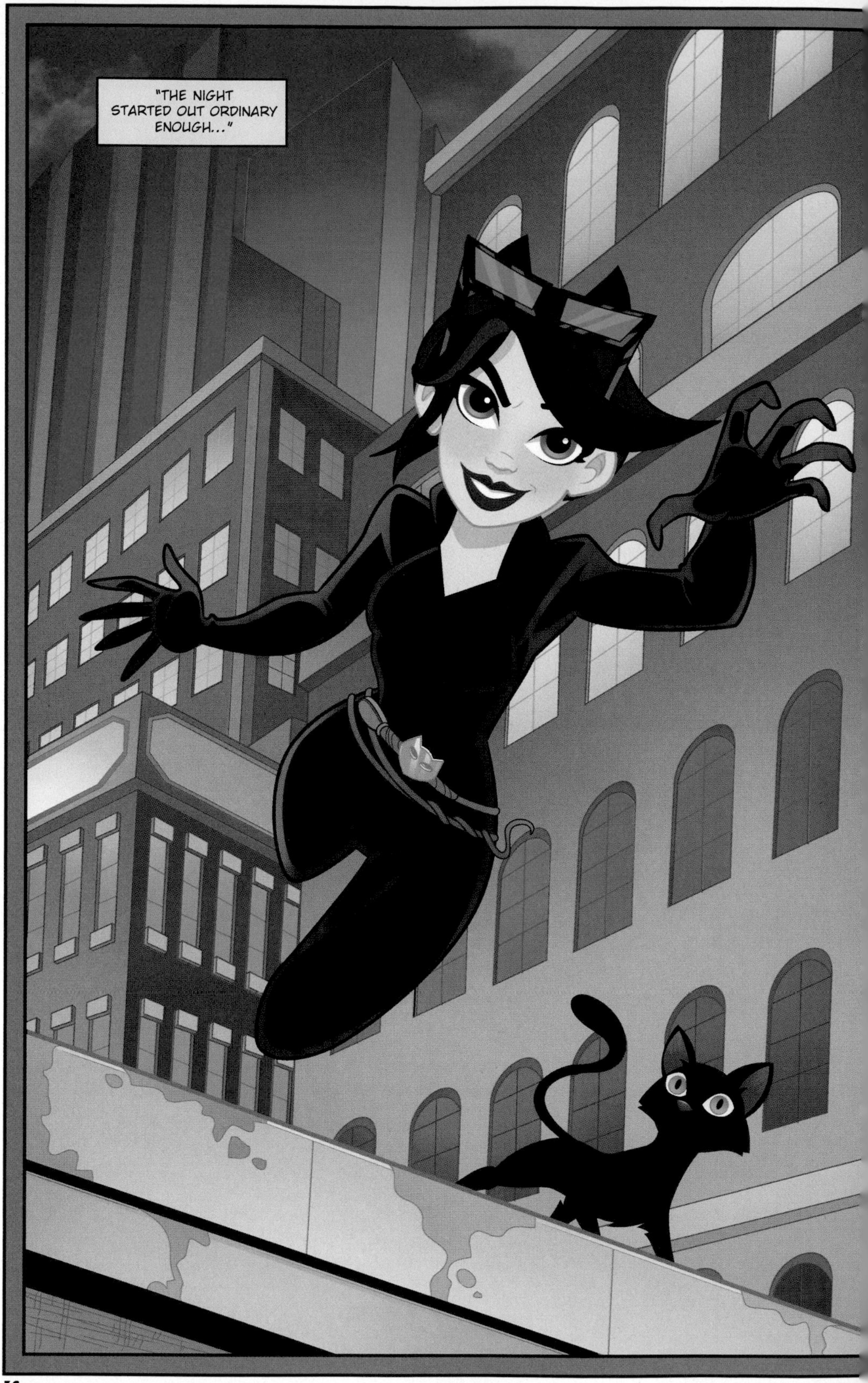
"THE NIGHT STARTED OUT ORDINARY ENOUGH..."

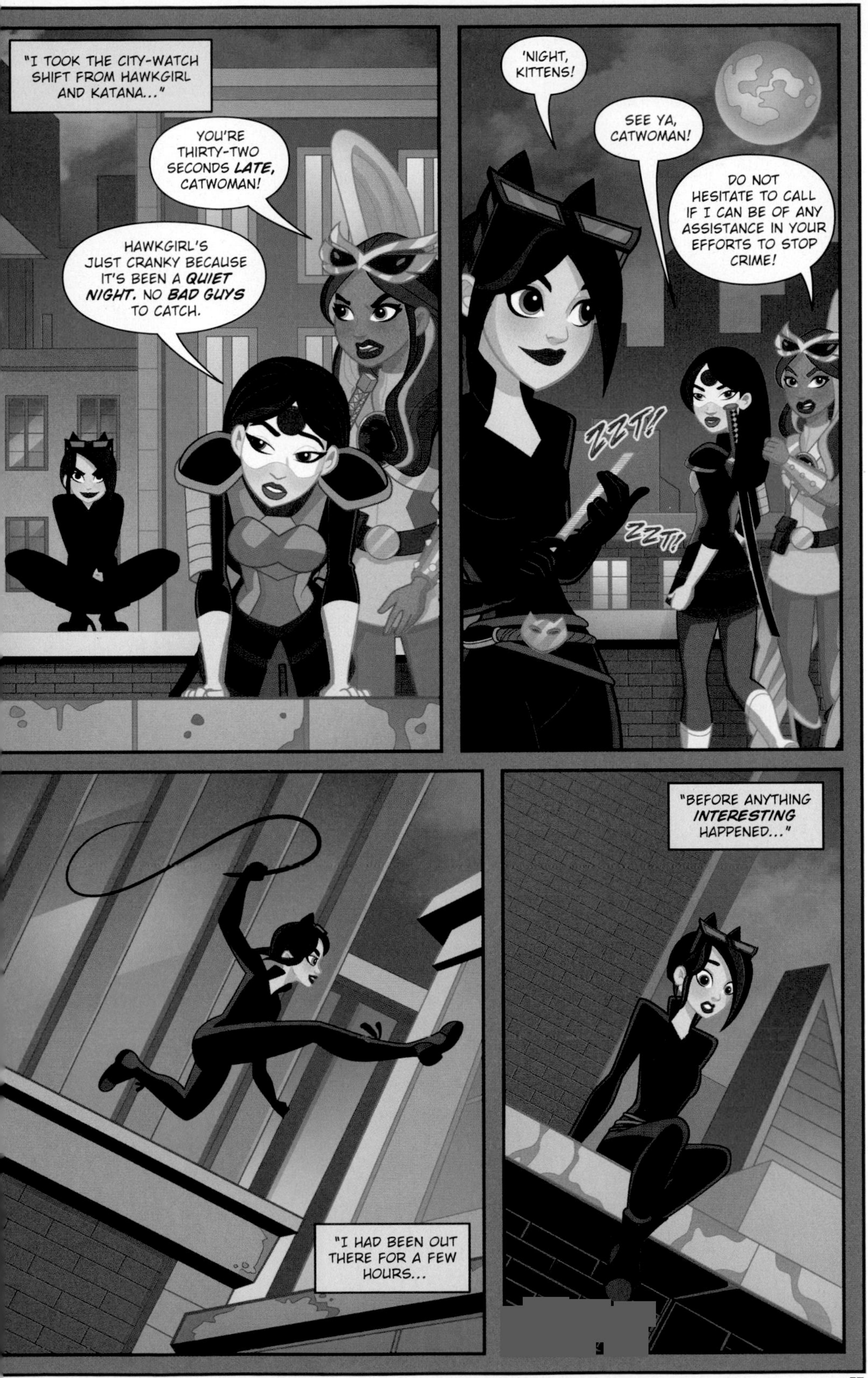
"I TOOK THE CITY-WATCH SHIFT FROM HAWKGIRL AND KATANA..."
YOU'RE THIRTY-TWO SECONDS **LATE,** CATWOMAN!
HAWKGIRL'S JUST CRANKY BECAUSE IT'S BEEN A **QUIET NIGHT.** NO **BAD GUYS** TO CATCH.
'NIGHT, KITTENS!
SEE YA, CATWOMAN!
DO NOT HESITATE TO CALL IF I CAN BE OF ANY ASSISTANCE IN YOUR EFFORTS TO STOP CRIME!
ZZZT!
ZZZT!
"I HAD BEEN OUT THERE FOR A FEW HOURS...
"BEFORE ANYTHING **INTERESTING** HAPPENED..."

"THAT WAS WHEN I SAW PRINCIPAL WALLER CANOODLING WITH SOME *MUSTACHIOED MAN!*"

OH, FLOYD! YOU SHOULDN'T HAVE!

HOW LUCKY AM I TO GET A MAN WHO BRINGS ME FLOWERS AND SMELLS LIKE *KETTLE CORN* AND *CARAMEL APPLES?*

WELL, *BLASTED BUTTONS!* YOU CAUGHT ME! GUESS IT'S OBVIOUS I'VE BEEN HANDING OUT TREATS AT THE CHILDREN'S HOSPITAL.

OH! YOU'RE SWEETER THAN COTTON CANDY!

I MEAN EVERY WORD, AMANDA.

I DON'T DO *GOSSIP* ON MY NEWS BLOG.

STICK TO THE RELEVANT DETAILS, CATWOMAN.

WHATEVER.

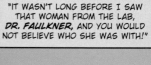

"IT WASN'T LONG BEFORE I SAW THAT WOMAN FROM THE LAB, *DR. FAULKNER,* AND YOU WOULD NOT BELIEVE WHO SHE WAS WITH!"

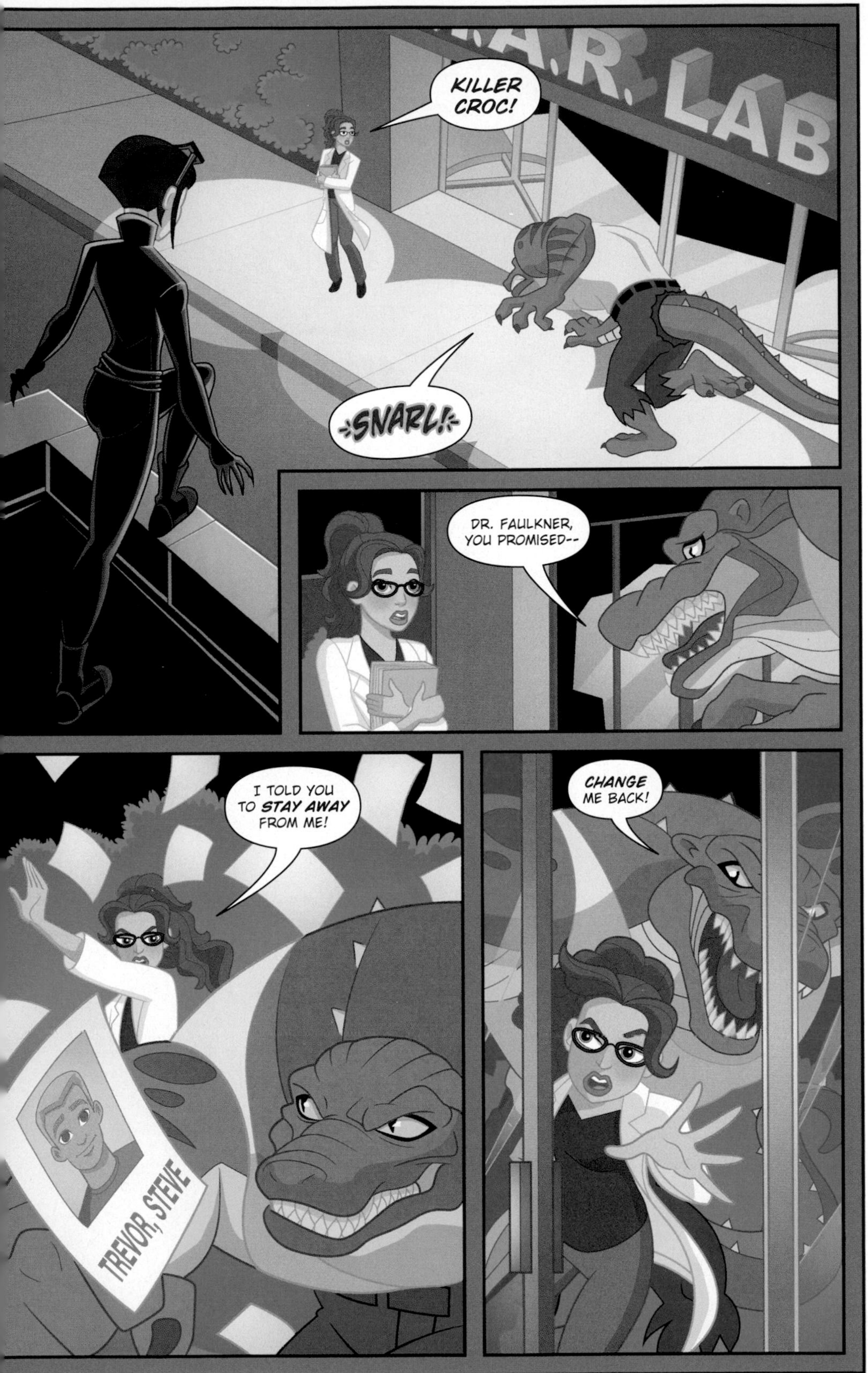
KILLER CROC!
-SNARL!-
DR. FAULKNER, YOU PROMISED--
I TOLD YOU TO STAY AWAY FROM ME!
TREVOR, STEVE
CHANGE ME BACK!

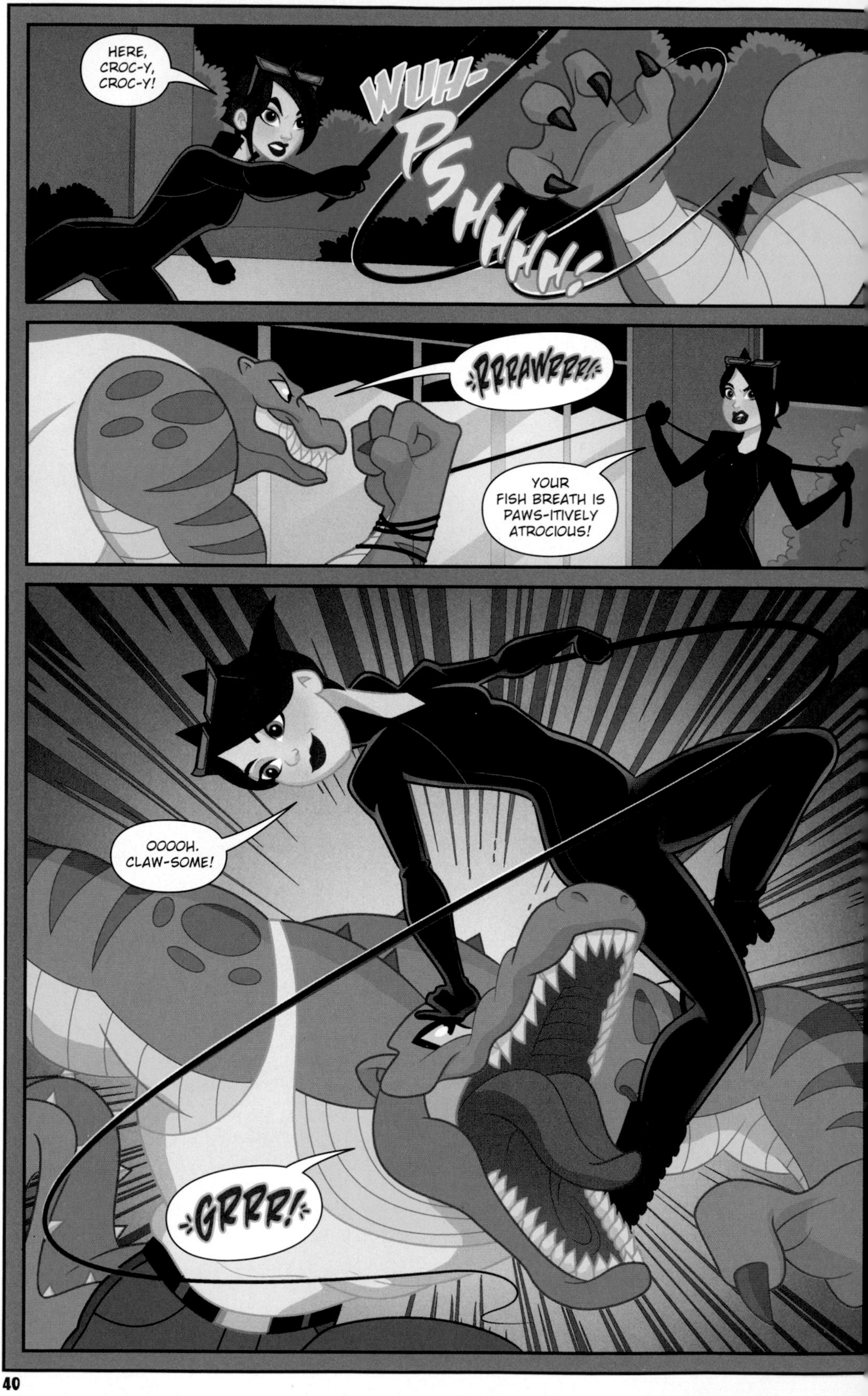
HERE, CROC-Y, CROC-Y!
WUH-PSHHHH!
RRRAWRRR!
YOUR FISH BREATH IS PAWS-ITIVELY ATROCIOUS!
OOOOH. CLAW-SOME!
GRRR!

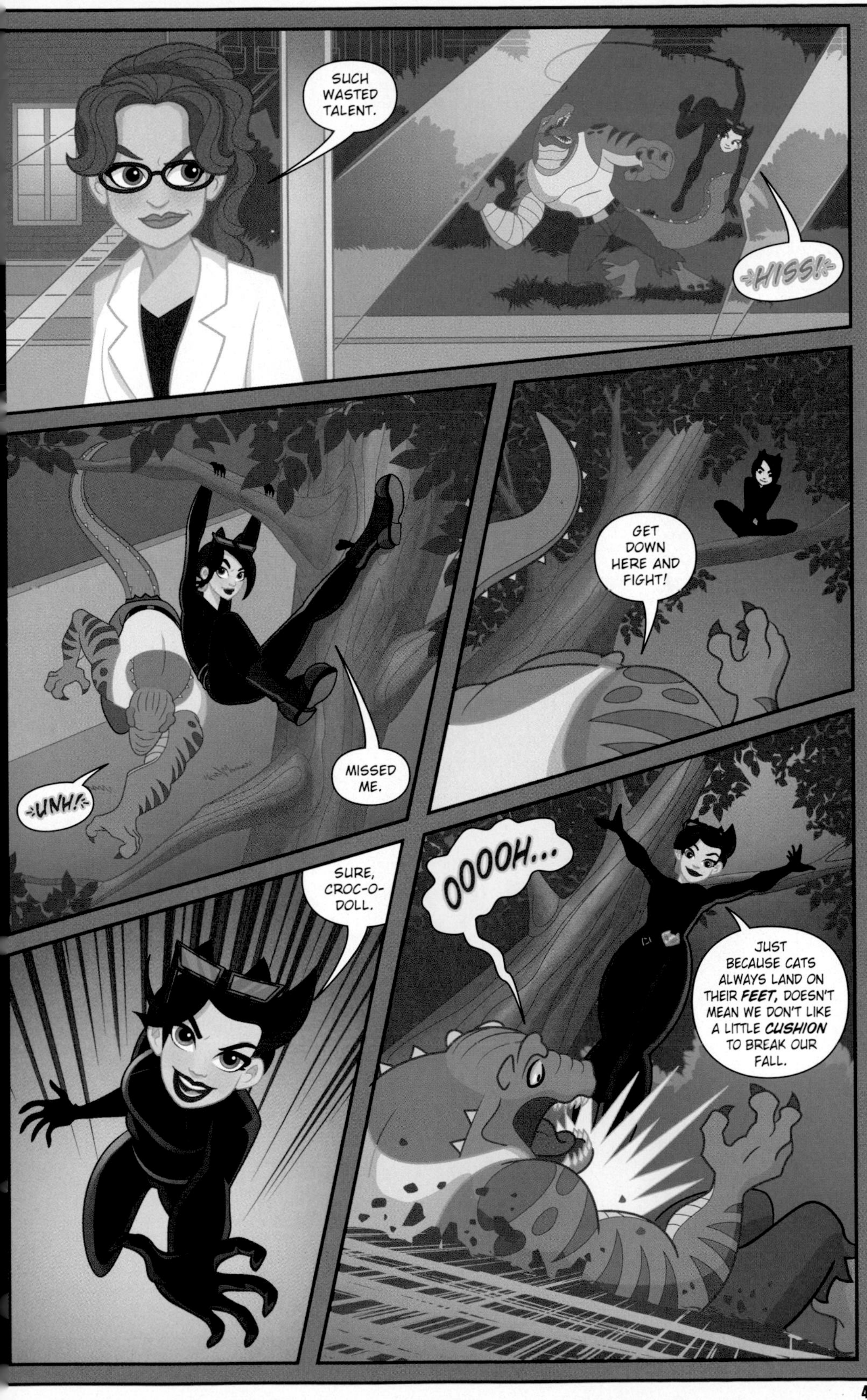
SUCH WASTED TALENT.
HISS!
UNH!
MISSED ME.
GET DOWN HERE AND FIGHT!
SURE, CROC-O-DOLL.
OOOOH...
JUST BECAUSE CATS ALWAYS LAND ON THEIR FEET, DOESN'T MEAN WE DON'T LIKE A LITTLE CUSHION TO BREAK OUR FALL.

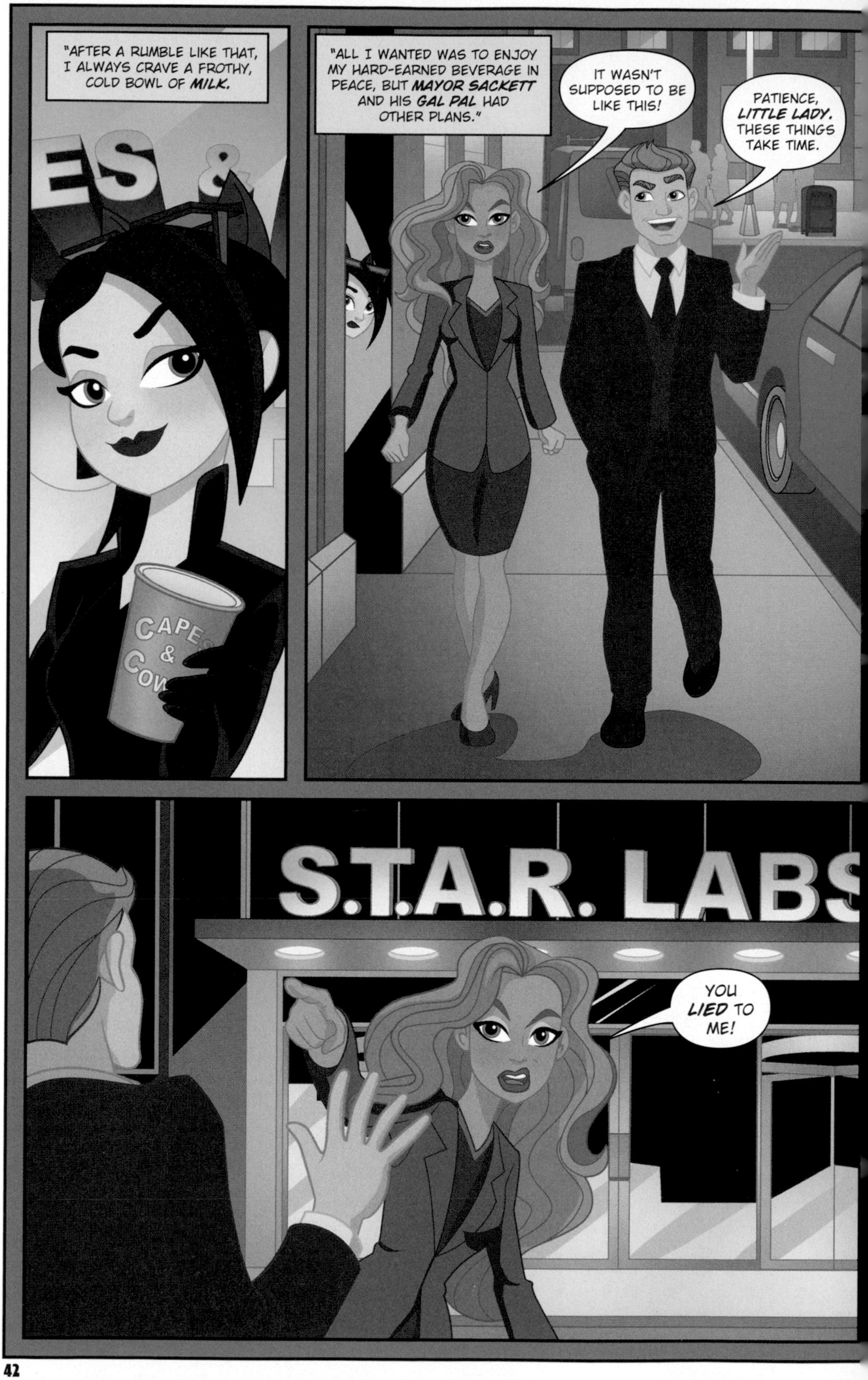
"AFTER A RUMBLE LIKE THAT, I ALWAYS CRAVE A FROTHY, COLD BOWL OF **MILK.**
"ALL I WANTED WAS TO ENJOY MY HARD-EARNED BEVERAGE IN PEACE, BUT **MAYOR SACKETT** AND HIS **GAL PAL** HAD OTHER PLANS."
IT WASN'T SUPPOSED TO BE LIKE THIS!
PATIENCE, **LITTLE LADY.** THESE THINGS TAKE TIME.
S.T.A.R. LABS
YOU **LIED** TO ME!

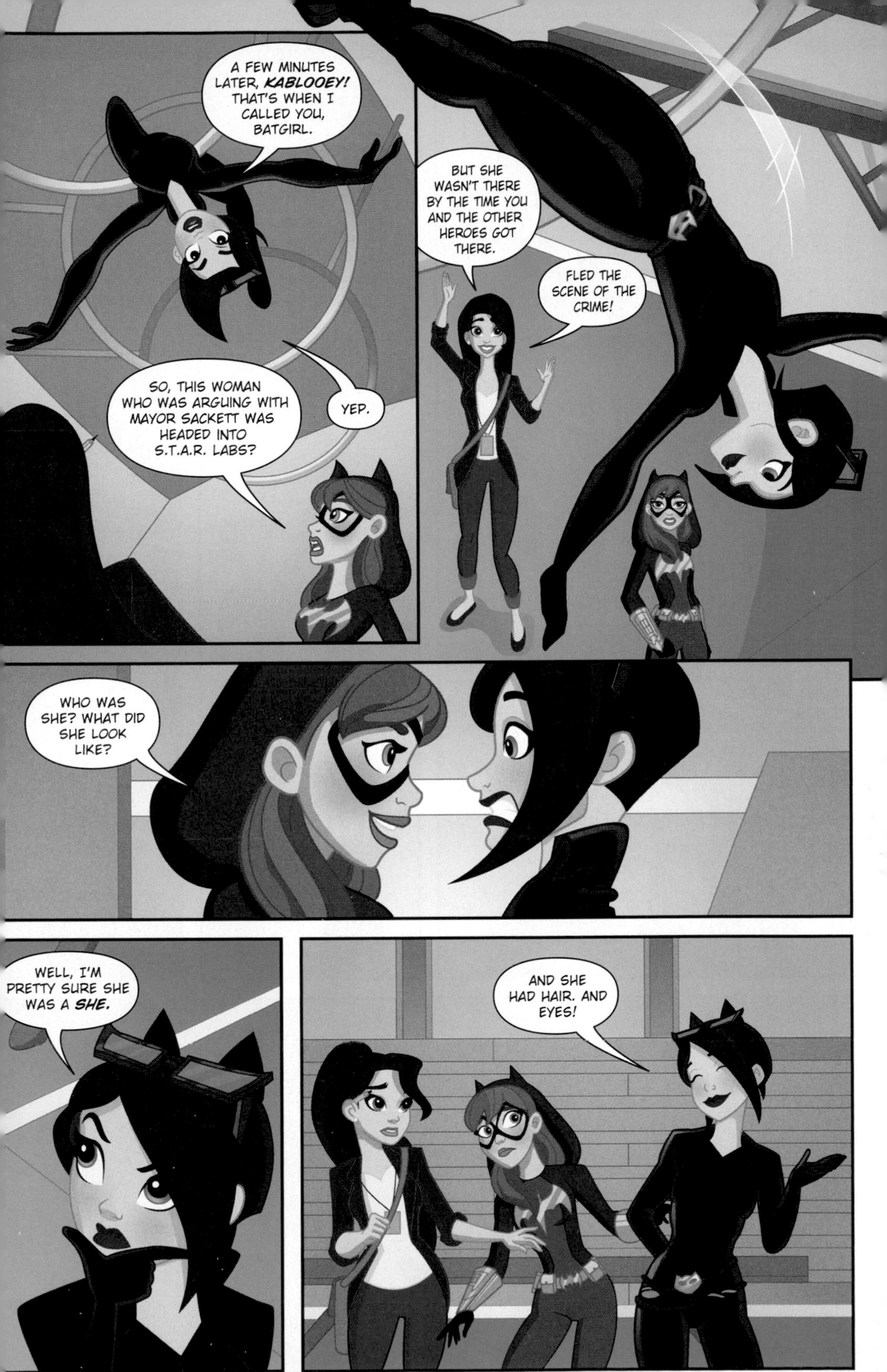

A FEW MINUTES LATER, KABLOOEY! THAT'S WHEN I CALLED YOU, BATGIRL.
BUT SHE WASN'T THERE BY THE TIME YOU AND THE OTHER HEROES GOT THERE.
FLED THE SCENE OF THE CRIME!
SO, THIS WOMAN WHO WAS ARGUING WITH MAYOR SACKETT WAS HEADED INTO S.T.A.R. LABS?
YEP.
WHO WAS SHE? WHAT DID SHE LOOK LIKE?
WELL, I'M PRETTY SURE SHE WAS A SHE.
AND SHE HAD HAIR. AND EYES!

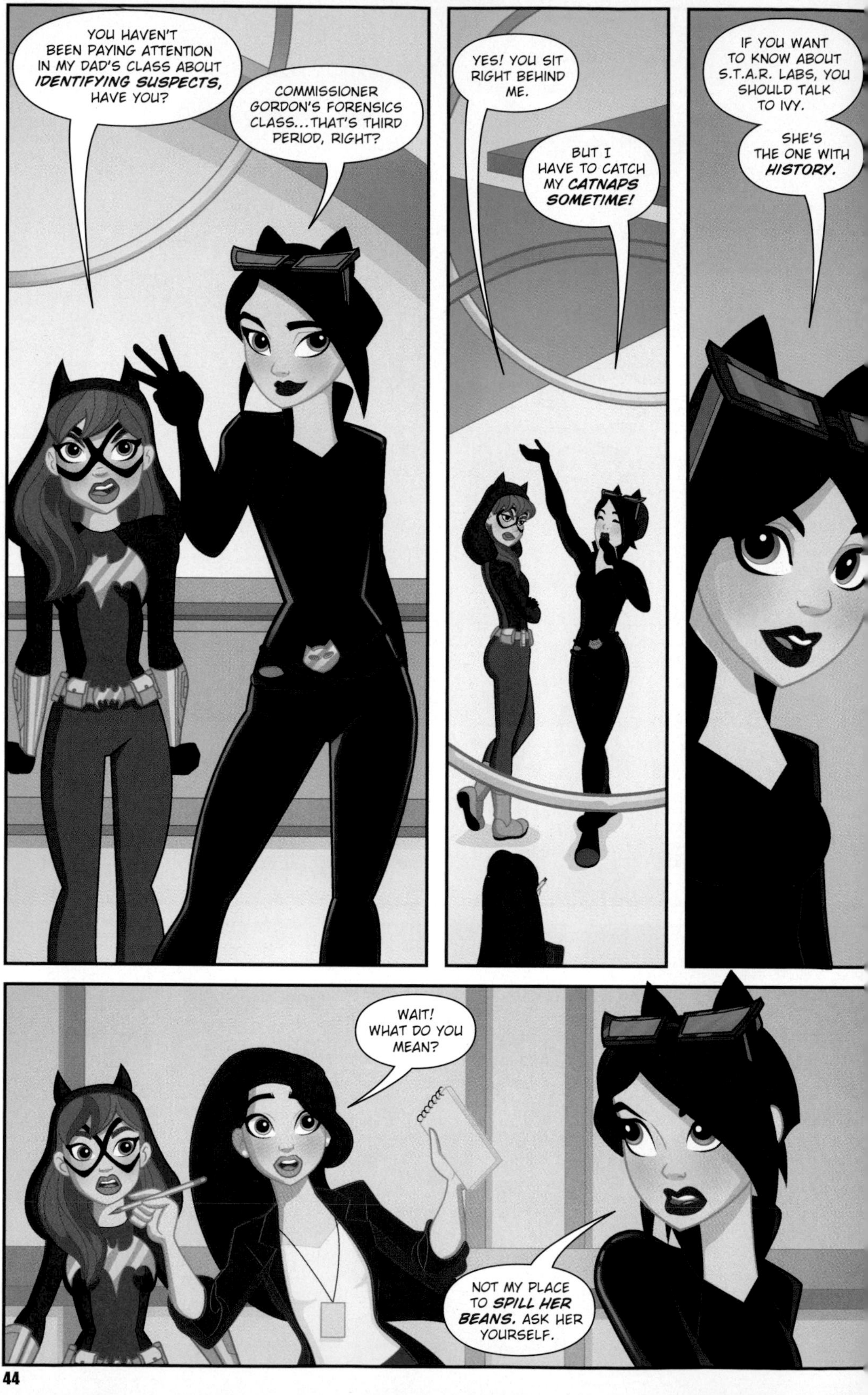
YOU HAVEN'T BEEN PAYING ATTENTION IN MY DAD'S CLASS ABOUT ***IDENTIFYING SUSPECTS,*** HAVE YOU?
COMMISSIONER GORDON'S FORENSICS CLASS...THAT'S THIRD PERIOD, RIGHT?
YES! YOU SIT RIGHT BEHIND ME.
BUT I HAVE TO CATCH MY ***CATNAPS SOMETIME!***
IF YOU WANT TO KNOW ABOUT S.T.A.R. LABS, YOU SHOULD TALK TO IVY.
SHE'S THE ONE WITH ***HISTORY.***
WAIT! WHAT DO YOU MEAN?
NOT MY PLACE TO ***SPILL HER BEANS.*** ASK HER YOURSELF.

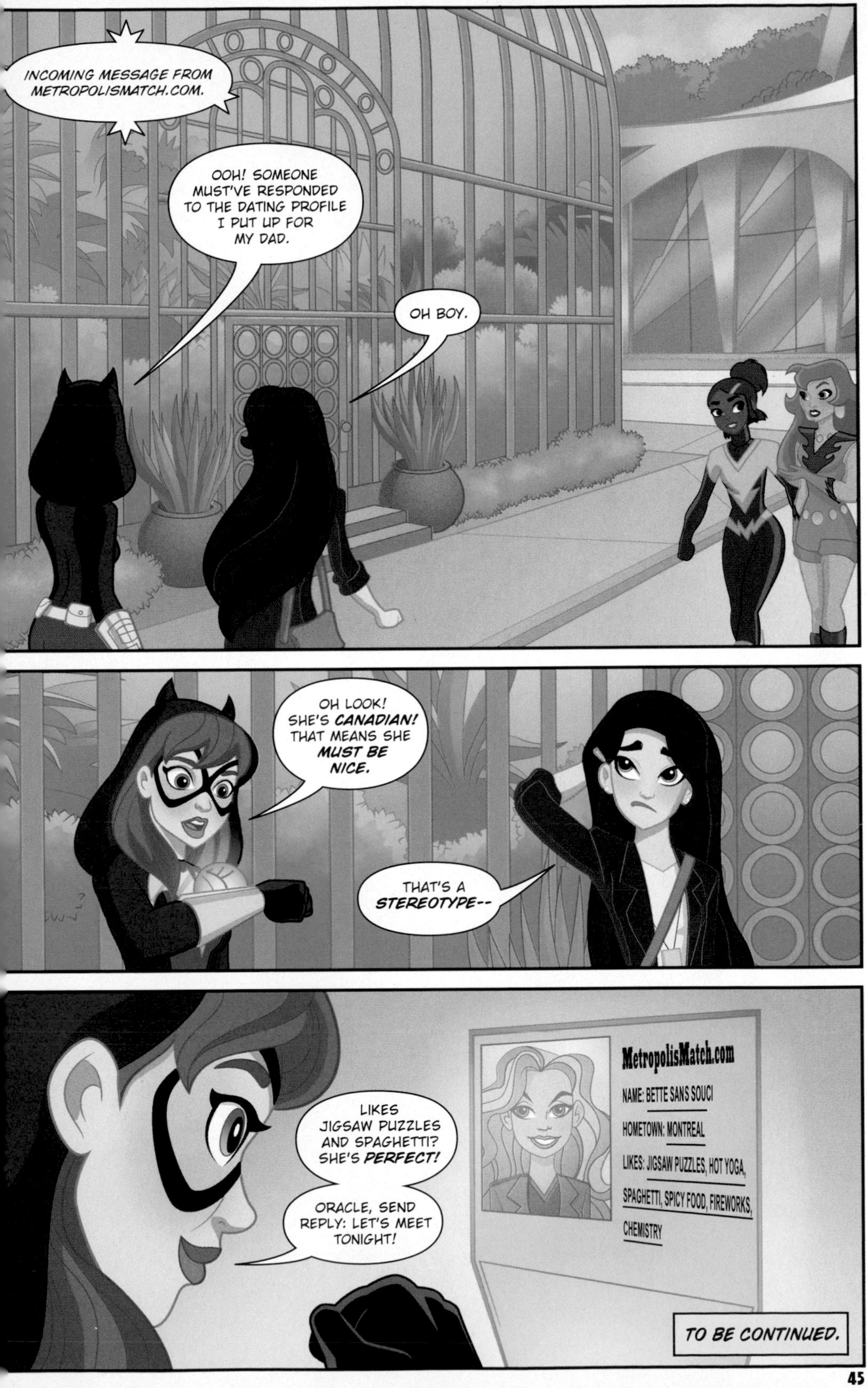
INCOMING MESSAGE FROM METROPOLISMATCH.COM.
OOH! SOMEONE MUST'VE RESPONDED TO THE DATING PROFILE I PUT UP FOR MY DAD.
OH BOY.
OH LOOK! SHE'S CANADIAN! THAT MEANS SHE MUST BE NICE.
THAT'S A STEREOTYPE--
MetropolisMatch.com
NAME: BETTE SANS SOUCI
HOMETOWN: MONTREAL
LIKES: JIGSAW PUZZLES, HOT YOGA, SPAGHETTI, SPICY FOOD, FIREWORKS, CHEMISTRY
LIKES JIGSAW PUZZLES AND SPAGHETTI? SHE'S PERFECT!
ORACLE, SEND REPLY: LET'S MEET TONIGHT!
TO BE CONTINUED.

CHAPTER 3
IVY'S ROOTS

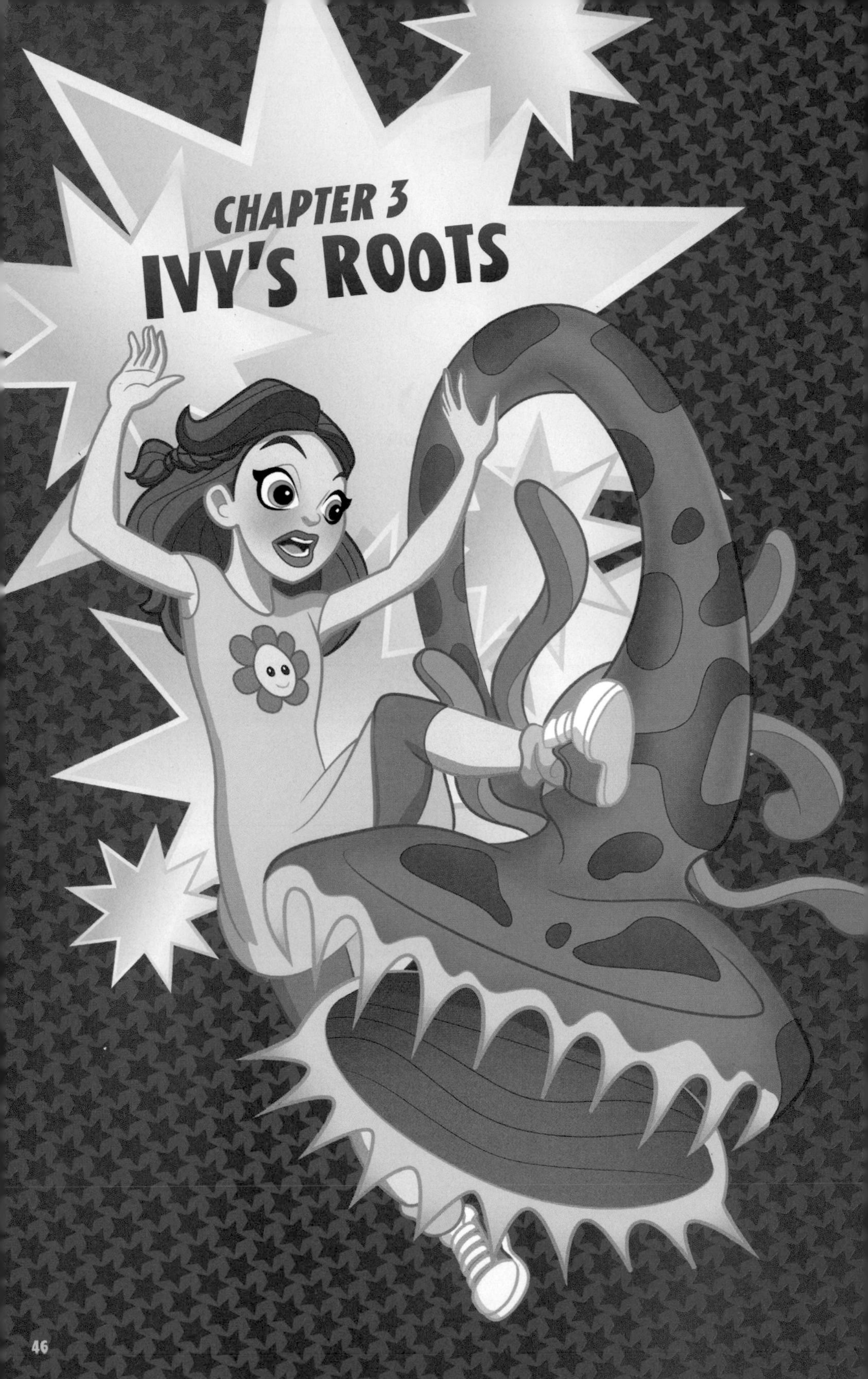

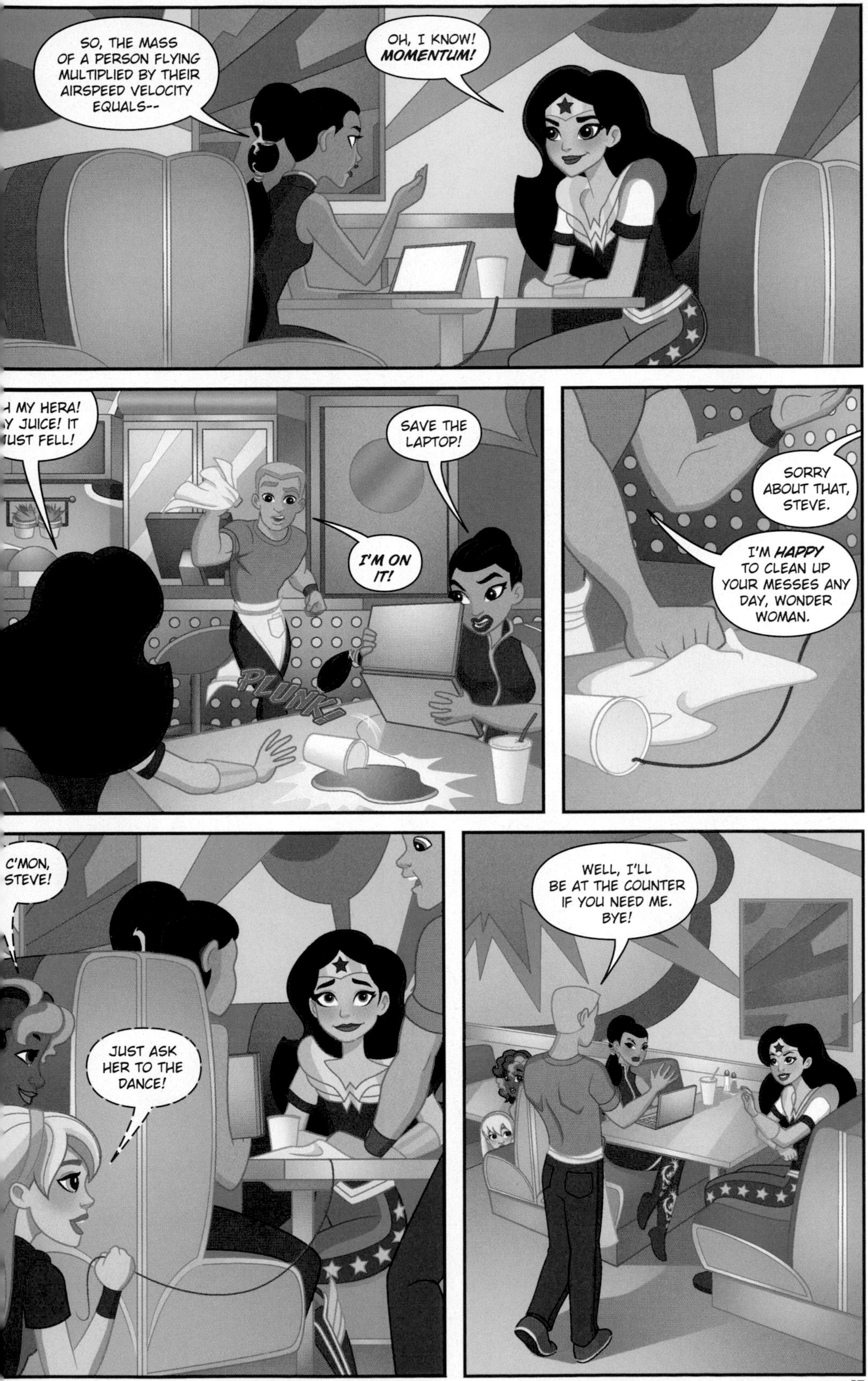
SO, THE MASS OF A PERSON FLYING MULTIPLIED BY THEIR AIRSPEED VELOCITY EQUALS--
OH, I KNOW! MOMENTUM!
H MY HERA! Y JUICE! IT UST FELL!
SAVE THE LAPTOP!
I'M ON IT!
PLUNK!
SORRY ABOUT THAT, STEVE.
I'M HAPPY TO CLEAN UP YOUR MESSES ANY DAY, WONDER WOMAN.
C'MON, STEVE!
JUST ASK HER TO THE DANCE!
WELL, I'LL BE AT THE COUNTER IF YOU NEED ME. BYE!

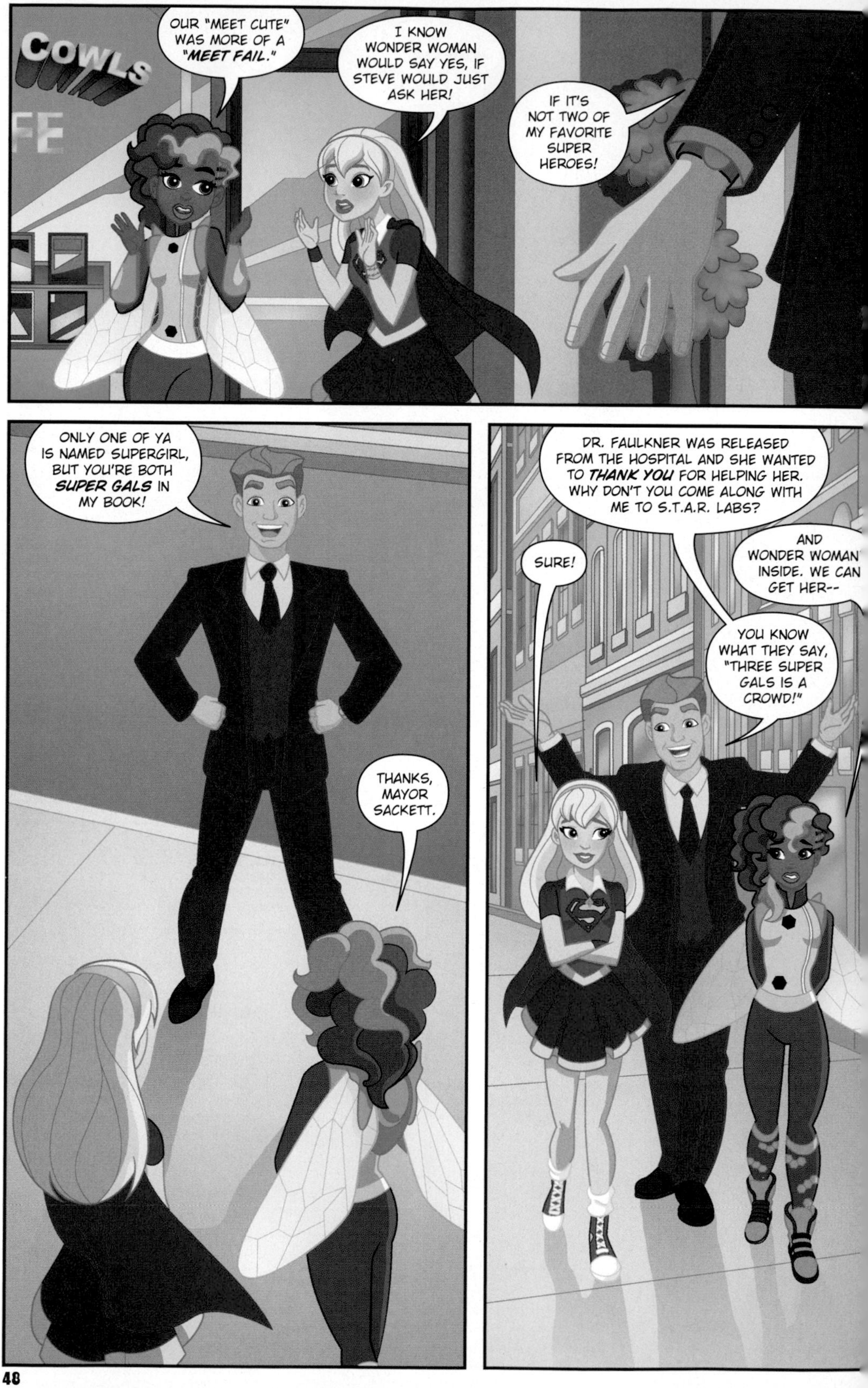
COWLS
FE
OUR "MEET CUTE" WAS MORE OF A "*MEET FAIL*."
I KNOW WONDER WOMAN WOULD SAY YES, IF STEVE WOULD JUST ASK HER!
IF IT'S NOT TWO OF MY FAVORITE SUPER HEROES!
ONLY ONE OF YA IS NAMED SUPERGIRL, BUT YOU'RE BOTH ***SUPER GALS*** IN MY BOOK!
THANKS, MAYOR SACKETT.
DR. FAULKNER WAS RELEASED FROM THE HOSPITAL AND SHE WANTED TO ***THANK YOU*** FOR HELPING HER. WHY DON'T YOU COME ALONG WITH ME TO S.T.A.R. LABS?
SURE!
AND WONDER WOMAN INSIDE. WE CAN GET HER--
YOU KNOW WHAT THEY SAY, "THREE SUPER GALS IS A CROWD!"

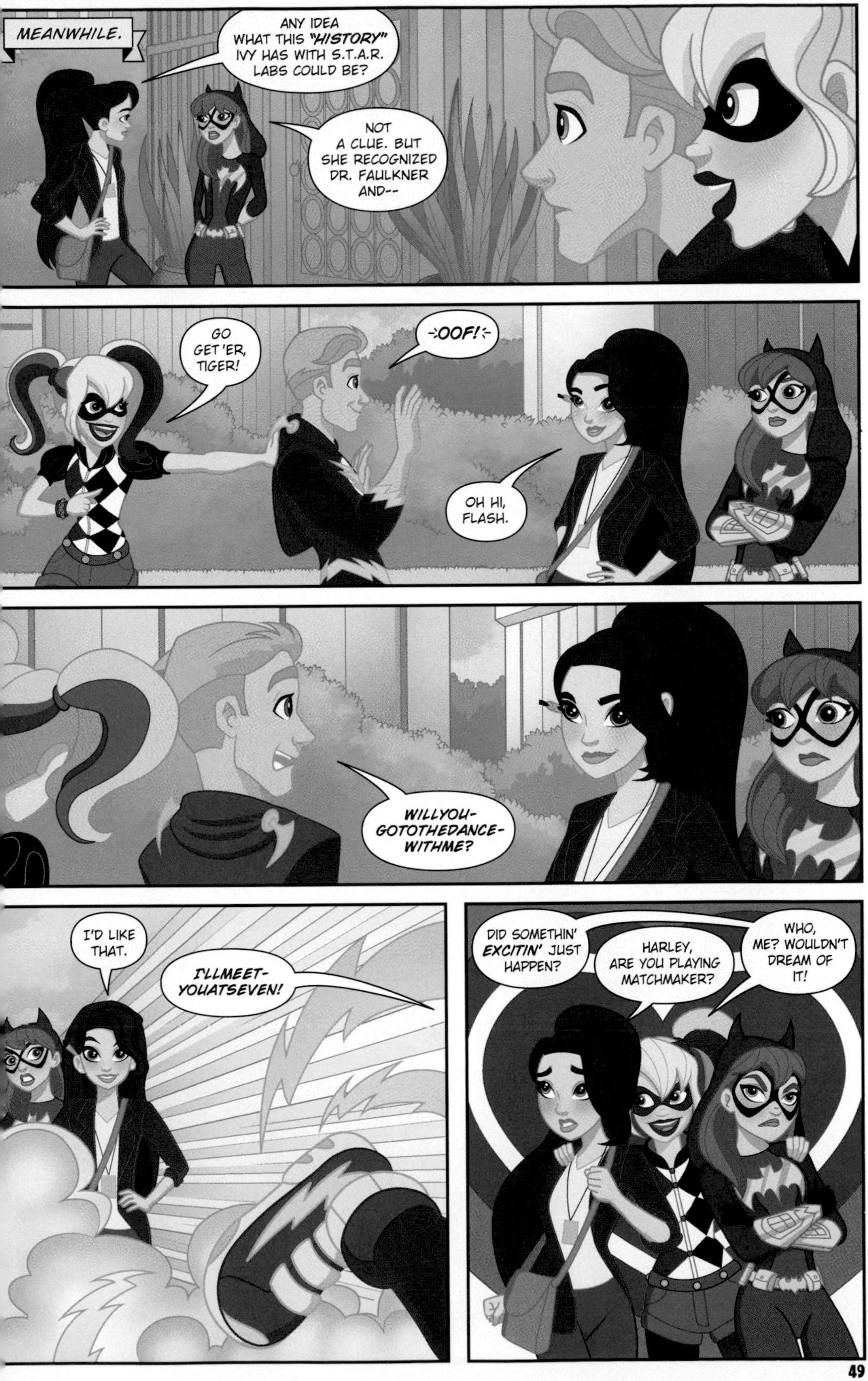
MEANWHILE.
ANY IDEA WHAT THIS "HISTORY" IVY HAS WITH S.T.A.R. LABS COULD BE?
NOT A CLUE. BUT SHE RECOGNIZED DR. FAULKNER AND--
GO GET 'ER, TIGER!
OOF!
OH HI, FLASH.
WILLYOU-GOTOTHEDANCE-WITHME?
I'D LIKE THAT.
I'LLMEET-YOUATSEVEN!
DID SOMETHIN' EXCITIN' JUST HAPPEN?
HARLEY, ARE YOU PLAYING MATCHMAKER?
WHO, ME? WOULDN'T DREAM OF IT!

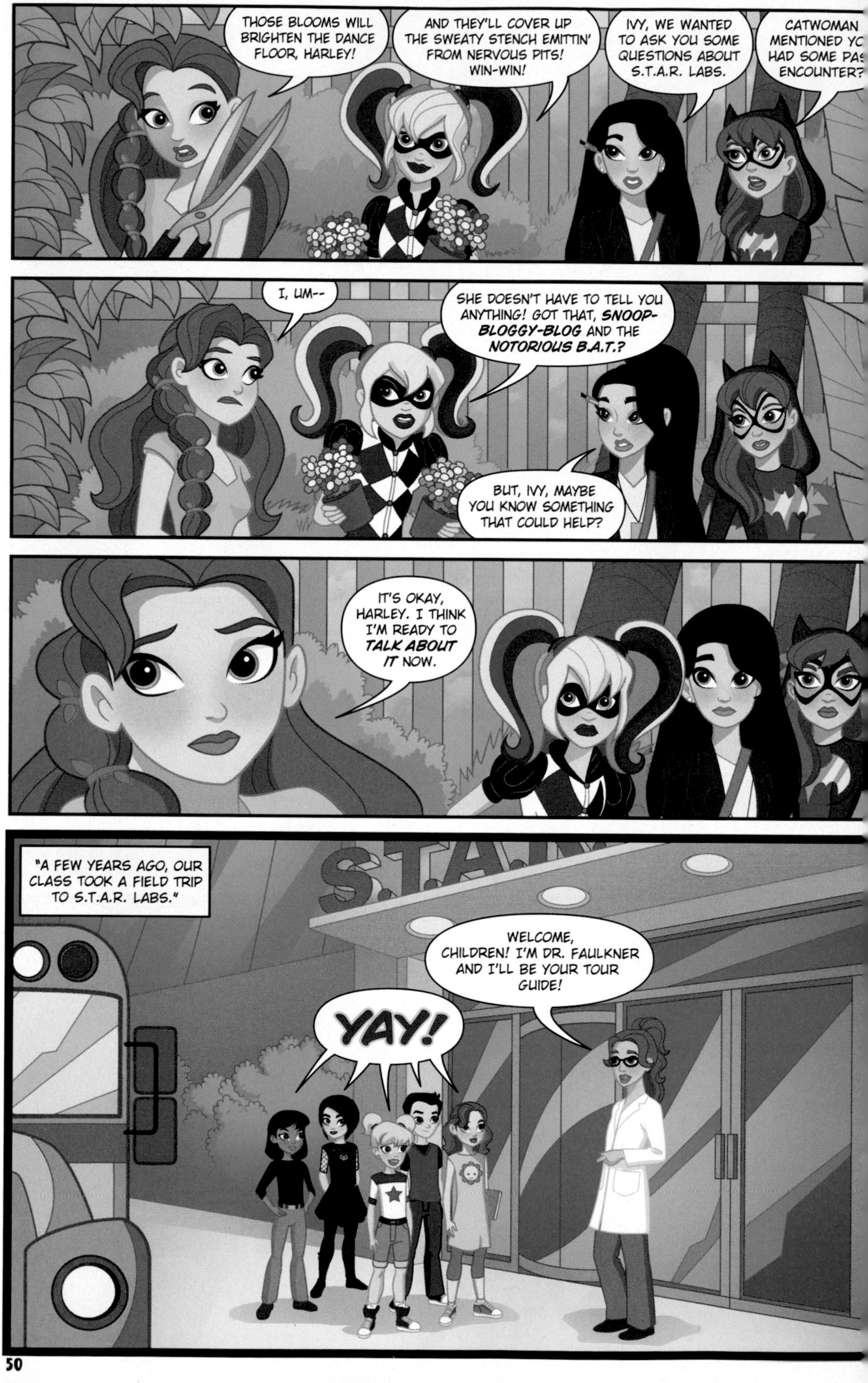
THOSE BLOOMS WILL BRIGHTEN THE DANCE FLOOR, HARLEY!
AND THEY'LL COVER UP THE SWEATY STENCH EMITTIN' FROM NERVOUS PITS! WIN-WIN!
IVY, WE WANTED TO ASK YOU SOME QUESTIONS ABOUT S.T.A.R. LABS.
CATWOMAN MENTIONED YO HAD SOME PAS ENCOUNTER?
I, UM--
SHE DOESN'T HAVE TO TELL YOU ANYTHING! GOT THAT, ***SNOOP-BLOGGY-BLOG*** AND THE ***NOTORIOUS B.A.T.***?
BUT, IVY, MAYBE YOU KNOW SOMETHING THAT COULD HELP?
IT'S OKAY, HARLEY. I THINK I'M READY TO ***TALK ABOUT IT*** NOW.
"A FEW YEARS AGO, OUR CLASS TOOK A FIELD TRIP TO S.T.A.R. LABS."
WELCOME, CHILDREN! I'M DR. FAULKNER AND I'LL BE YOUR TOUR GUIDE!
YAY!

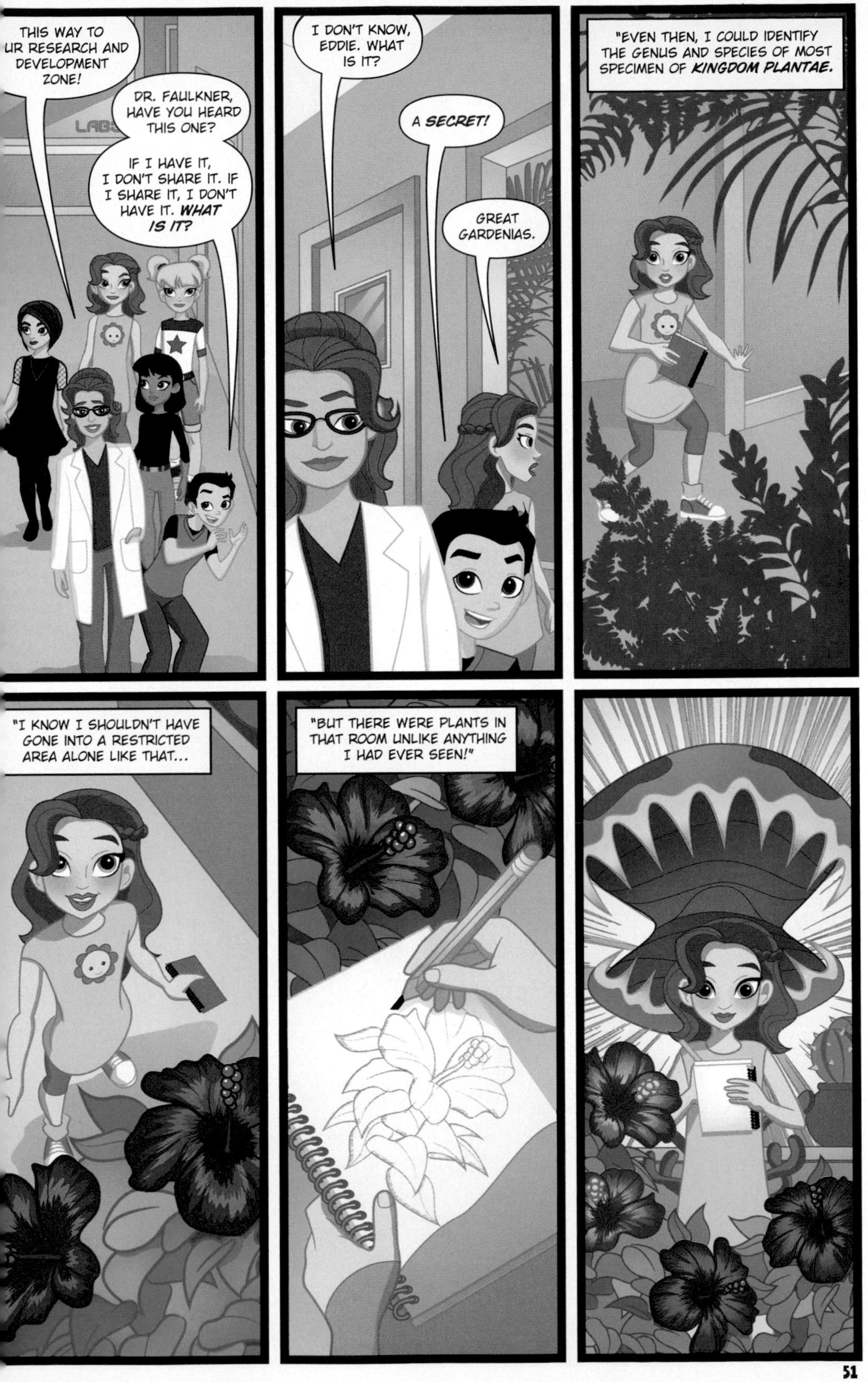
THIS WAY TO UR RESEARCH AND DEVELOPMENT ZONE!
DR. FAULKNER, HAVE YOU HEARD THIS ONE?
IF I HAVE IT, I DON'T SHARE IT. IF I SHARE IT, I DON'T HAVE IT. WHAT IS IT?
I DON'T KNOW, EDDIE. WHAT IS IT?
A SECRET!
GREAT GARDENIAS.
"EVEN THEN, I COULD IDENTIFY THE GENUS AND SPECIES OF MOST SPECIMEN OF KINGDOM PLANTAE.
"I KNOW I SHOULDN'T HAVE GONE INTO A RESTRICTED AREA ALONE LIKE THAT...
"BUT THERE WERE PLANTS IN THAT ROOM UNLIKE ANYTHING I HAD EVER SEEN!"

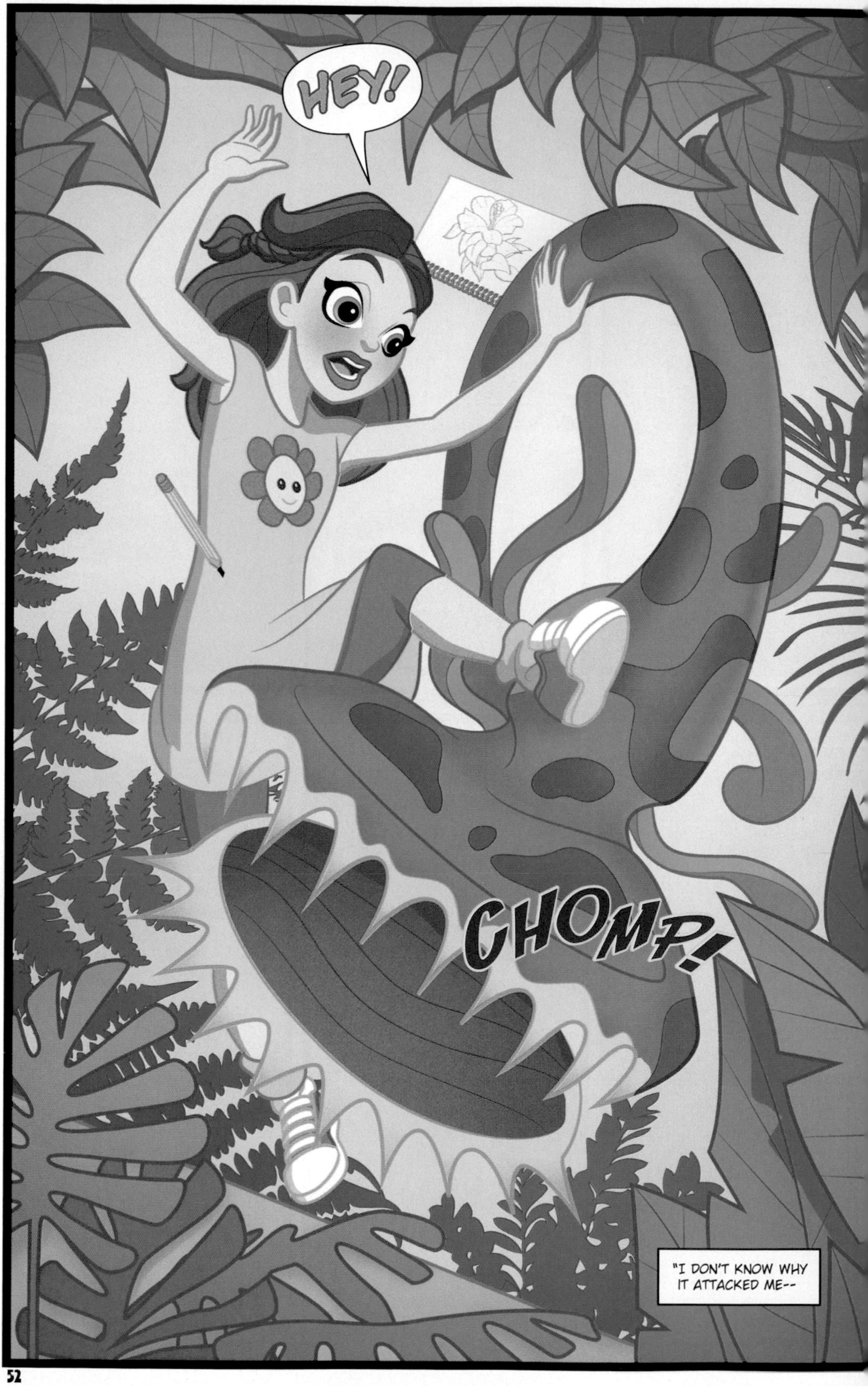
HEY!
CHOMP!
"I DON'T KNOW WHY IT ATTACKED ME--

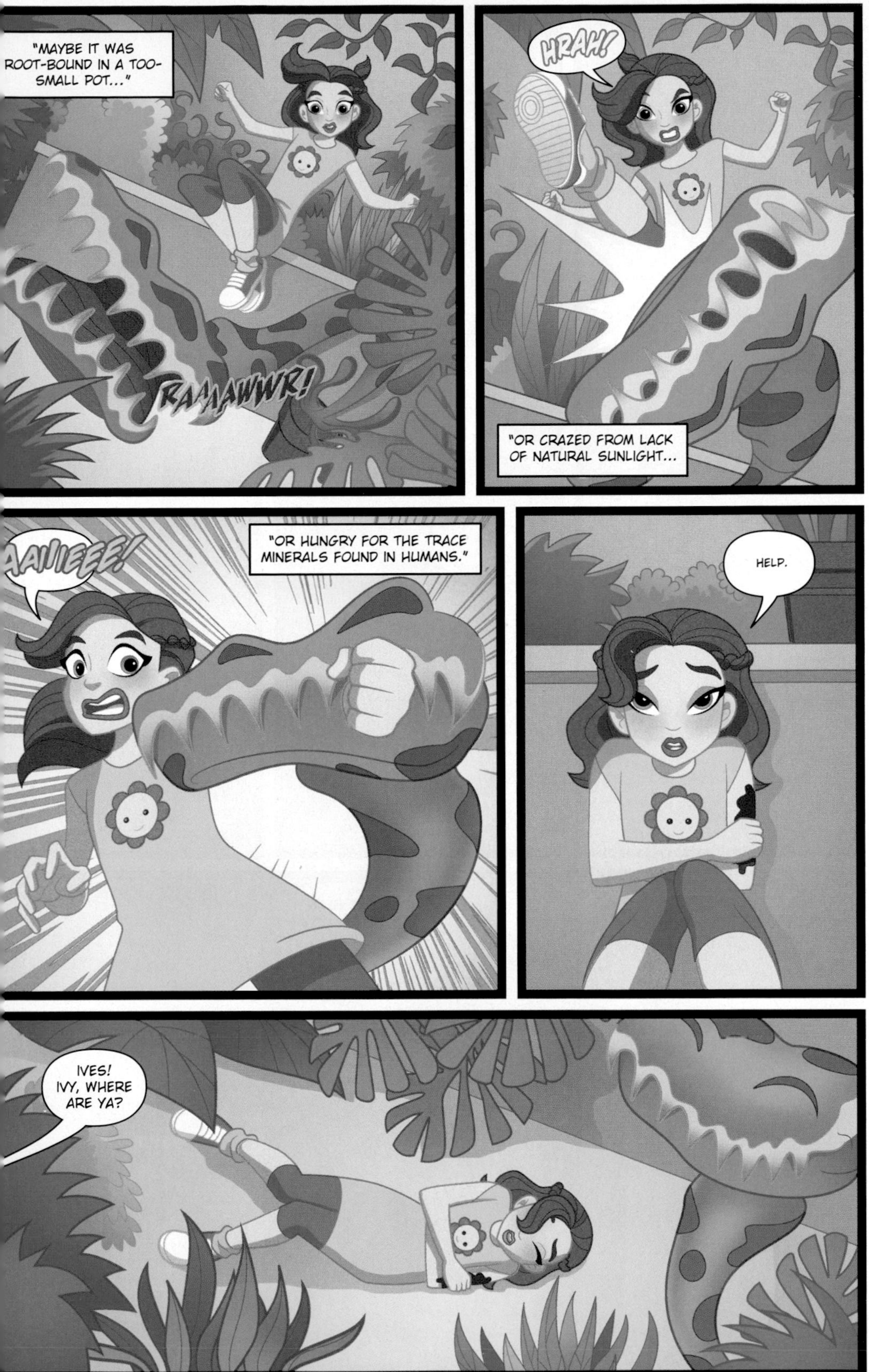
"MAYBE IT WAS ROOT-BOUND IN A TOO-SMALL POT..."
RAAAAWWR!
HRAH!
"OR CRAZED FROM LACK OF NATURAL SUNLIGHT...
AAIIIEEE!
"OR HUNGRY FOR THE TRACE MINERALS FOUND IN HUMANS."
HELP.
IVES! IVY, WHERE ARE YA?

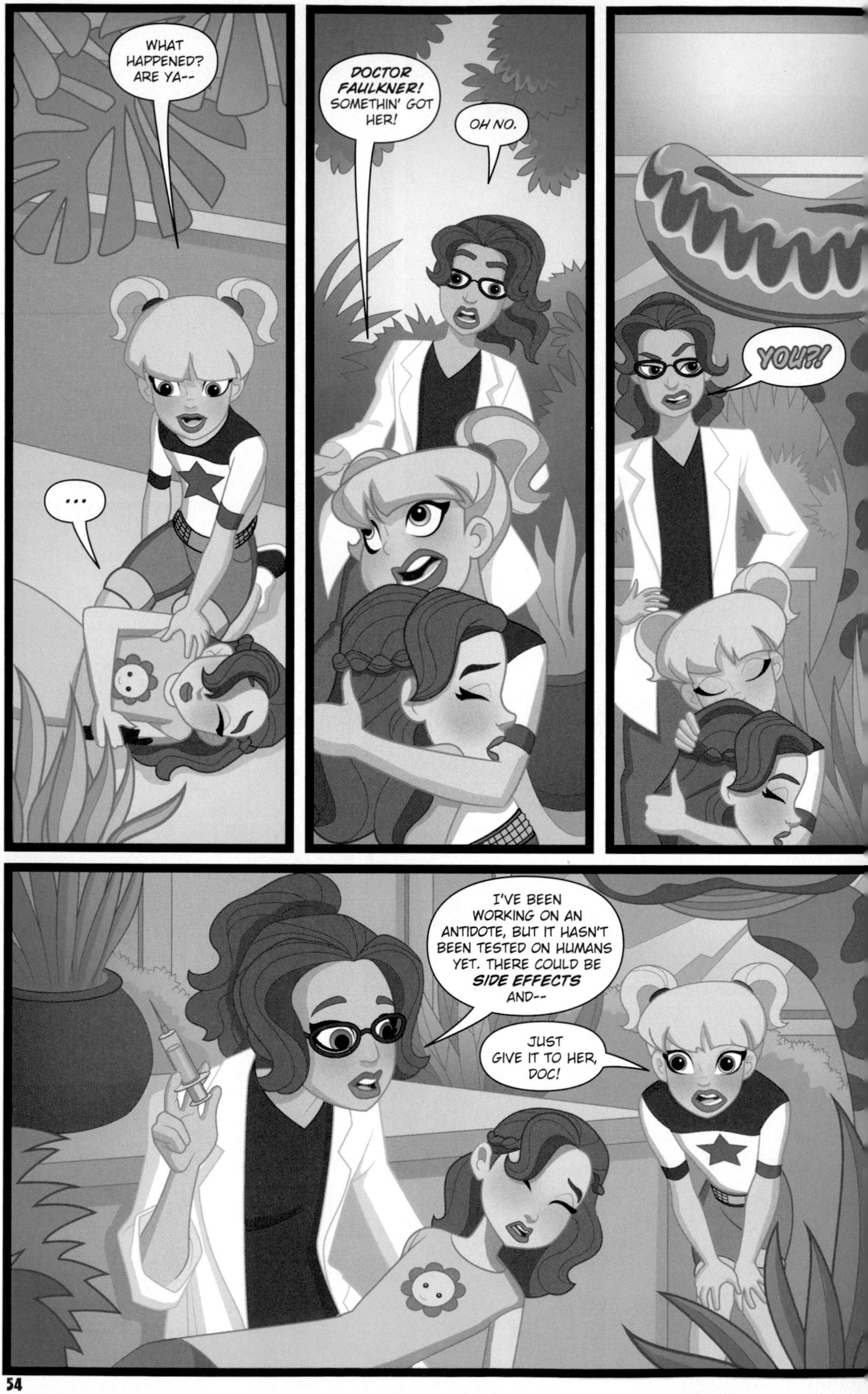
WHAT HAPPENED? ARE YA--
...
DOCTOR FAULKNER! SOMETHIN' GOT HER!
OH NO.
YOU?!
I'VE BEEN WORKING ON AN ANTIDOTE, BUT IT HASN'T BEEN TESTED ON HUMANS YET. THERE COULD BE SIDE EFFECTS AND--
JUST GIVE IT TO HER, DOC!

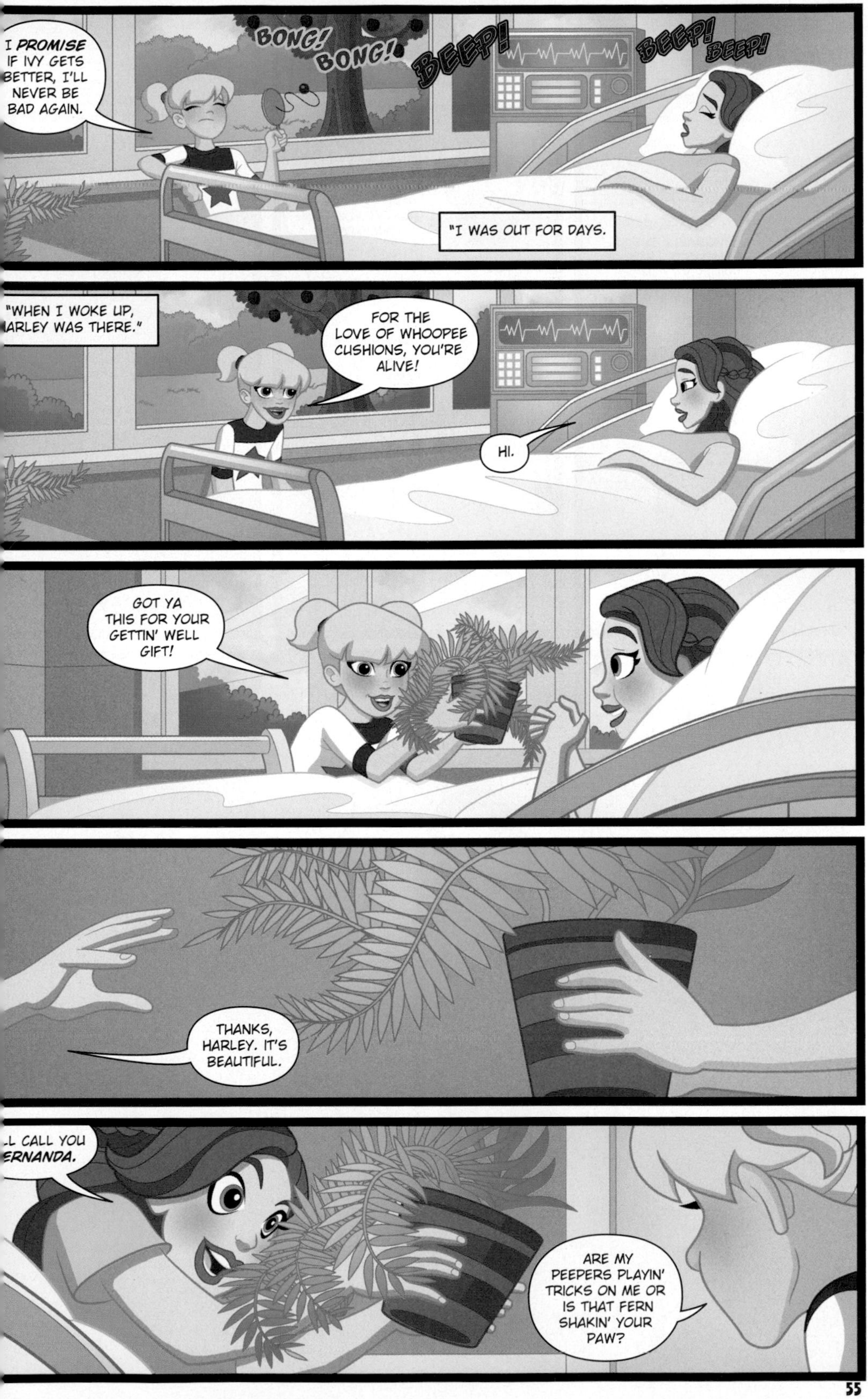
I PROMISE IF IVY GETS BETTER, I'LL NEVER BE BAD AGAIN.
BONG! BONG!
BEEP!
BEEP! BEEP!
"I WAS OUT FOR DAYS.
"WHEN I WOKE UP, ARLEY WAS THERE."
FOR THE LOVE OF WHOOPEE CUSHIONS, YOU'RE ALIVE!
HI.
GOT YA THIS FOR YOUR GETTIN' WELL GIFT!
THANKS, HARLEY. IT'S BEAUTIFUL.
L CALL YOU ERNANDA.
ARE MY PEEPERS PLAYIN' TRICKS ON ME OR IS THAT FERN SHAKIN' YOUR PAW?

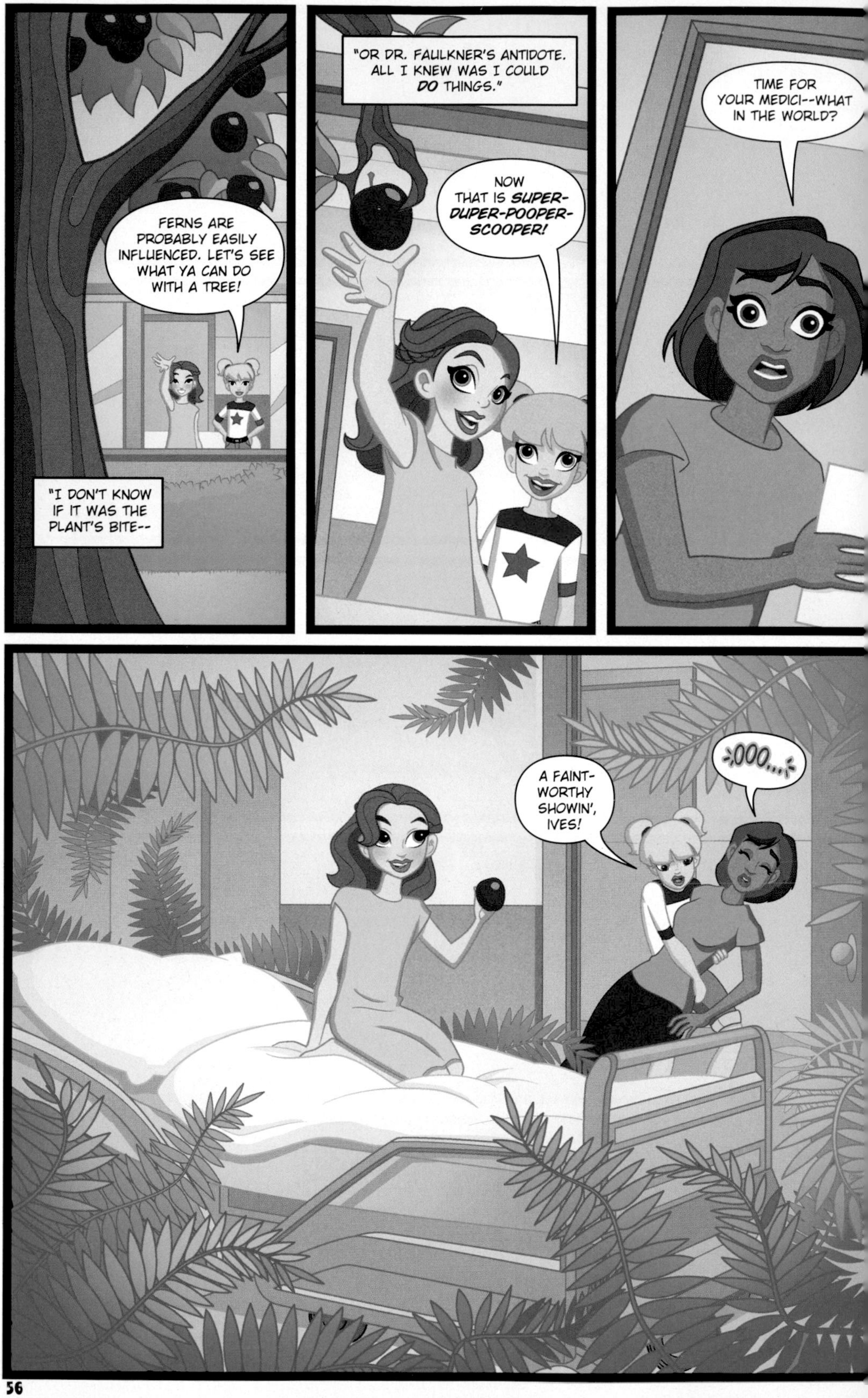
FERNS ARE PROBABLY EASILY INFLUENCED. LET'S SEE WHAT YA CAN DO WITH A TREE!
"I DON'T KNOW IF IT WAS THE PLANT'S BITE--
"OR DR. FAULKNER'S ANTIDOTE. ALL I KNEW WAS I COULD DO THINGS."
NOW THAT IS SUPER-DUPER-POOPER-SCOOPER!
TIME FOR YOUR MEDICI--WHAT IN THE WORLD?
A FAINT-WORTHY SHOWIN', IVES!
OOO...

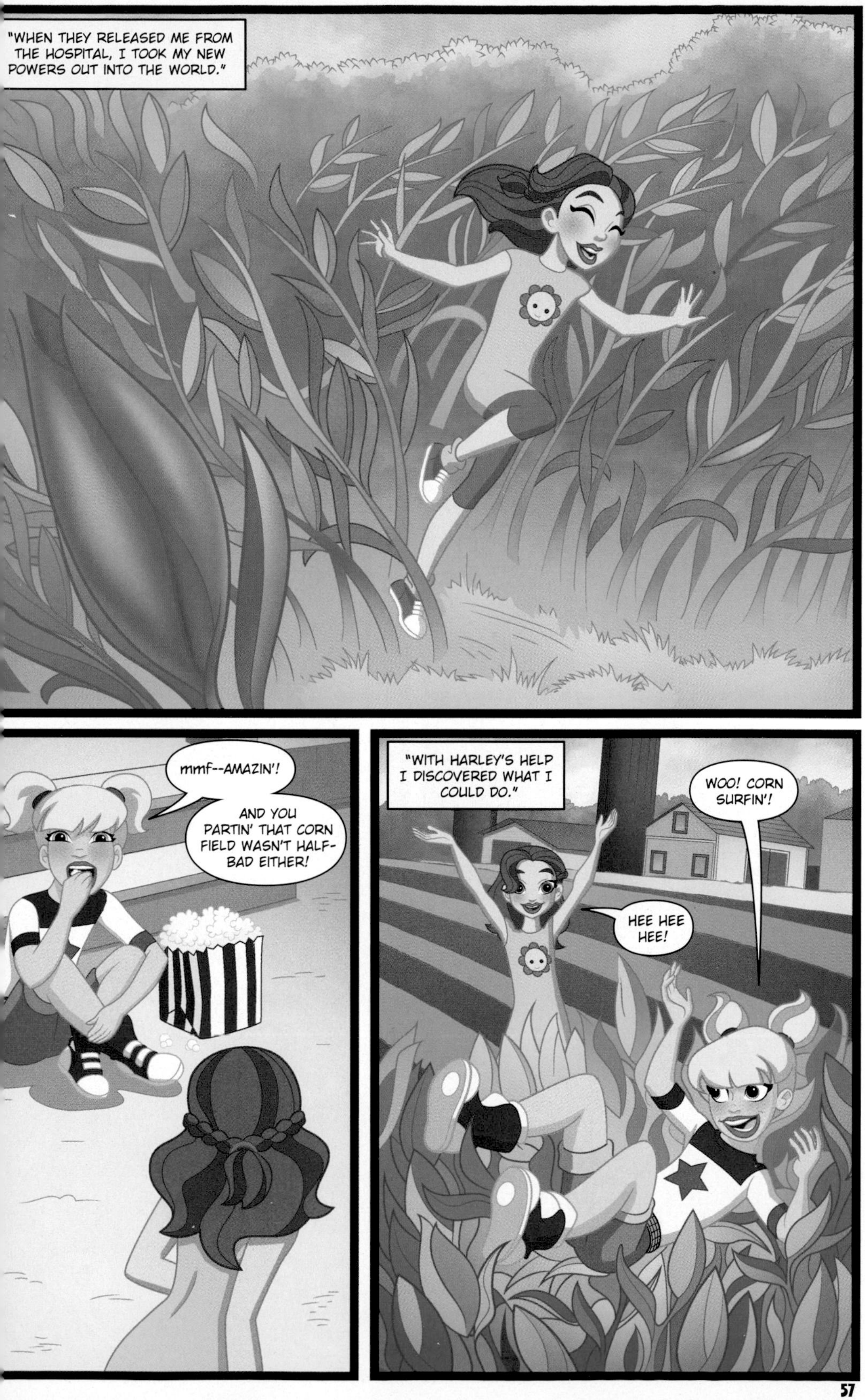
"WHEN THEY RELEASED ME FROM THE HOSPITAL, I TOOK MY NEW POWERS OUT INTO THE WORLD."
mmf--AMAZIN'!
AND YOU PARTIN' THAT CORN FIELD WASN'T HALF-BAD EITHER!
"WITH HARLEY'S HELP I DISCOVERED WHAT I COULD DO."
WOO! CORN SURFIN'!
HEE HEE HEE!

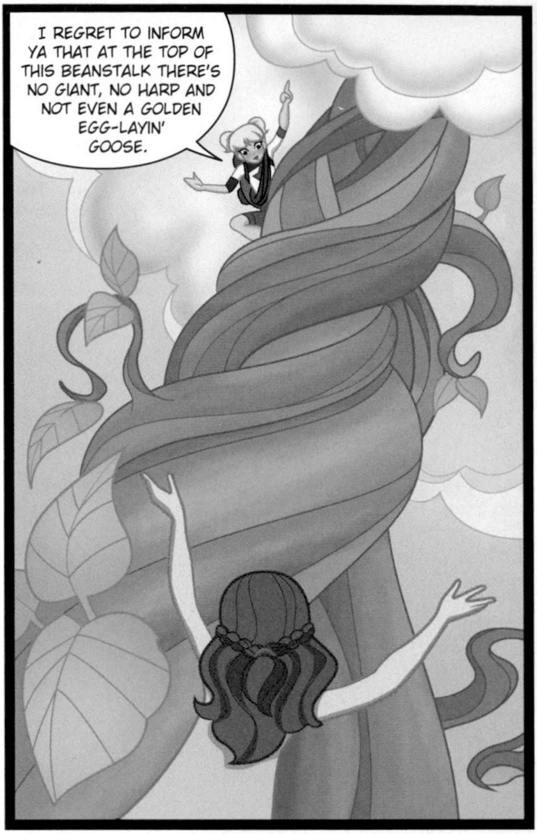
I REGRET TO INFORM YA THAT AT THE TOP OF THIS BEANSTALK THERE'S NO GIANT, NO HARP AND NOT EVEN A GOLDEN EGG-LAYIN' GOOSE.

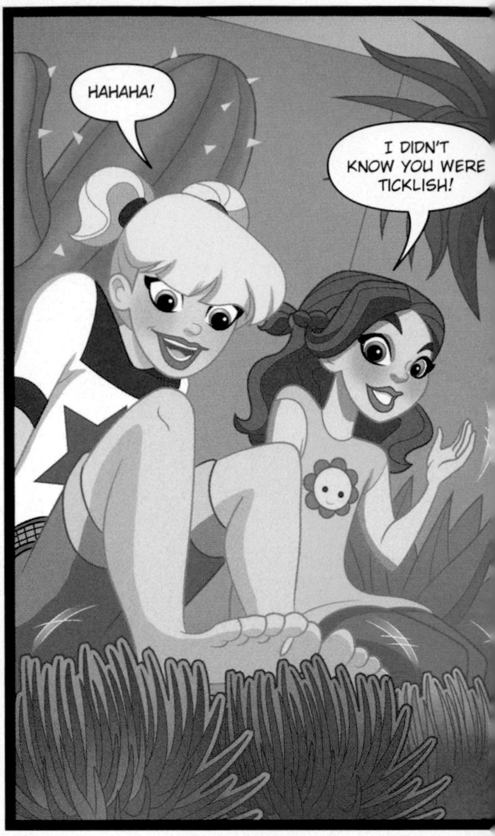
HAHAHA!
I DIDN'T KNOW YOU WERE TICKLISH!

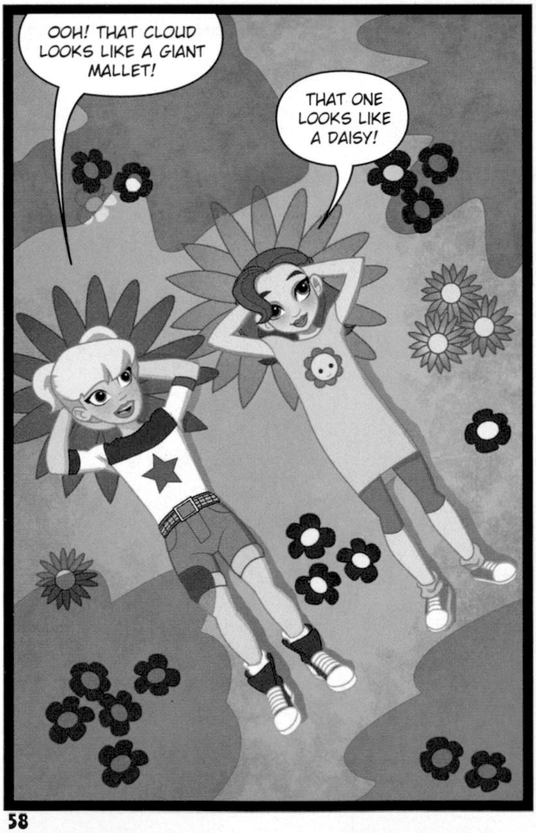
OOH! THAT CLOUD LOOKS LIKE A GIANT MALLET!
THAT ONE LOOKS LIKE A DAISY!

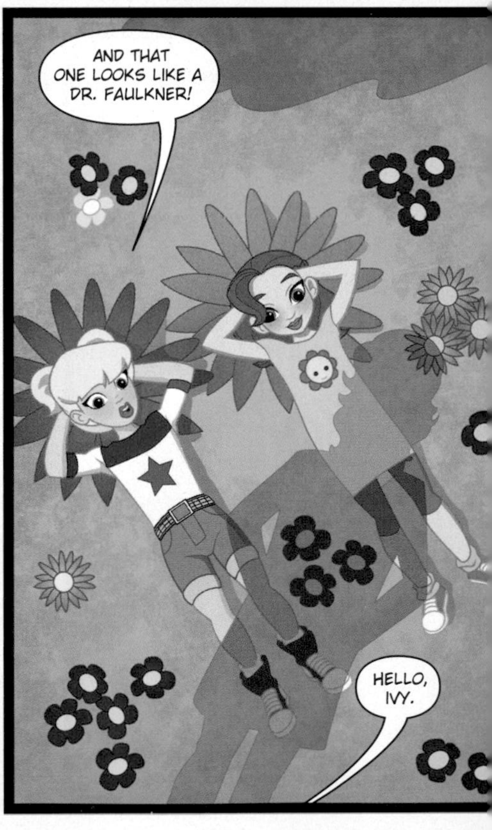
AND THAT ONE LOOKS LIKE A DR. FAULKNER!
HELLO, IVY.

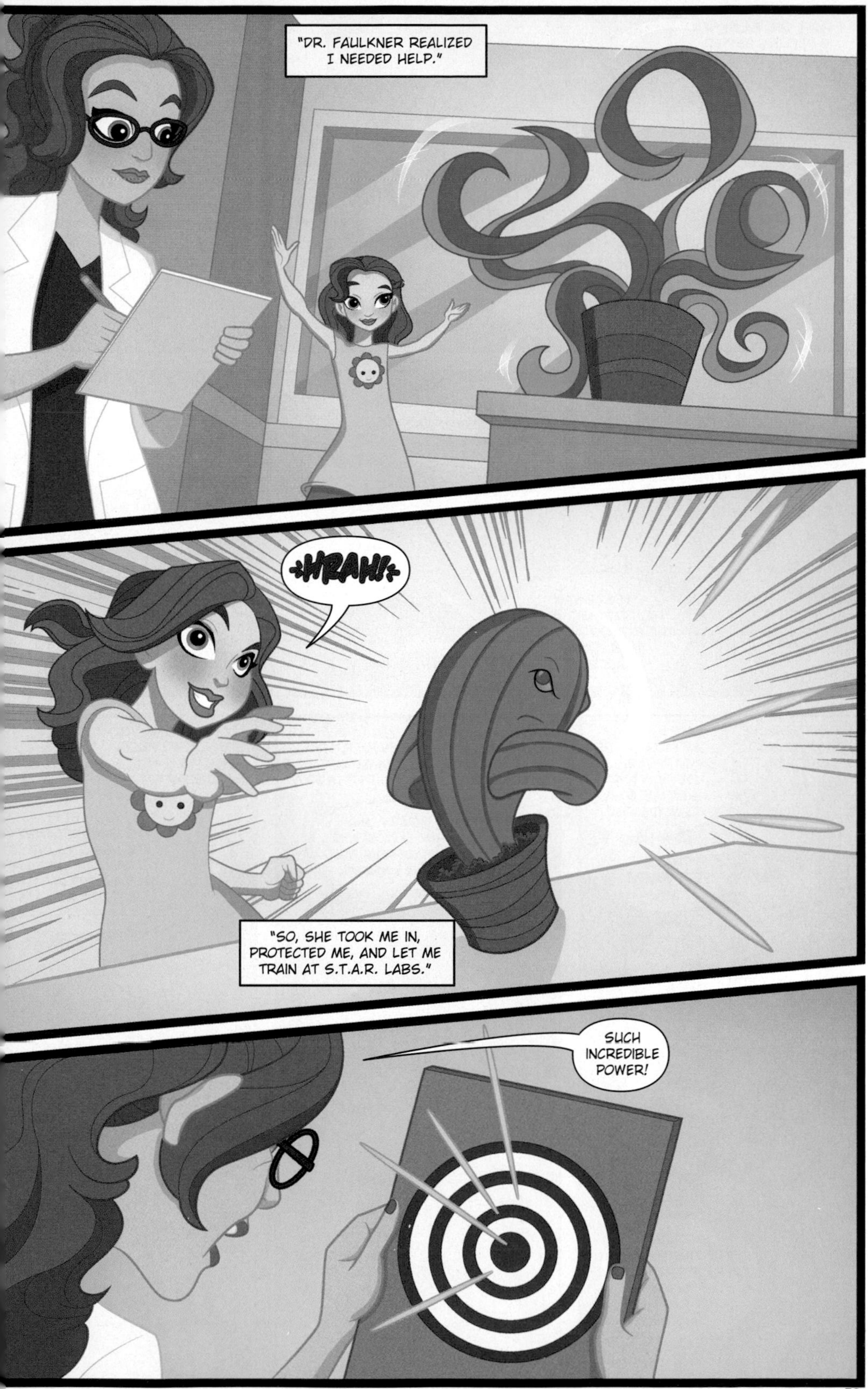
"DR. FAULKNER REALIZED I NEEDED HELP."
HRAH!
"SO, SHE TOOK ME IN, PROTECTED ME, AND LET ME TRAIN AT S.T.A.R. LABS."
SUCH INCREDIBLE POWER!

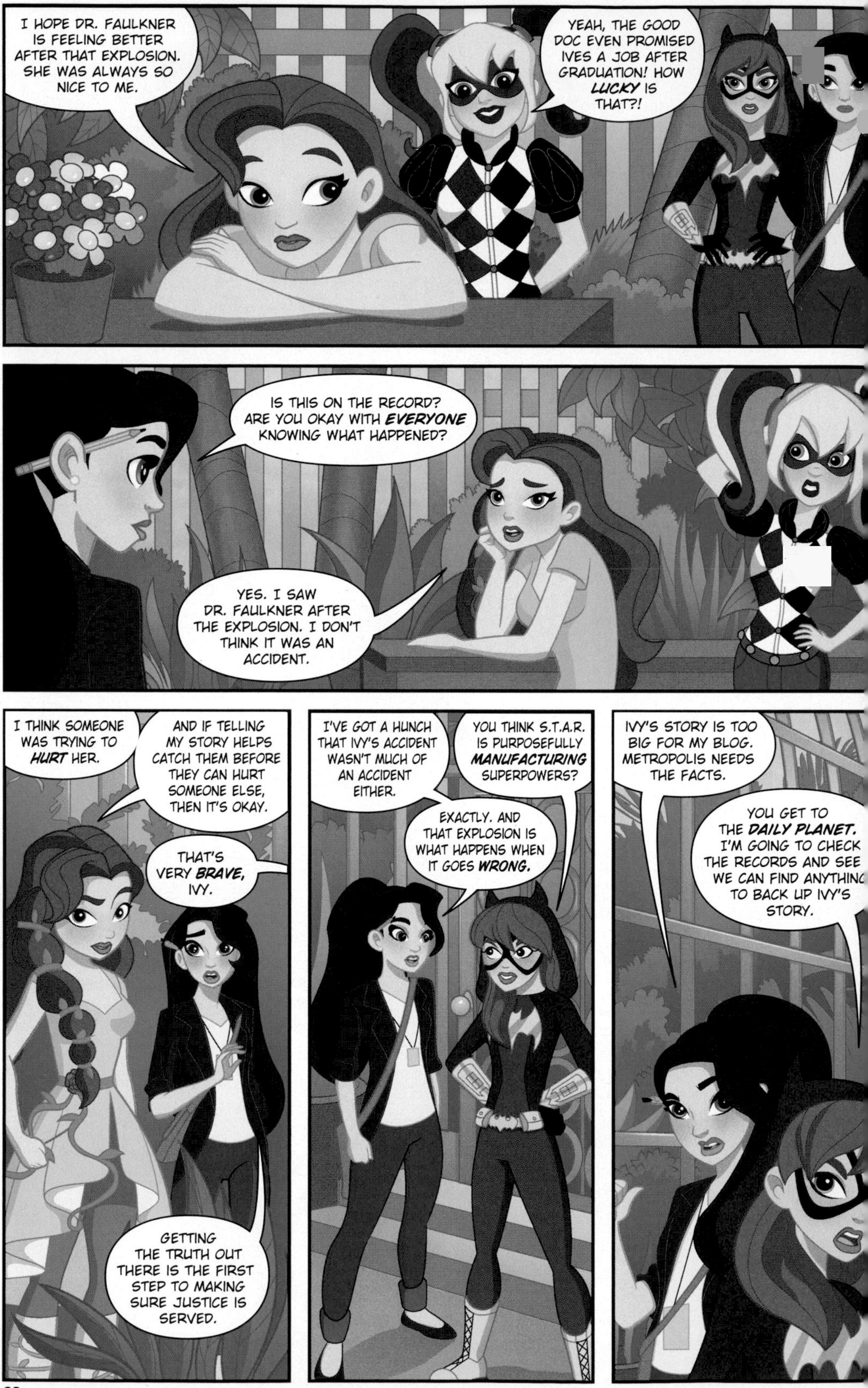

I HOPE DR. FAULKNER IS FEELING BETTER AFTER THAT EXPLOSION. SHE WAS ALWAYS SO NICE TO ME.
YEAH, THE GOOD DOC EVEN PROMISED IVES A JOB AFTER GRADUATION! HOW *LUCKY* IS THAT?!
IS THIS ON THE RECORD? ARE YOU OKAY WITH *EVERYONE* KNOWING WHAT HAPPENED?
YES. I SAW DR. FAULKNER AFTER THE EXPLOSION. I DON'T THINK IT WAS AN ACCIDENT.
I THINK SOMEONE WAS TRYING TO *HURT* HER.
AND IF TELLING MY STORY HELPS CATCH THEM BEFORE THEY CAN HURT SOMEONE ELSE, THEN IT'S OKAY.
THAT'S VERY *BRAVE,* IVY.
GETTING THE TRUTH OUT THERE IS THE FIRST STEP TO MAKING SURE JUSTICE IS SERVED.
I'VE GOT A HUNCH THAT IVY'S ACCIDENT WASN'T MUCH OF AN ACCIDENT EITHER.
YOU THINK S.T.A.R. IS PURPOSEFULLY *MANUFACTURING* SUPERPOWERS?
EXACTLY. AND THAT EXPLOSION IS WHAT HAPPENS WHEN IT GOES *WRONG.*
IVY'S STORY IS TOO BIG FOR MY BLOG. METROPOLIS NEEDS THE FACTS.
YOU GET TO THE *DAILY PLANET.* I'M GOING TO CHECK THE RECORDS AND SEE WE CAN FIND ANYTHIN TO BACK UP IVY'S STORY.

Clack!
Clack!
Clack!

FF!
RFF!

HELLO? IS SOMEONE THERE? HARLEY, ARE YOU TRYING TO PRANK ME? DID YOU GET STUCK SMALL AGAIN, BUMBLEBEE?

YOU MUST BE BATGIRL. PLEASED TO MEET YOU.

MEANWHILE AT S.T.A.R. LABS.

RIGHT THIS WAY!

THE ELEVATOR?

I'M SO USED TO FLYING EVERYWHERE, I ALMOST FORGOT THESE THINGS EXISTED!

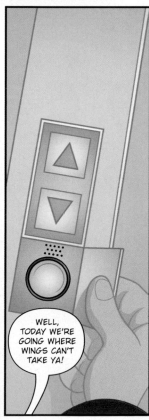

WELL, TODAY WE'RE GOING WHERE WINGS CAN'T TAKE YA!

SECURITY CLEARANCE CONFIRMED

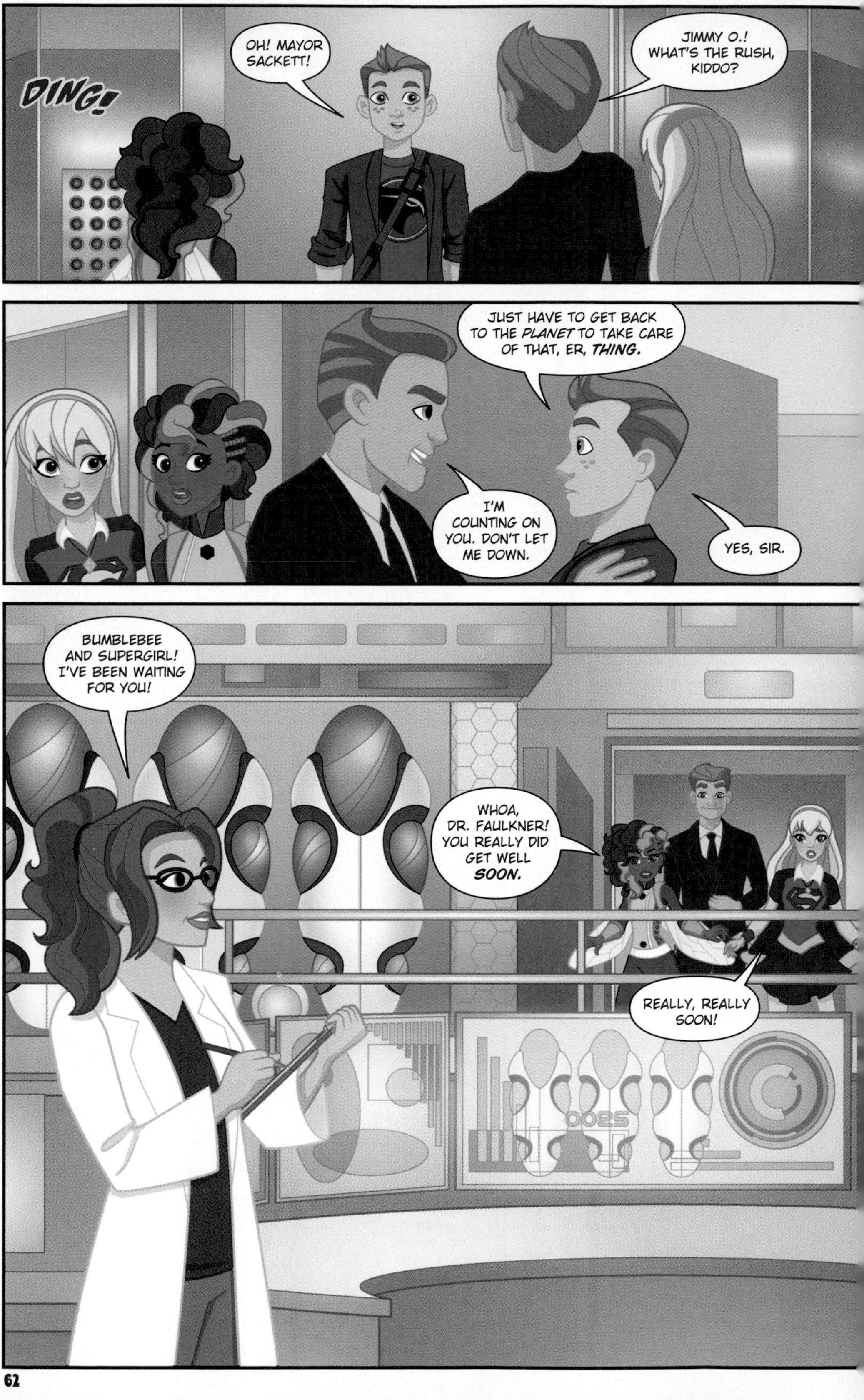
DING!
OH! MAYOR SACKETT!
JIMMY O.! WHAT'S THE RUSH, KIDDO?
JUST HAVE TO GET BACK TO THE *PLANET* TO TAKE CARE OF THAT, ER, ***THING.***
I'M COUNTING ON YOU. DON'T LET ME DOWN.
YES, SIR.
BUMBLEBEE AND SUPERGIRL! I'VE BEEN WAITING FOR YOU!
WHOA, DR. FAULKNER! YOU REALLY DID GET WELL ***SOON.***
REALLY, REALLY SOON!

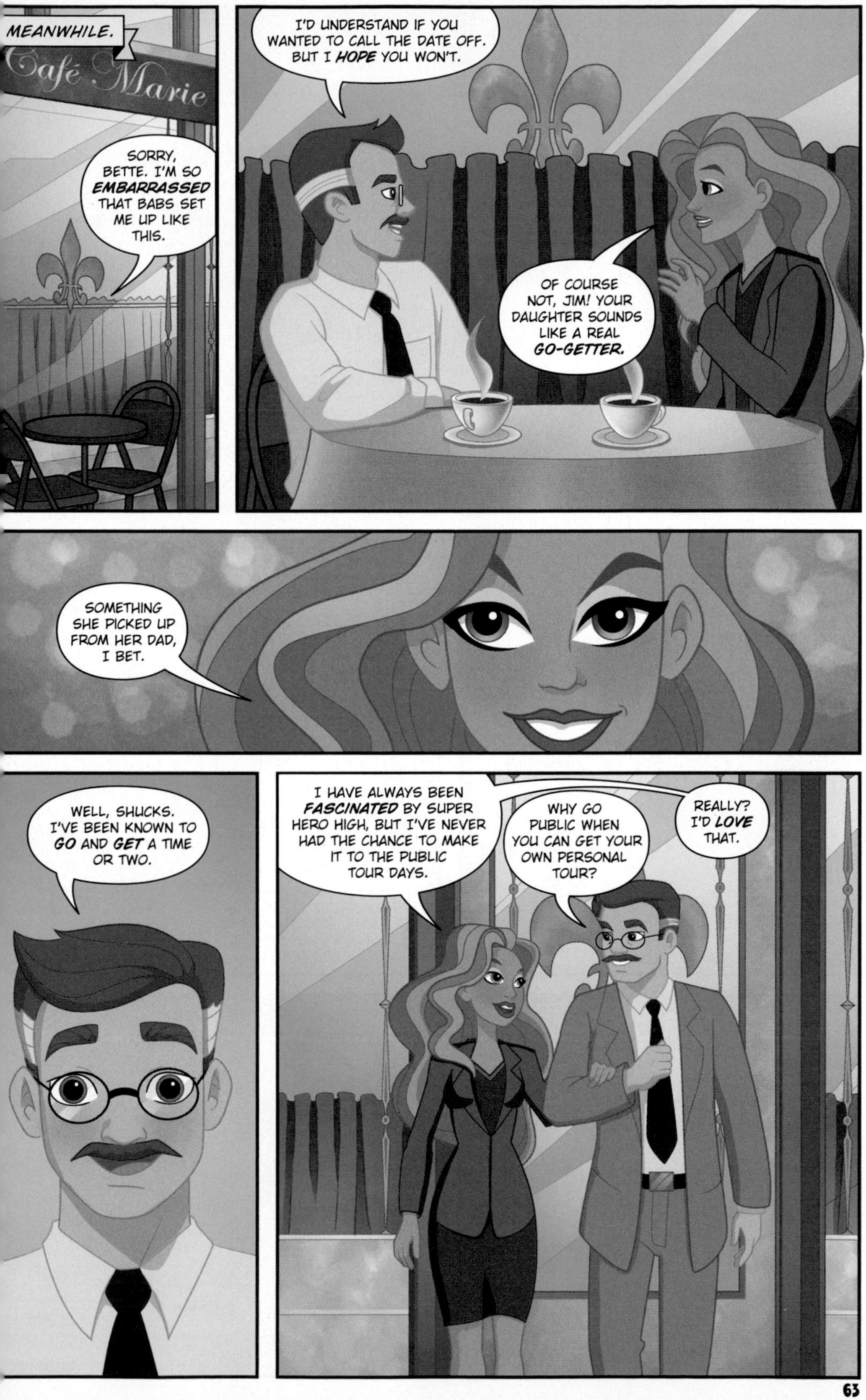
MEANWHILE.
Café Marie
SORRY, BETTE. I'M SO EMBARRASSED THAT BABS SET ME UP LIKE THIS.
I'D UNDERSTAND IF YOU WANTED TO CALL THE DATE OFF. BUT I HOPE YOU WON'T.
OF COURSE NOT, JIM! YOUR DAUGHTER SOUNDS LIKE A REAL GO-GETTER.
SOMETHING SHE PICKED UP FROM HER DAD, I BET.
WELL, SHUCKS. I'VE BEEN KNOWN TO GO AND GET A TIME OR TWO.
I HAVE ALWAYS BEEN FASCINATED BY SUPER HERO HIGH, BUT I'VE NEVER HAD THE CHANCE TO MAKE IT TO THE PUBLIC TOUR DAYS.
WHY GO PUBLIC WHEN YOU CAN GET YOUR OWN PERSONAL TOUR?
REALLY? I'D LOVE THAT.

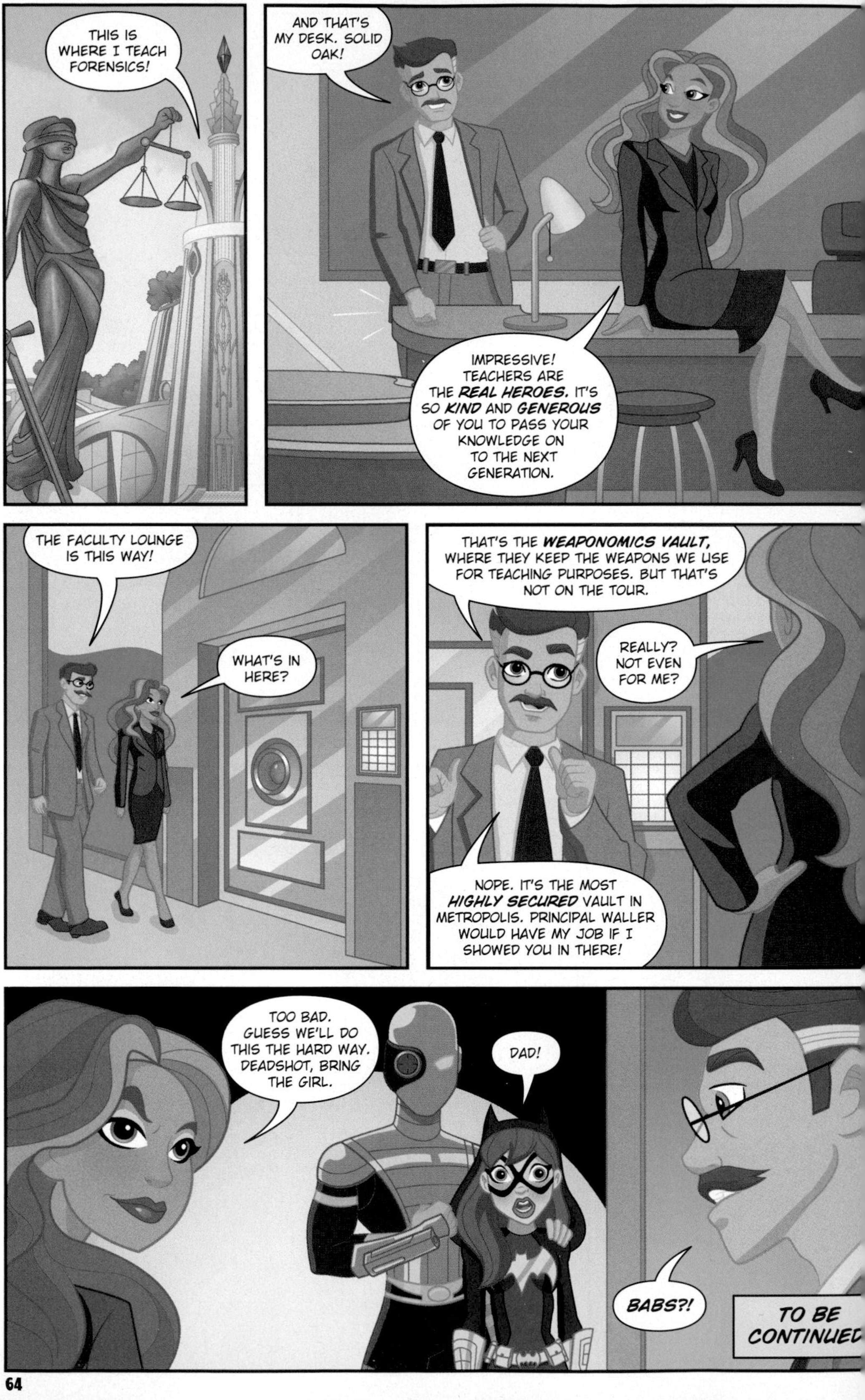
THIS IS WHERE I TEACH FORENSICS!
AND THAT'S MY DESK. SOLID OAK!
IMPRESSIVE! TEACHERS ARE THE **REAL HEROES.** IT'S SO **KIND** AND **GENEROUS** OF YOU TO PASS YOUR KNOWLEDGE ON TO THE NEXT GENERATION.
THE FACULTY LOUNGE IS THIS WAY!
WHAT'S IN HERE?
THAT'S THE **WEAPONOMICS VAULT,** WHERE THEY KEEP THE WEAPONS WE USE FOR TEACHING PURPOSES. BUT THAT'S NOT ON THE TOUR.
REALLY? NOT EVEN FOR ME?
NOPE. IT'S THE MOST **HIGHLY SECURED** VAULT IN METROPOLIS. PRINCIPAL WALLER WOULD HAVE MY JOB IF I SHOWED YOU IN THERE!
TOO BAD. GUESS WE'LL DO THIS THE HARD WAY. DEADSHOT, BRING THE GIRL.
DAD!
BABS?!
TO BE CONTINUED

CHAPTER 4
THE WHOLE TRUTH

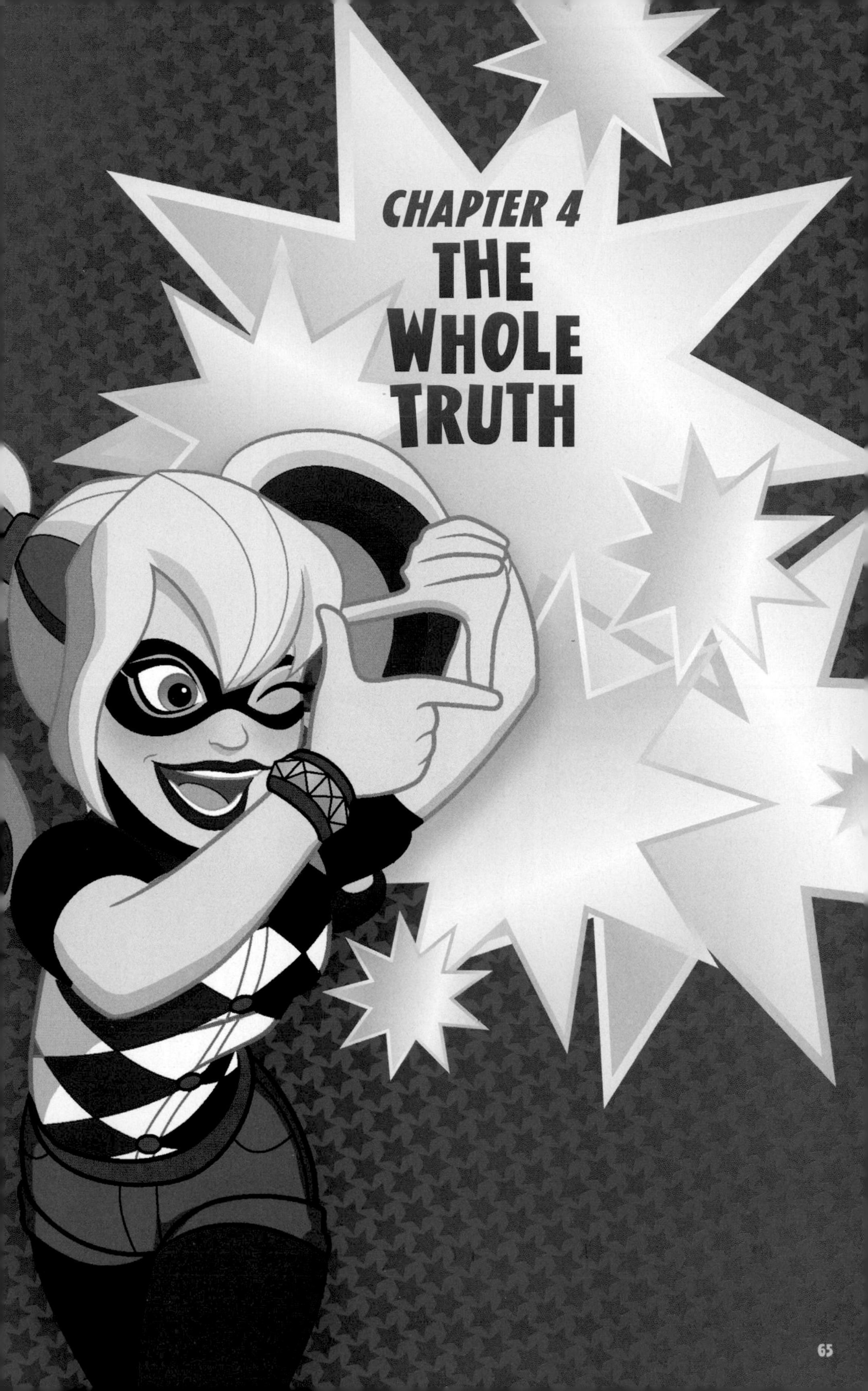

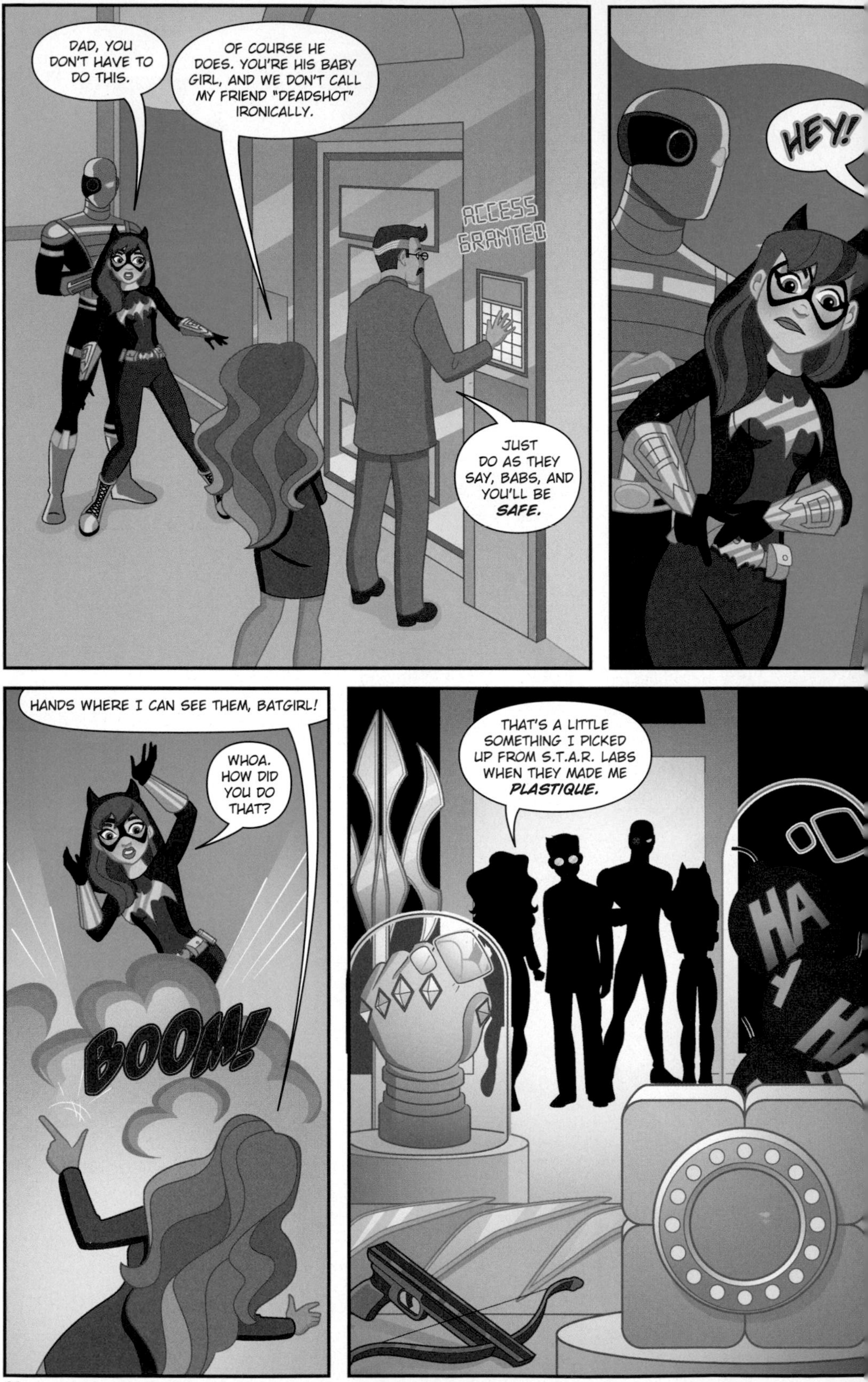
DAD, YOU DON'T HAVE TO DO THIS.
OF COURSE HE DOES. YOU'RE HIS BABY GIRL, AND WE DON'T CALL MY FRIEND "DEADSHOT" IRONICALLY.
ACCESS GRANTED
JUST DO AS THEY SAY, BABS, AND YOU'LL BE SAFE.
HEY!
HANDS WHERE I CAN SEE THEM, BATGIRL!
WHOA. HOW DID YOU DO THAT?
BOOM!
THAT'S A LITTLE SOMETHING I PICKED UP FROM S.T.A.R. LABS WHEN THEY MADE ME PLASTIQUE.
HA
HA

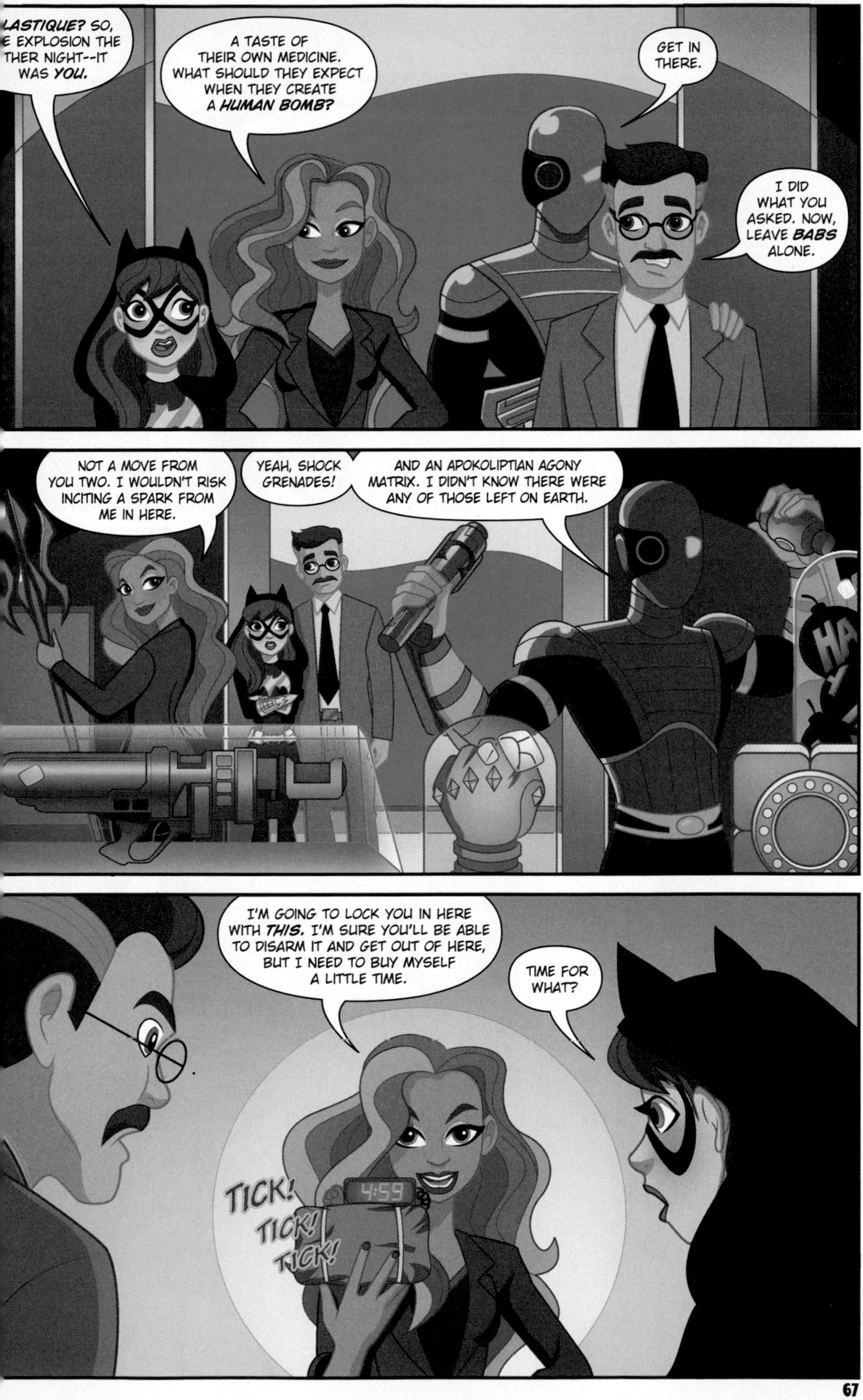
LASTIQUE? SO, E EXPLOSION THE THER NIGHT--IT WAS YOU.
A TASTE OF THEIR OWN MEDICINE. WHAT SHOULD THEY EXPECT WHEN THEY CREATE A HUMAN BOMB?
GET IN THERE.
I DID WHAT YOU ASKED. NOW, LEAVE BABS ALONE.
NOT A MOVE FROM YOU TWO. I WOULDN'T RISK INCITING A SPARK FROM ME IN HERE.
YEAH, SHOCK GRENADES!
AND AN APOKOLIPTIAN AGONY MATRIX. I DIDN'T KNOW THERE WERE ANY OF THOSE LEFT ON EARTH.
I'M GOING TO LOCK YOU IN HERE WITH THIS. I'M SURE YOU'LL BE ABLE TO DISARM IT AND GET OUT OF HERE, BUT I NEED TO BUY MYSELF A LITTLE TIME.
TIME FOR WHAT?
4:59
TICK! TICK! TICK!

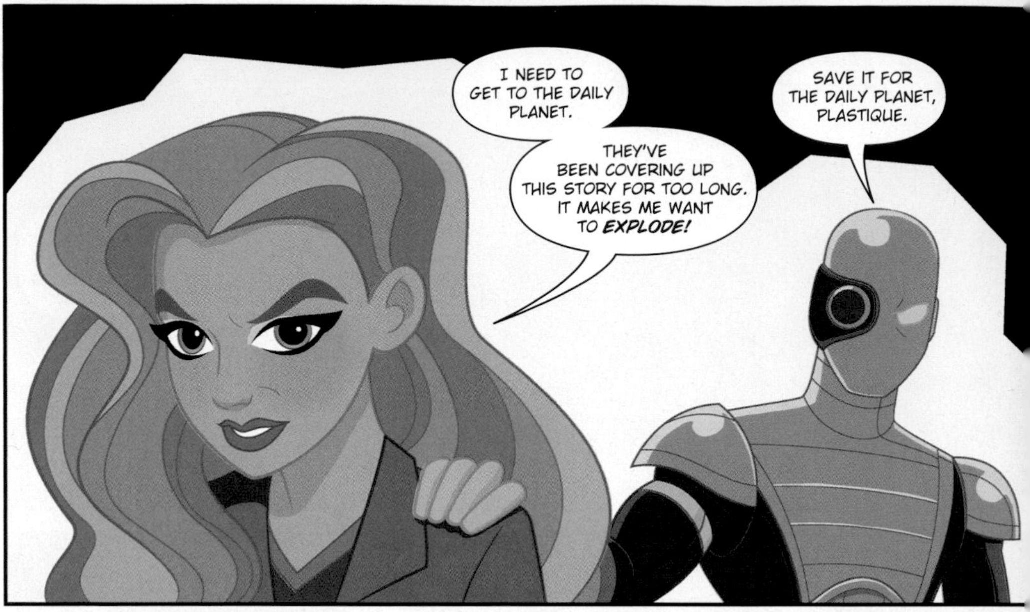
I NEED TO GET TO THE DAILY PLANET.
THEY'VE BEEN COVERING UP THIS STORY FOR TOO LONG. IT MAKES ME WANT TO *EXPLODE!*
SAVE IT FOR THE DAILY PLANET, PLASTIQUE.

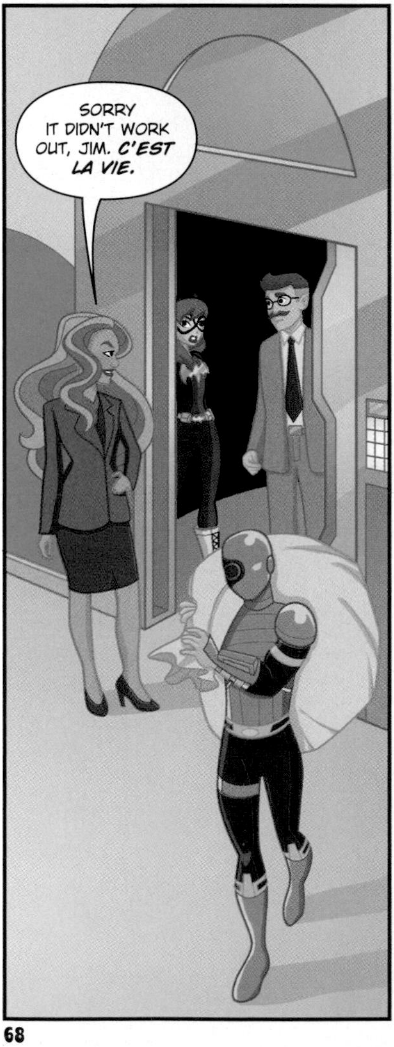
SORRY IT DIDN'T WORK OUT, JIM. *C'EST LA VIE.*

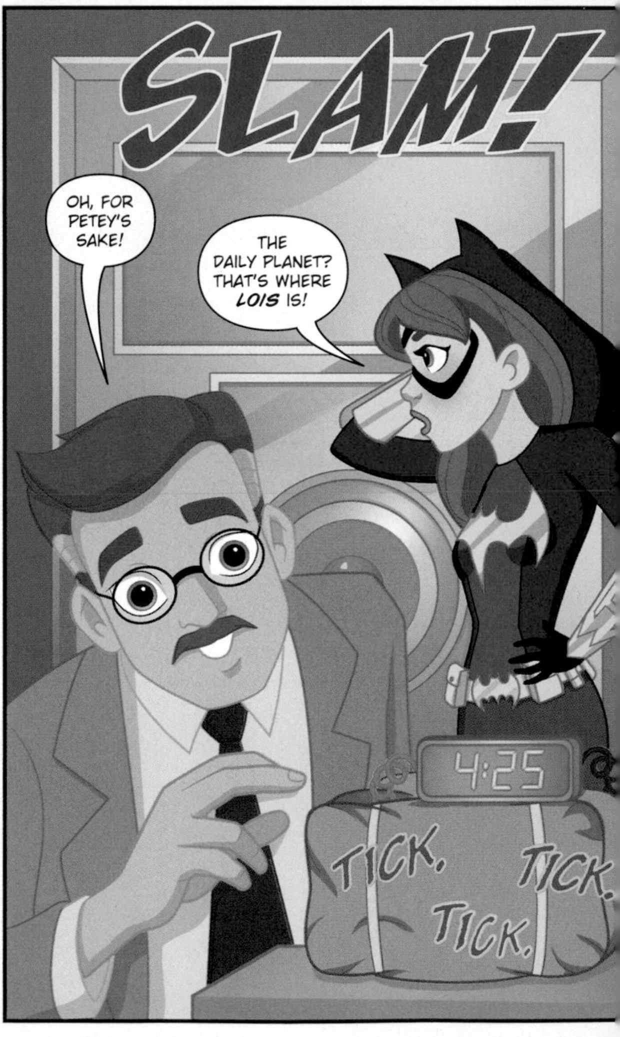
SLAM!
OH, FOR PETEY'S SAKE!
THE DAILY PLANET? THAT'S WHERE *LOIS* IS!
4:25
TICK. TICK. TICK.

LOOKIN' LOVELIER THAN WAKIN' UP TO A TWELVE-PACK OF WHOOPEE CUSHIONS AND AN INDUSTRIAL-SIZED ROLL OF PLASTIC WRAP ON APRIL FOOL'S DAY!

SHNKT

WITH *PRECISELY* TWO HOURS AND 33 MINUTES UNTIL THE DANCE, I HYPOTHESIZE THAT WE'LL FINISH DECORATING JUST IN TIME.

BUT WE COULD'VE USED *SUPERGIRL* AND *BUMBLEBEE'S* HELP.

YEAH, WHERE ARE THEY? DON'T THEY KNOW THAT BEIN' *TARDY* IS MY THING!

DEADSHOT, THIS WAY!

WHO IS--

...AY OUT THIS, ...IDS!

BLASTED BUTTONS! THERE'S MORE OF 'EM!

NO WAY! I'M HARLEY QUINN, AND *NOT* STAYIN' OUT OF STUFF IS MY SPECIALTY!

FREEZE!

~GUH!~

AGGGH!

FROST, FROST, SHE'S OUR SUPER! WATCH HER FREEZE THAT PARTY POOPER!

UM, GUYS?

69

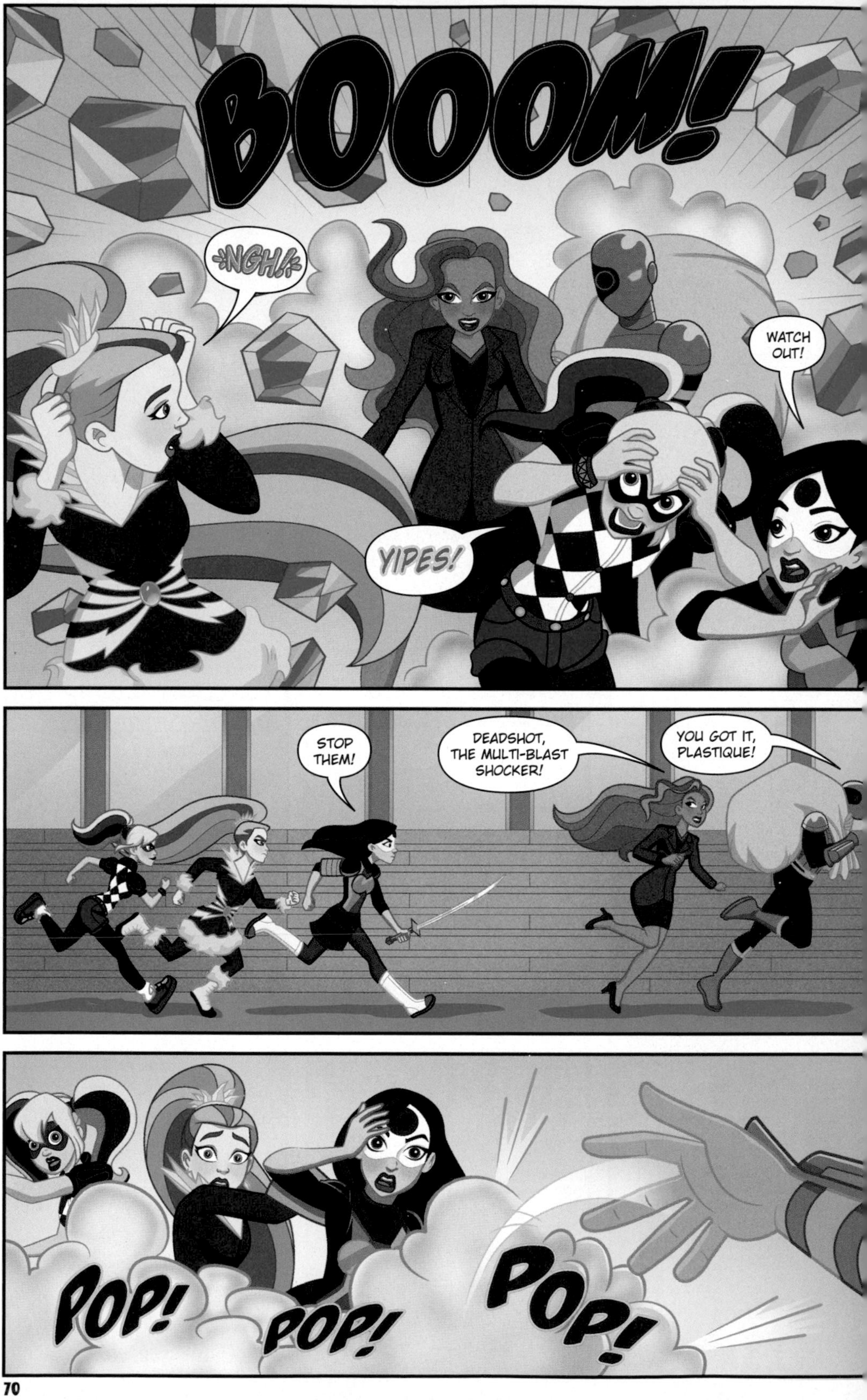
BOOOM!
NGH!
WATCH OUT!
YIPES!
STOP THEM!
DEADSHOT, THE MULTI-BLAST SHOCKER!
YOU GOT IT, PLASTIQUE!
POP!
POP!
POP!

MEANWHILE AT S.T.A.R. LABS.

YOU GIRLS SHOWED SUCH IMPRESSIVE SKILLS RESCUING DR. FAULKNER THE OTHER NIGHT THAT WE WANTED TO INVITE YOU TO BE PART OF A *SUPER HERO CLUB* WE'RE PUTTING TOGETHER.

SO, PLEASE COME THIS WAY AND TAKE A SEAT.

WAIT, GO BACK, *REWIND.* WE'RE NOT DOING ANYTHING UNTIL WE GET SOME ANSWERS.

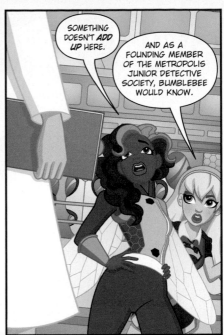

SOMETHING DOESN'T *ADD UP* HERE.

AND AS A FOUNDING MEMBER OF THE METROPOLIS JUNIOR DETECTIVE SOCIETY, BUMBLEBEE WOULD KNOW.

WHAT DOESN'T ADD UP?

DR. FAULKNER WAS IN REALLY *BAD SHAPE* WHEN YOU FLEW HER TO THE HOSPITAL.

NOW, SHE DOESN'T EVEN HAVE A SCRATCH ON HER!

YEAH! WHAT ARE YOU, SOME SORT OF SUPER DOCTOR?

YOU COULD SAY THAT.

71

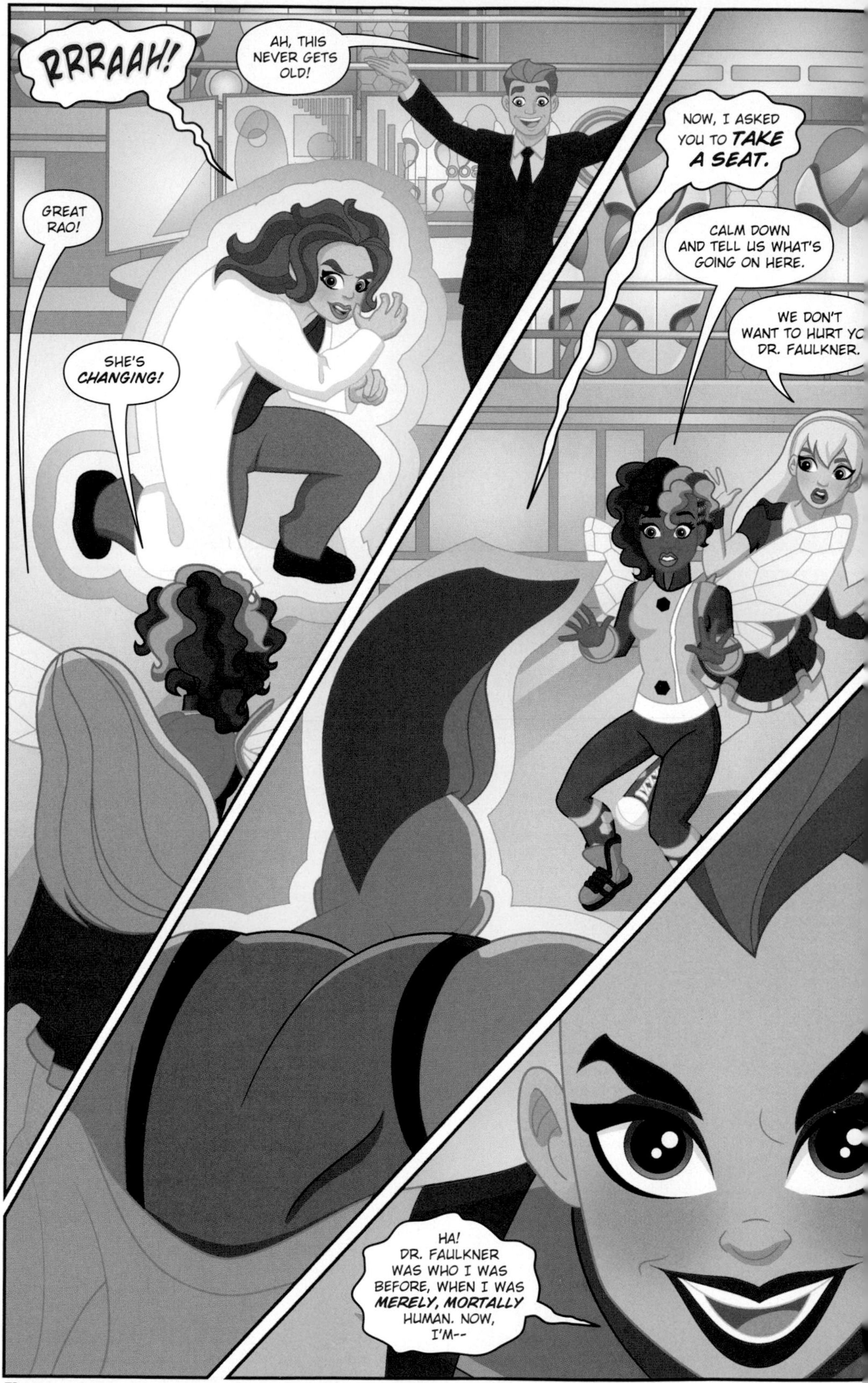
RRRAAH!
AH, THIS NEVER GETS OLD!
GREAT RAO!
SHE'S CHANGING!
NOW, I ASKED YOU TO TAKE A SEAT.
CALM DOWN AND TELL US WHAT'S GOING ON HERE.
WE DON'T WANT TO HURT YO DR. FAULKNER.
HA! DR. FAULKNER WAS WHO I WAS BEFORE, WHEN I WAS MERELY, MORTALLY HUMAN. NOW, I'M--

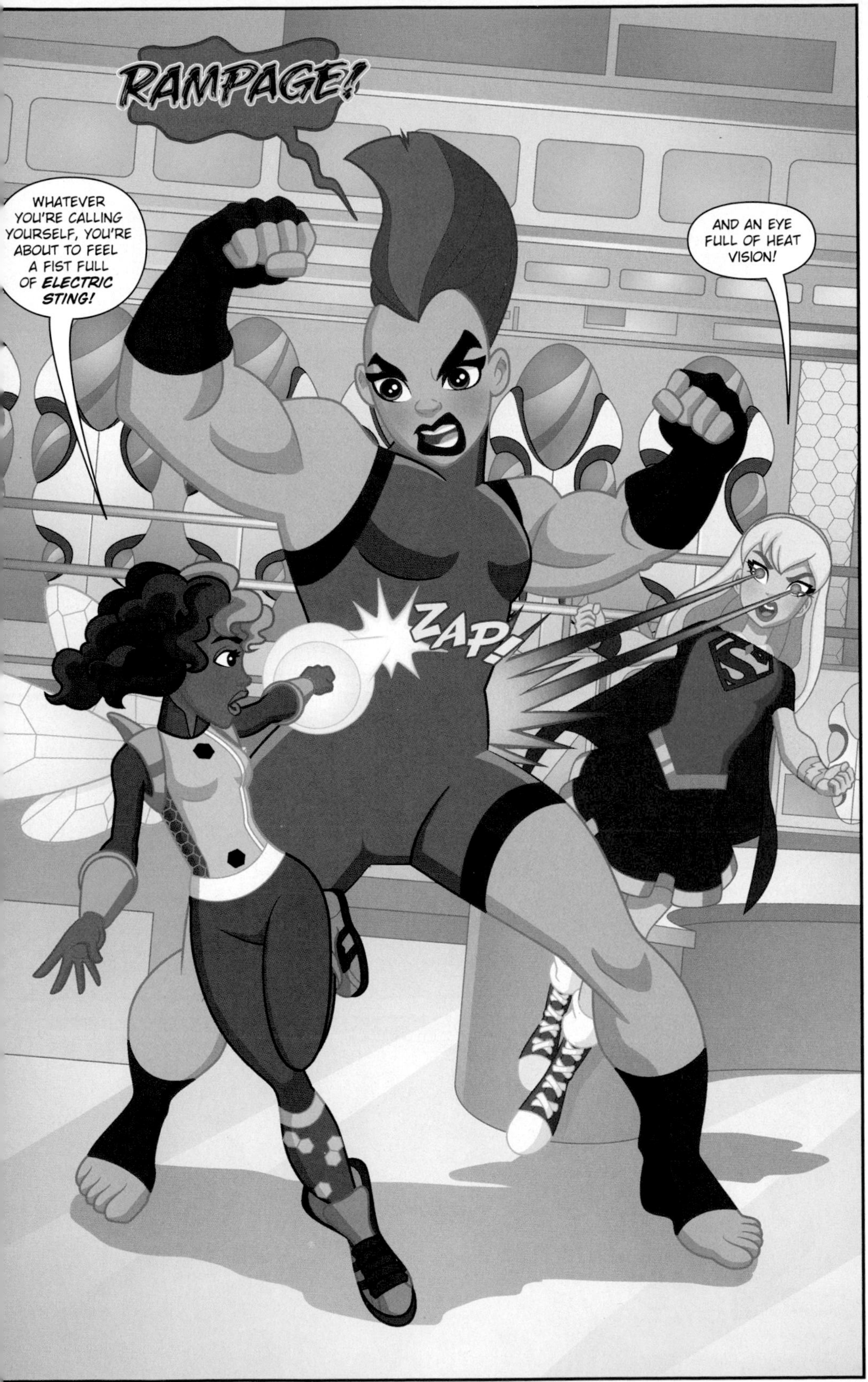
RAMPAGE!
WHATEVER YOU'RE CALLING YOURSELF, YOU'RE ABOUT TO FEEL A FIST FULL OF ELECTRIC STING!
AND AN EYE FULL OF HEAT VISION!
ZAP!

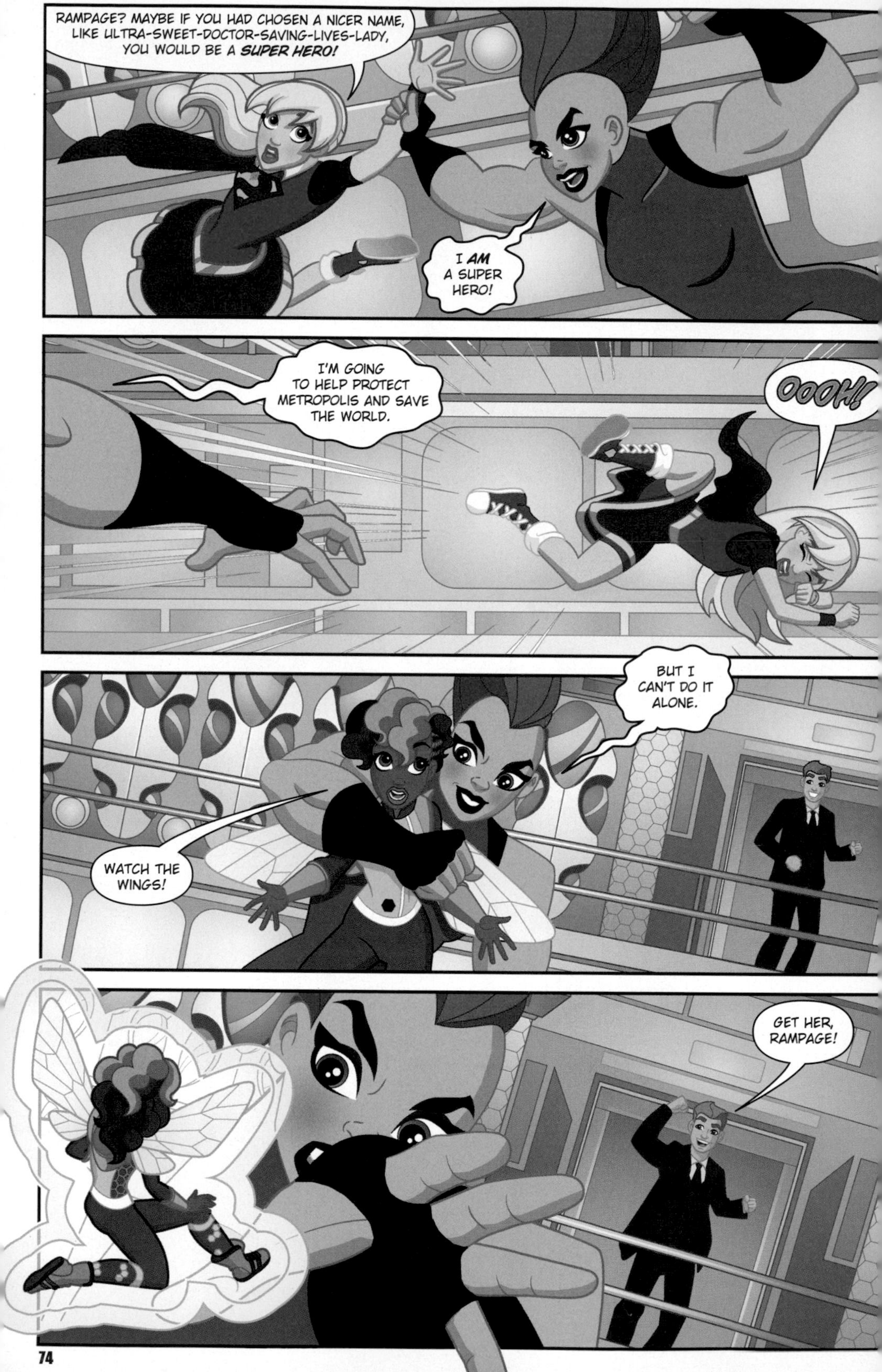
RAMPAGE? MAYBE IF YOU HAD CHOSEN A NICER NAME, LIKE ULTRA-SWEET-DOCTOR-SAVING-LIVES-LADY, YOU WOULD BE A SUPER HERO!
I AM A SUPER HERO!
I'M GOING TO HELP PROTECT METROPOLIS AND SAVE THE WORLD.
OOOH!
BUT I CAN'T DO IT ALONE.
WATCH THE WINGS!
GET HER, RAMPAGE!

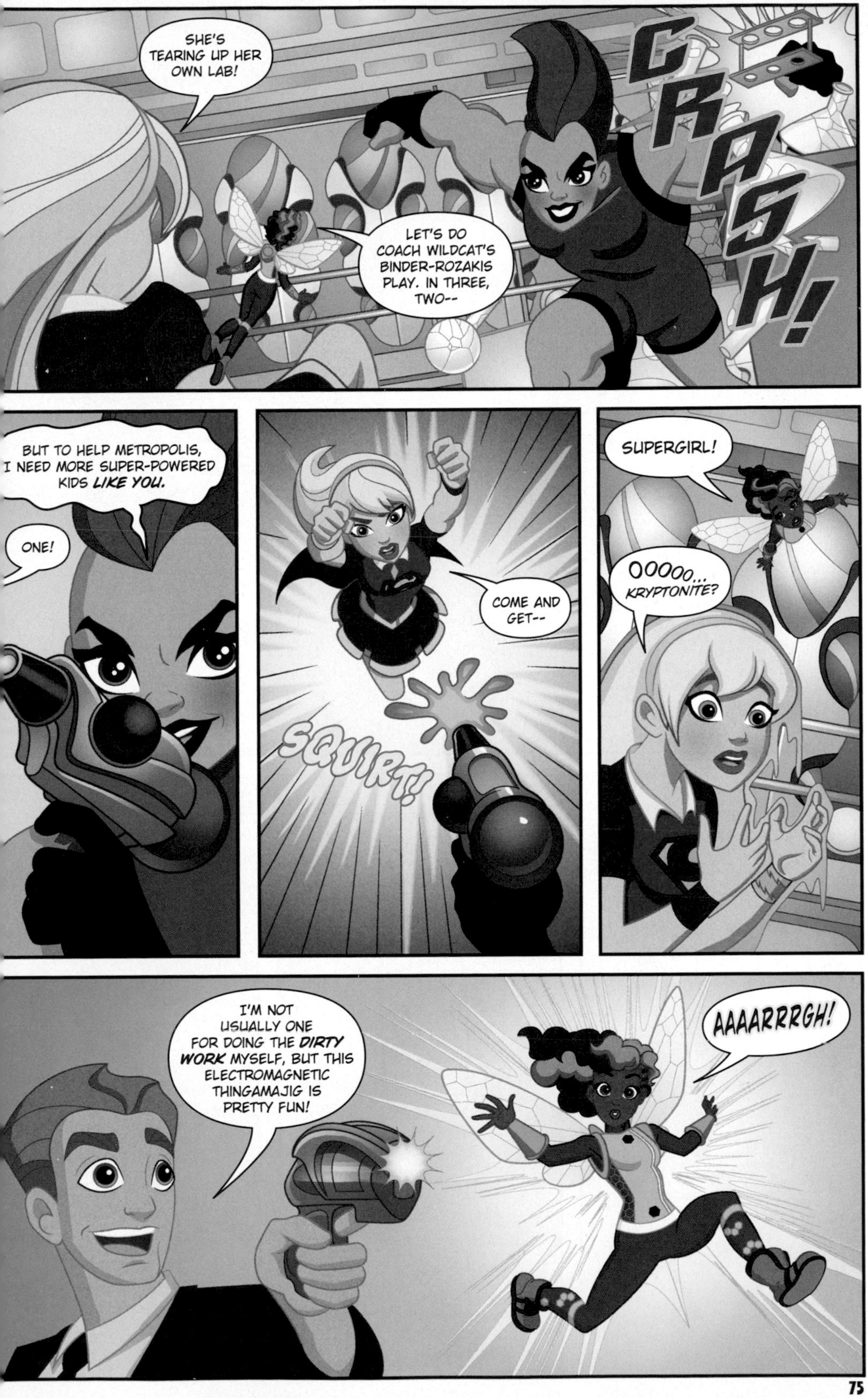
SHE'S TEARING UP HER OWN LAB!
LET'S DO COACH WILDCAT'S BINDER-ROZAKIS PLAY. IN THREE, TWO--
CRASH!
BUT TO HELP METROPOLIS, I NEED MORE SUPER-POWERED KIDS LIKE YOU.
ONE!
COME AND GET--
SQUIRT!
SUPERGIRL!
OOOOO... KRYPTONITE?
I'M NOT USUALLY ONE FOR DOING THE DIRTY WORK MYSELF, BUT THIS ELECTROMAGNETIC THINGAMAJIG IS PRETTY FUN!
AAAARRRGH!

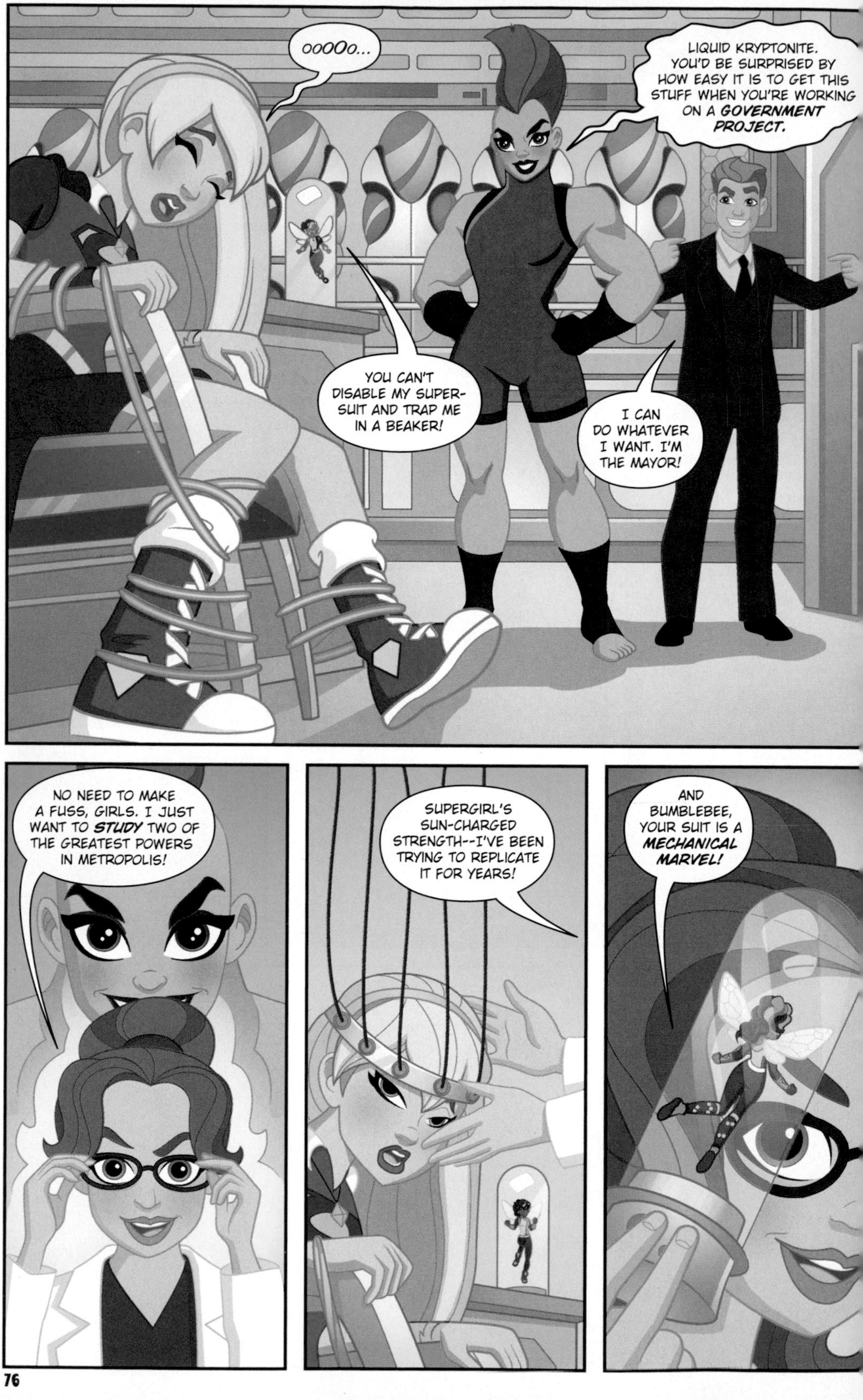
oooOo...
LIQUID KRYPTONITE. YOU'D BE SURPRISED BY HOW EASY IT IS TO GET THIS STUFF WHEN YOU'RE WORKING ON A **GOVERNMENT PROJECT.**
YOU CAN'T DISABLE MY SUPER-SUIT AND TRAP ME IN A BEAKER!
I CAN DO WHATEVER I WANT. I'M THE MAYOR!
NO NEED TO MAKE A FUSS, GIRLS. I JUST WANT TO ***STUDY*** TWO OF THE GREATEST POWERS IN METROPOLIS!
SUPERGIRL'S SUN-CHARGED STRENGTH--I'VE BEEN TRYING TO REPLICATE IT FOR YEARS!
AND BUMBLEBEE, YOUR SUIT IS A ***MECHANICAL MARVEL!***

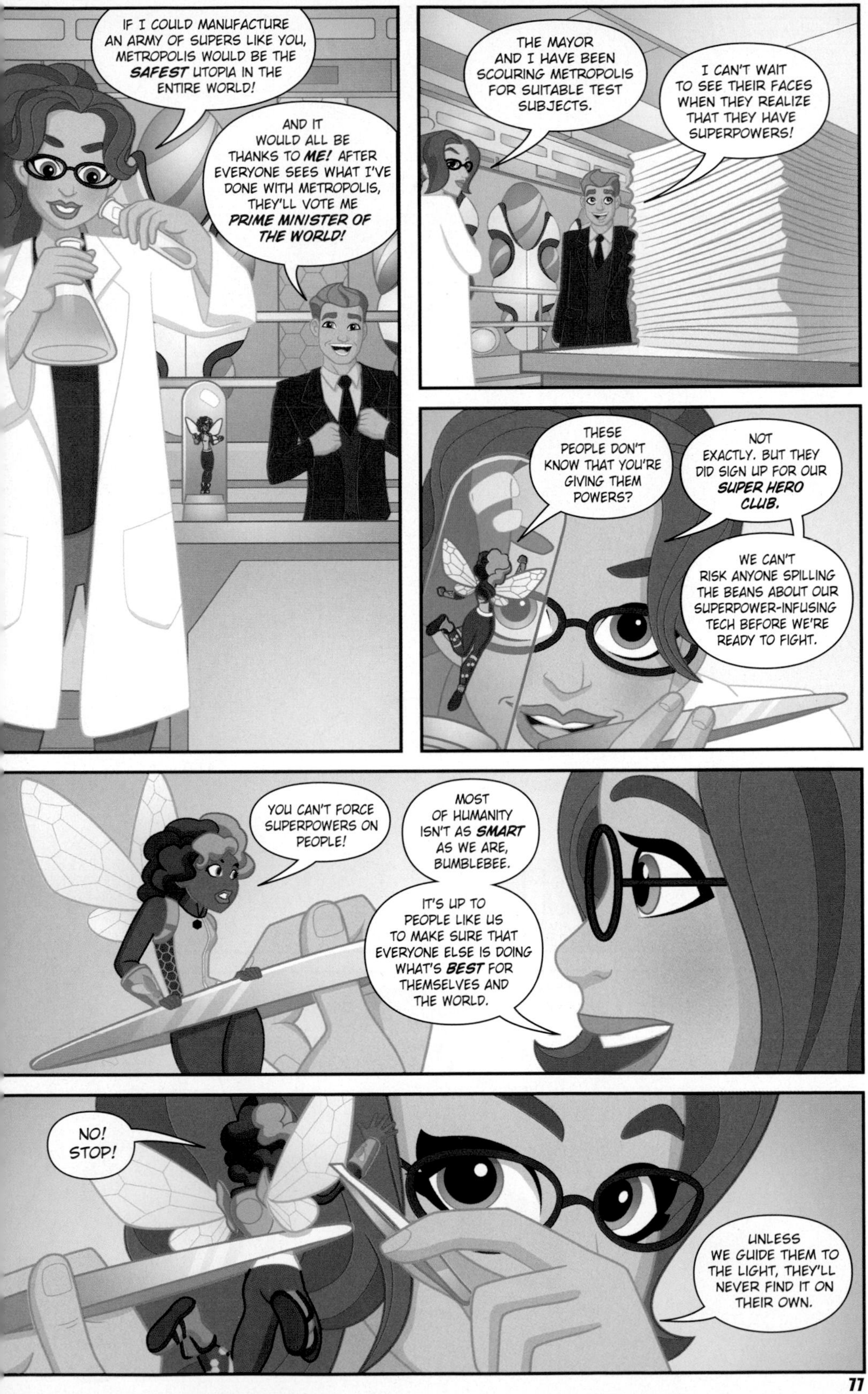
IF I COULD MANUFACTURE AN ARMY OF SUPERS LIKE YOU, METROPOLIS WOULD BE THE SAFEST UTOPIA IN THE ENTIRE WORLD!
AND IT WOULD ALL BE THANKS TO ME! AFTER EVERYONE SEES WHAT I'VE DONE WITH METROPOLIS, THEY'LL VOTE ME PRIME MINISTER OF THE WORLD!
THE MAYOR AND I HAVE BEEN SCOURING METROPOLIS FOR SUITABLE TEST SUBJECTS.
I CAN'T WAIT TO SEE THEIR FACES WHEN THEY REALIZE THAT THEY HAVE SUPERPOWERS!
THESE PEOPLE DON'T KNOW THAT YOU'RE GIVING THEM POWERS?
NOT EXACTLY. BUT THEY DID SIGN UP FOR OUR SUPER HERO CLUB.
WE CAN'T RISK ANYONE SPILLING THE BEANS ABOUT OUR SUPERPOWER-INFUSING TECH BEFORE WE'RE READY TO FIGHT.
YOU CAN'T FORCE SUPERPOWERS ON PEOPLE!
MOST OF HUMANITY ISN'T AS SMART AS WE ARE, BUMBLEBEE.
IT'S UP TO PEOPLE LIKE US TO MAKE SURE THAT EVERYONE ELSE IS DOING WHAT'S BEST FOR THEMSELVES AND THE WORLD.
NO! STOP!
UNLESS WE GUIDE THEM TO THE LIGHT, THEY'LL NEVER FIND IT ON THEIR OWN.

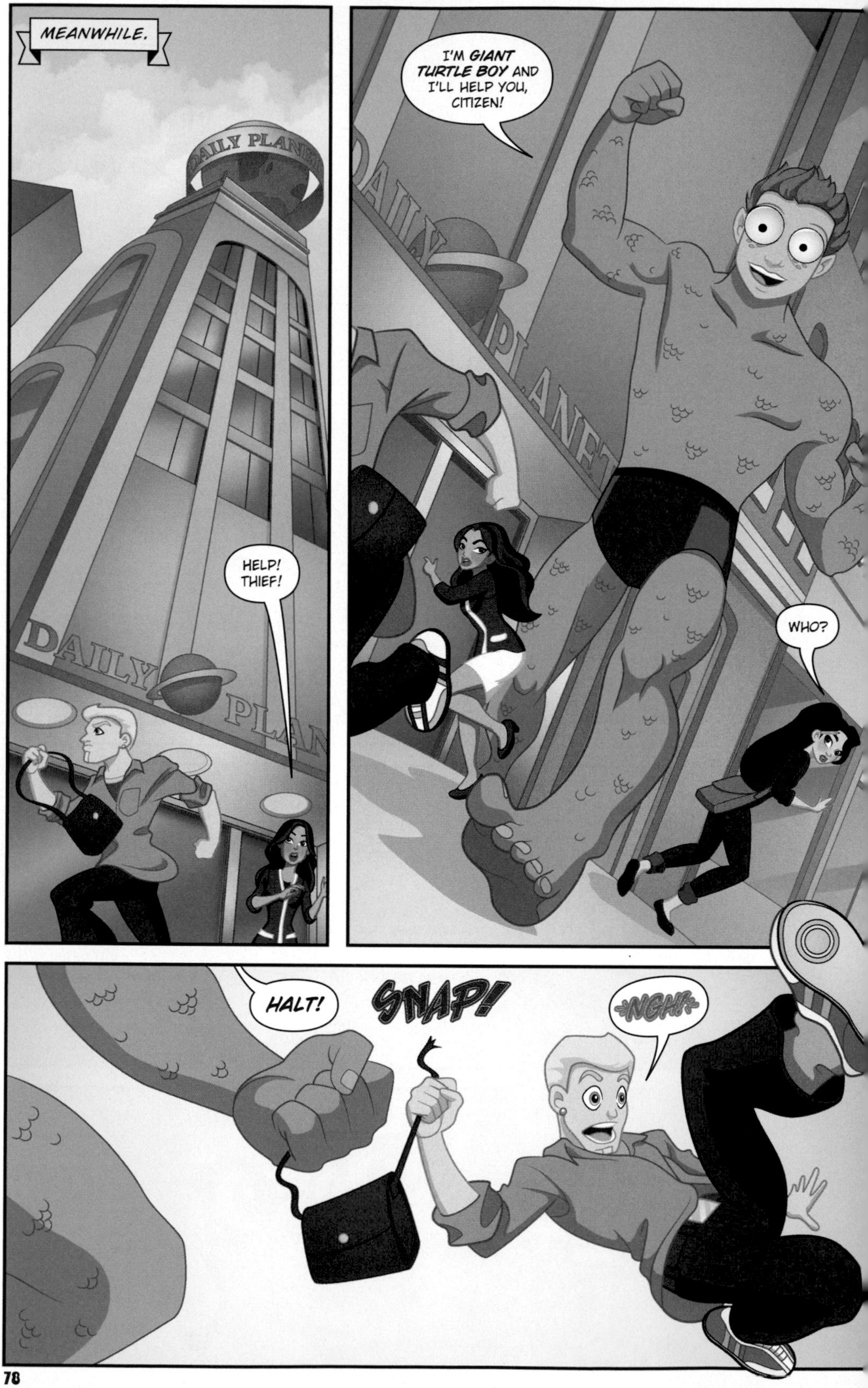
MEANWHILE.
DAILY PLANET
HELP! THIEF!
I'M GIANT TURTLE BOY AND I'LL HELP YOU, CITIZEN!
WHO?
HALT!
SNAP!
NGH!

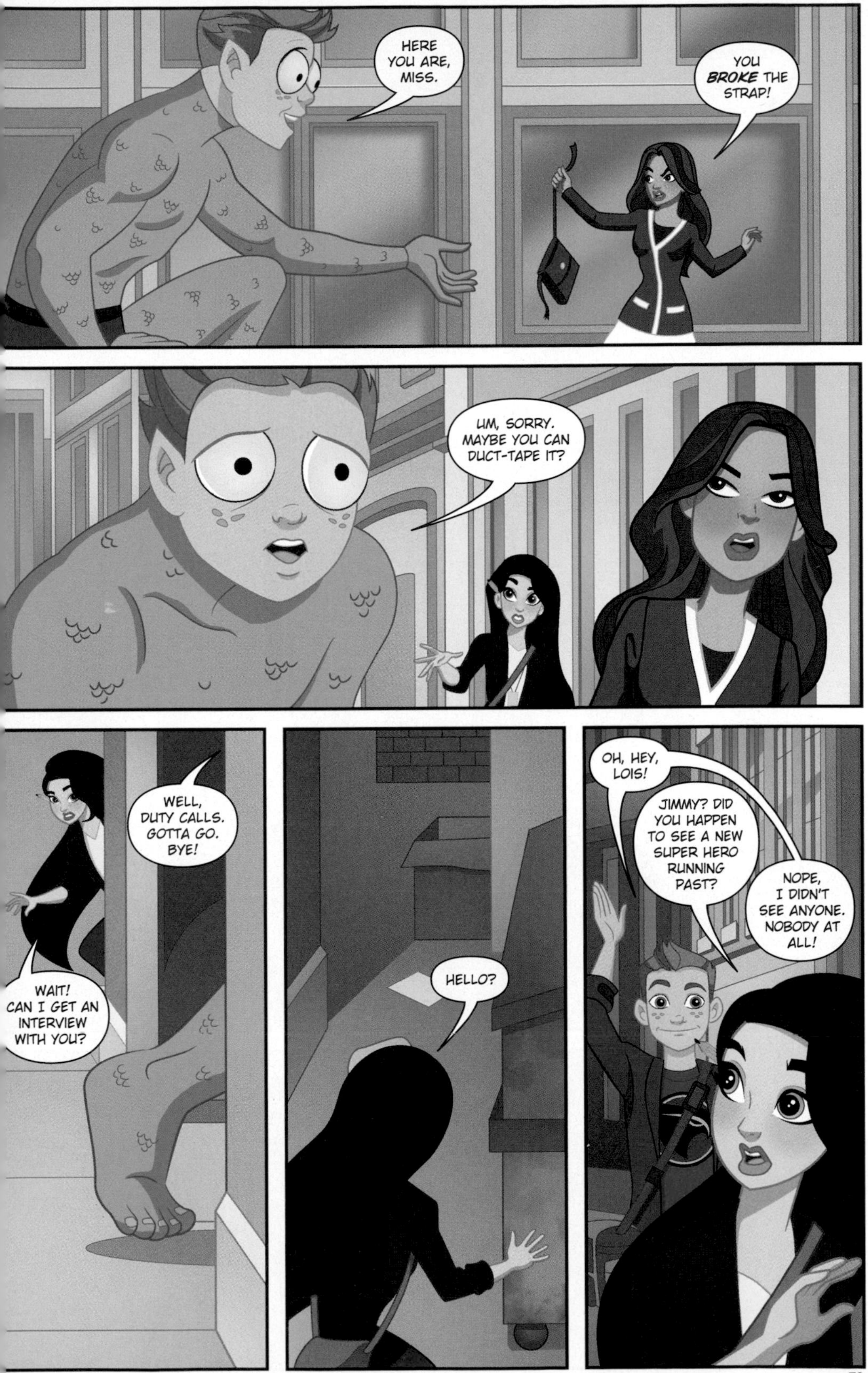
HERE YOU ARE, MISS.
YOU BROKE THE STRAP!
UM, SORRY. MAYBE YOU CAN DUCT-TAPE IT?
WELL, DUTY CALLS. GOTTA GO. BYE!
WAIT! CAN I GET AN INTERVIEW WITH YOU?
HELLO?
OH, HEY, LOIS!
JIMMY? DID YOU HAPPEN TO SEE A NEW SUPER HERO RUNNING PAST?
NOPE, I DIDN'T SEE ANYONE. NOBODY AT ALL!

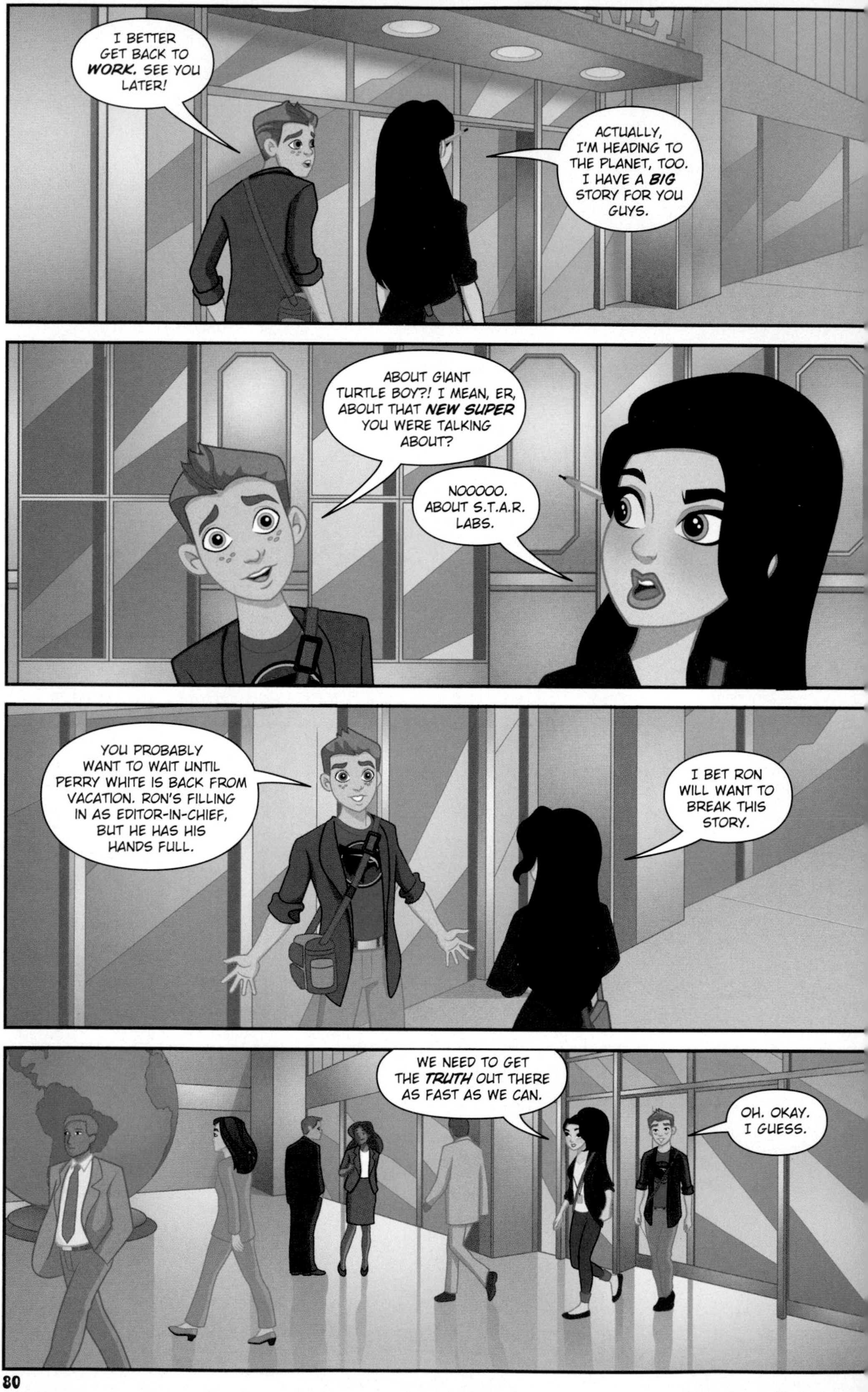
I BETTER GET BACK TO WORK. SEE YOU LATER!
ACTUALLY, I'M HEADING TO THE PLANET, TOO. I HAVE A BIG STORY FOR YOU GUYS.
ABOUT GIANT TURTLE BOY?! I MEAN, ER, ABOUT THAT NEW SUPER YOU WERE TALKING ABOUT?
NOOOOO. ABOUT S.T.A.R. LABS.
YOU PROBABLY WANT TO WAIT UNTIL PERRY WHITE IS BACK FROM VACATION. RON'S FILLING IN AS EDITOR-IN-CHIEF, BUT HE HAS HIS HANDS FULL.
I BET RON WILL WANT TO BREAK THIS STORY.
WE NEED TO GET THE TRUTH OUT THERE AS FAST AS WE CAN.
OH. OKAY. I GUESS.

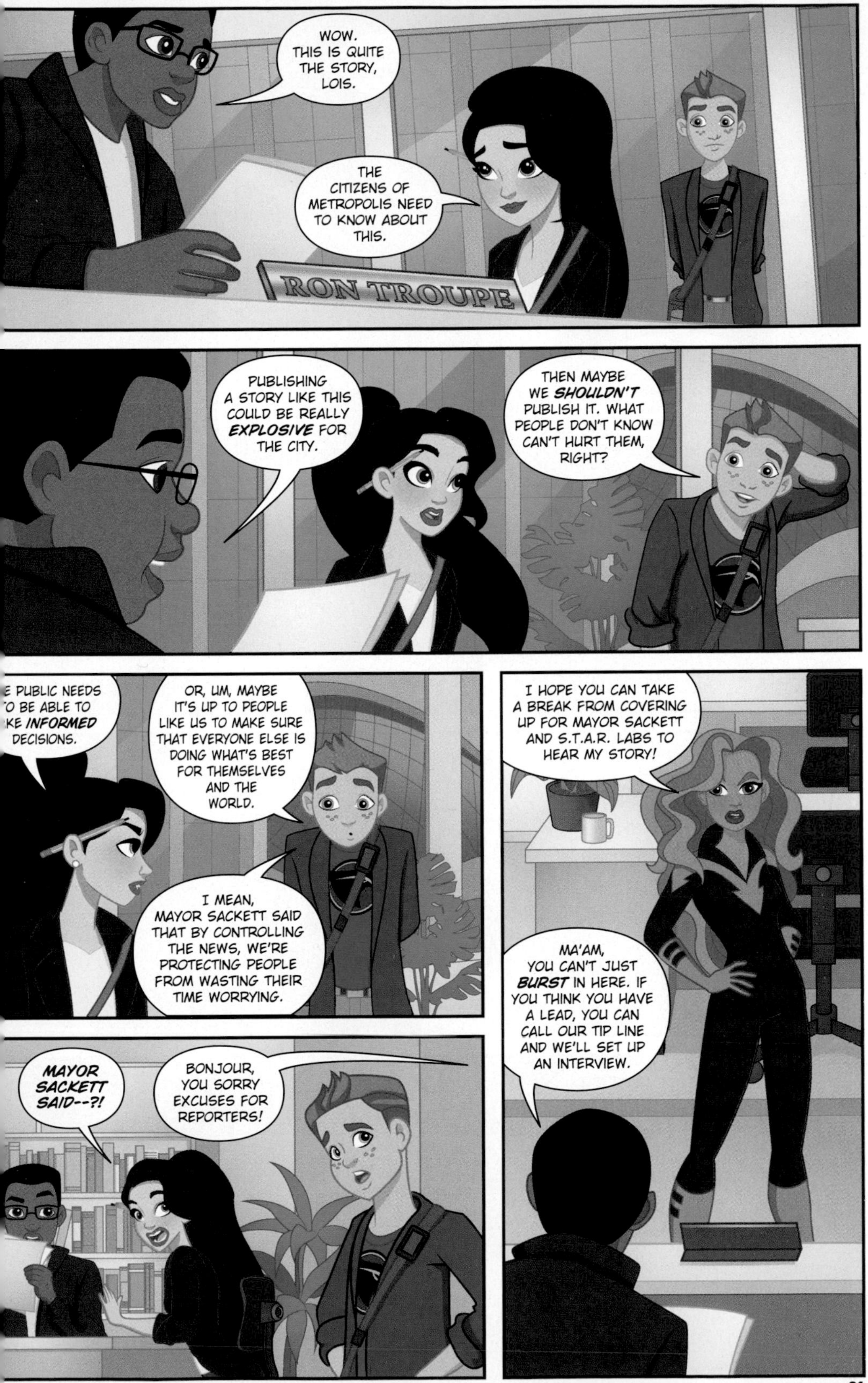
WOW. THIS IS QUITE THE STORY, LOIS.
THE CITIZENS OF METROPOLIS NEED TO KNOW ABOUT THIS.
RON TROUPE
PUBLISHING A STORY LIKE THIS COULD BE REALLY EXPLOSIVE FOR THE CITY.
THEN MAYBE WE SHOULDN'T PUBLISH IT. WHAT PEOPLE DON'T KNOW CAN'T HURT THEM, RIGHT?
E PUBLIC NEEDS O BE ABLE TO KE INFORMED DECISIONS.
OR, UM, MAYBE IT'S UP TO PEOPLE LIKE US TO MAKE SURE THAT EVERYONE ELSE IS DOING WHAT'S BEST FOR THEMSELVES AND THE WORLD.
I MEAN, MAYOR SACKETT SAID THAT BY CONTROLLING THE NEWS, WE'RE PROTECTING PEOPLE FROM WASTING THEIR TIME WORRYING.
MAYOR SACKETT SAID--?!
BONJOUR, YOU SORRY EXCUSES FOR REPORTERS!
I HOPE YOU CAN TAKE A BREAK FROM COVERING UP FOR MAYOR SACKETT AND S.T.A.R. LABS TO HEAR MY STORY!
MA'AM, YOU CAN'T JUST BURST IN HERE. IF YOU THINK YOU HAVE A LEAD, YOU CAN CALL OUR TIP LINE AND WE'LL SET UP AN INTERVIEW.

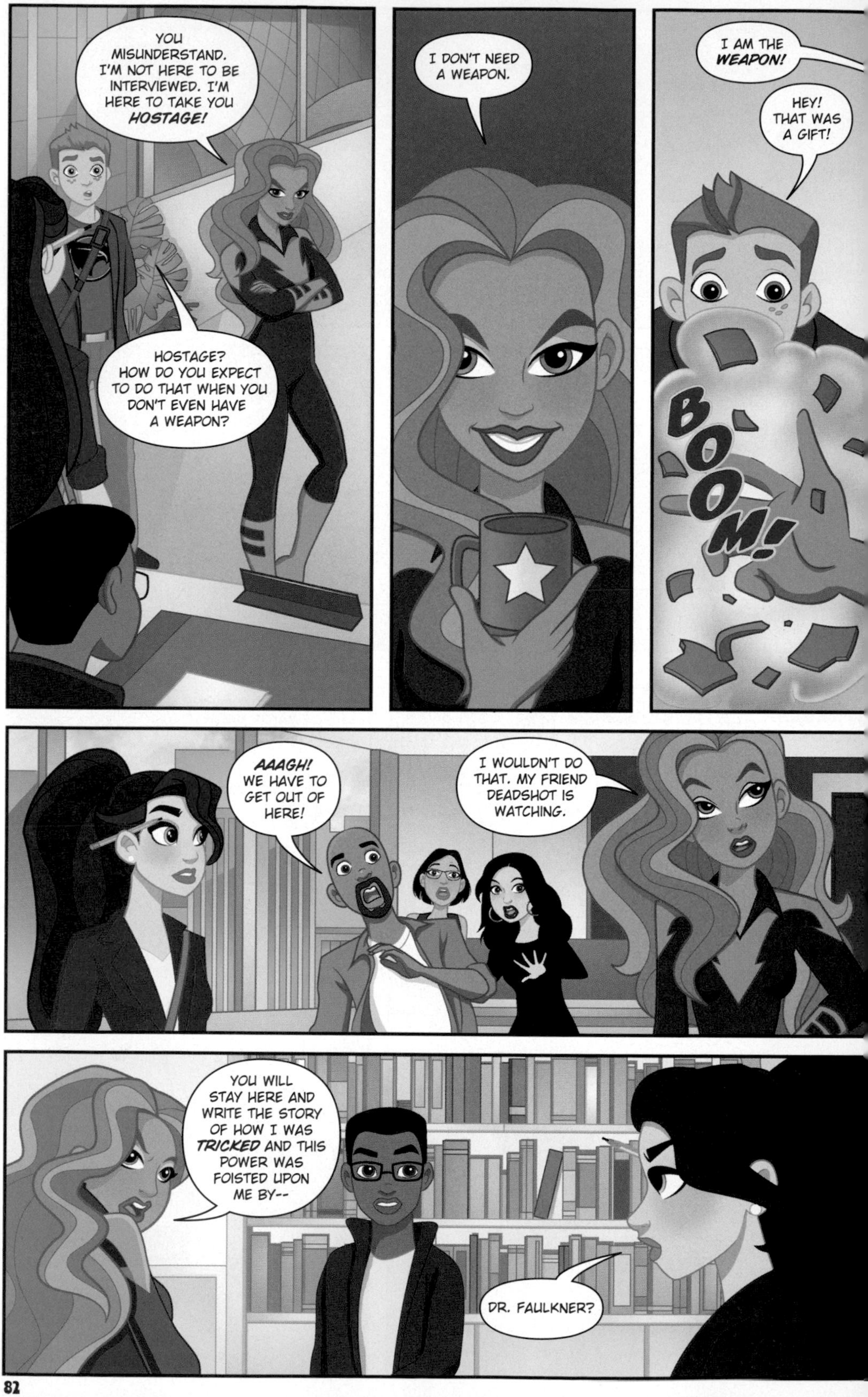
YOU MISUNDERSTAND. I'M NOT HERE TO BE INTERVIEWED. I'M HERE TO TAKE YOU HOSTAGE!
HOSTAGE? HOW DO YOU EXPECT TO DO THAT WHEN YOU DON'T EVEN HAVE A WEAPON?
I DON'T NEED A WEAPON.
I AM THE WEAPON!
HEY! THAT WAS A GIFT!
BOOM!
AAAGH! WE HAVE TO GET OUT OF HERE!
I WOULDN'T DO THAT. MY FRIEND DEADSHOT IS WATCHING.
YOU WILL STAY HERE AND WRITE THE STORY OF HOW I WAS TRICKED AND THIS POWER WAS FOISTED UPON ME BY--
DR. FAULKNER?

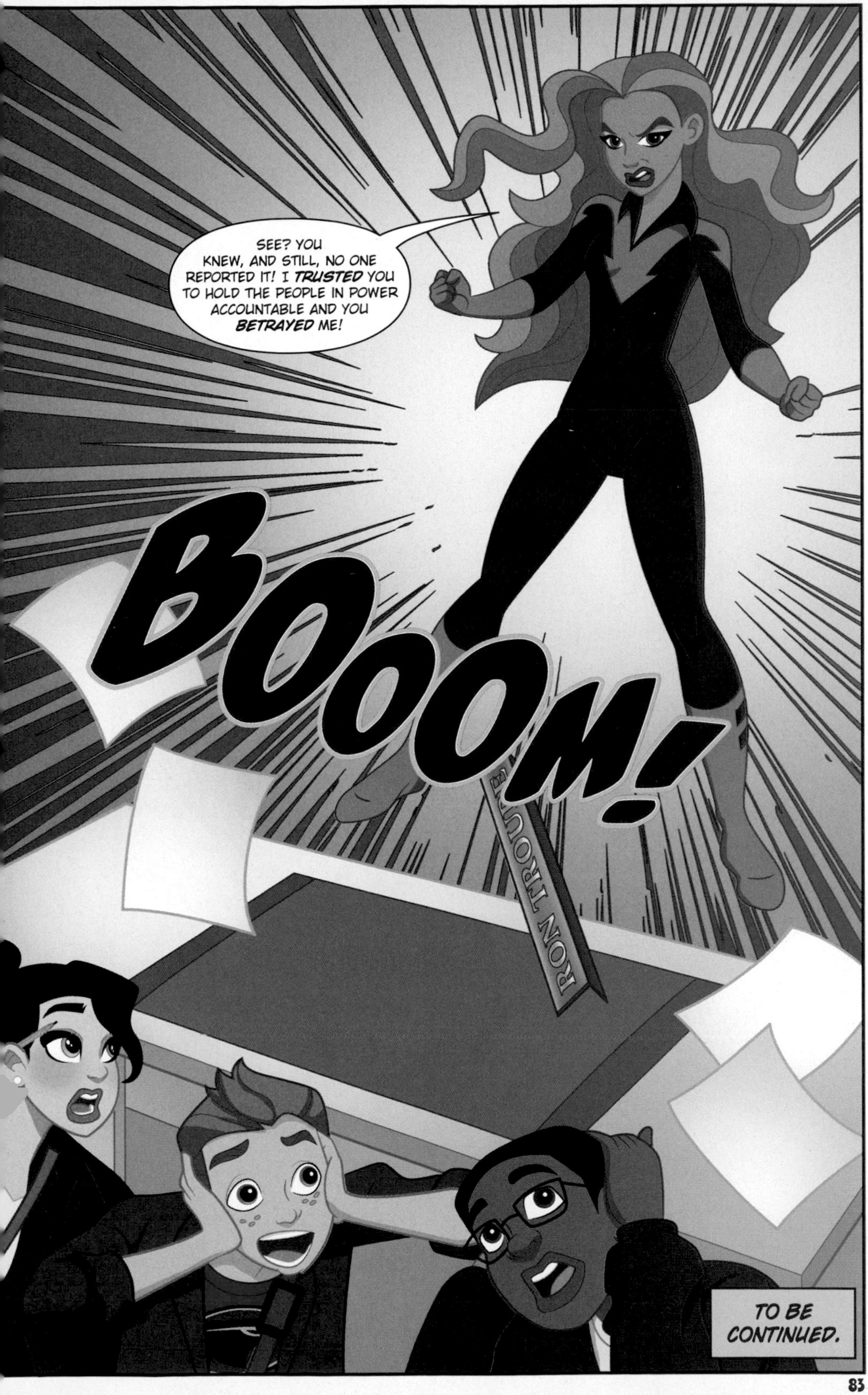
SEE? YOU KNEW, AND STILL, NO ONE REPORTED IT! I *TRUSTED* YOU TO HOLD THE PEOPLE IN POWER ACCOUNTABLE AND YOU *BETRAYED* ME!
BOOOM!
RON TROUPE
TO BE CONTINUED.

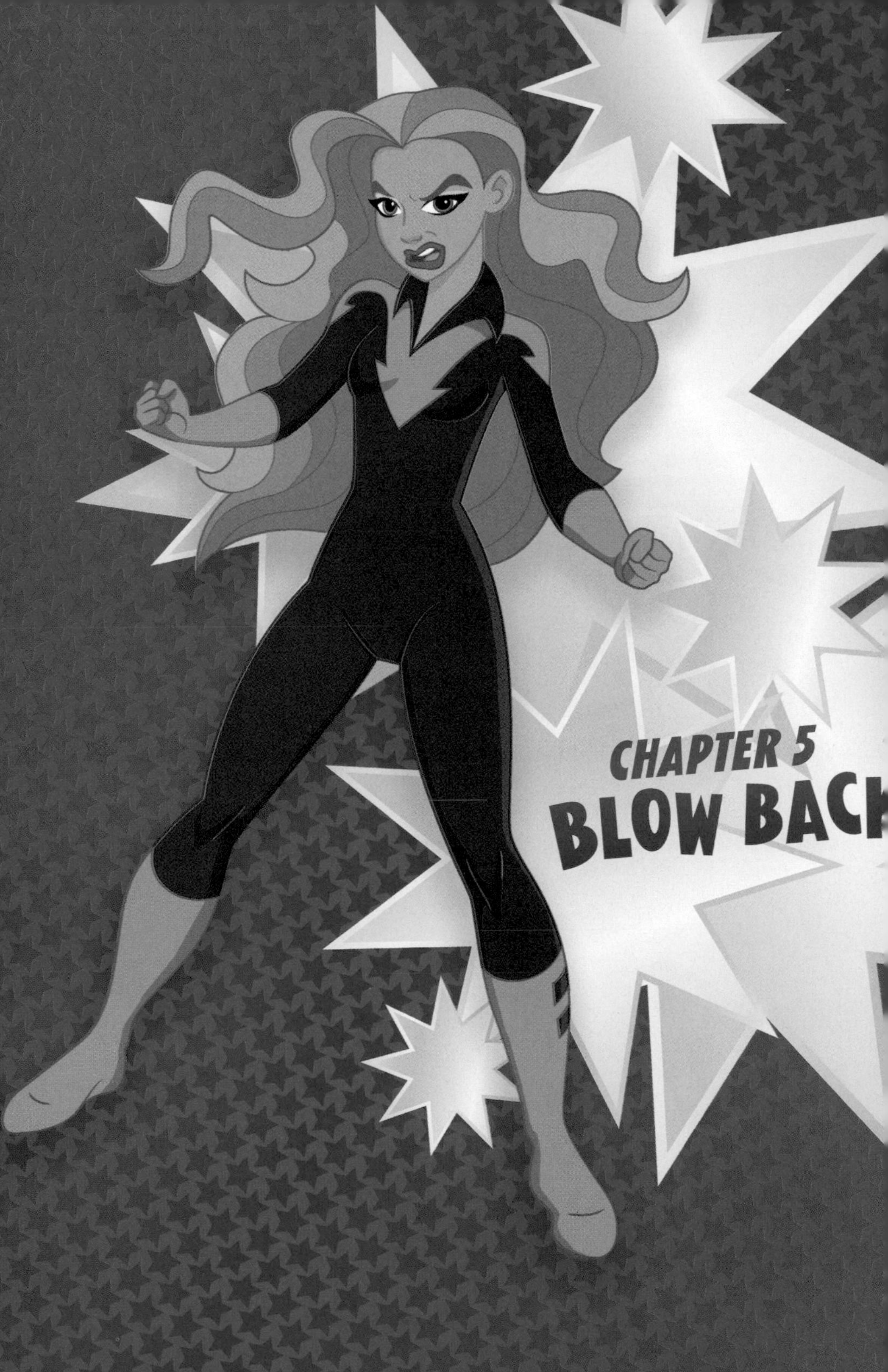

CHAPTER 5
BLOW BACK

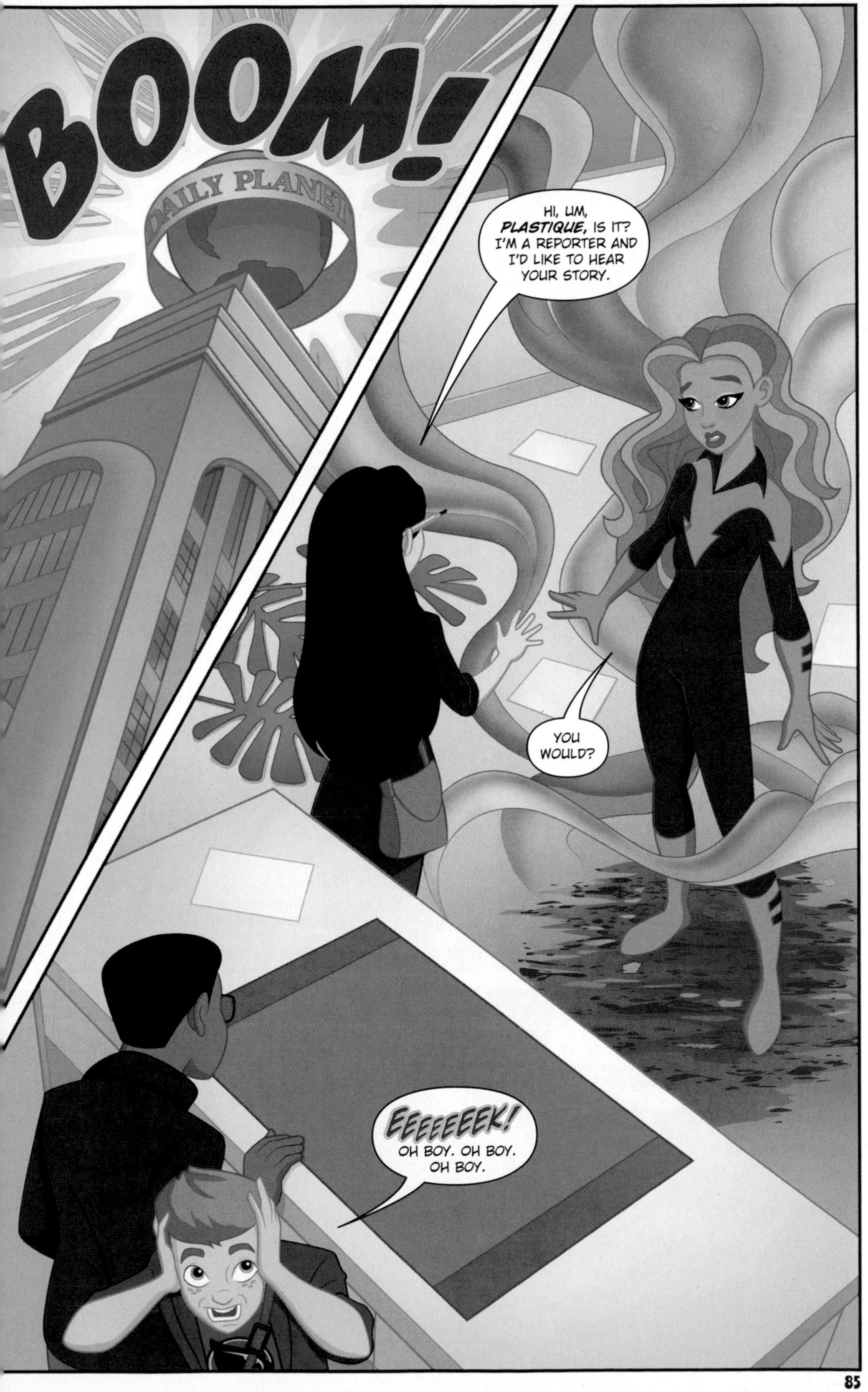
BOOM!
DAILY PLANET
HI, UM, PLASTIQUE, IS IT? I'M A REPORTER AND I'D LIKE TO HEAR YOUR STORY.
YOU WOULD?
EEEEEEEK! OH BOY. OH BOY. OH BOY.

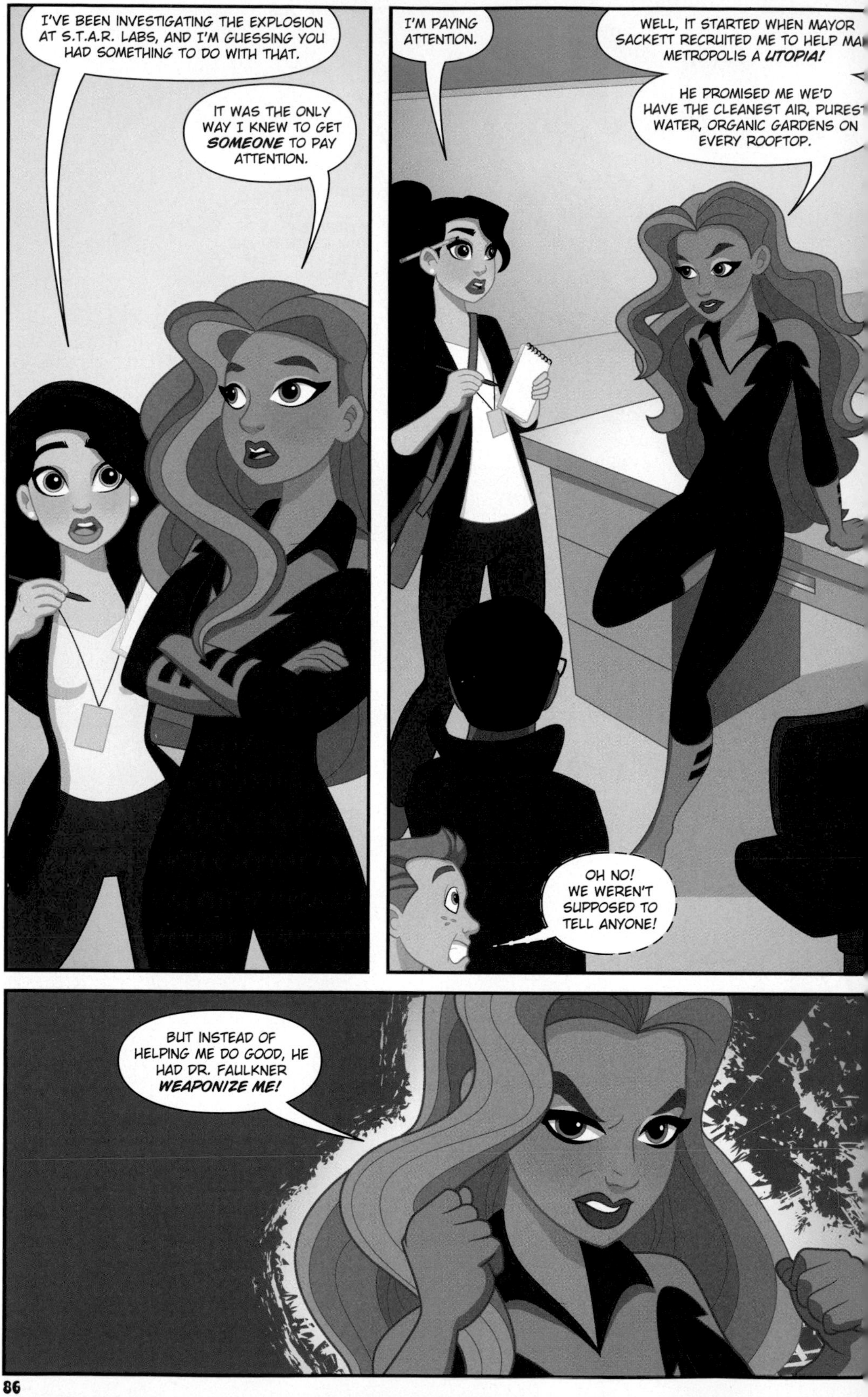
I'VE BEEN INVESTIGATING THE EXPLOSION AT S.T.A.R. LABS, AND I'M GUESSING YOU HAD SOMETHING TO DO WITH THAT.
IT WAS THE ONLY WAY I KNEW TO GET **SOMEONE** TO PAY ATTENTION.
I'M PAYING ATTENTION.
WELL, IT STARTED WHEN MAYOR SACKETT RECRUITED ME TO HELP MA METROPOLIS A ***UTOPIA!***
HE PROMISED ME WE'D HAVE THE CLEANEST AIR, PUREST WATER, ORGANIC GARDENS ON EVERY ROOFTOP.
OH NO! WE WEREN'T SUPPOSED TO TELL ANYONE!
BUT INSTEAD OF HELPING ME DO GOOD, HE HAD DR. FAULKNER ***WEAPONIZE ME!***

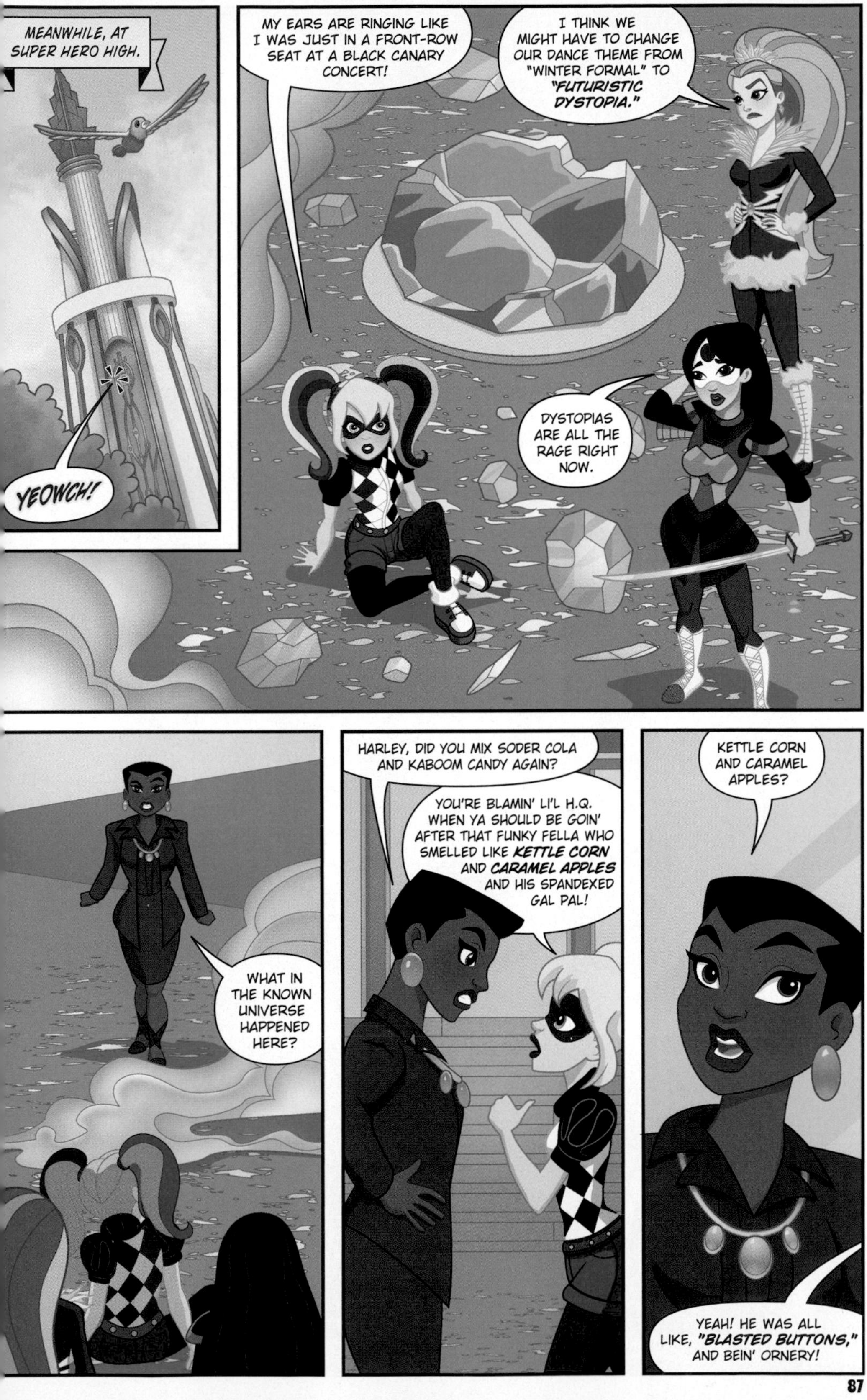

MEANWHILE, AT SUPER HERO HIGH.
YEOWCH!
MY EARS ARE RINGING LIKE I WAS JUST IN A FRONT-ROW SEAT AT A BLACK CANARY CONCERT!
I THINK WE MIGHT HAVE TO CHANGE OUR DANCE THEME FROM "WINTER FORMAL" TO "FUTURISTIC DYSTOPIA."
DYSTOPIAS ARE ALL THE RAGE RIGHT NOW.
WHAT IN THE KNOWN UNIVERSE HAPPENED HERE?
HARLEY, DID YOU MIX SODER COLA AND KABOOM CANDY AGAIN?
YOU'RE BLAMIN' LI'L H.Q. WHEN YA SHOULD BE GOIN' AFTER THAT FUNKY FELLA WHO SMELLED LIKE KETTLE CORN AND CARAMEL APPLES AND HIS SPANDEXED GAL PAL!
KETTLE CORN AND CARAMEL APPLES?
YEAH! HE WAS ALL LIKE, "BLASTED BUTTONS," AND BEIN' ORNERY!

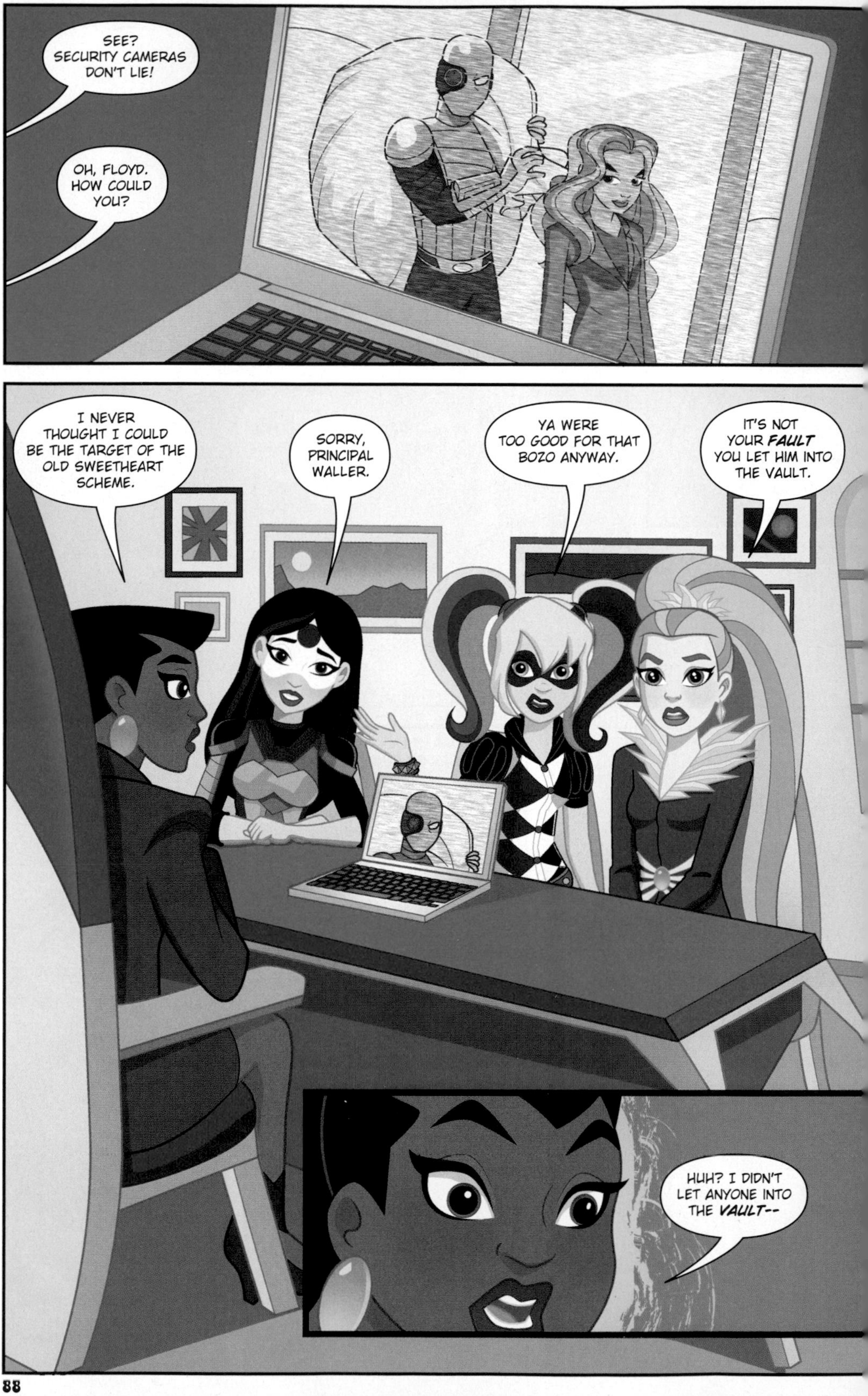
SEE? SECURITY CAMERAS DON'T LIE!
OH, FLOYD. HOW COULD YOU?
I NEVER THOUGHT I COULD BE THE TARGET OF THE OLD SWEETHEART SCHEME.
SORRY, PRINCIPAL WALLER.
YA WERE TOO GOOD FOR THAT BOZO ANYWAY.
IT'S NOT YOUR ***FAULT*** YOU LET HIM INTO THE VAULT.
HUH? I DIDN'T LET ANYONE INTO THE ***VAULT--***

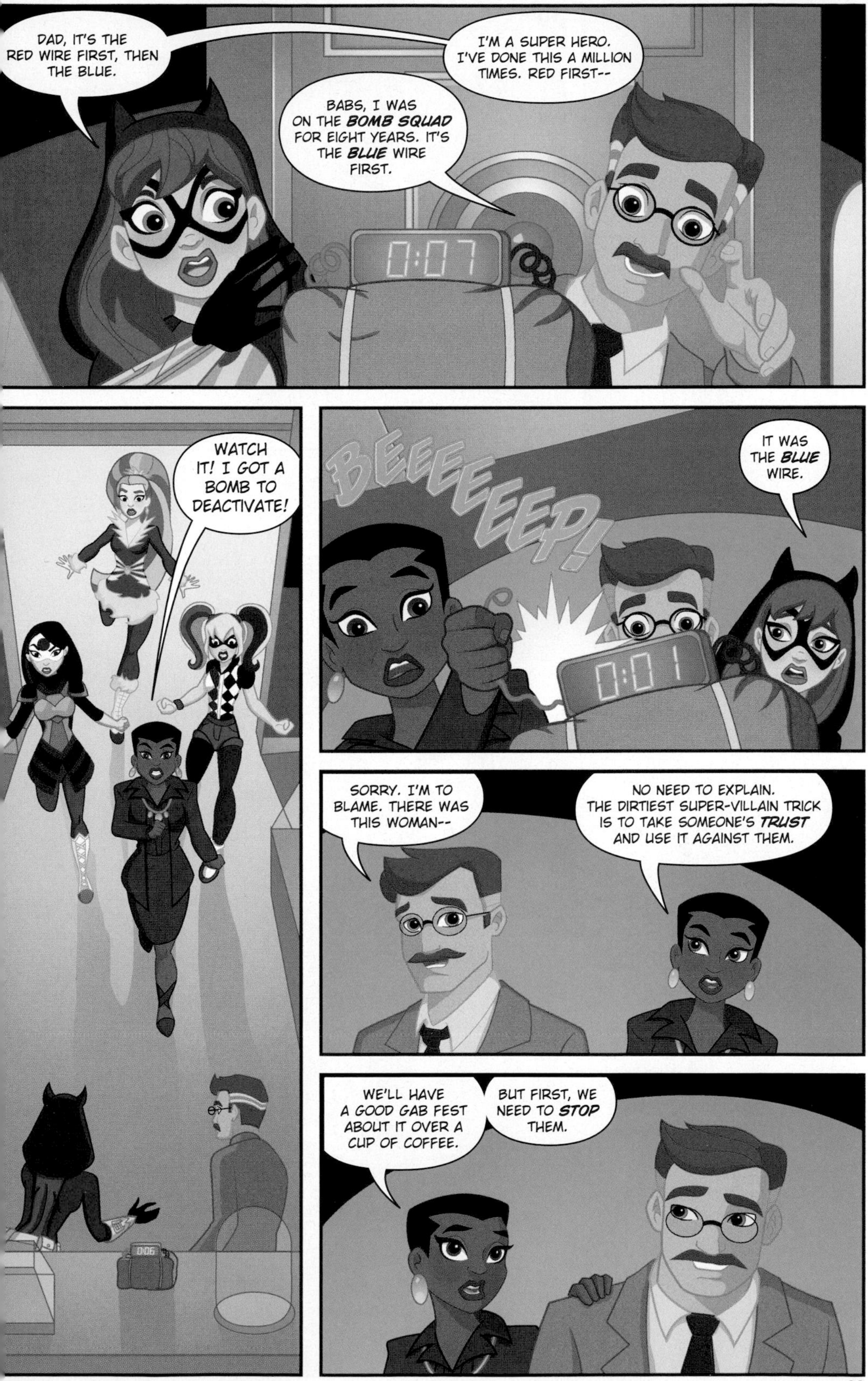
DAD, IT'S THE RED WIRE FIRST, THEN THE BLUE.
I'M A SUPER HERO. I'VE DONE THIS A MILLION TIMES. RED FIRST--
BABS, I WAS ON THE BOMB SQUAD FOR EIGHT YEARS. IT'S THE BLUE WIRE FIRST.
0:07
WATCH IT! I GOT A BOMB TO DEACTIVATE!
0:06
BEEEEEEP!
IT WAS THE BLUE WIRE.
0:01
SORRY. I'M TO BLAME. THERE WAS THIS WOMAN--
NO NEED TO EXPLAIN. THE DIRTIEST SUPER-VILLAIN TRICK IS TO TAKE SOMEONE'S TRUST AND USE IT AGAINST THEM.
WE'LL HAVE A GOOD GAB FEST ABOUT IT OVER A CUP OF COFFEE.
BUT FIRST, WE NEED TO STOP THEM.

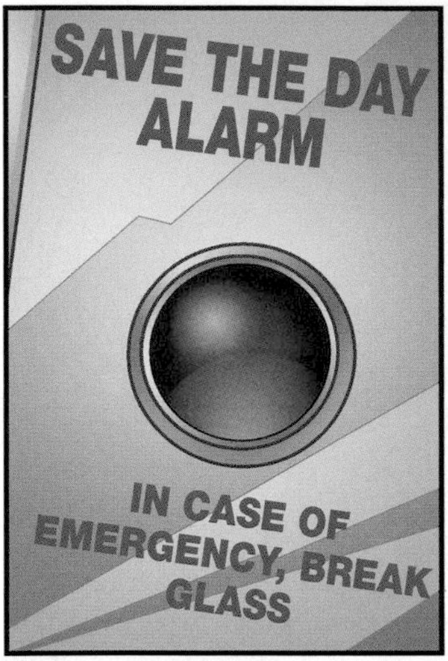
SAVE THE DAY ALARM
IN CASE OF EMERGENCY, BREAK GLASS

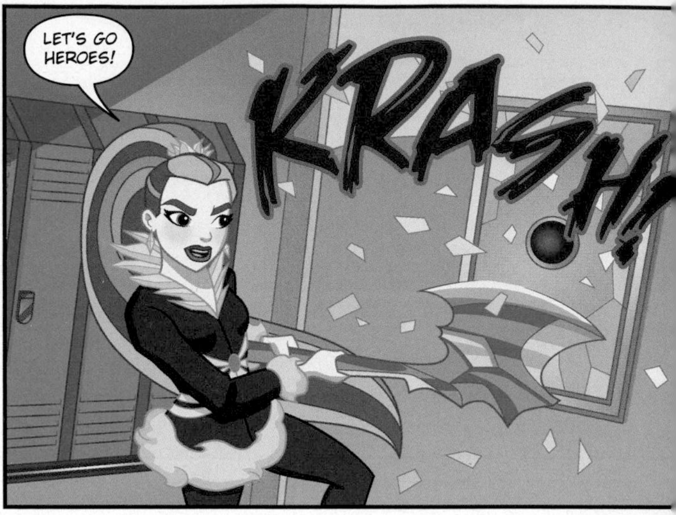
LET'S GO HEROES!
KRASH!

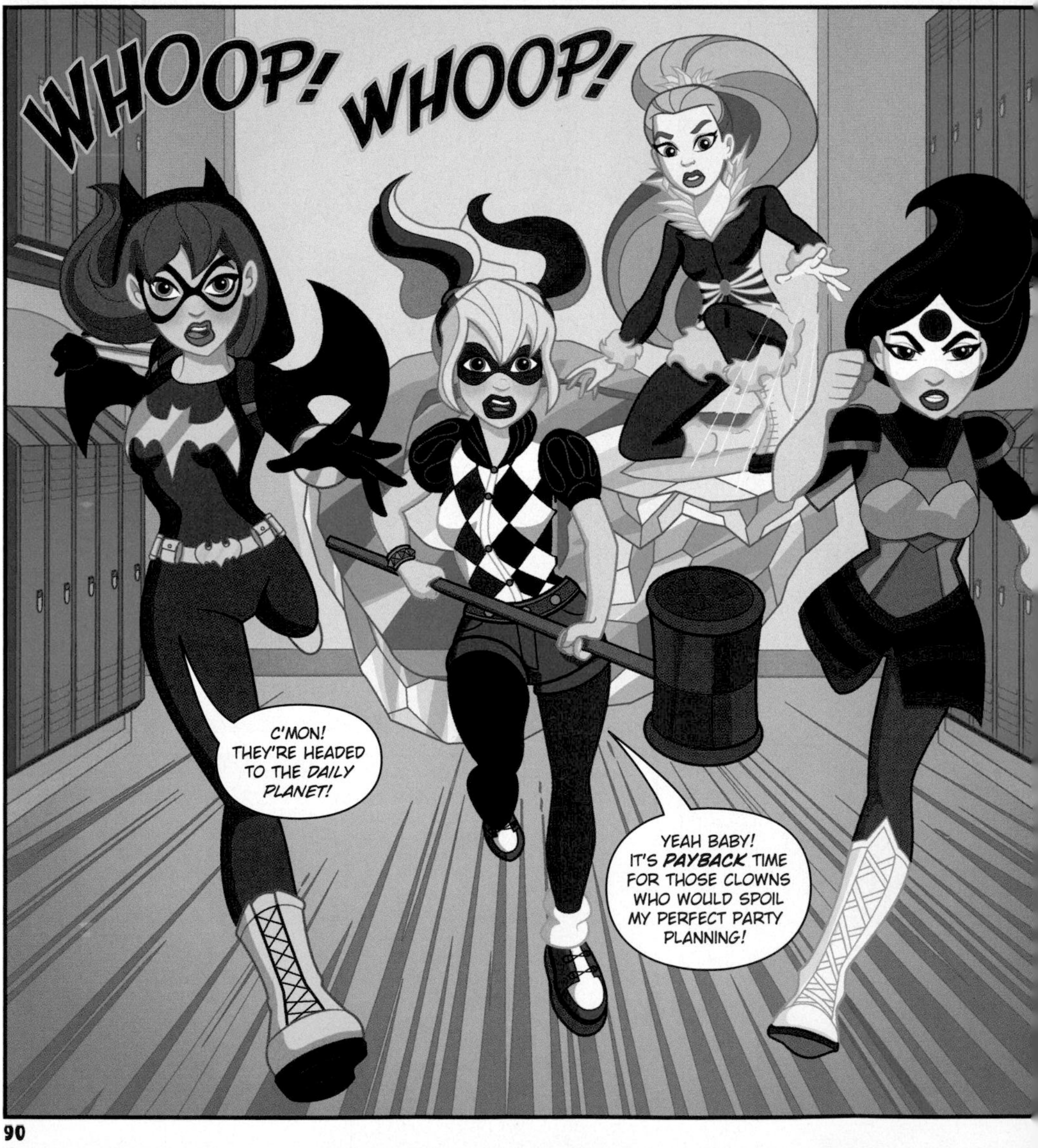
WHOOP! WHOOP!
C'MON! THEY'RE HEADED TO THE *DAILY PLANET!*
YEAH BABY! IT'S ***PAYBACK*** TIME FOR THOSE CLOWNS WHO WOULD SPOIL MY PERFECT PARTY PLANNING!

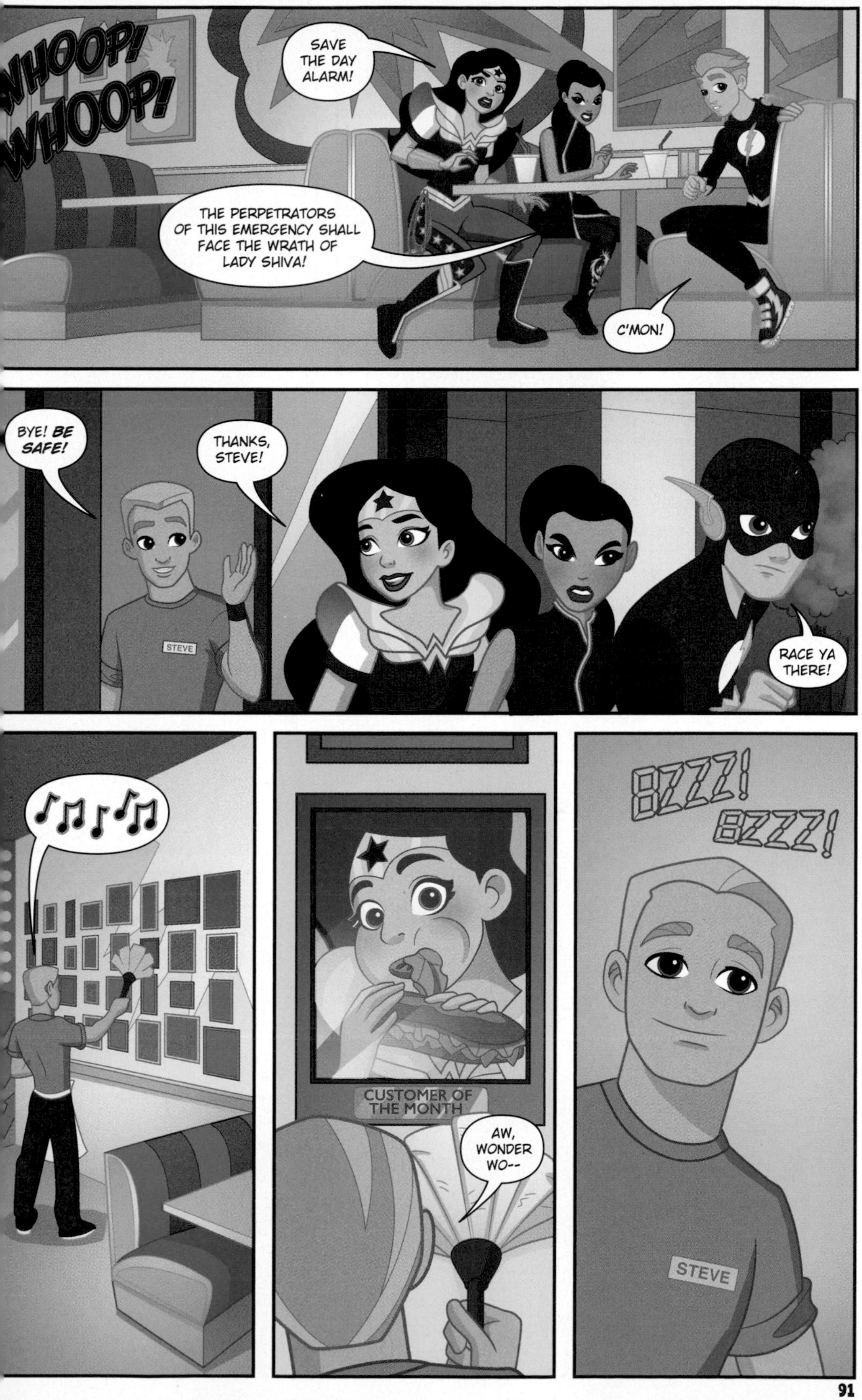
WHOOP! WHOOP!
SAVE THE DAY ALARM!
THE PERPETRATORS OF THIS EMERGENCY SHALL FACE THE WRATH OF LADY SHIVA!
C'MON!
BYE! BE SAFE!
THANKS, STEVE!
STEVE
RACE YA THERE!
CUSTOMER OF THE MONTH
AW, WONDER WO--
BZZZ! BZZZ!
STEVE

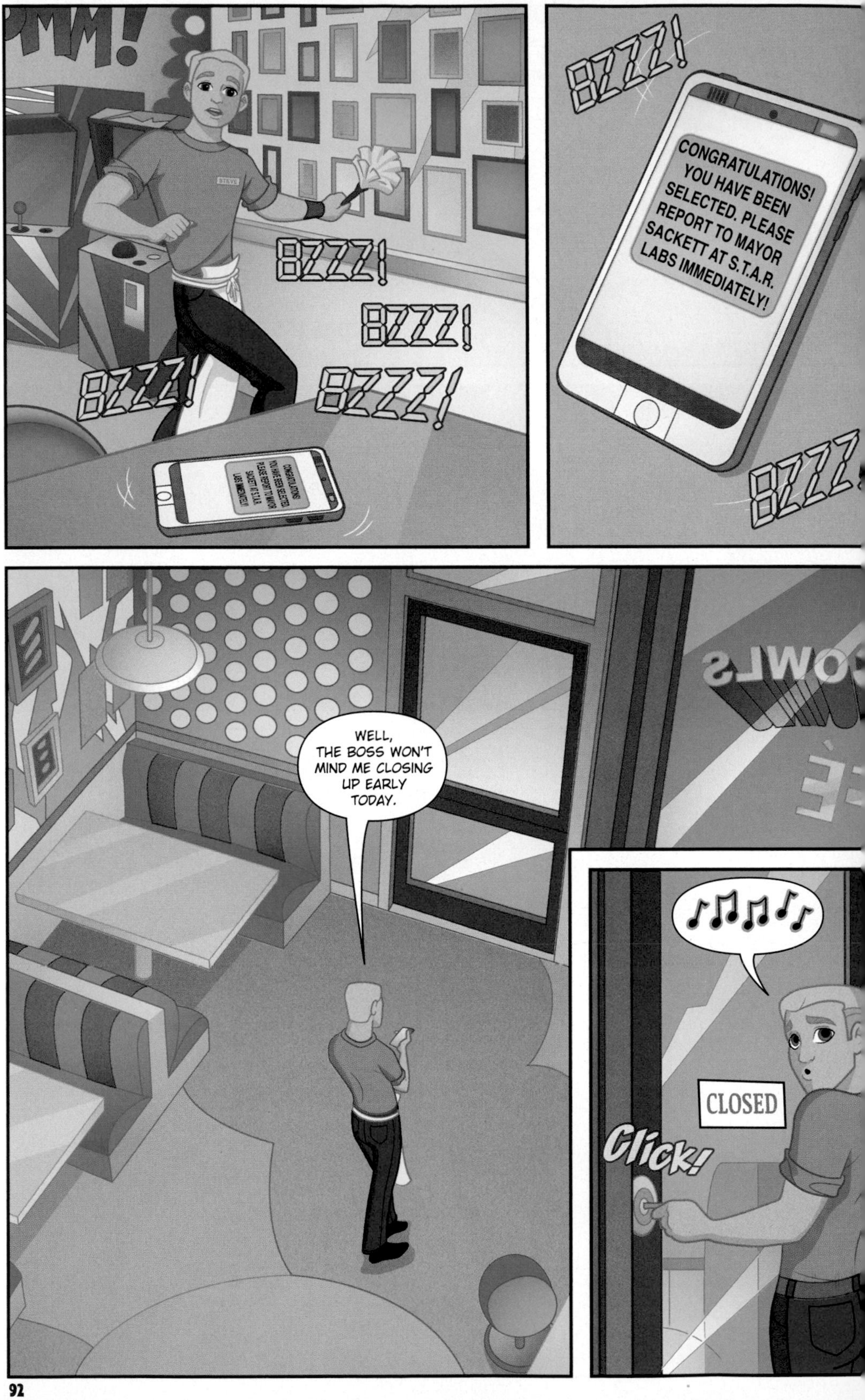
BZZZ!
BZZZ!
BZZZ!
BZZZ!
BZZZ!
CONGRATULATIONS! YOU HAVE BEEN SELECTED. PLEASE REPORT TO MAYOR SACKETT AT S.T.A.R. LABS IMMEDIATELY!
WELL, THE BOSS WON'T MIND ME CLOSING UP EARLY TODAY.
CLOSED
Click!

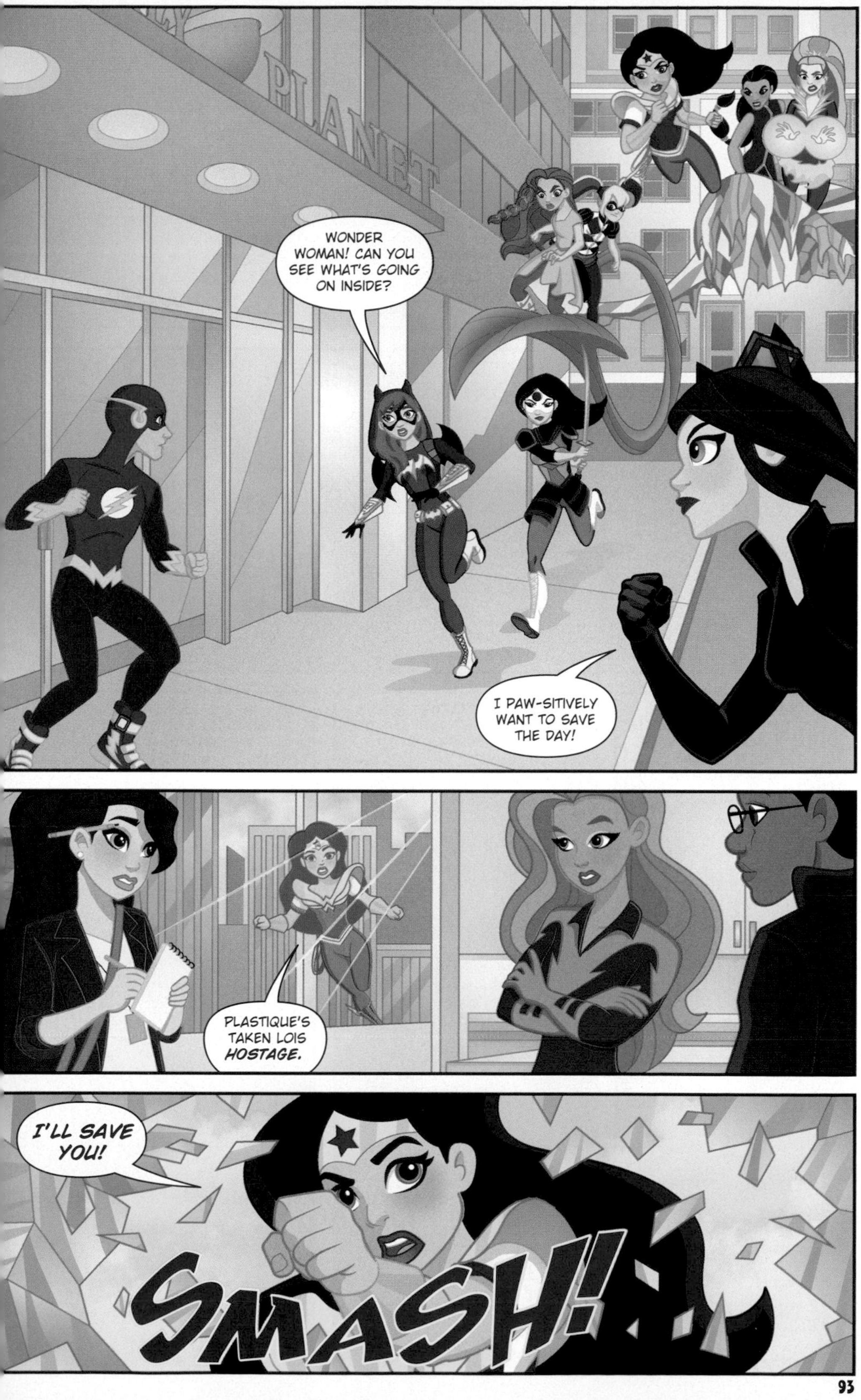
PLANET
WONDER WOMAN! CAN YOU SEE WHAT'S GOING ON INSIDE?
I PAW-SITIVELY WANT TO SAVE THE DAY!
PLASTIQUE'S TAKEN LOIS *HOSTAGE.*
I'LL SAVE YOU!
SMASH!

THIS WAY!

STOP!

OOF!

WHAT'S THE BIG IDEA?

FOR WHAT REASON ARE WE HALTING?!

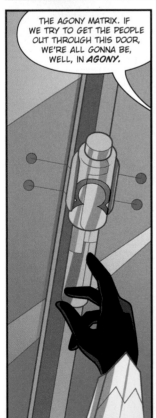

THE AGONY MATRIX. IF WE TRY TO GET THE PEOPLE OUT THROUGH THIS DOOR, WE'RE ALL GONNA BE, WELL, IN *AGONY.*

I'VE NEVER MET A LOCK I COULDN'T PICK, BUT THIS BAD BOY IS--

STEP AWAY FROM THE BUILDING, HEROES.

DEADSHOT?

DO AS I SAY OR YOU'LL FIND THE AGONY MATRIX ISN'T THE ONLY THING THAT WILL PUT AN *"OUCH"* IN YOUR STEP.

KETTLE CORN

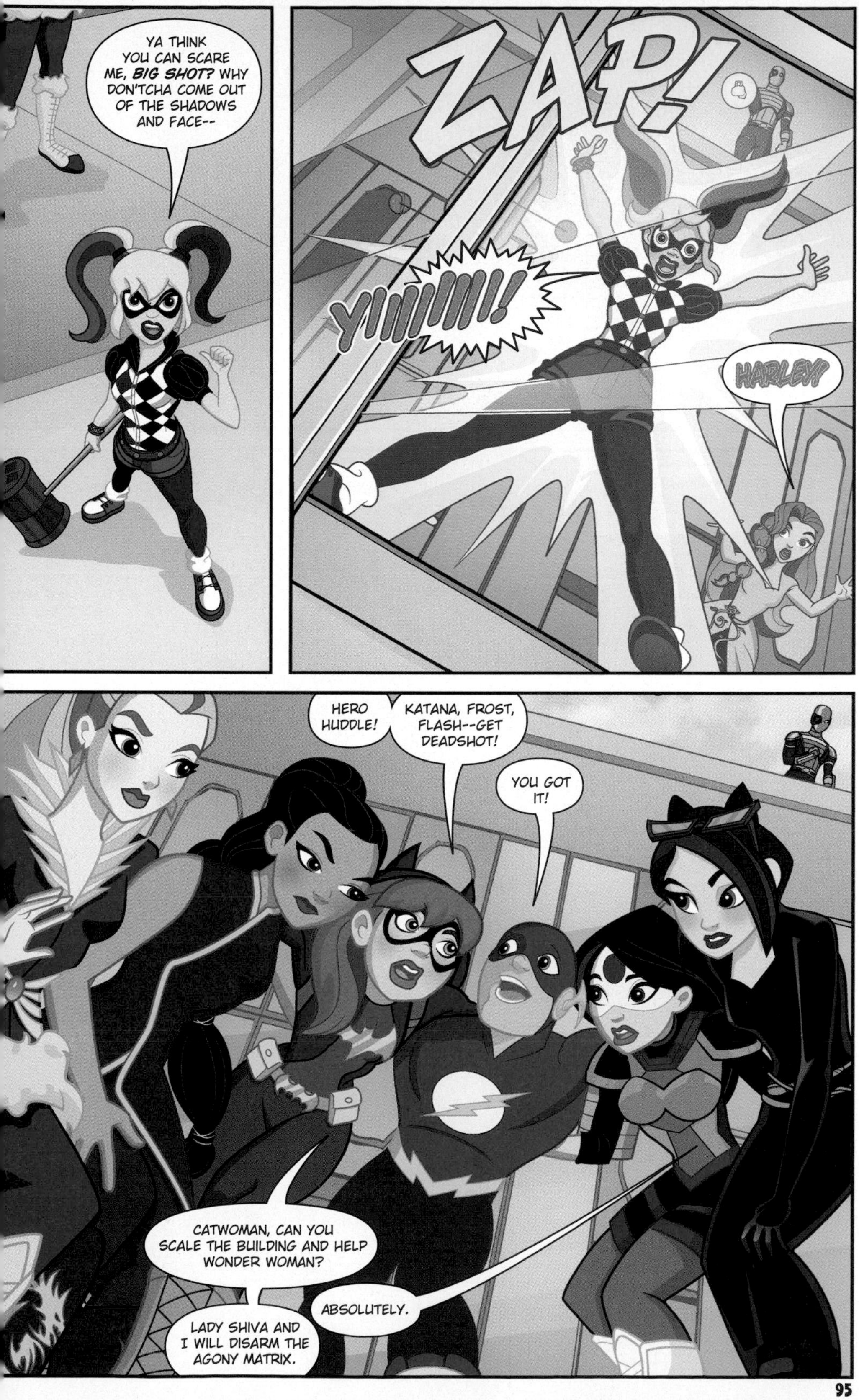
YA THINK YOU CAN SCARE ME, BIG SHOT? WHY DON'TCHA COME OUT OF THE SHADOWS AND FACE--
ZAP!
YIIIIIIII!
HARLEY!
HERO HUDDLE!
KATANA, FROST, FLASH--GET DEADSHOT!
YOU GOT IT!
CATWOMAN, CAN YOU SCALE THE BUILDING AND HELP WONDER WOMAN?
ABSOLUTELY.
LADY SHIVA AND I WILL DISARM THE AGONY MATRIX.

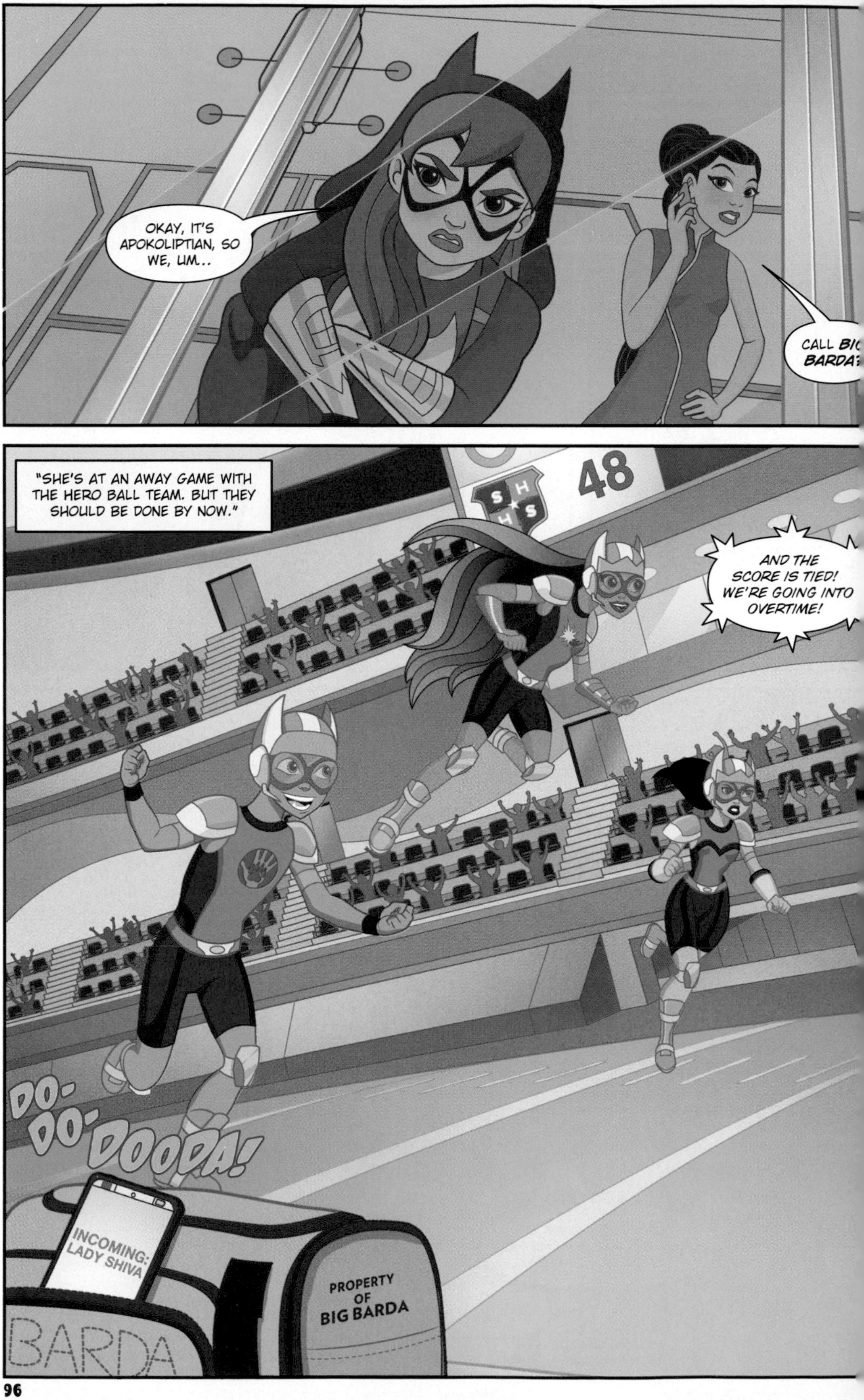
OKAY, IT'S APOKOLIPTIAN, SO WE, UM...
CALL BIG BARDA?
"SHE'S AT AN AWAY GAME WITH THE HERO BALL TEAM. BUT THEY SHOULD BE DONE BY NOW."
48
AND THE SCORE IS TIED! WE'RE GOING INTO OVERTIME!
DO-DO-DOODA!
INCOMING: LADY SHIVA
PROPERTY OF BIG BARDA
BARDA

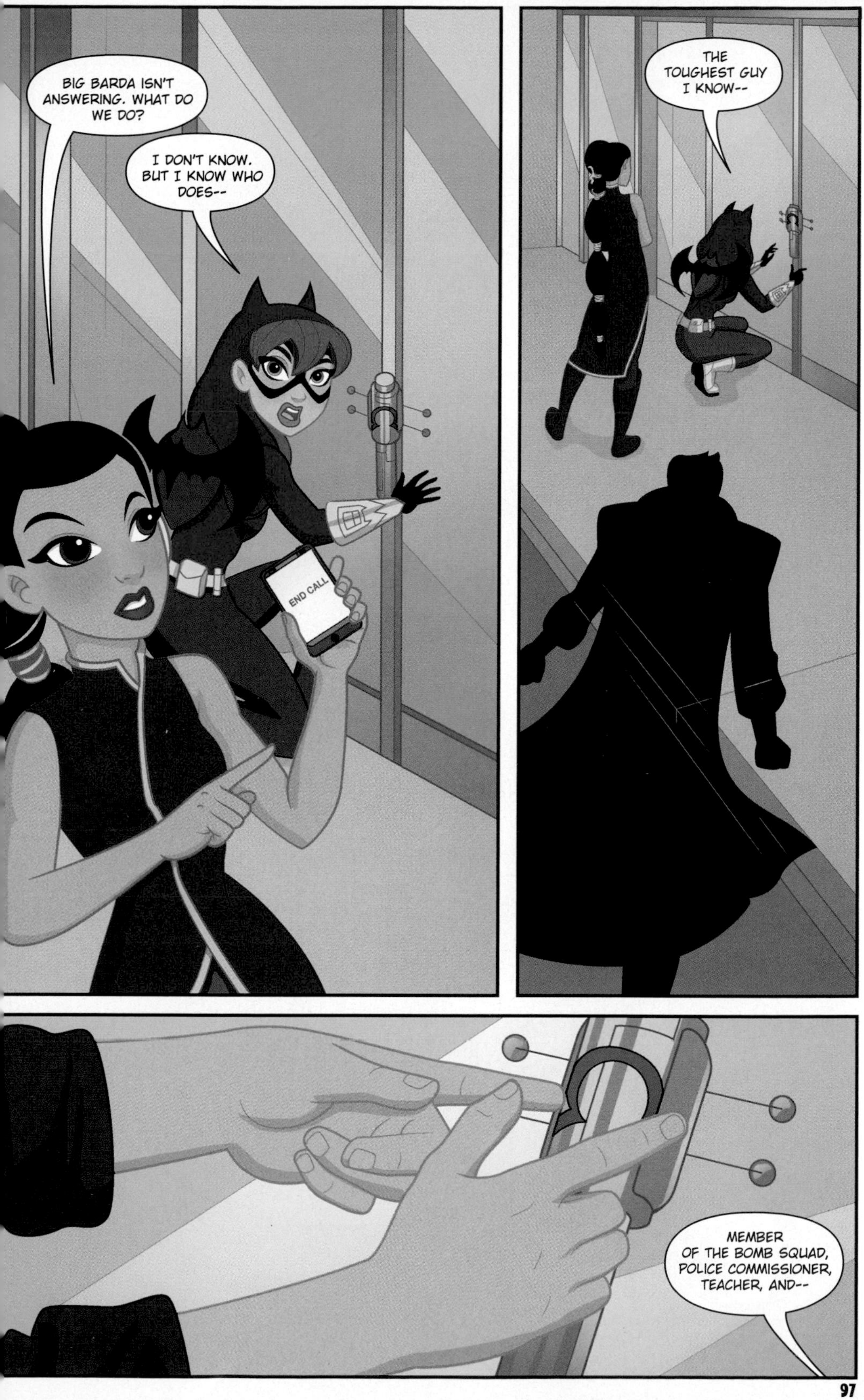
BIG BARDA ISN'T ANSWERING. WHAT DO WE DO?
I DON'T KNOW. BUT I KNOW WHO DOES--
END CALL
THE TOUGHEST GUY I KNOW--
MEMBER OF THE BOMB SQUAD, POLICE COMMISSIONER, TEACHER, AND--

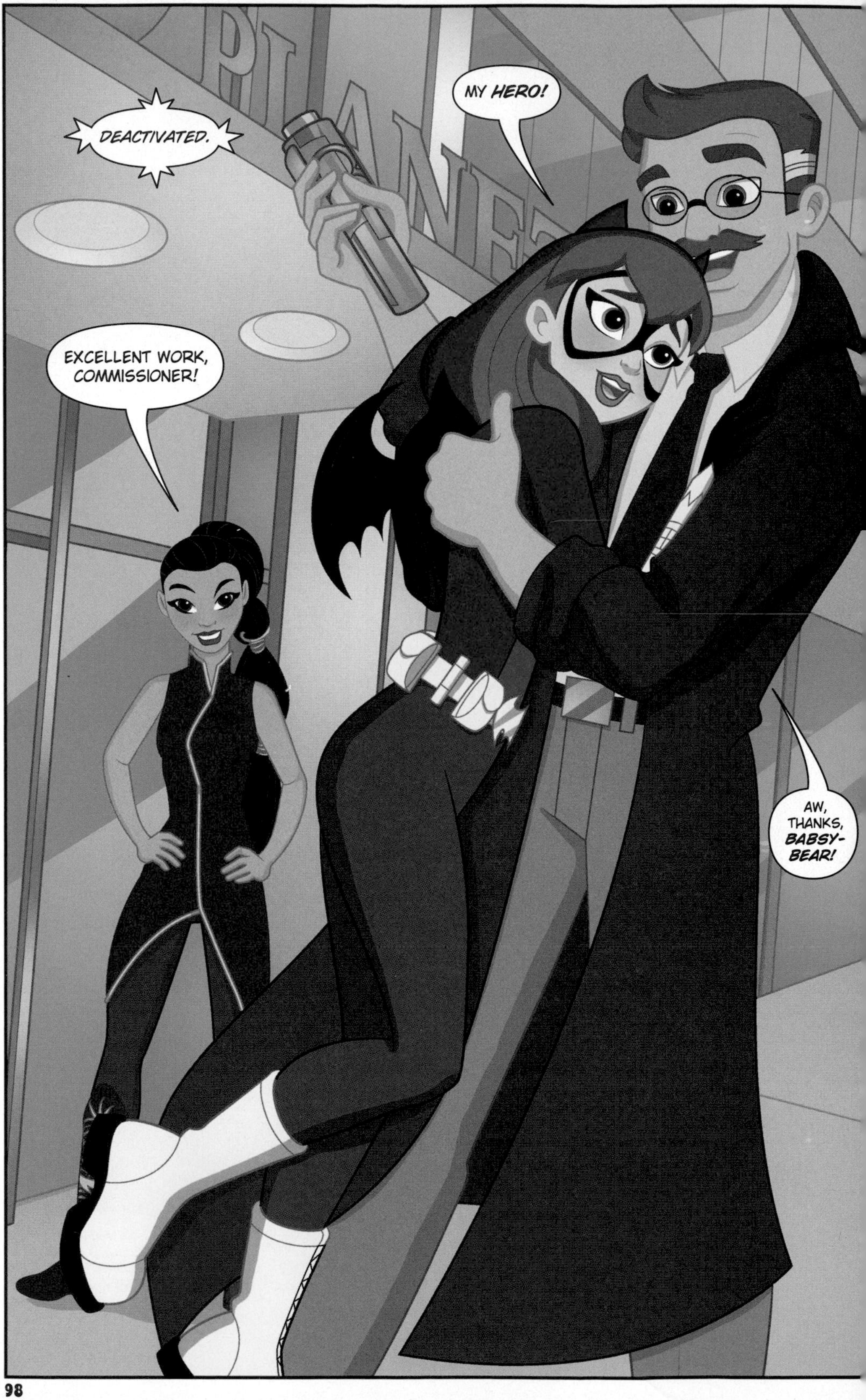
DEACTIVATED.
MY HERO!
EXCELLENT WORK, COMMISSIONER!
AW, THANKS, BABSY-BEAR!

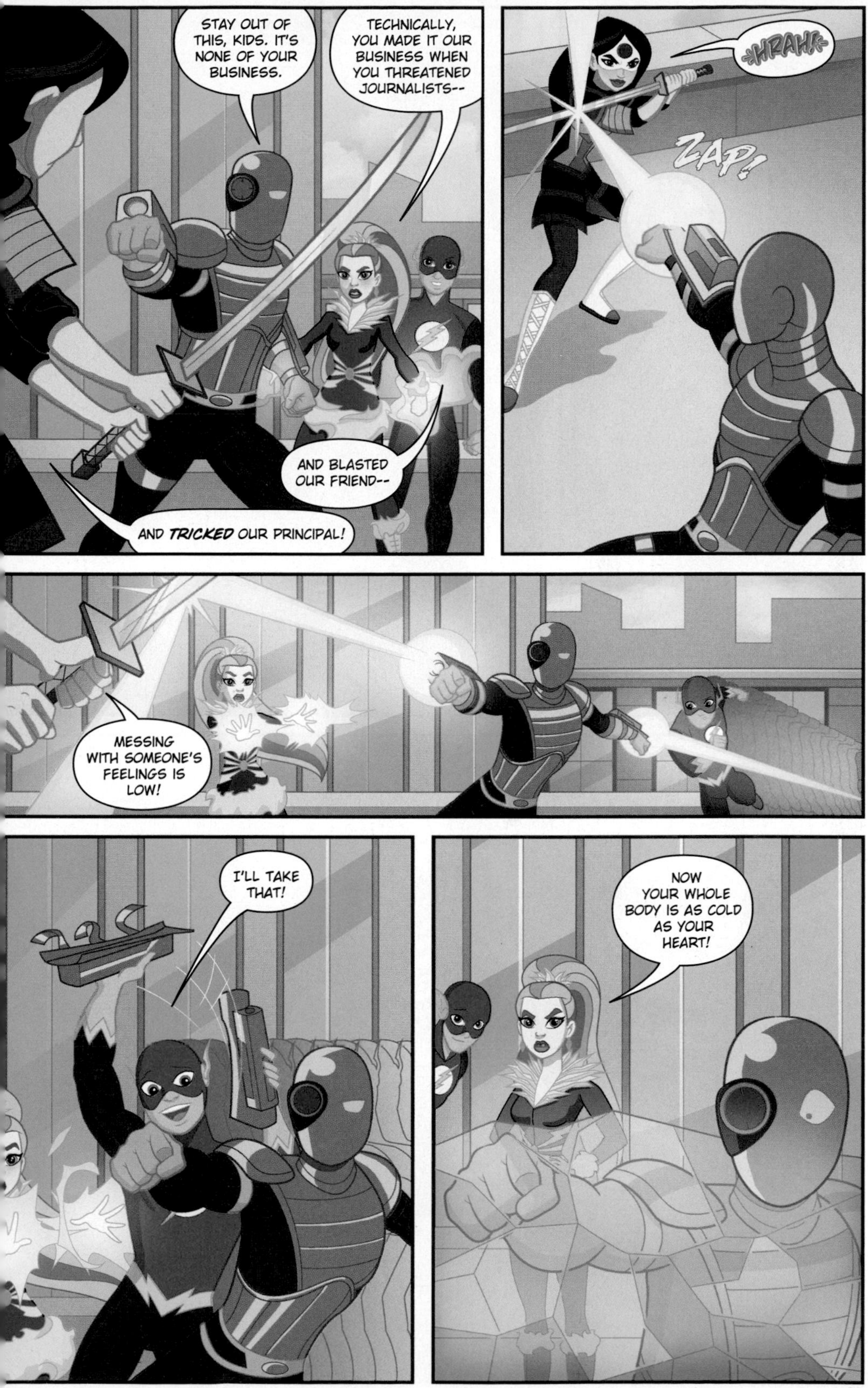
STAY OUT OF THIS, KIDS. IT'S NONE OF YOUR BUSINESS.
TECHNICALLY, YOU MADE IT OUR BUSINESS WHEN YOU THREATENED JOURNALISTS--
AND BLASTED OUR FRIEND--
AND TRICKED OUR PRINCIPAL!
HRAH!
ZAP!
MESSING WITH SOMEONE'S FEELINGS IS LOW!
I'LL TAKE THAT!
NOW YOUR WHOLE BODY IS AS COLD AS YOUR HEART!

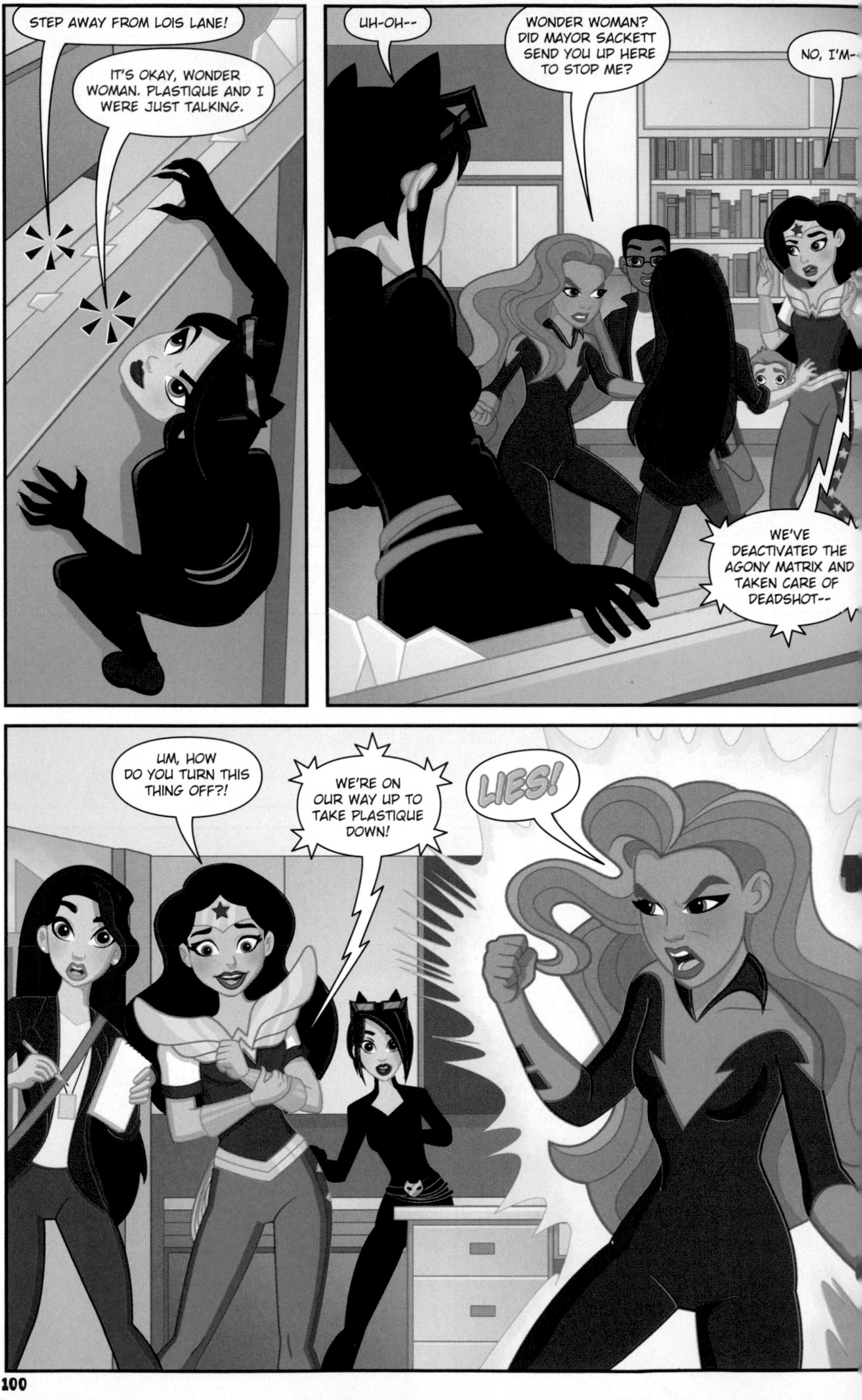
STEP AWAY FROM LOIS LANE!
IT'S OKAY, WONDER WOMAN. PLASTIQUE AND I WERE JUST TALKING.
UH-OH--
WONDER WOMAN? DID MAYOR SACKETT SEND YOU UP HERE TO STOP ME?
NO, I'M--
WE'VE DEACTIVATED THE AGONY MATRIX AND TAKEN CARE OF DEADSHOT--
UM, HOW DO YOU TURN THIS THING OFF?!
WE'RE ON OUR WAY UP TO TAKE PLASTIQUE DOWN!
LIES!

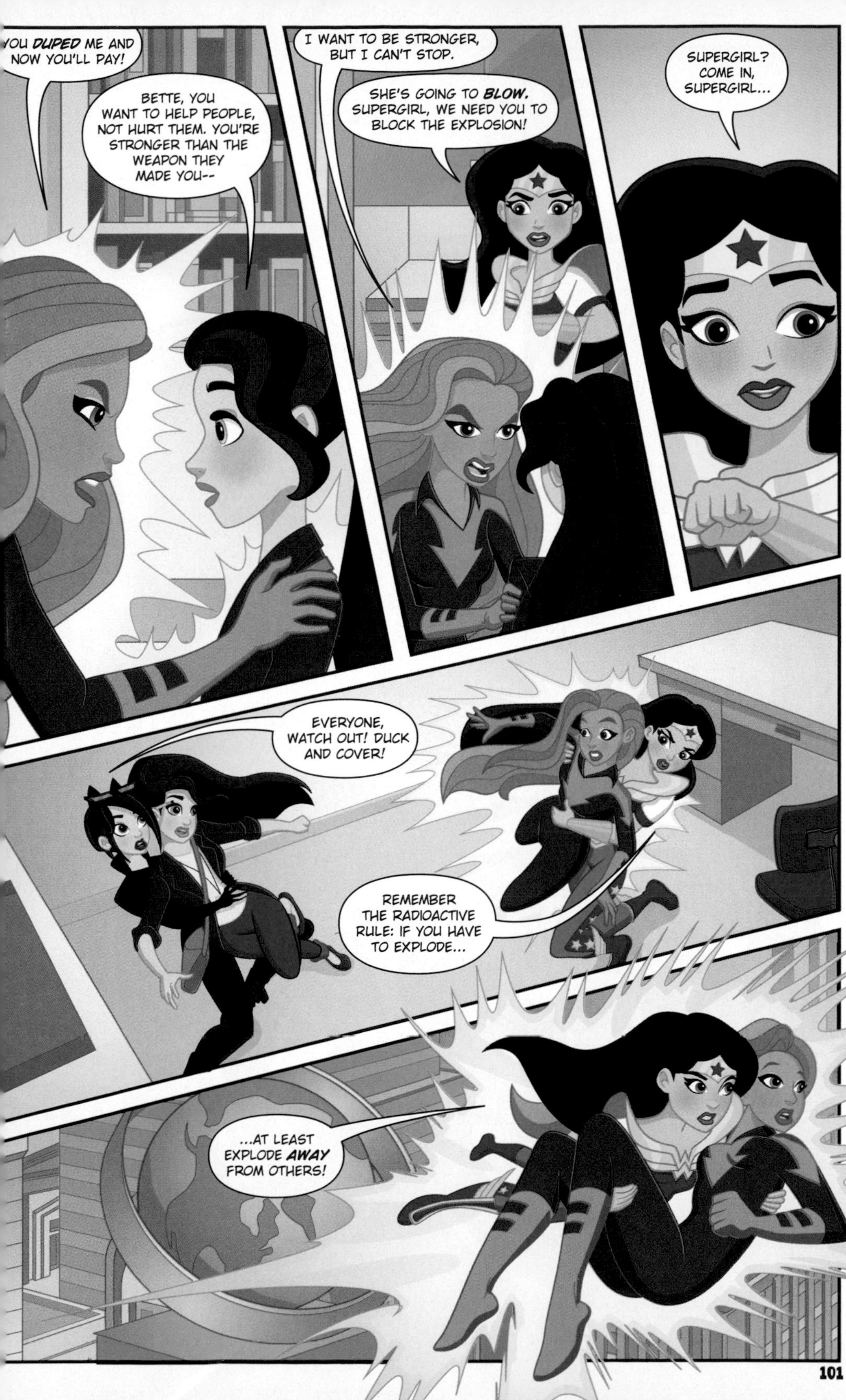

YOU DUPED ME AND NOW YOU'LL PAY!
BETTE, YOU WANT TO HELP PEOPLE, NOT HURT THEM. YOU'RE STRONGER THAN THE WEAPON THEY MADE YOU--
I WANT TO BE STRONGER, BUT I CAN'T STOP.
SHE'S GOING TO BLOW. SUPERGIRL, WE NEED YOU TO BLOCK THE EXPLOSION!
SUPERGIRL? COME IN, SUPERGIRL...
EVERYONE, WATCH OUT! DUCK AND COVER!
REMEMBER THE RADIOACTIVE RULE: IF YOU HAVE TO EXPLODE...
...AT LEAST EXPLODE AWAY FROM OTHERS!

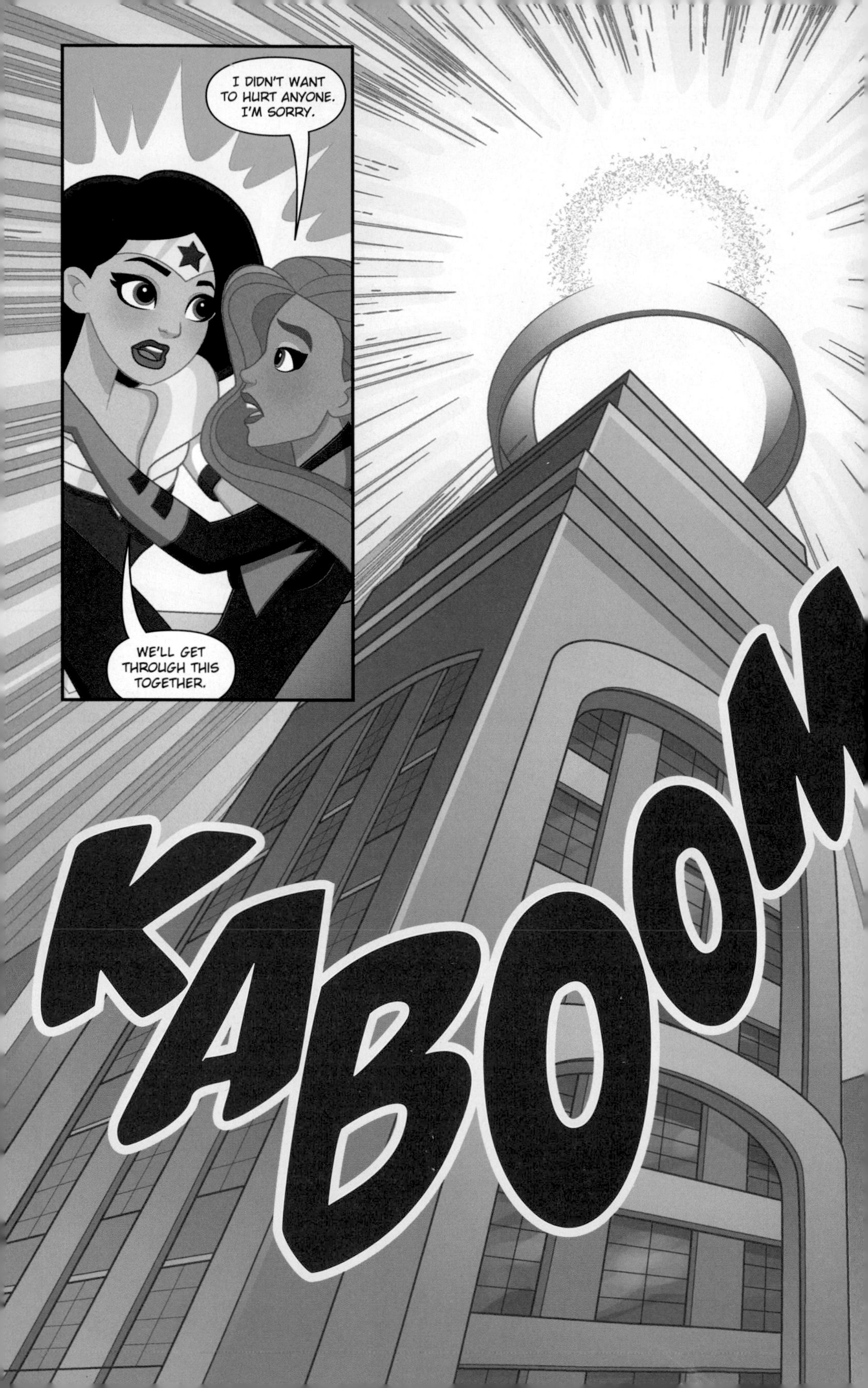
I DIDN'T WANT TO HURT ANYONE. I'M SORRY.
WE'LL GET THROUGH THIS TOGETHER.
KABOOM

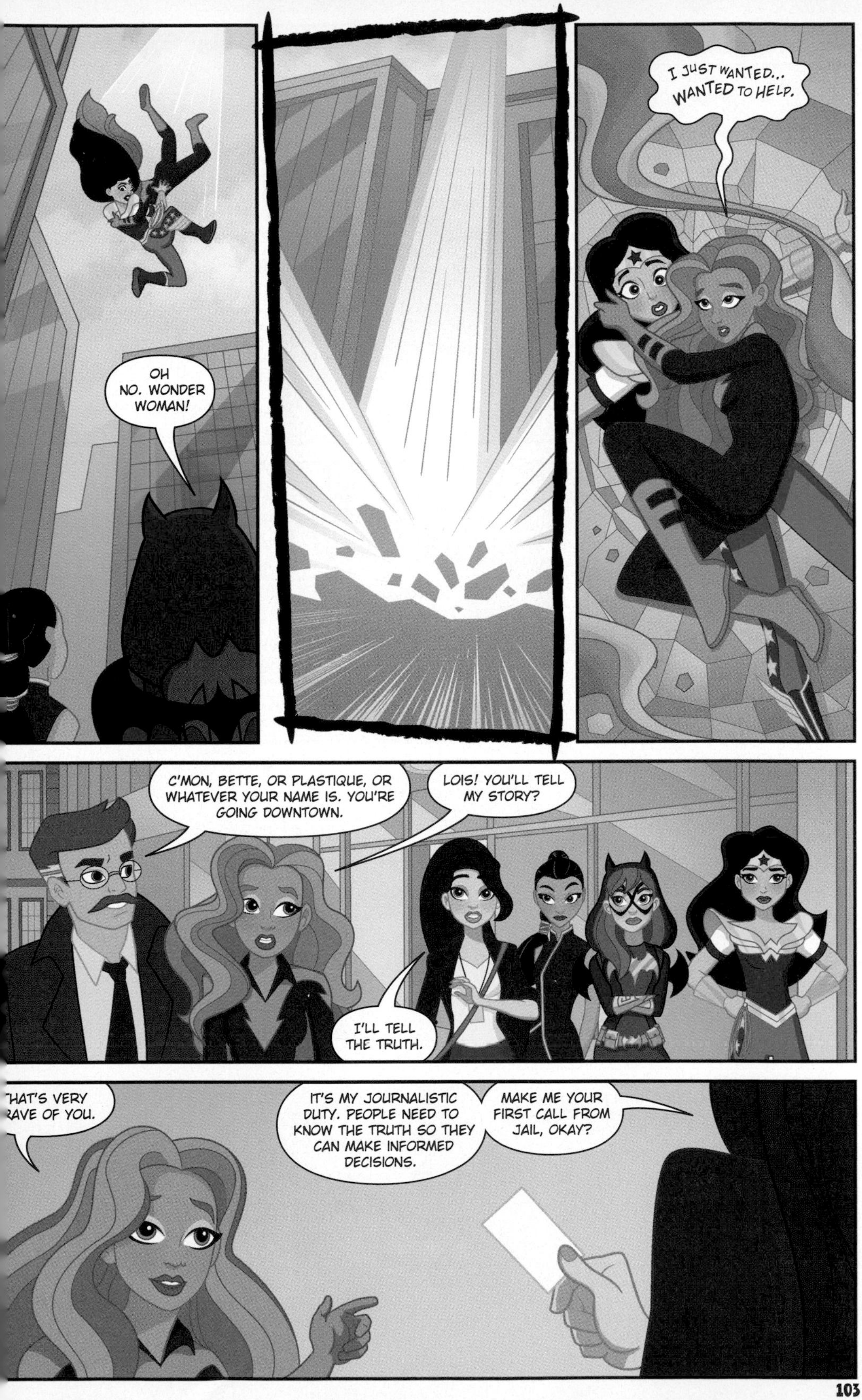
OH NO. WONDER WOMAN!
I JUST WANTED... WANTED TO HELP.
C'MON, BETTE, OR PLASTIQUE, OR WHATEVER YOUR NAME IS. YOU'RE GOING DOWNTOWN.
LOIS! YOU'LL TELL MY STORY?
I'LL TELL THE TRUTH.
HAT'S VERY
AVE OF YOU.
IT'S MY JOURNALISTIC DUTY. PEOPLE NEED TO KNOW THE TRUTH SO THEY CAN MAKE INFORMED DECISIONS.
MAKE ME YOUR FIRST CALL FROM JAIL, OKAY?

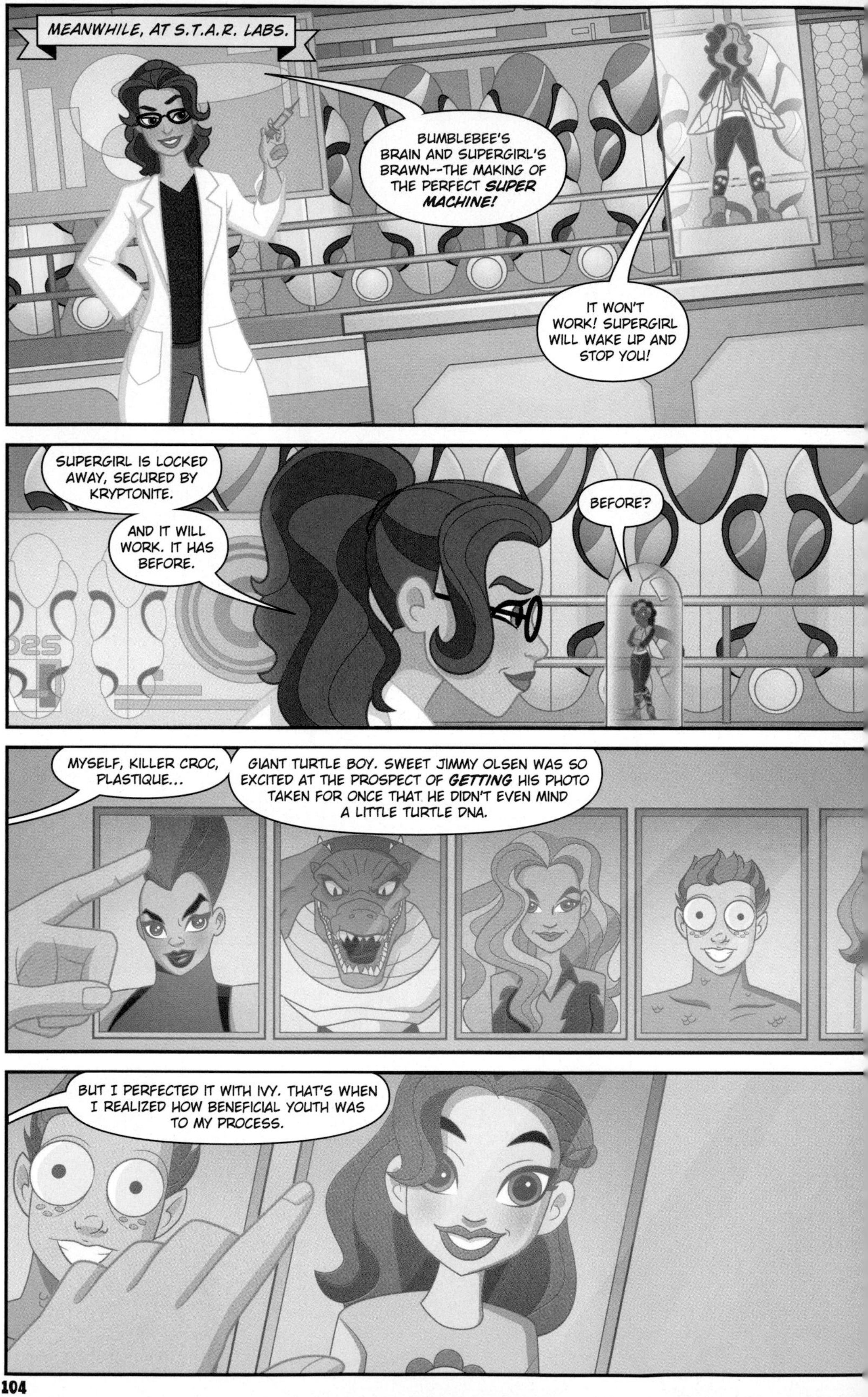
MEANWHILE, AT S.T.A.R. LABS.
BUMBLEBEE'S BRAIN AND SUPERGIRL'S BRAWN--THE MAKING OF THE PERFECT SUPER MACHINE!
IT WON'T WORK! SUPERGIRL WILL WAKE UP AND STOP YOU!
SUPERGIRL IS LOCKED AWAY, SECURED BY KRYPTONITE.
AND IT WILL WORK. IT HAS BEFORE.
BEFORE?
MYSELF, KILLER CROC, PLASTIQUE...
GIANT TURTLE BOY. SWEET JIMMY OLSEN WAS SO EXCITED AT THE PROSPECT OF GETTING HIS PHOTO TAKEN FOR ONCE THAT HE DIDN'T EVEN MIND A LITTLE TURTLE DNA.
BUT I PERFECTED IT WITH IVY. THAT'S WHEN I REALIZED HOW BENEFICIAL YOUTH WAS TO MY PROCESS.

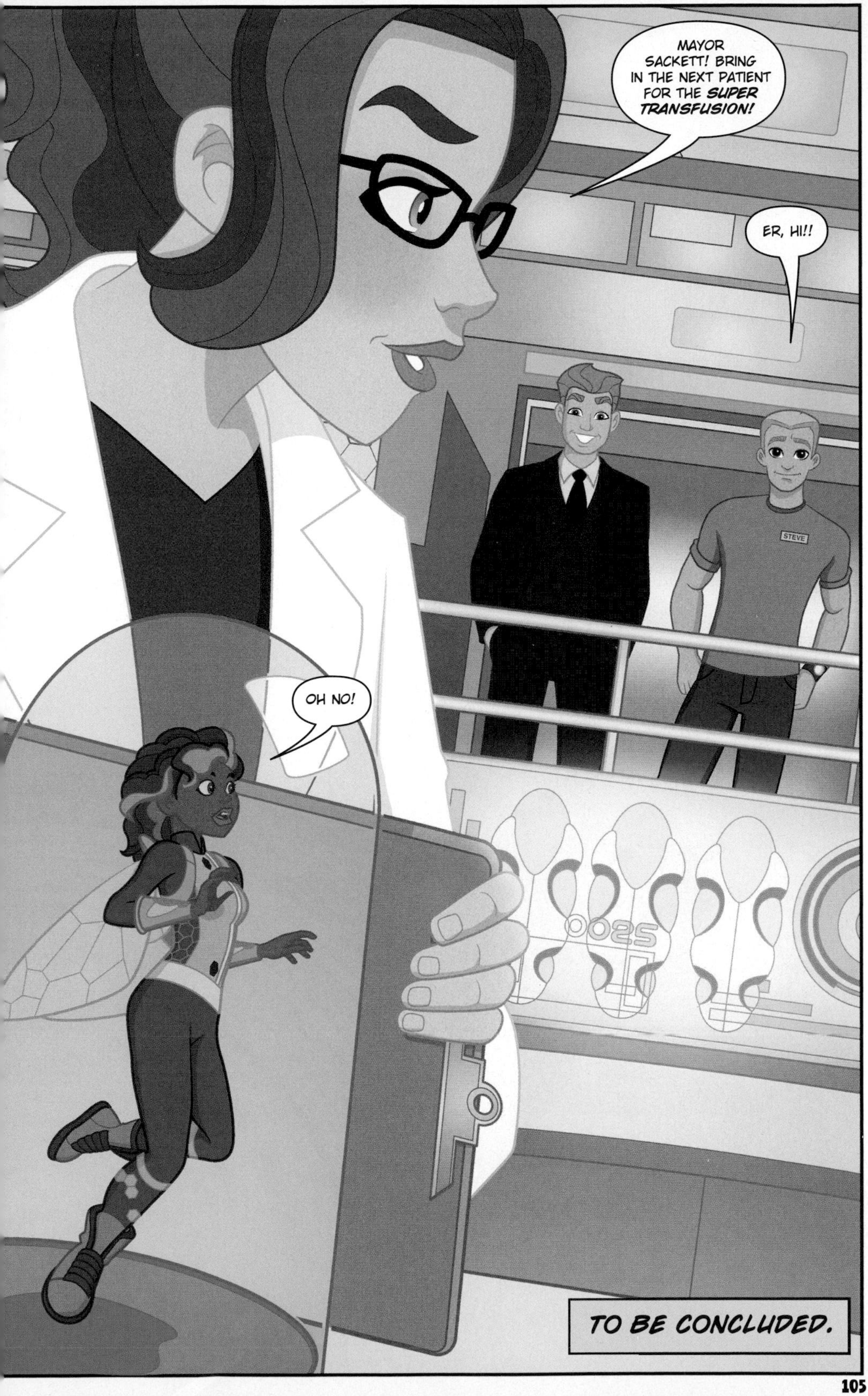
MAYOR SACKETT! BRING IN THE NEXT PATIENT FOR THE SUPER TRANSFUSION!
ER, HI!!
STEVE
OH NO!
0025
TO BE CONCLUDED.

CHAPTER 6
CONSEQUENCES

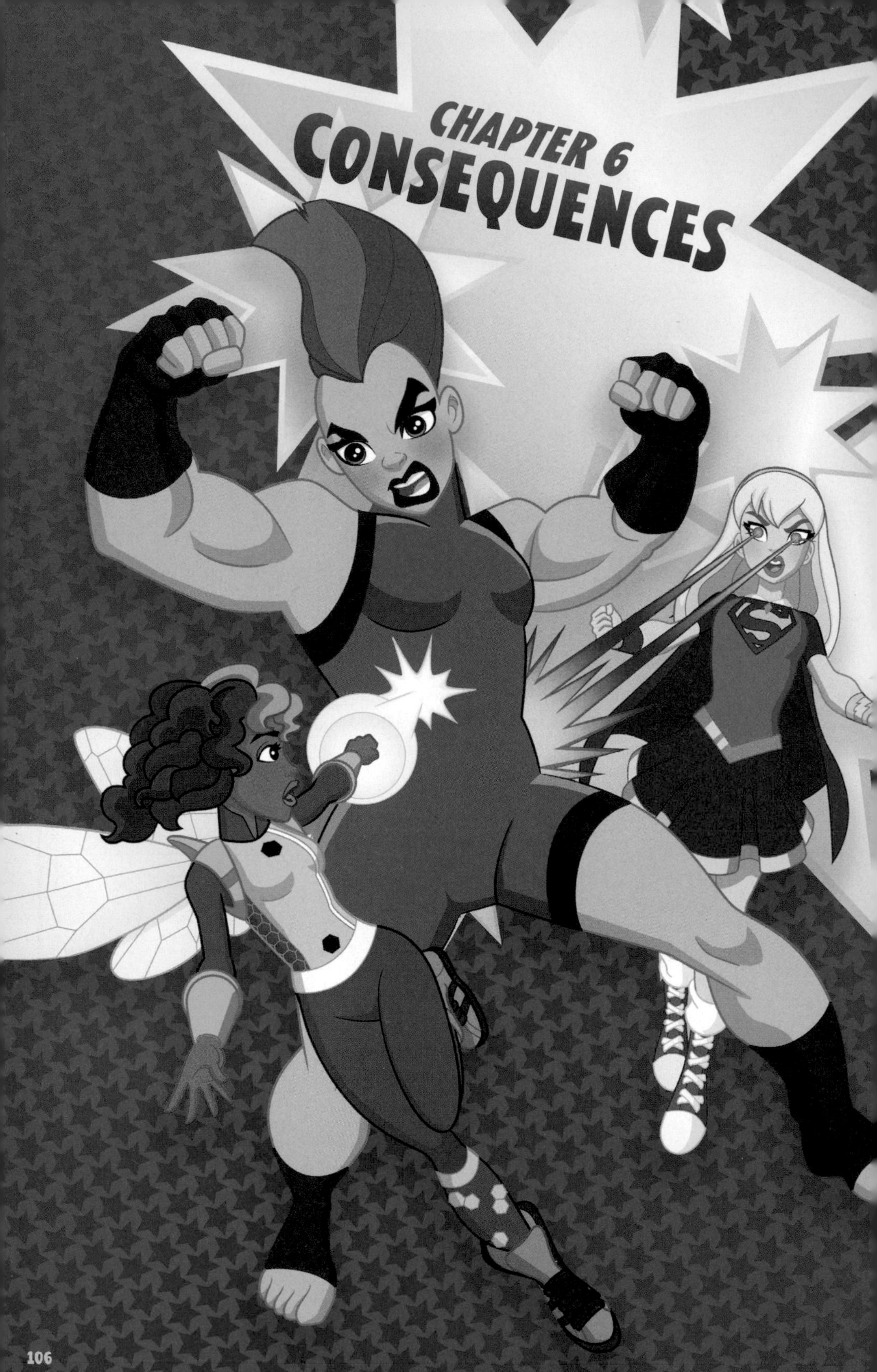

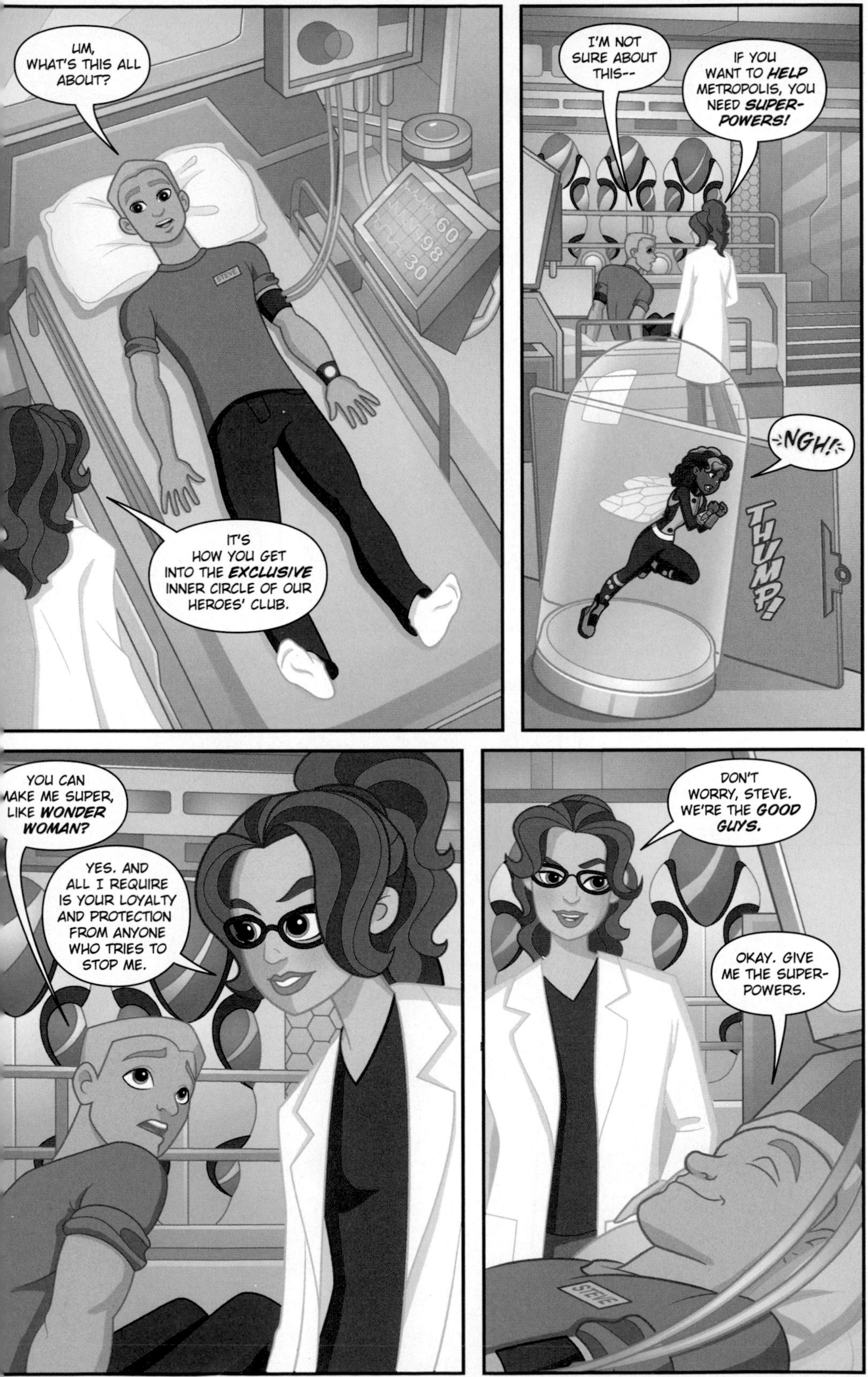

UM, WHAT'S THIS ALL ABOUT?
IT'S HOW YOU GET INTO THE EXCLUSIVE INNER CIRCLE OF OUR HEROES' CLUB.
I'M NOT SURE ABOUT THIS--
IF YOU WANT TO HELP METROPOLIS, YOU NEED SUPER-POWERS!
NGH!
THUMP!
YOU CAN MAKE ME SUPER, LIKE WONDER WOMAN?
YES. AND ALL I REQUIRE IS YOUR LOYALTY AND PROTECTION FROM ANYONE WHO TRIES TO STOP ME.
DON'T WORRY, STEVE. WE'RE THE GOOD GUYS.
OKAY. GIVE ME THE SUPER-POWERS.

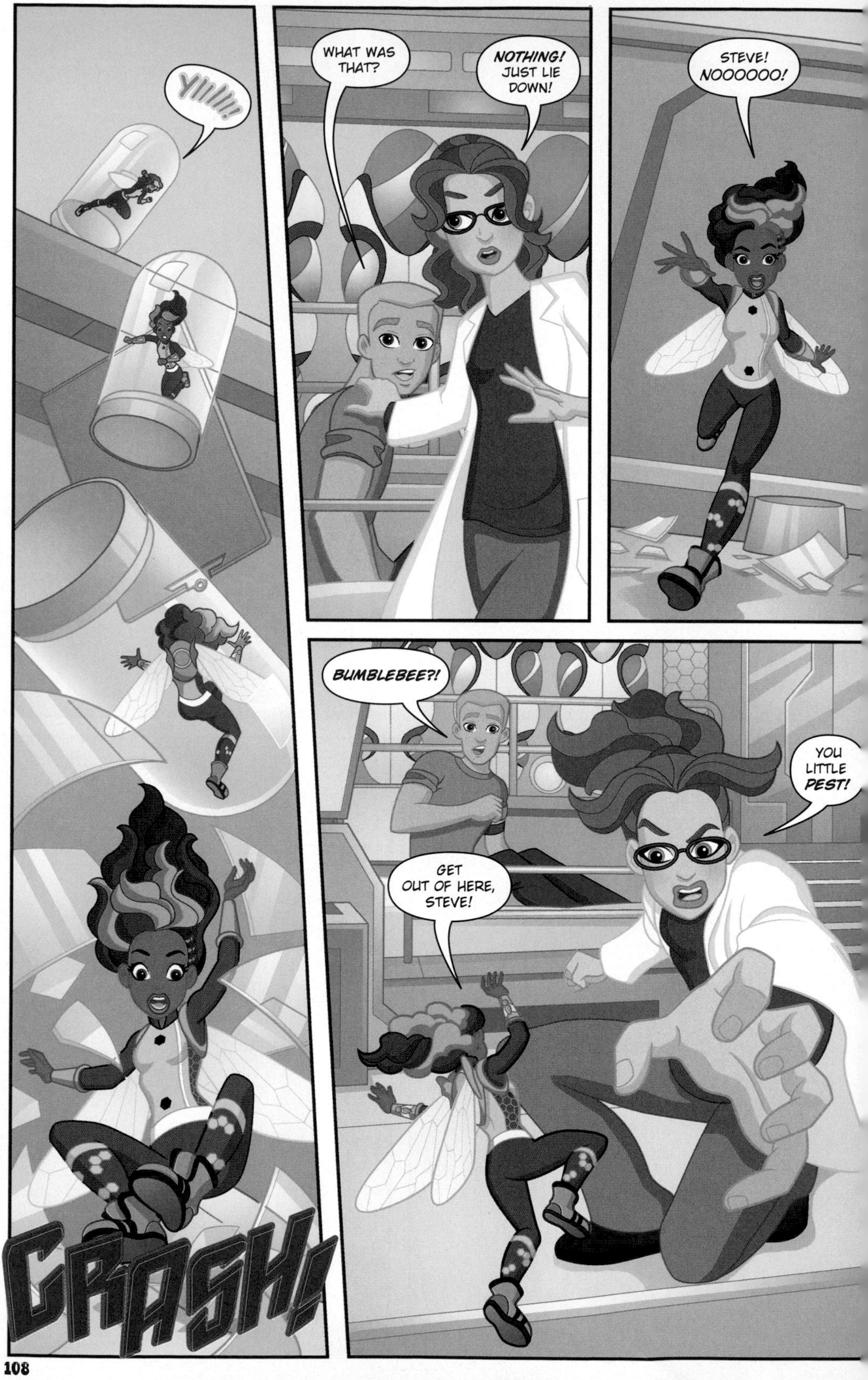
YIII!!!
WHAT WAS THAT?
NOTHING! JUST LIE DOWN!
STEVE! NOOOOOO!
CRASH!
BUMBLEBEE?!
YOU LITTLE PEST!
GET OUT OF HERE, STEVE!

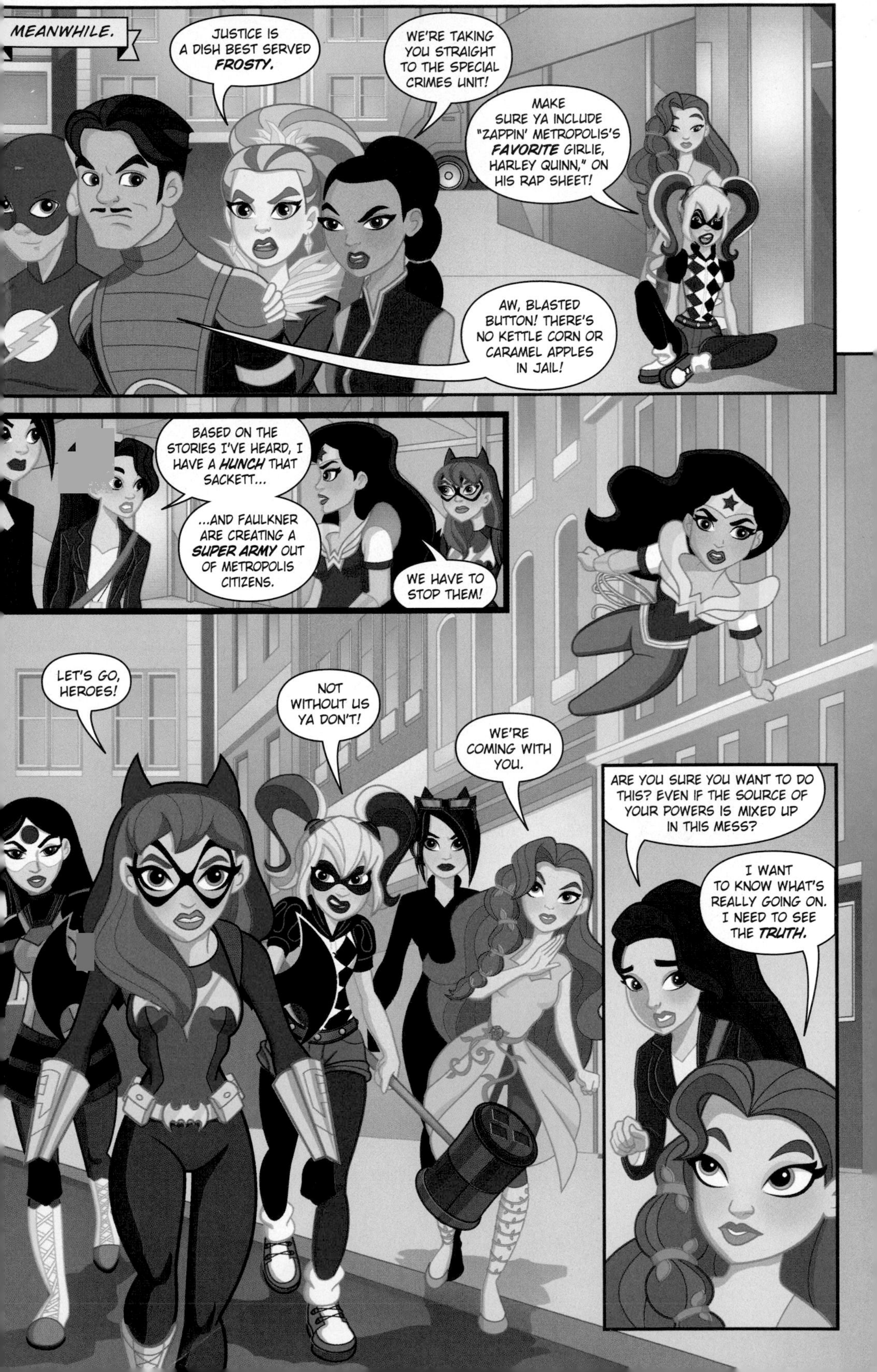
MEANWHILE.
JUSTICE IS A DISH BEST SERVED FROSTY.
WE'RE TAKING YOU STRAIGHT TO THE SPECIAL CRIMES UNIT!
MAKE SURE YA INCLUDE "ZAPPIN' METROPOLIS'S FAVORITE GIRLIE, HARLEY QUINN," ON HIS RAP SHEET!
AW, BLASTED BUTTON! THERE'S NO KETTLE CORN OR CARAMEL APPLES IN JAIL!
BASED ON THE STORIES I'VE HEARD, I HAVE A HUNCH THAT SACKETT...
...AND FAULKNER ARE CREATING A SUPER ARMY OUT OF METROPOLIS CITIZENS.
WE HAVE TO STOP THEM!
LET'S GO, HEROES!
NOT WITHOUT US YA DON'T!
WE'RE COMING WITH YOU.
ARE YOU SURE YOU WANT TO DO THIS? EVEN IF THE SOURCE OF YOUR POWERS IS MIXED UP IN THIS MESS?
I WANT TO KNOW WHAT'S REALLY GOING ON. I NEED TO SEE THE TRUTH.

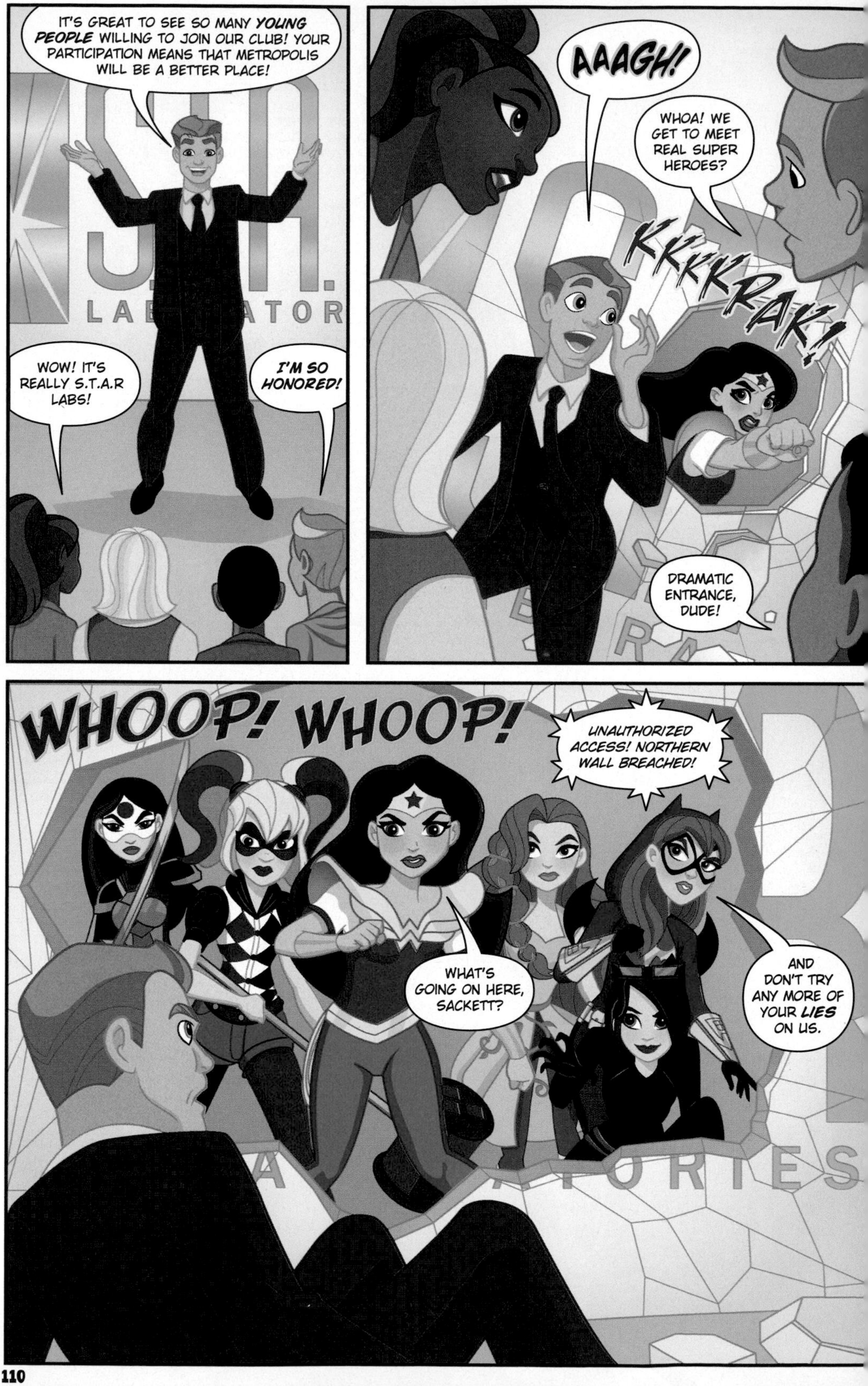
IT'S GREAT TO SEE SO MANY *YOUNG PEOPLE* WILLING TO JOIN OUR CLUB! YOUR PARTICIPATION MEANS THAT METROPOLIS WILL BE A BETTER PLACE!
WOW! IT'S REALLY S.T.A.R LABS!
I'M SO HONORED!
AAAGH!
WHOA! WE GET TO MEET REAL SUPER HEROES?
KKKKRAK!
DRAMATIC ENTRANCE, DUDE!
WHOOP! WHOOP!
UNAUTHORIZED ACCESS! NORTHERN WALL BREACHED!
WHAT'S GOING ON HERE, SACKETT?
AND DON'T TRY ANY MORE OF YOUR *LIES* ON US.

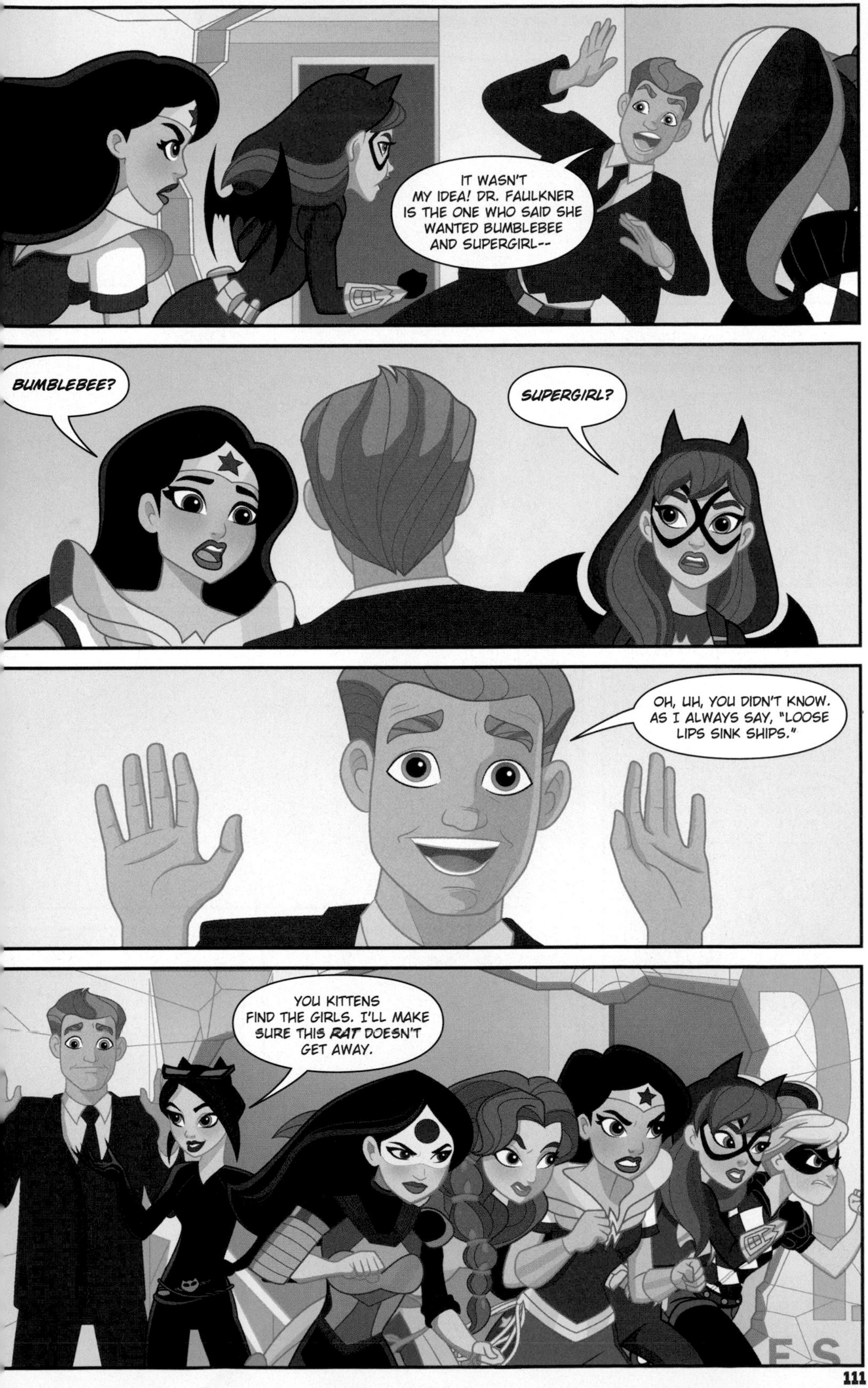
IT WASN'T MY IDEA! DR. FAULKNER IS THE ONE WHO SAID SHE WANTED BUMBLEBEE AND SUPERGIRL--
BUMBLEBEE?
SUPERGIRL?
OH, UH, YOU DIDN'T KNOW. AS I ALWAYS SAY, "LOOSE LIPS SINK SHIPS."
YOU KITTENS FIND THE GIRLS. I'LL MAKE SURE THIS RAT DOESN'T GET AWAY.

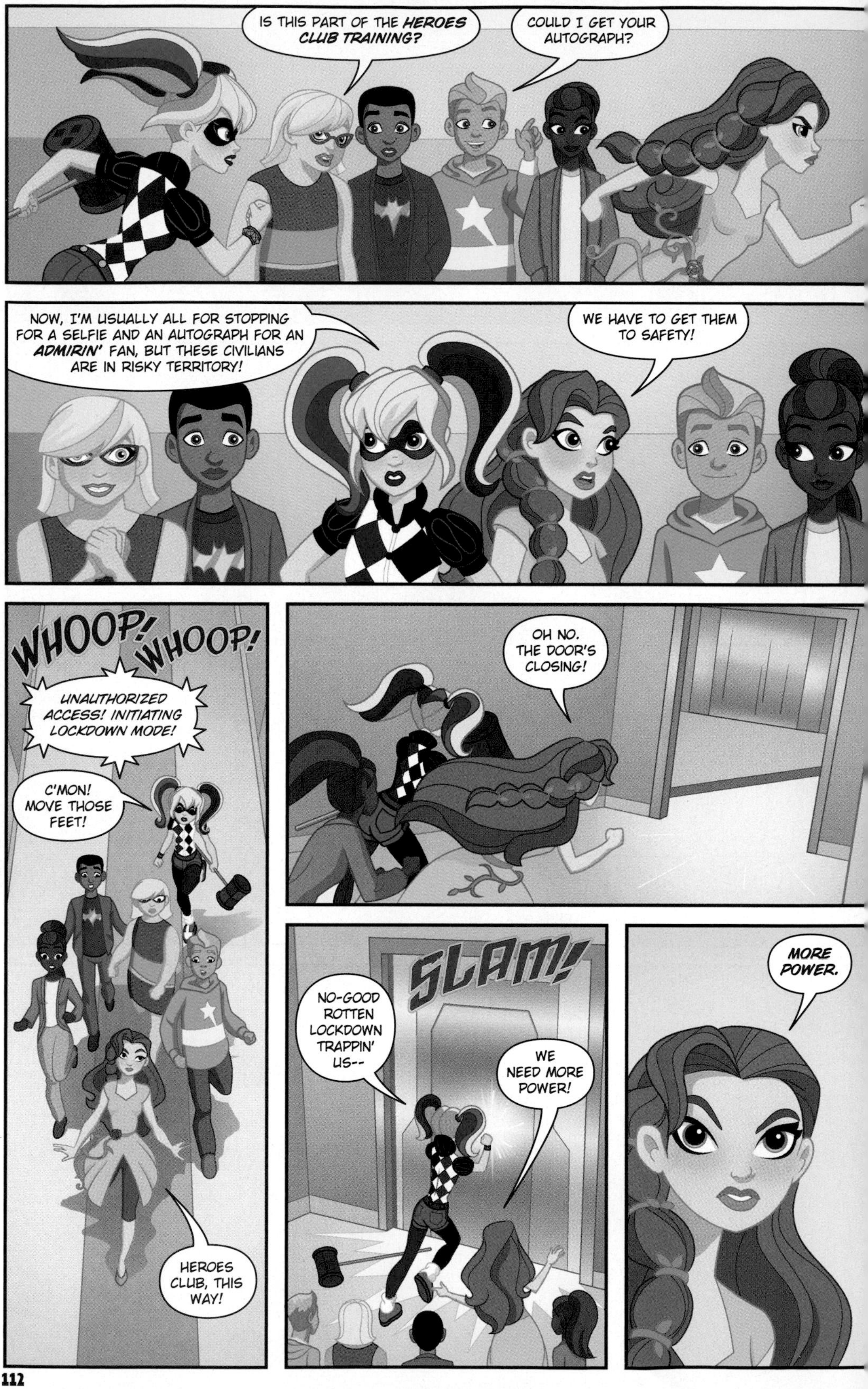
IS THIS PART OF THE HEROES CLUB TRAINING?
COULD I GET YOUR AUTOGRAPH?
NOW, I'M USUALLY ALL FOR STOPPING FOR A SELFIE AND AN AUTOGRAPH FOR AN ADMIRIN' FAN, BUT THESE CIVILIANS ARE IN RISKY TERRITORY!
WE HAVE TO GET THEM TO SAFETY!
WHOOP! WHOOP!
UNAUTHORIZED ACCESS! INITIATING LOCKDOWN MODE!
C'MON! MOVE THOSE FEET!
HEROES CLUB, THIS WAY!
OH NO. THE DOOR'S CLOSING!
SLAM!
NO-GOOD ROTTEN LOCKDOWN TRAPPIN' US--
WE NEED MORE POWER!
MORE POWER.

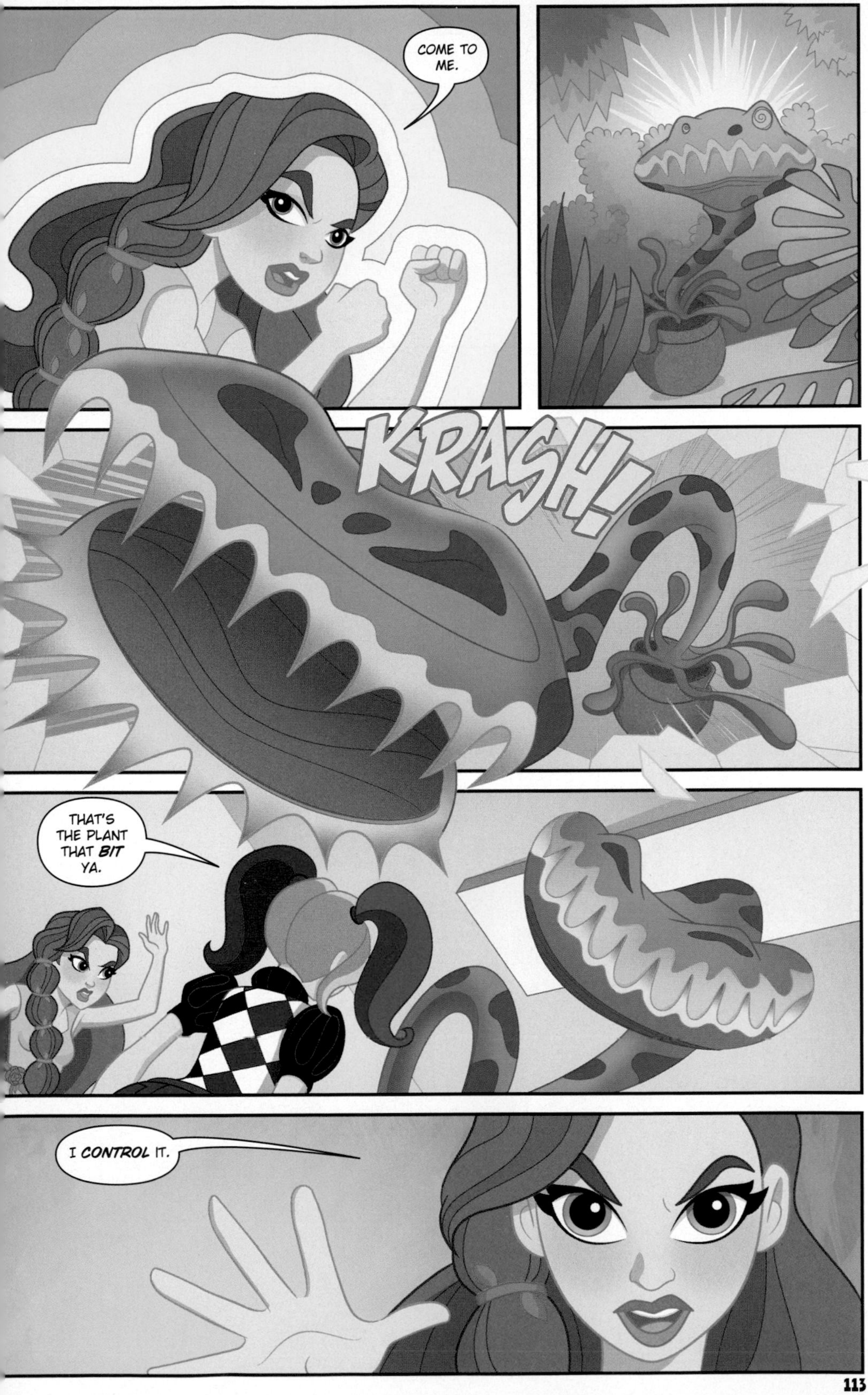
COME TO ME.
KRASH!
THAT'S THE PLANT THAT *BIT* YA.
I *CONTROL* IT.

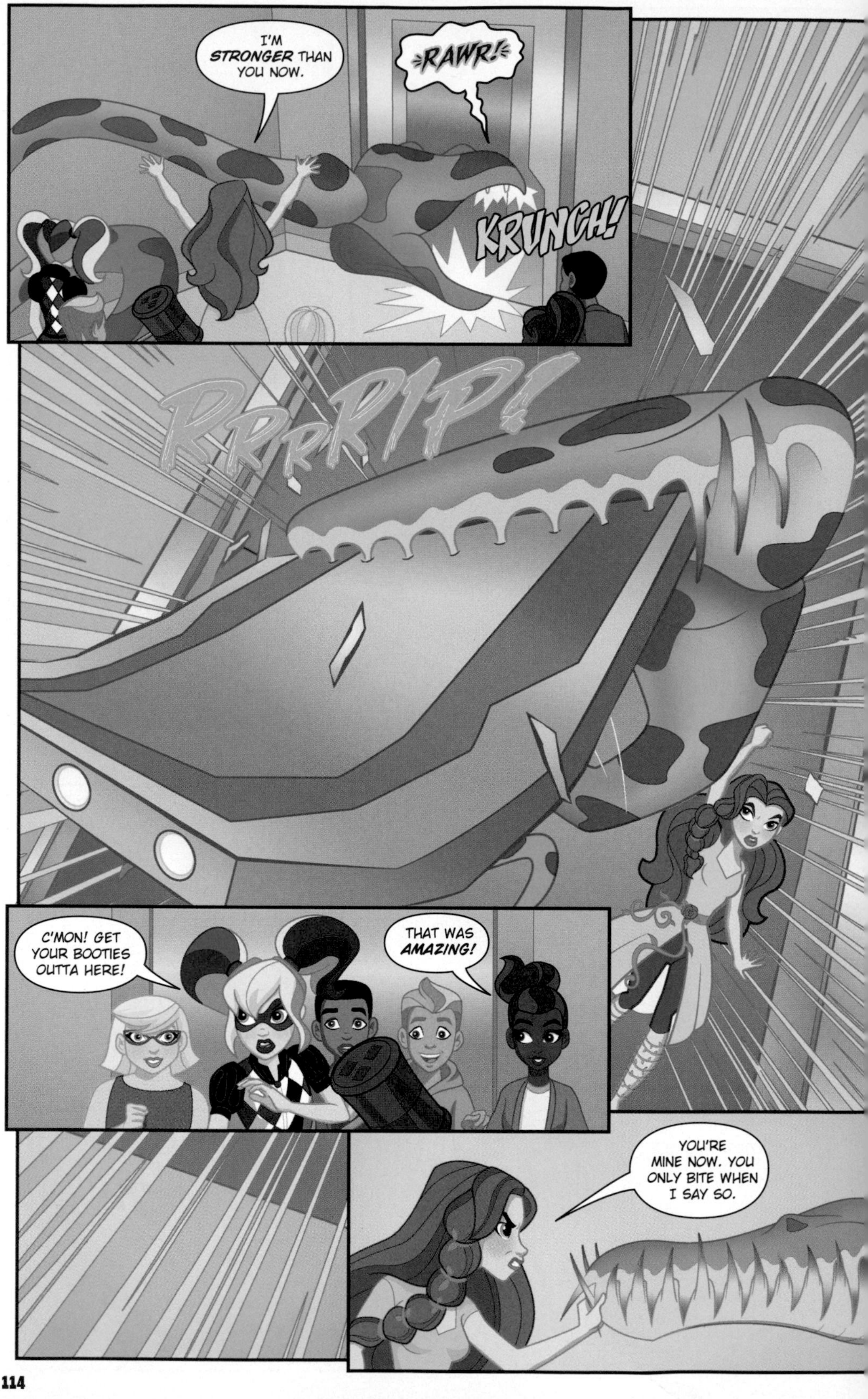
I'M STRONGER THAN YOU NOW.
RAWR!
KRUNCH!
RRRRIP!
C'MON! GET YOUR BOOTIES OUTTA HERE!
THAT WAS AMAZING!
YOU'RE MINE NOW. YOU ONLY BITE WHEN I SAY SO.

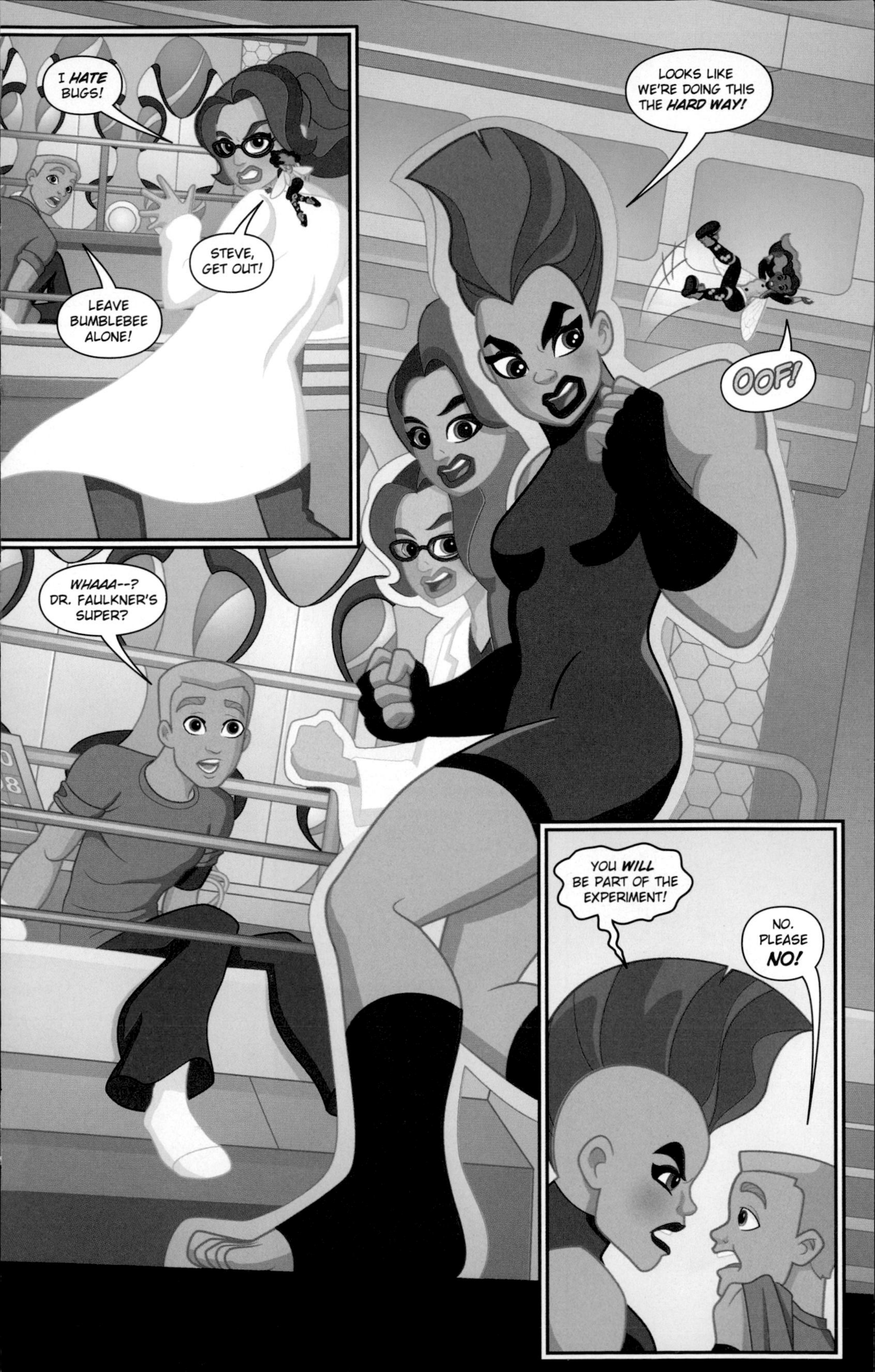
I HATE BUGS!
STEVE, GET OUT!
LEAVE BUMBLEBEE ALONE!
LOOKS LIKE WE'RE DOING THIS THE HARD WAY!
OOF!
WHAAA--? DR. FAULKNER'S SUPER?
YOU WILL BE PART OF THE EXPERIMENT!
NO. PLEASE NO!

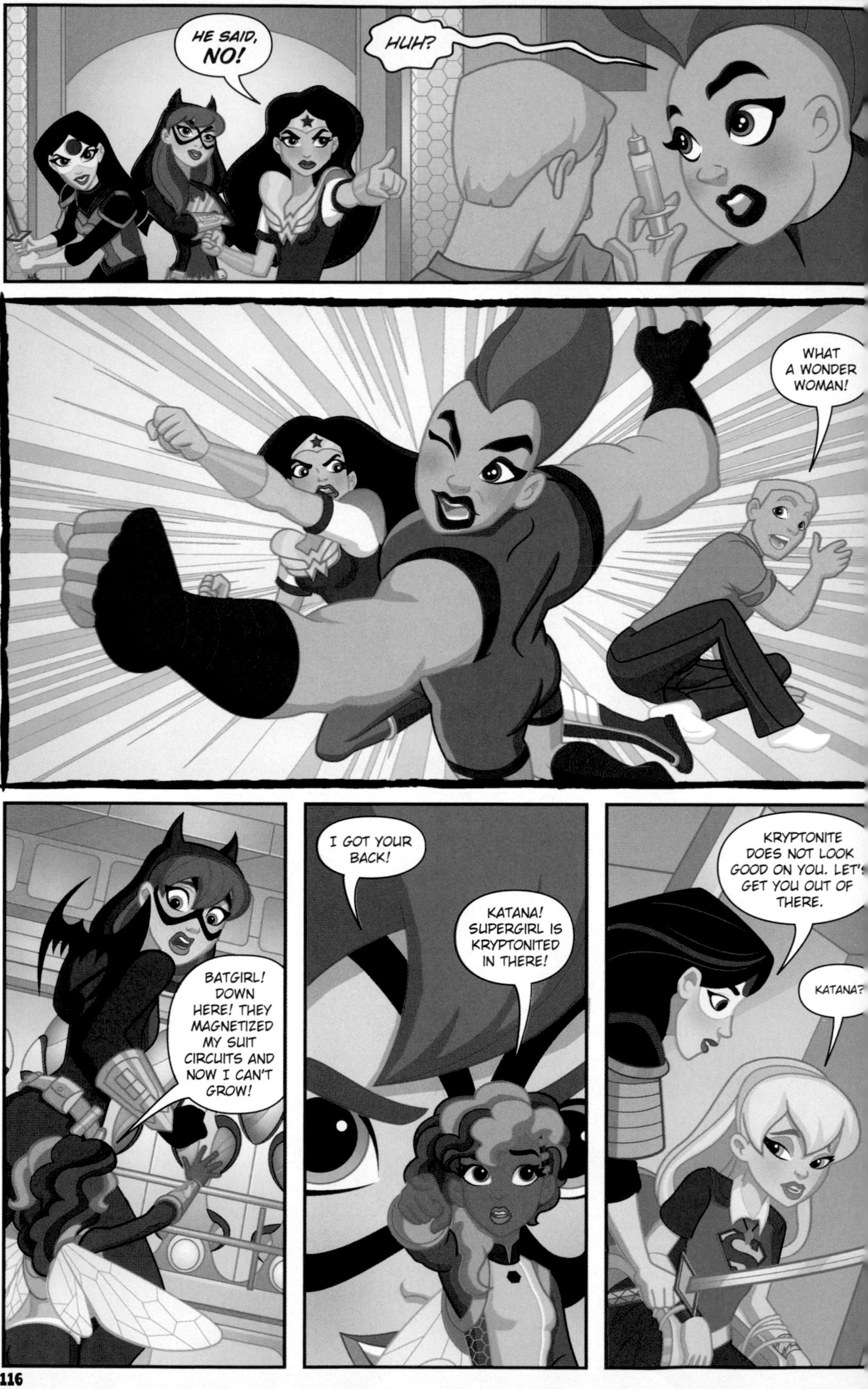
HE SAID, NO!
HUH?
WHAT A WONDER WOMAN!
BATGIRL! DOWN HERE! THEY MAGNETIZED MY SUIT CIRCUITS AND NOW I CAN'T GROW!
I GOT YOUR BACK!
KATANA! SUPERGIRL IS KRYPTONITED IN THERE!
KRYPTONITE DOES NOT LOOK GOOD ON YOU. LET'S GET YOU OUT OF THERE.
KATANA?

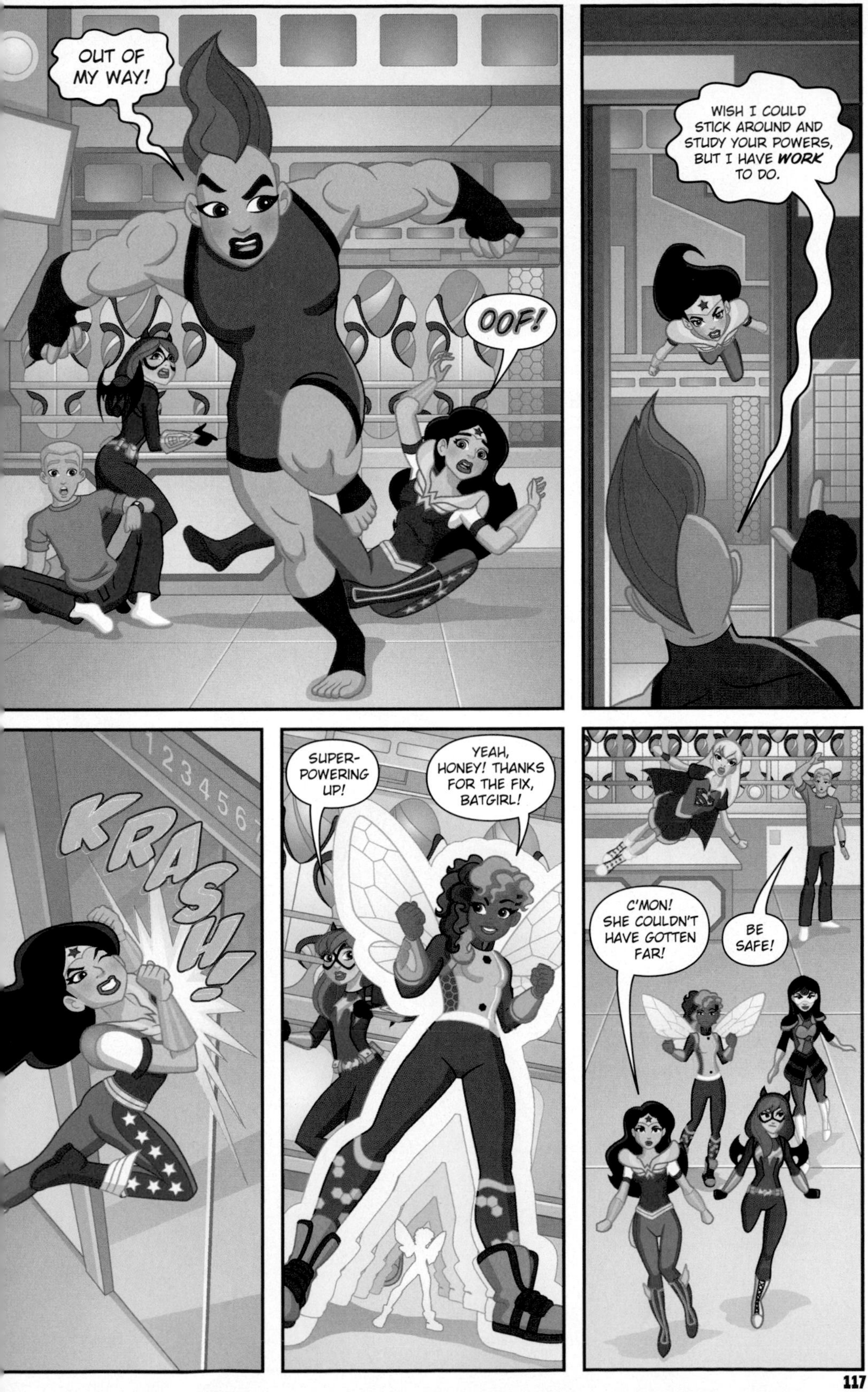
OUT OF MY WAY!
OOF!
WISH I COULD STICK AROUND AND STUDY YOUR POWERS, BUT I HAVE WORK TO DO.
KRASH!
SUPER-POWERING UP!
YEAH, HONEY! THANKS FOR THE FIX, BATGIRL!
C'MON! SHE COULDN'T HAVE GOTTEN FAR!
BE SAFE!

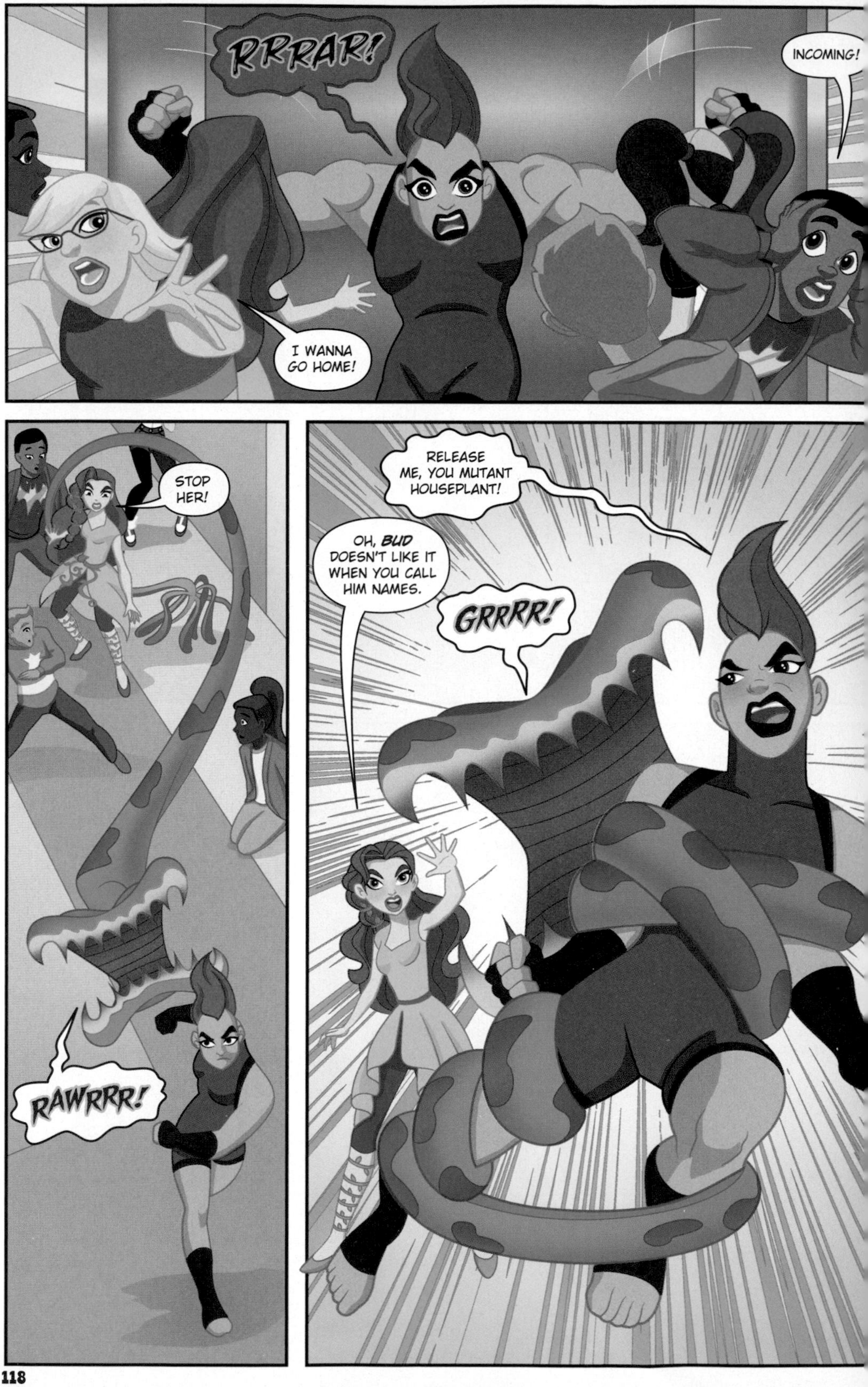
RRRAR!
I WANNA GO HOME!
INCOMING!
STOP HER!
RAWRRR!
RELEASE ME, YOU MUTANT HOUSEPLANT!
OH, BUD DOESN'T LIKE IT WHEN YOU CALL HIM NAMES.
GRRRR!

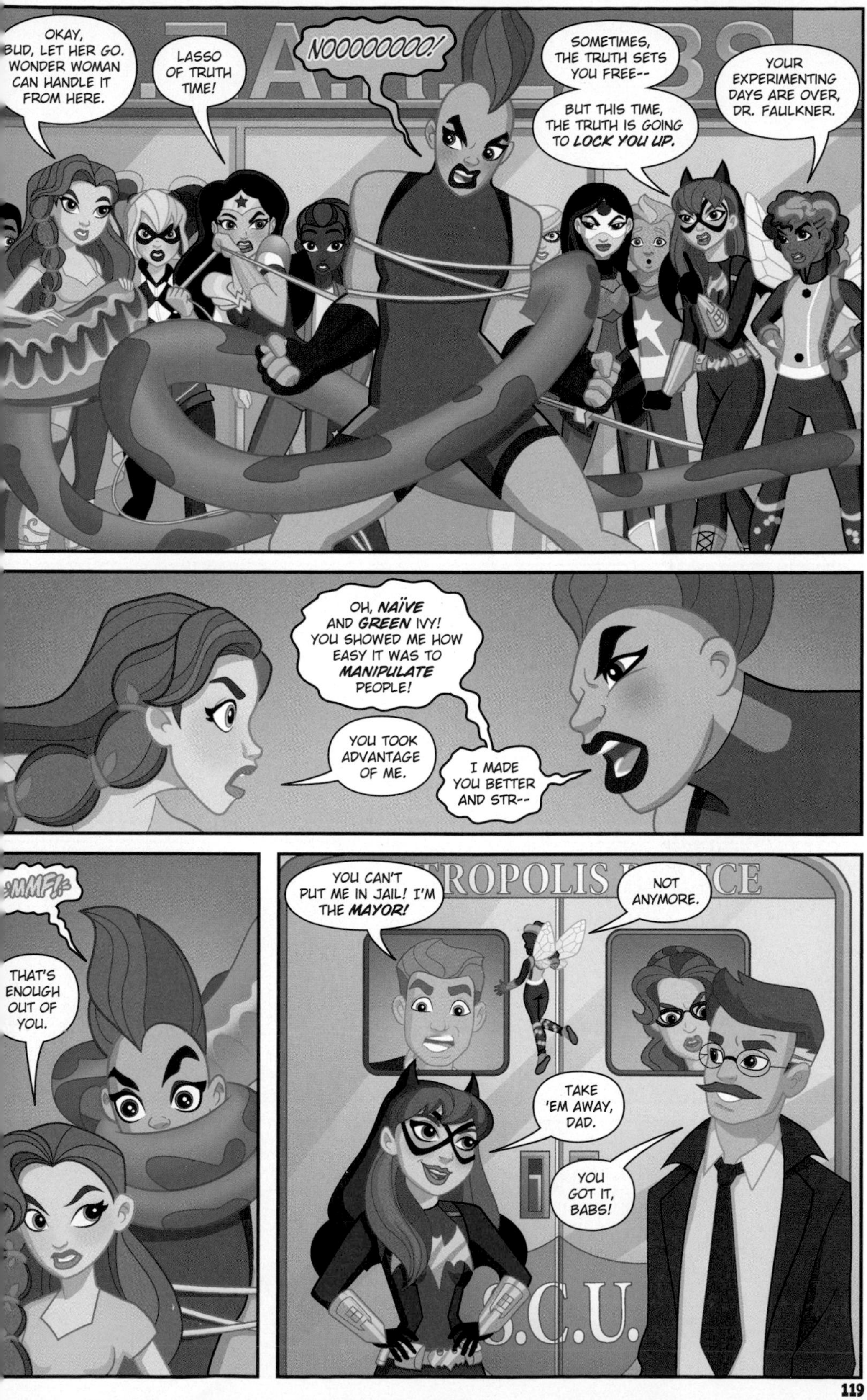
OKAY, BUD, LET HER GO. WONDER WOMAN CAN HANDLE IT FROM HERE.
LASSO OF TRUTH TIME!
NOOOOOOOO!
SOMETIMES, THE TRUTH SETS YOU FREE--
BUT THIS TIME, THE TRUTH IS GOING TO LOCK YOU UP.
YOUR EXPERIMENTING DAYS ARE OVER, DR. FAULKNER.
OH, NAÏVE AND GREEN IVY! YOU SHOWED ME HOW EASY IT WAS TO MANIPULATE PEOPLE!
YOU TOOK ADVANTAGE OF ME.
I MADE YOU BETTER AND STR--
MMF!!
THAT'S ENOUGH OUT OF YOU.
ROPOLIS ICE
YOU CAN'T PUT ME IN JAIL! I'M THE MAYOR!
NOT ANYMORE.
TAKE 'EM AWAY, DAD.
YOU GOT IT, BABS!
S.C.U.

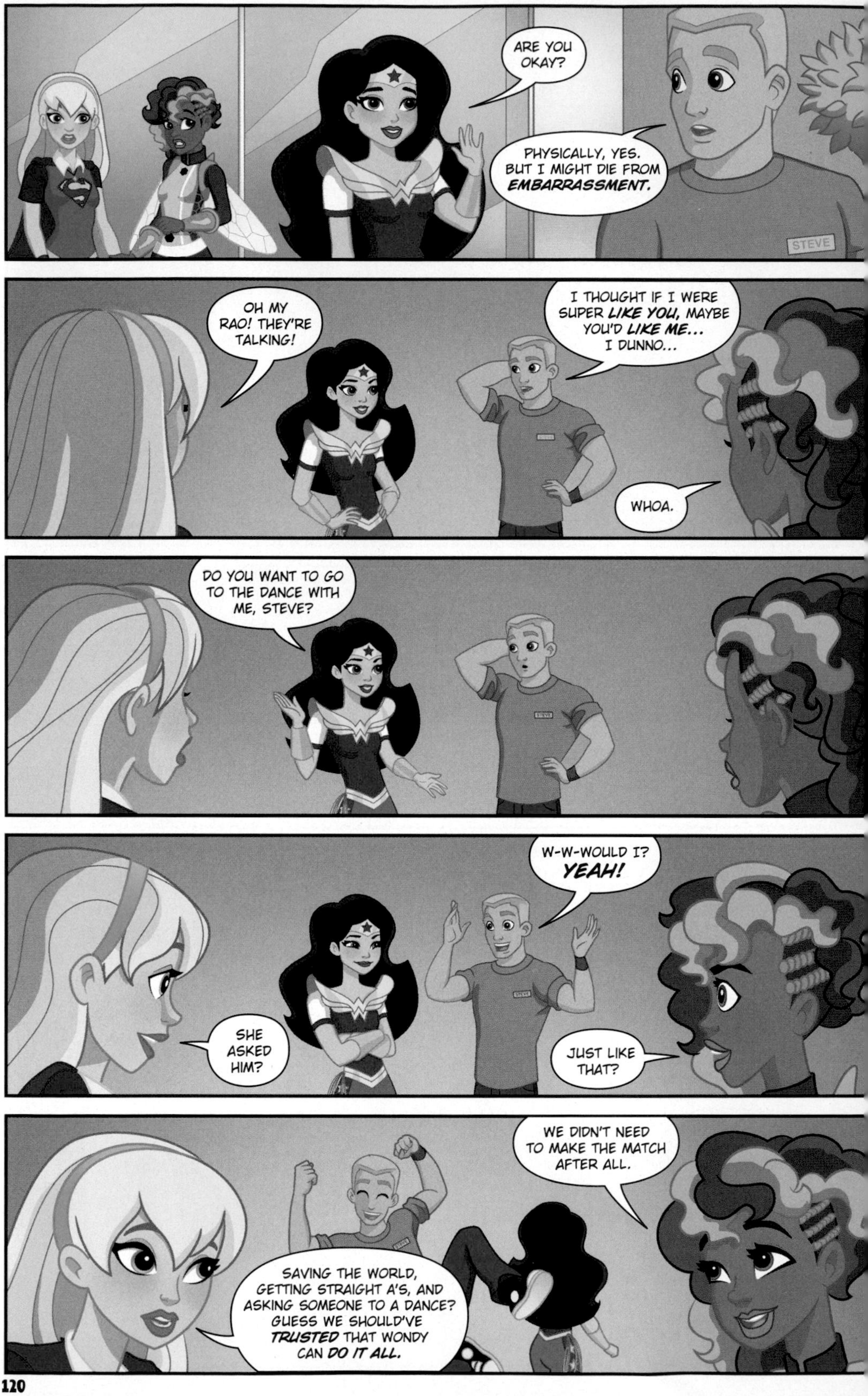
ARE YOU OKAY?
PHYSICALLY, YES. BUT I MIGHT DIE FROM **EMBARRASSMENT.**
STEVE
OH MY RAO! THEY'RE TALKING!
I THOUGHT IF I WERE SUPER ***LIKE YOU,*** MAYBE YOU'D ***LIKE ME...*** I DUNNO...
WHOA.
DO YOU WANT TO GO TO THE DANCE WITH ME, STEVE?
W-W-WOULD I? ***YEAH!***
SHE ASKED HIM?
JUST LIKE THAT?
WE DIDN'T NEED TO MAKE THE MATCH AFTER ALL.
SAVING THE WORLD, GETTING STRAIGHT A'S, AND ASKING SOMEONE TO A DANCE? GUESS WE SHOULD'VE ***TRUSTED*** THAT WONDY CAN ***DO IT ALL.***

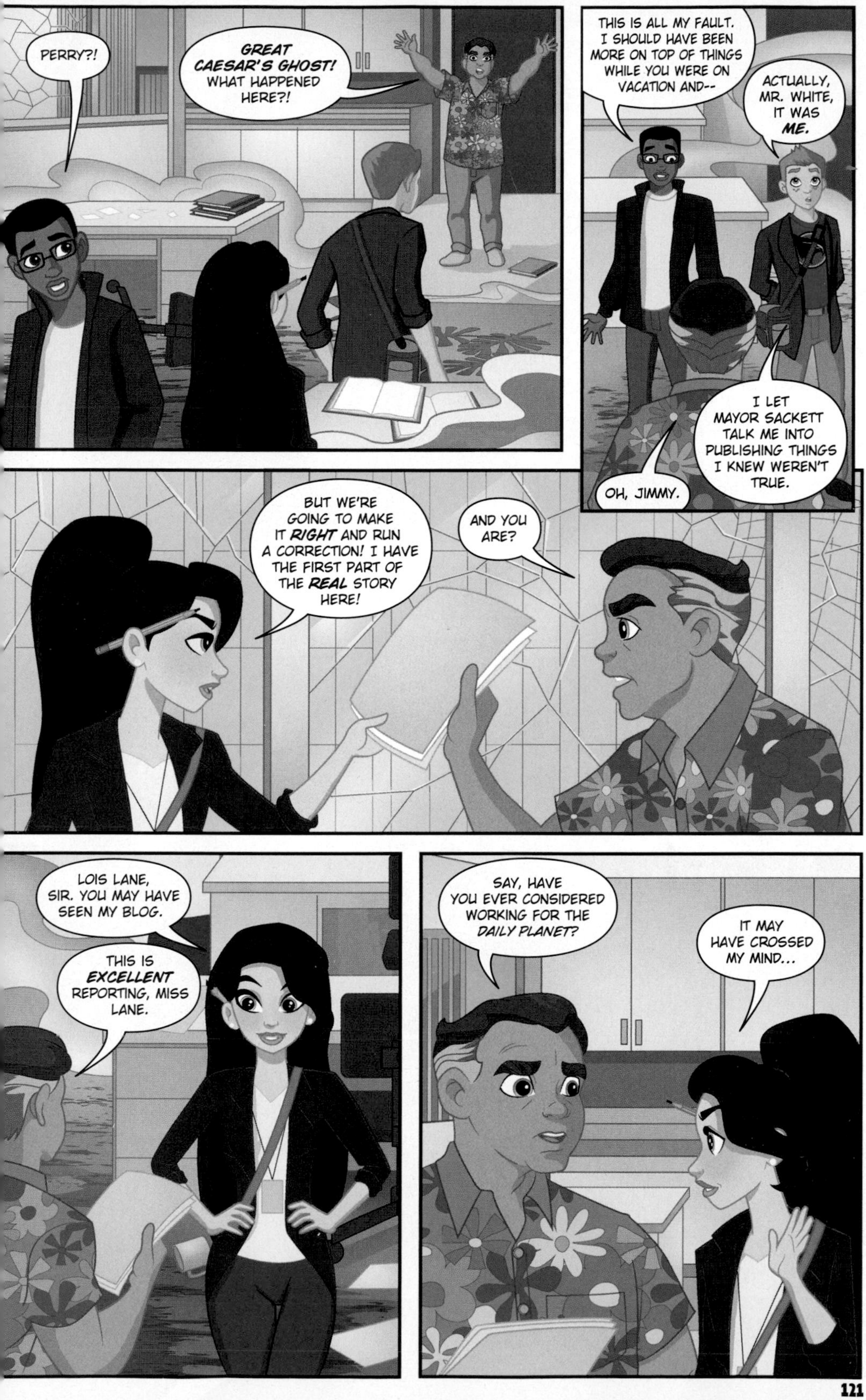
PERRY?!
GREAT CAESAR'S GHOST! WHAT HAPPENED HERE?!
THIS IS ALL MY FAULT. I SHOULD HAVE BEEN MORE ON TOP OF THINGS WHILE YOU WERE ON VACATION AND--
ACTUALLY, MR. WHITE, IT WAS ME.
I LET MAYOR SACKETT TALK ME INTO PUBLISHING THINGS I KNEW WEREN'T TRUE.
OH, JIMMY.
BUT WE'RE GOING TO MAKE IT RIGHT AND RUN A CORRECTION! I HAVE THE FIRST PART OF THE REAL STORY HERE!
AND YOU ARE?
LOIS LANE, SIR. YOU MAY HAVE SEEN MY BLOG.
THIS IS EXCELLENT REPORTING, MISS LANE.
SAY, HAVE YOU EVER CONSIDERED WORKING FOR THE DAILY PLANET?
IT MAY HAVE CROSSED MY MIND...

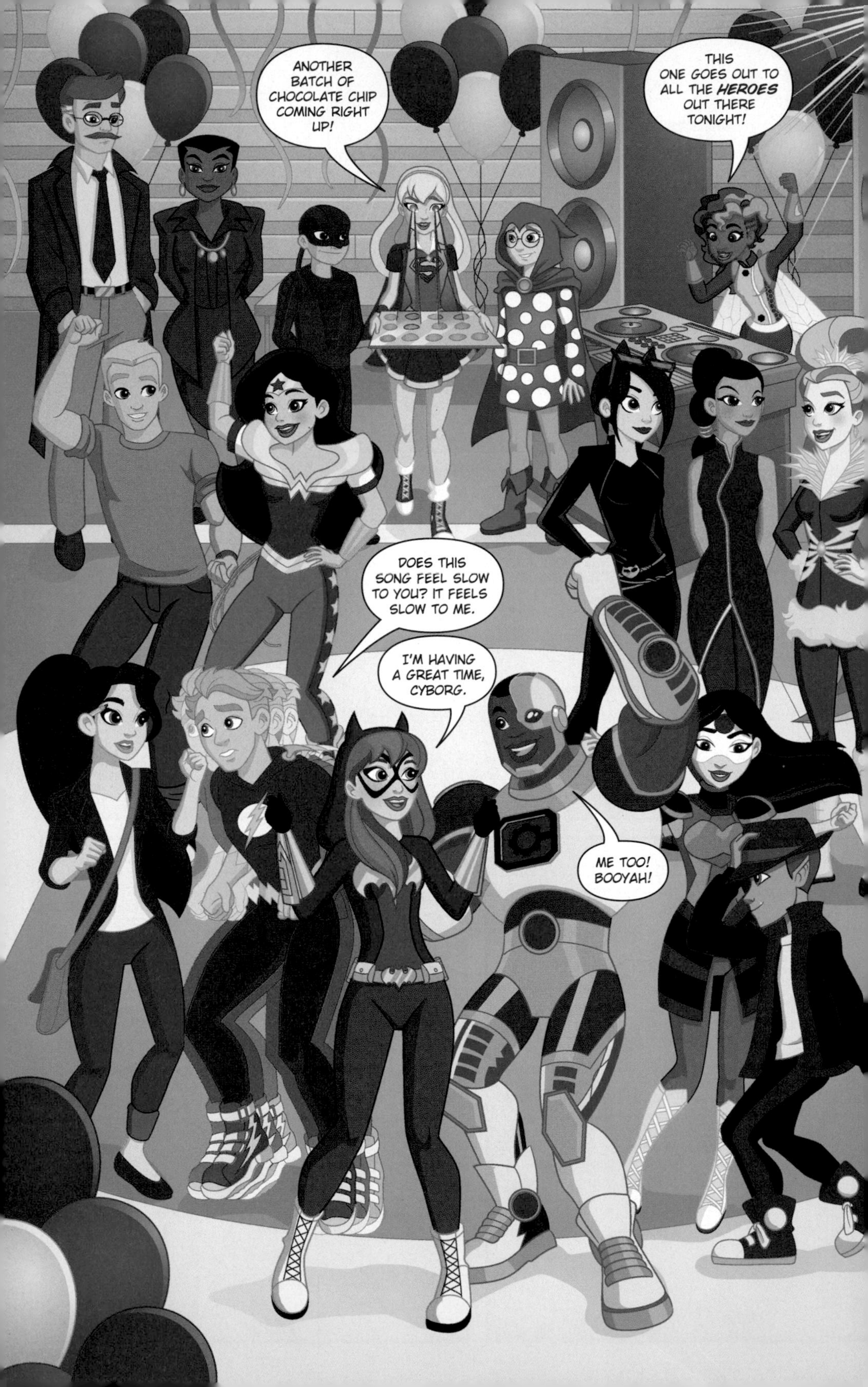
ANOTHER BATCH OF CHOCOLATE CHIP COMING RIGHT UP!
THIS ONE GOES OUT TO ALL THE **HEROES** OUT THERE TONIGHT!
DOES THIS SONG FEEL SLOW TO YOU? IT FEELS SLOW TO ME.
I'M HAVING A GREAT TIME, CYBORG.
ME TOO! BOOYAH!

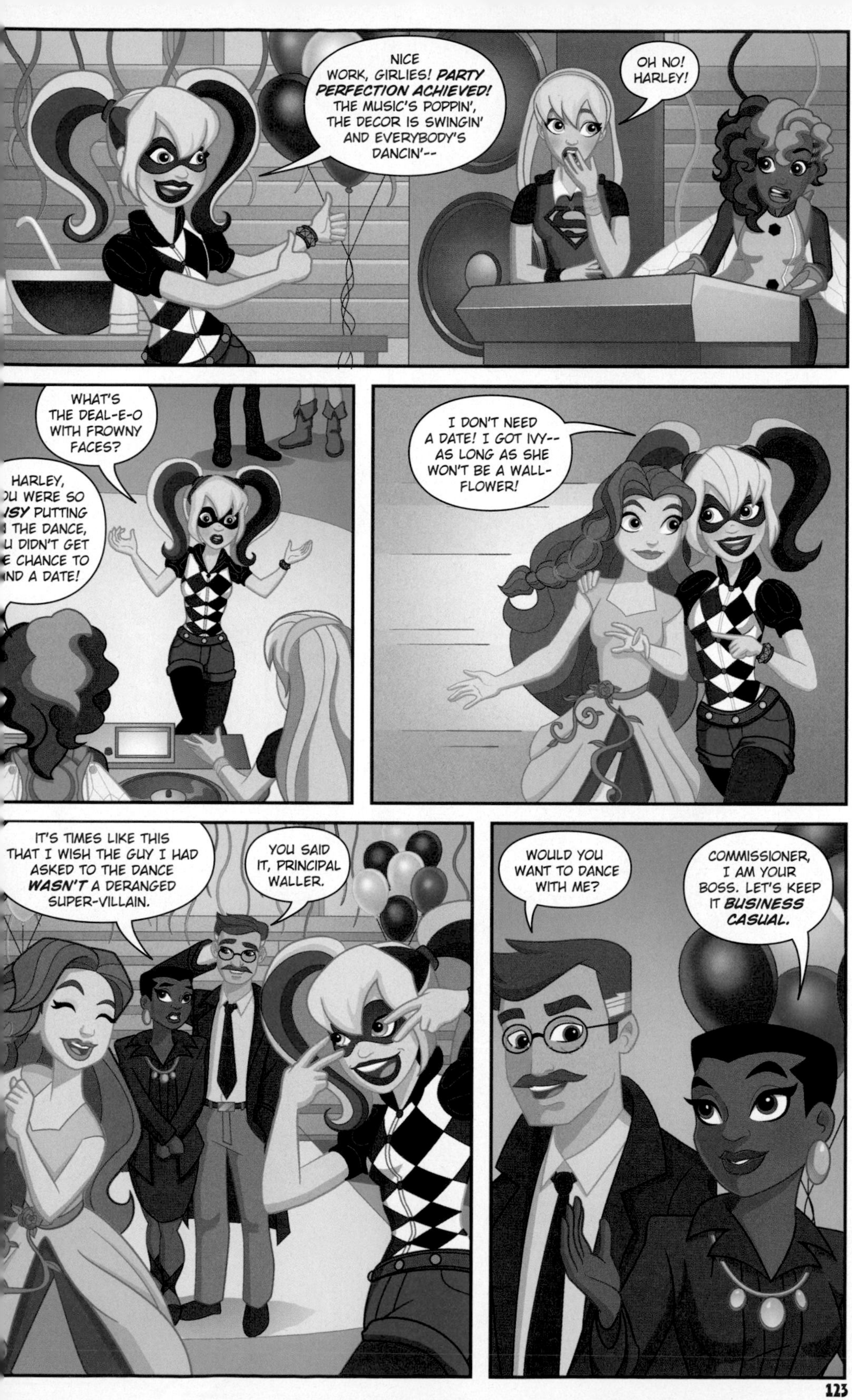

NICE WORK, GIRLIES! ***PARTY PERFECTION ACHIEVED!*** THE MUSIC'S POPPIN', THE DECOR IS SWINGIN' AND EVERYBODY'S DANCIN'--
OH NO! HARLEY!
WHAT'S THE DEAL-E-O WITH FROWNY FACES?
HARLEY, OU WERE SO ***ISY*** PUTTING THE DANCE, U DIDN'T GET E CHANCE TO ND A DATE!
I DON'T NEED A DATE! I GOT IVY-- AS LONG AS SHE WON'T BE A WALL-FLOWER!
IT'S TIMES LIKE THIS THAT I WISH THE GUY I HAD ASKED TO THE DANCE ***WASN'T*** A DERANGED SUPER-VILLAIN.
YOU SAID IT, PRINCIPAL WALLER.
WOULD YOU WANT TO DANCE WITH ME?
COMMISSIONER, I AM YOUR BOSS. LET'S KEEP IT ***BUSINESS CASUAL.***

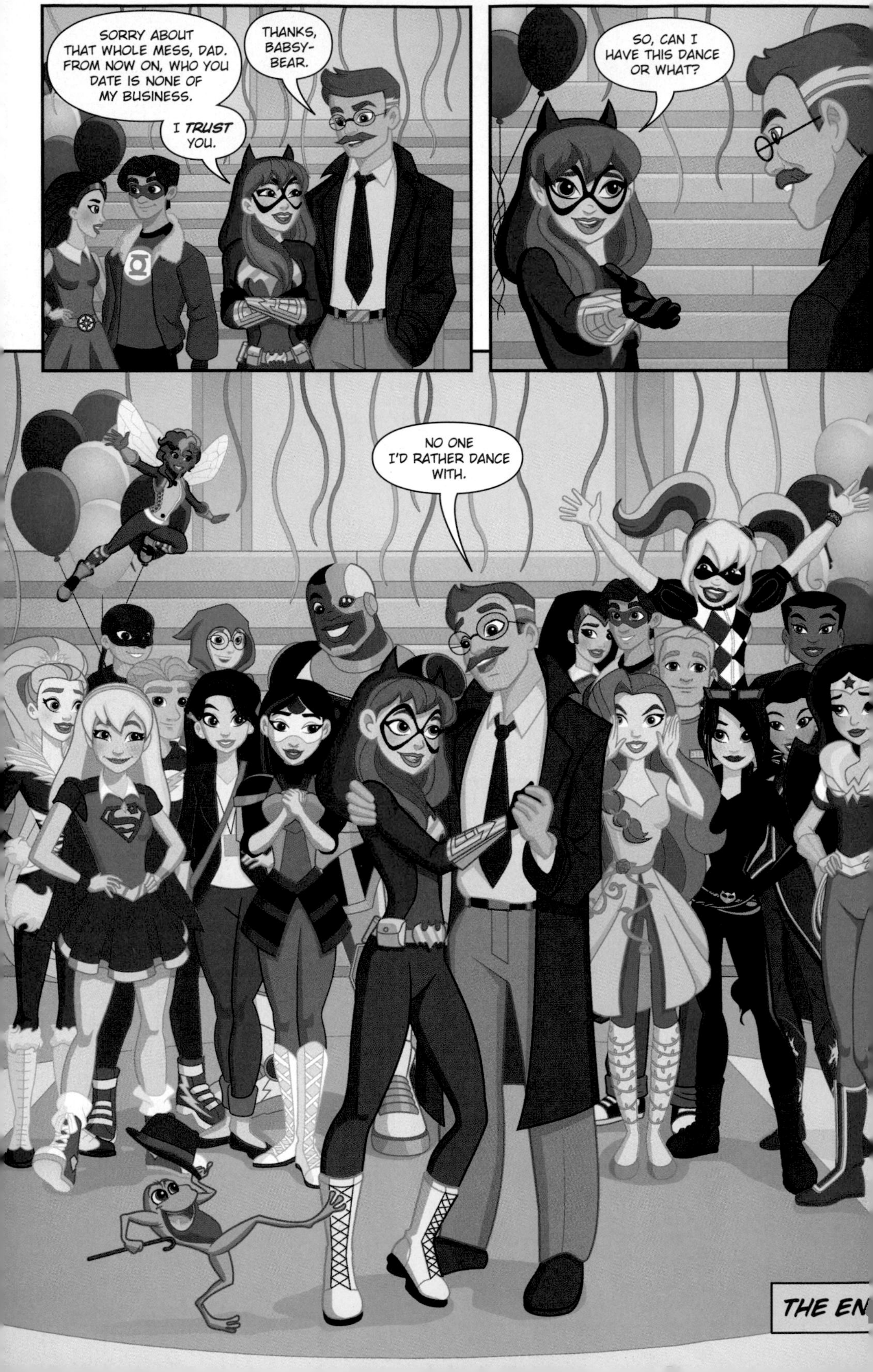
SORRY ABOUT THAT WHOLE MESS, DAD. FROM NOW ON, WHO YOU DATE IS NONE OF MY BUSINESS.
I *TRUST* YOU.
THANKS, BABSY-BEAR.
SO, CAN I HAVE THIS DANCE OR WHAT?
NO ONE I'D RATHER DANCE WITH.
THE EN

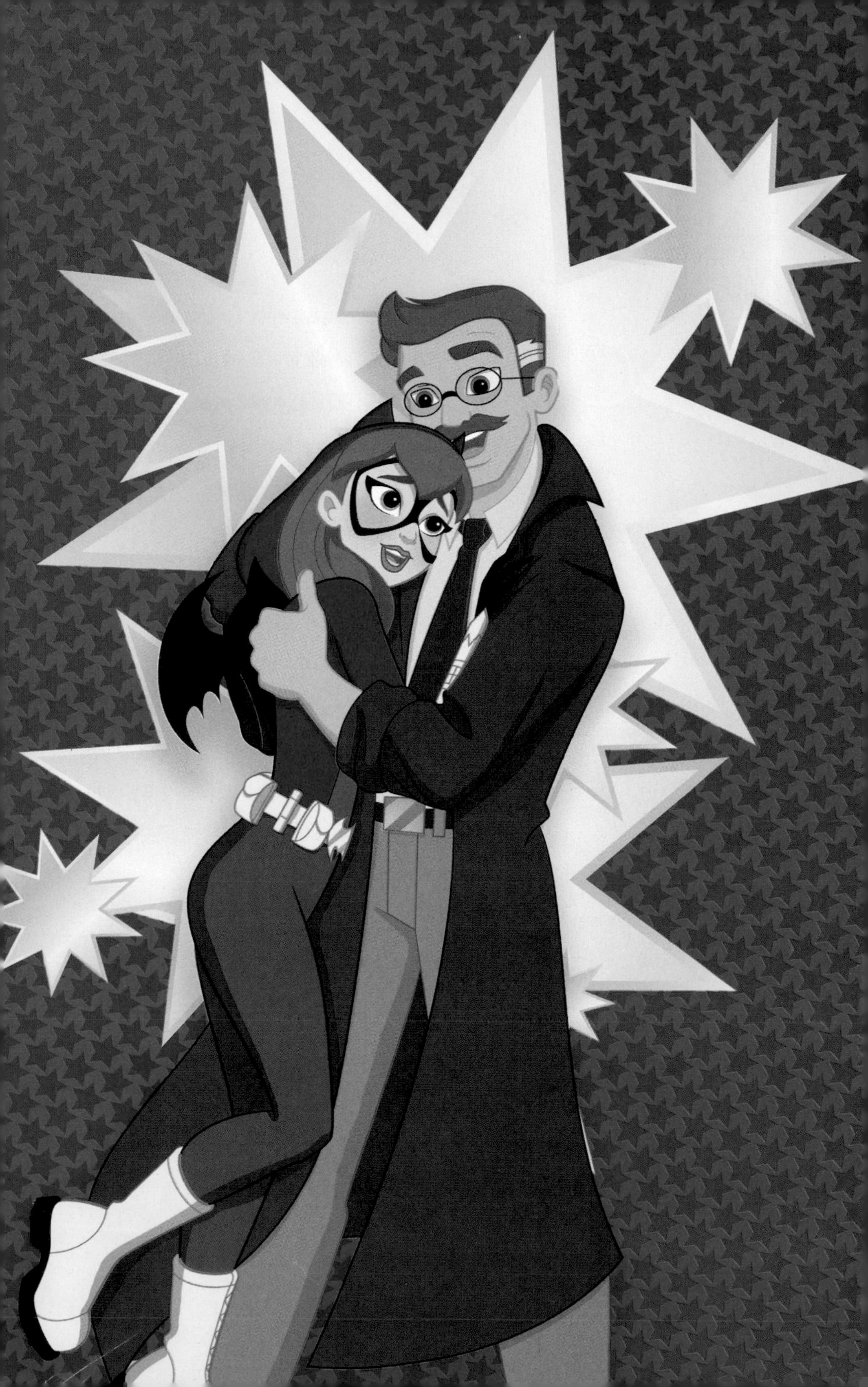

Shea Fontana is a writer for film, television, and graphic novels. In addition to the DC SUPER HERO GIRLS graphic novels, she also writes the DC Super Hero Girls animated shorts, TV specials, and movies. Her other credits include *Polly Pocket*, *Doc McStuffins*, *Dorothy and the Wizard of Oz*, *Whisker Haven Tales with the Palace Pets*, live shows for Disney on Ice, and some of DC's most iconic comic book series including WONDER WOMAN and JUSTICE LEAGUE. She lives in sunny Los Angeles, where she enjoys playing roller derby, hiking, hanging out with her dog, Moxie, and changing her hair color. ★

ABOUT THE COLORIST

Monica Kubina

has colored countless comics, including super hero series, manga titles, kids' comics, and science fiction stories. She's colored *Phineas and Ferb*, *Spongebob*, THE 99, and *Star Wars: Forces of Destiny*. Monica's favorite activities are bike riding and going to museums with her husband and two young sons.

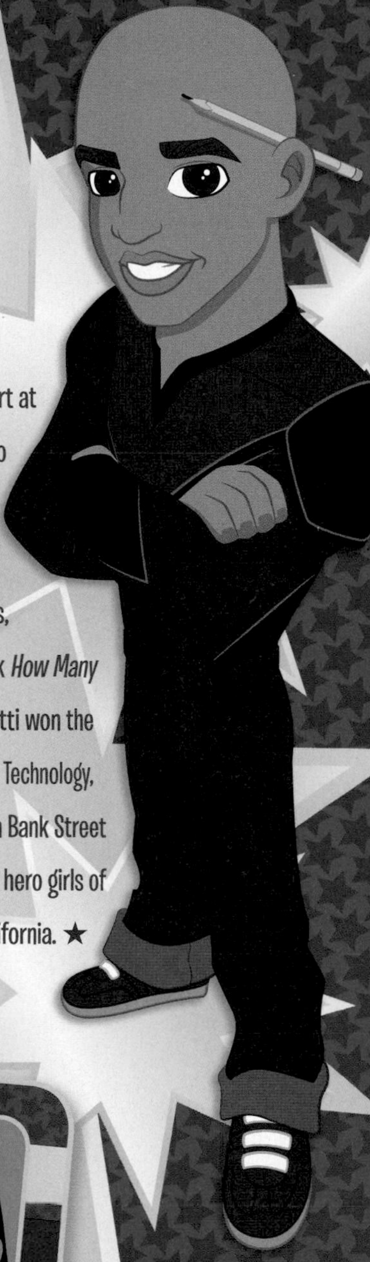

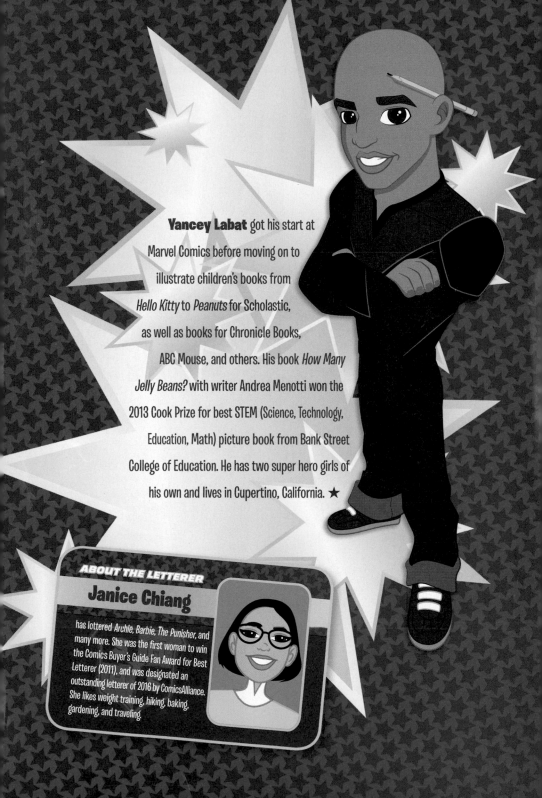

Yancey Labat got his start at Marvel Comics before moving on to illustrate children's books from *Hello Kitty* to *Peanuts* for Scholastic, as well as books for Chronicle Books, ABC Mouse, and others. His book *How Many Jelly Beans?* with writer Andrea Menotti won the 2013 Cook Prize for best STEM (Science, Technology, Education, Math) picture book from Bank Street College of Education. He has two super hero girls of his own and lives in Cupertino, California. ★

ABOUT THE LETTERER

Janice Chiang

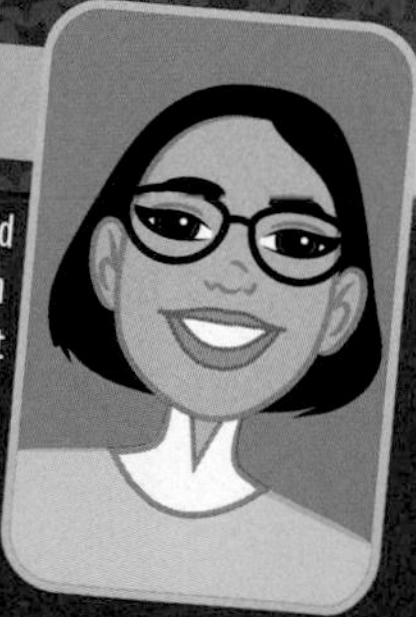

has lettered *Archie, Barbie, The Punisher,* and many more. She was the first woman to win the Comics Buyer's Guide Fan Award for Best Letterer (2011), and was designated an outstanding letterer of 2016 by ComicsAlliance. She likes weight training, hiking, baking, gardening, and traveling.

ALSO AVAILABLE!

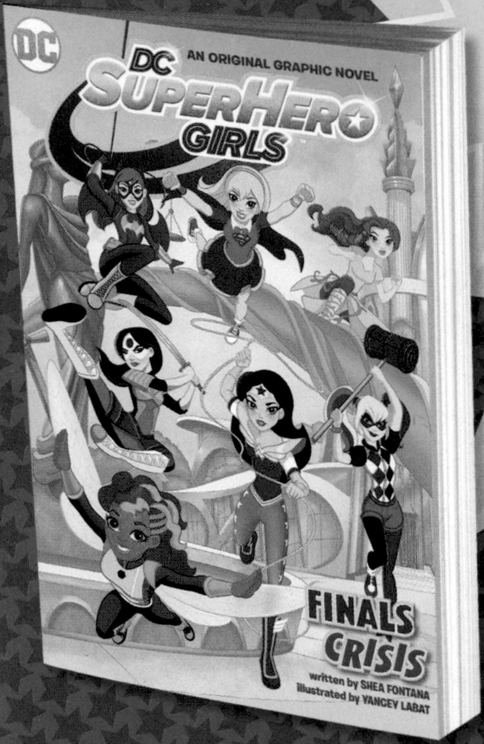
DC
AN ORIGINAL GRAPHIC NOVEL
DC SUPERHERO GIRLS
FINALS CRISIS
written by SHEA FONTANA
illustrated by YANCEY LABAT

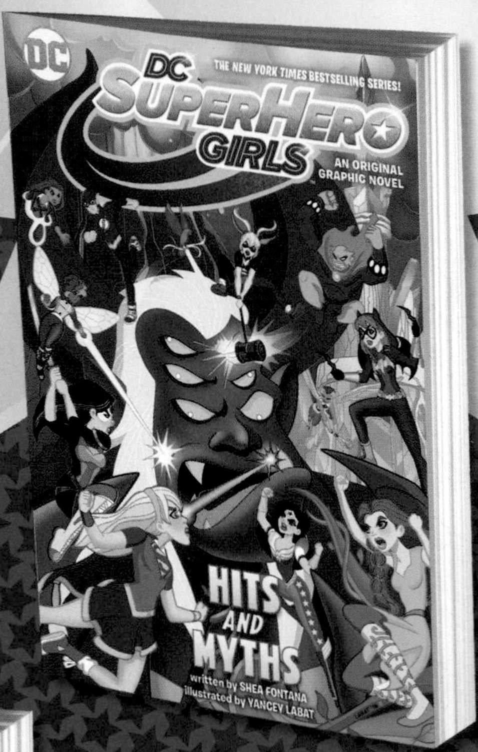
DC
THE NEW YORK TIMES BESTSELLING SERIES!
DC SUPERHERO GIRLS
AN ORIGINAL GRAPHIC NOVEL
HITS AND MYTHS
written by SHEA FONTANA
illustrated by YANCEY LABAT

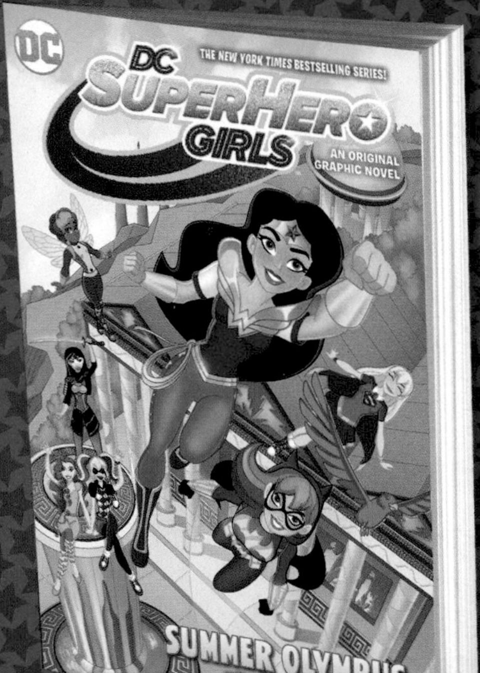
DC
THE NEW YORK TIMES BESTSELLING SERIES!
DC SUPERHERO GIRLS
AN ORIGINAL GRAPHIC NOVEL
SUMMER OLYMPUS
written by SHEA FONTANA
illustrated by YANCEY LABAT

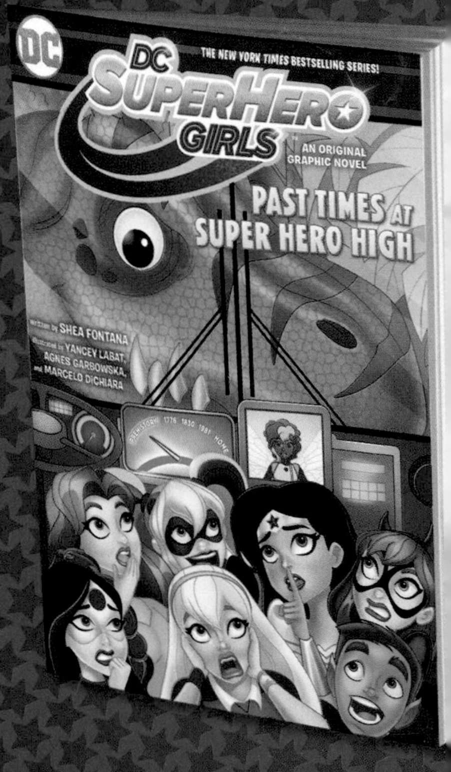
DC
THE NEW YORK TIMES BESTSELLING SERIES!
DC SUPERHERO GIRLS
AN ORIGINAL GRAPHIC NOVEL
PAST TIMES AT SUPER HERO HIGH
written by SHEA FONTANA
illustrated by YANCEY LABAT, AGNES GARBOWSKA, and MARCELO DICHIARA

DC Super Hero Girls: Finals Crisis
DC Super Hero Girls: Hits and Myths
DC Super Hero Girls: Summer Olympus
DC Super Hero Girls: Past Times at Super Hero High

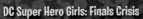